Norwood, Frank.

The man in the moon

DATE			

The Man in the Moon

The MAN in the MOON

Frank Norwood

A THOMAS DUNNE BOOK

St. Martin's Press / New York

 For information, address St. Martin's Press, 175 Fifth Avenue, New York, N.Y. 10010.

Library of Congress Cataloging-in-Publication Data

Norwood, Frank.
The man in the moon / Frank Norwood.
p. cm.
"A Thomas Dunne book."
ISBN 0-312-03393-1
I. Title.
PS3564.O78M36 1989
813'.54—dc20 89-33029
CIP

First Edition

10 9 8 7 6 5 4 3 2 1

For Diane, Dad, Johnny & Mid

And the man in the moon
sings for his supper

The Man in the Moon

1

Short Change

Joe had been feeling bad, but now he was feeling better. A cold had been beating him down for a week, the kind that leaves you blood-dead and blue, and that's pretty tough for a fat man with a bond and a limp, so Joe had gone on down to the Corral to share a few brewskies and the lousy lighting with Eddie Mikenas, which was a helluva lot better'n slugging orange juice and Bayers, and Eddie had told him a couple things, so after a while Joe had rung up JFK and suggested the two of them get together at the Glo-Lite laundry, and they sat there rapping about Ragman and scag and watching the colors toss, and after a while Joe had cozied up to what Eddie had told him and JFK thought maybe it was something, although maybe not so much, but still JFK had promised Joe a bill, and back behind the dryers where the studs would throw the used Mary Janes, Joe had found a shiny bright quarter, which he just knew was good luck, and that's what Joe was tossing under a dirty Christmas moon as he took his fat man's shortcut home from the laundry down the street with the eucalyptus and the tracts and hi there kitty under a bush with your Jack o'-lantern eyes, down toward the tunnel that snuggles under the 405, the one with all the dirty writing on the walls, and there was this bum in there back away from the glare and swaying to a tune nobody else could hear and you could get the smell of him for a block, but Joe liked bums, he knew the turf, so he gave the guy a smile since it had been Joe's night for sharing, and sharing was what Christmas was all about, wasn't it?

Sergeant Sam Dodd wouldn't have found him if it hadn't been for the cat.

Sam was cruising alone in a black-and-white when he saw it lying on the street near the underpass. Parking, he left his low beams on, climbed out of his car and balanced on his heels beside the dead young calico and the skid marks. The tire tracks veered only a foot or so. Whoever had struck it hadn't tried very hard to avoid it. The cat had tried harder—its claws were extended as if still struggling for traction on the asphalt.

Sam liked cats and, although it didn't matter now, he gently lifted the stiffening, arched body to place it by the side of the road, where it wouldn't be struck again. Then, as he started up from his crouch, he spotted the other, larger body. The man in the underpass was slumped in such a way that he could have been a drunk sleeping it off, could have been except for the blood touched by the sleeves of light reaching from Sam's car.

There was too much blood; Sam knew that the instant he was in the tunnel. His flashlight found it everywhere he looked. It was spattered on the grainy cement of floor and curved walls, it had splashed the blocks of Mexican graffiti, deepening the edges of scratched love. It had pooled under the fat man's body, which, like the cat's, was still warm to the touch. It had flecked his loafers and trousers and spilled laundry and filled the pockets of his cheap coat, but it wasn't the blood, it wasn't even the hands severed at the wrists and folded over the dead man's lap as if in penance for some irrevocable sin, that turned Sam's grimace into an involuntary smile that was more like a tic, and it wasn't the right eye, staring and bloodshot and glassy, that produced the sick grin, but the left where someone had placed, as a joke better suited for Halloween, a quarter, a gleam of bright, shiny silver under the harsh artificial mesmerizing light.

2

Moon Shuffle

Charley glanced up at the sky as he ran. The man in the moon had a smile on his face. Charley smiled back—just Charley and the moon, and Ali, of course, shuffling along.

He ran easily, his floppy gray sneakers slapping in time against the cement, his breathing even and deep as he jogged past the shuttered concession stands lining the boardwalk. A solitary seagull blotted the moon for a frozen second before swooping down toward the green-black, gently swelling ocean. The Santa Monica night was turning cold. Charley watched his breath feather the air. He and Ali always ran late, after the exhaust fumes had subsided, leaving only the good strong scents of sand and brine. Moving at this pace, they could cover three miles in twenty-five minutes. They used to be able to do it in twenty, but both of them were getting older.

Charley noticed that Ali was no longer at his heels—having stopped to chase a moth, he lunged and missed, the white wings fluttering away from the spread claws. Ali sat down, amazed. The cat was the color of coal, shorthair black from his paws to the tip of his tail. It was ten years since Charley had picked him up as a stray starving kitten on Friday the thirteenth, superstition not being one of Charley's defects. Ali's coat had lost some of its gloss and he'd added a few pounds and sags, but his eyes were still copper studs.

"C'mon, Ali," Charley said, showing compassion. Ali meowed once, pretending to object. Give me another crack at that moth and he's supper, his bright eyes said, but he scurried after Charley, glad he wouldn't have to prove it. Charley knew he was embarrassed and tried not to look at him. When Ali was younger, he had rarely missed anything that moved, but then neither had Charley. Getting older, Charley thought, drawing in his stomach as he ran.

At thirty-eight, Charley looked close to fifty, but then he'd looked close to fifty when he was eighteen and probably would in the grave; he had that kind of face. People said he resembled Charles Bronson, but he never gave it much thought, except maybe that was what you got being Mex and Irish, Indian skin and County Cork eyes. The scar under the right one he'd earned, compliments of a Marvelous Hagler left hook; the thin mustache that wouldn't stay balanced he was starting to regret. The body he was still buying with sweat, worth the price, but yeah getting older, just Charley and Ali and the moon shuffling along, rumpled and tattered and set in their ways.

"Good evening, Charley." Charley's mood, as elusive as white wings, broke as he heard the voice scratching down a hill.

"Evening, Mrs. Kravitz," he called out as he and Ali swung left and started up the sidewalk.

Mrs. Kravitz was just up ahead, walking her chihuahua Max, named for her late husband. Charley's landlady was ninety if a day—the dog couldn't be much younger—her stick figure cheating the long cardigan she wore, crackles of casual calamity drifting from the radio she held in her hand.

Seeing Ali, whom he was terrified of, Max immediately fell into a quaking fit; straining to escape, he jerked Mrs. Kravitz into a garbage can. Cursing, she recovered with amazing speed, unlike Max, who continued to tremble and piss. Ali, however, had long ago decided the dog was beneath his attention. He no longer hissed or flared up into a monster of electric black fur, but merely kept pace beside Charley, who touched the brim of his flat denim cap in greeting as he trotted past Mrs. Kravitz.

"They butchered a thirteen-year-old girl in Compton," Mrs. Kravitz said, showing her teeth, "they" being the sinister forces prowling the streets and the old woman's imagination. Charley would've said killed instead of butchered, but then he wasn't up on newsspeak.

"Yes, ma'am," he replied, not breaking stride. He wanted to get by with Ali before Max completely panicked and yanked her rolling down the hill the way he almost had last week.

"And savagely raped her," Mrs. Kravitz called after him.

"Yes, ma'am." In her kitchen, she kept a corkboard happy with grisly killings clipped from the L.A. *Times*. Tragedy was her way of making conversation.

Charley looked back over his shoulder. Mrs. Kravitz was hurrying grimly down the hill, cloppy shoes struggling for traction as Max pulled her along. Charley guessed she was afraid of missing the Channel 9 news—the world might have ended. With the possibility lingering like a sore throat, Charley finished his run in double time; before he realized it, he was home.

Home was near the Santa Monica pier, with its nautical restaurants, trinket shops, and merry-go-round. On summer nights, you could unlatch a window and listen to the old-fashioned songs, but the carousel was closed for the winter. Home was also up a flight of outside stairs as rickety as the eight-unit yellow slatboard; the place had charm, if you liked red latticing, Depression glass, the 1930s, and $325 a month. Charley did, although he didn't care for the circumstances. He had moved here after separating from his wife.

As he started to climb the stairs, Charley saw something else he didn't particularly care for. The empty squad car was parked behind the building, playing it cute. The Santa Monica cops drove white Chevies with snazzy blue striping. This one was a bled-dry black-and-white, out of its jurisdiction. Maybe they were here for the girl next door, better known as the Migrant Angel Dust Maniac. The possibility brought a sweet smile to Charley's face; then, through the rungs, he saw Mrs. Kravitz peering out from behind the curtains of her apartment. Her eyes somewhere between hurt and anger, she was glaring up at him with the expression she usually reserved for mug shots on the late news.

It took five minutes before there was a knock at Charley's door. The cops were clones and young; their voices kept climbing into unwanted registers. They tortured Charley with displays of aimlessness for a few minutes, the way cops like to do, then they told him that a client of his, Joe Torelli, had been found murdered near Joe's home in the San Fernando Valley. Charley's bailbondsman's card had been on the body. So had Joe's wallet. Robbery hadn't been the motive. Charley didn't believe them at first—only bikers and hopes got killed in the Valley. After a while, they convinced him. Charley told them Joe had been in his office that afternoon. One of the cops jotted the info down in a notepad. The pad had a wasted Jesus stenciled on the front and the cop kept smirking. Having Jesus in your pocket could do that to you. His partner's eyes kept smoking the room. It was obvious he wanted to find something in the situation, a decaying corpse in the closet, a bloody paw print under the rug.

Along about twelve, the cops seemed to decide Charley wasn't a suspect. Maybe it was because his eyes didn't cross and he fed his cat. Maybe they thought he was as dumb as dog biscuits. Sighing in disgust, the cops left, slamming the door, not quite hard enough to break any glass.

3

An Offer

It took Charley thirty-five minutes to drive to the morgue. His car was a restored four-door 1954 Packard Clipper, bronze chassis, black hardtop. It had a sculptured hood, full-width grille, horned headlight rims, swept-back fins, and nickel plating. He had gotten it in one of his better boxing years, when money was easier, the future brighter. It had held up well—two dings in the doors, one disturbing, but all the curves still in the right places. The upholstery was a deep beige, with the kind of wrinkles that come from good leather. In the summer, the seats could stick to you like glue, but the rest of the year they offered a seasoned comfort vinyl couldn't provide.

At the moment the car was acting up. It was two days before Christmas and the engine was turning into rock and roll soup. Looking for sympathy wherever he could find it, Charley glanced up at the man in the moon—the wise silver face did a slow turn around a cloud and snickered.

Charley arrived at a little past one. County General was a conspiracy of bleak buildings in an even bleaker neighborhood, where bullet and stab wounds were as common as the common cold. The coroner's office was housed in a white granite one-story that reminded Charley of a tombstone. The lot was full and it took him five minutes to find a spot. Locking his car against resident poltergeists, he went past a fragged garden and entered the morgue.

They were having a Christmas party inside. At least he could hear the sounds from behind a partition, laughter, jazzy talk, and a radio playing bad disco. Reception was nice, clean and bright, with potted geraniums on a coffee table. Charley walked to the counter and rang the kind of button-bell you find in hotel lobbies and doctors' offices. The results were no better; no one came. He rang the bell again. No one came.

Shrugging, he ambled into a corridor labeled AUTHORIZED PERSONNEL ONLY. A big black guy with a gold earring and gunboats for arms was yelling at an attendant at the far end. Where's my fuckin' old lady? he kept bellowing. The attendant, who had a store dummy's dead face, was trying to tell him where his fucking old lady was, but couldn't make himself heard.

Charley politely asked where he might find a body. The black guy stopped between fuckin's, goggled at Charley, and just as politely replied, Don't know, man. The attendant asked Charley if he'd been cleared up front. Charley told him, Definitely. The attendant asked who he was looking for. Charley told him and the attendant said, Cold Storage, to your left then to your right, just follow your nose. Short trip, Charley replied, thanking him. Where's my fuckin' old lady? the black guy was shouting as Charley sauntered away. Somewhere, they were playing the Bee Gees' "Staying Alive."

Turning left, Charley strolled down a corridor where shadow fell without apparent source. He would've thought the walls would be a dignified gray or at least a neutral white, but they were painted a Halloween pumpkin orange. Taking a right, he went past the scale—blood still shiny on the metal—where Joe's body had been weighed, measured, and fingerprinted. There were double doors at the end of the corridor stamped, as the man had promised, COLD STORAGE. Charley went through them, the doors swinging in with a lazy unhinged slickness.

It was very cold inside. The lighting was overhead fluorescent, with a bluish cast that made it seem even colder. So did the bodies.

There were say three hundred, stacked on trays five to eight tiers high. Each corpse was covered by a sheet, with the feet sticking out. Every big right toe was tagged with a number. An Oriental M.E. in short sleeves, tie, and clipboard was giving directions to a forklift driver between the tiers, which threw shadows as hard as left hooks. The forklift was pumpkin orange, like the walls outside, and had a gritty, grating energy to its engine. The driver, burly in overalls, maneuvered his machine deftly between the shrouded stacks.

There were a few other people still breathing in the room. A civilian was standing near the double doors, sipping from a bottle in a brown paper bag. A plain, skinny girl was making small talk with a dark, dapper attendant who had the cheap charm of a small-town gigolo. They were lounging beside a stiff on a stainless steel table, a gross, hairy guy in heavy pancake makeup and a frilly white dress with two neat bullet holes through the bosom. The small town gigolo made a bad joke about drag queens—he went Gee-oh, gee-ah—and the homely girl laughed as if it was the funniest thing she'd ever heard, a squeaky, Minnie Mouse titter.

"Night's a carnival," Charley muttered to himself. "A cheap one," he added, for he liked to be accurate whenever possible. He said things like that sometimes. When he did, people usually raised their brows and gave him the time.

The civilian simply said, "Yeah," and nodded in agreement. He was wearing chinos and a flannel shirt unbuttoned over a green T-shirt with the slogan Contractors Do It Better. He looked like a husky young JFK without the energy. He offered Charley the brown paper bag but Charley declined.

"Somebody gave it to me back there," JFK explained, jerking a thumb back over his shoulder. His voice was street gritty, but a little on the patronizing side, something in a minor key. "They're having a party," he added.

"I heard."

"Pretty good stuff. Southern Comfort," JFK said, peeking inside the bag at the label, then taking a swig. "Who're you here for?"

"Guy named Joe Torelli."

JFK focused on him for the first time. Tilting his head, he gave Charley a long, curious look before saying, "Funny, so am I." He glanced at the M.E. and the forklift.

"They're getting him now. You related?"

"Sorta. He owed me. What about you? You related?"

JFK shook his head. "Cop I know asked me to identify the body. Seems Joe's mother wasn't up to it, which you can understand. Name's Phil Peterson, by the way."

"Charley Tone." Charley shook the hand Peterson offered. He still didn't understand his connection to Joe, but he let the question hang.

"How'd you hear about this?" Peterson took another belt. He seemed to be getting a little high.

"Same as you, the law. They thought I might've been the last one to see him alive, but I wasn't."

"Know who was?"

"Guy named Eddie Mikenas."

Peterson measured him with that curious look again, then looked away, his eyes distant, tracking miles. "You know Eddie?"

"In passing." Eddie was a friend of Joe's, a small, dark guy with an accent, wore soiled wingtips and knew how to keep in the shade. Joe was going to meet him at a local watering hole, the Corral, after leaving Charley's office. Joe had asked Charley to go along, but Charley had to go home to feed the cat.

"You think the cops'll catch the guy who killed Joe?"

Peterson made a face. "Valley cops can't catch a cold."

"He had one."

"Found a cure."

"The surest."

Light footsteps and a mechanical growl closed in. The M.E., frail and scrutable, strolled over, trailed by the forklift carrying Joe on a stainless steel tray. Joe's bulk was draped by a not-so-clean white sheet, stomach as big as a pregnant woman's in her ninth month. His bare feet needed a bath, maybe two.

The M.E. read from the tag on Joe's toe. "Number two nine three. That's who you wanted, right?"

Tight-lipped, Peterson nodded. They waited while the driver, who had the *Racing Form* in his shirt pocket, drew back a lever, lowering the steel prongs. The M.E. put up a hand, stopping the tray at waist level. Off to the left, there was a sudden flash as the plain girl took a snap of the guy in drag. Charley guessed the picture would serve some purpose.

"Like ice in here." Peterson hugged himself, shifted his feet.

"You get use to it," said the M.E. His voice and self-conscious shrug showed he hadn't. He pulled the sheet back from Joe's face and naked torso for inspection. The sheet smelled of disinfectant and other odors Charley hoped wouldn't be defined. Joe didn't look good. Ditches looked better. His face was bled dry, his breasts like an old lady's, saggy with stretch marks. Four grouped gashes scarred his belly where the blade had gone in. Charley had seen a few stabbings when he was growing up in the barrio. Most knife wounds are as even as a razor slit. These were long and ragged. Whoever killed Joe had done so with a cool fury.

Peterson took a short pull on the bottle, wiped his lips dry, and said softly, "Yeah, that's Joe, all right. Looks like a dartboard, huh?"

"More like a butchered cow." For once, Mrs. Kravitz's TV hyperbole seemed to apply, and that was even before Charley saw the stumps. "Jesus, what happened to his hands?"

"They're in a plastic bag," the M.E. told him. "Want a look?"

"Another time." Charley shivered. He felt very cold.

Peterson said, "What'd he use? A goddamn hatchet?"

"We'll know more at the autopsy in the morning, but offhand, I'd say an ax or a large knife, if the man was exceptionally strong. He probably knows something about anatomy." The M.E. held up one of Joe's arms. "You see, the killer cut through here at the wrist, right at the point where the radius and the ulna terminate, so he didn't have to go through much bone. He would have held the arm on the ground and cut down, like a butcher with a slab of beef on the block. I would say an ax because the severance of both hands appears to be clean—I noticed when the body was brought in that the coat sleeves were spattered with blood, indicating a single sharp, chopping blow." He returned the arm to Joe's side, rested his case.

"Yes, he cut through the easiest place, but even so, a knife only if the man was very, very strong."

"According to a cop I know," Peterson said, "the guy left Joe praying and with a little change over one eye."

"Nice sense of humor." The M.E.'s chuckle didn't clear his throat.

"Yeah, and not much regard for animals." Peterson was getting caught up in details. "He also mashed a cat driving from the scene."

"Kill the cat?" Charley asked, concerned.

"All nine lives."

Charley grimaced.

"Seen enough?" The M.E. was itchy, Peterson's nod was quick. The M.E. pulled the sheet back over Joe's torso and face. The forklift driver, who had waited out the exchange bored, backed up his machine. The M.E. shambled after him, one hand idle on a prong. Peterson watched Joe's sheet darken under the shadows of the tiers. Without facing him, he offered the brown bag to Charley. Charley hesitated, then he took a healthy pull. The hot bite of Southern Comfort crowded his throat and senses, momentarily cloaking the room's atmosphere of factory death. Returning the bag, he glanced to his left. The girl had finished taking her snaps. She was raptly watching the attendant strip the transvestite, giggling in her Minnie Mouse squeal at his sick jokes. Charley turned to Peterson, waiting until he had drained what was left in the bottle before he spoke:

"Okay if I ask you something?"

"Feel free."

"What's your involvement with Joe?"

"Well, we weren't exactly lovers. C'mon, let's go outside. We'll talk."

Charley followed him from the room. Peterson dropped the empty bottle into a wastebasket crammed with bloody gauze pads as they went out into the corridor. The attendant with the mannequin face came down the hallway, with the big black on his heels. "Where's my fuckin' old lady?" the black guy demanded. "Number two six seven," the attendant crisply replied.

Peterson waited until they'd gone into Cold Storage, then he took out his wallet, opened it, and handed it to Charley. He slouched against the wall, arms folded across his chest, while Charley looked inside.

Charley stared down at the card. It showed a young Phil Peterson, blue eyes clearer, sandy hair shorter. The card also carried a familiar name.

"FBI?" Charley said. His eyes were wide as he returned the wallet.

"Don't exactly look the part, do I?" Peterson said with a hint of pride. "Joe was on our payroll. I was his contact. By the way, Eddie Mikenas wasn't the last guy to see him alive. I was, except for—"

"I don't understand."

"Joe was an informer."

"An informer?"

"An informer."

Charley tried to decide if he was surprised. Joe had been a nice enough guy with a bum leg and a wheeze and a few bad habits; no reason selling street secrets couldn't be one of them. "That what got him killed?" Charley asked.

"Could be, but I doubt it. Joe had some loose mob connections, very loose—he hung around people who hung around. Once in a while he'd give us something to play with, but never enough to put him in there. Maybe somebody caught on he was passing on tidbits and decided to make an example."

"Helluva way to score a point."

"Yeah, but it doesn't figure. Joe was a nobody. Hell, he didn't even have a nickname! You ever hear of anybody who was anybody who didn't have a nickname?"

"I wouldn't know."

Peterson studied his own feet, scratched an ear. "Mind if I ask *you* a question, Charley?"

"Feel free."

"You said Joe owed you?"

"On his bond, what I do for a living." Joe had been busted for selling geriatric porn. Maybe a Gray Panther—

"You had collateral, right?"

"Uh-uh. Dumb, huh?"

"Maybe it just means you're a nice guy."

"Like I said, dumb."

"How much he owe you?"

"Seven fifty."

Peterson whistled softly. "That's sizable."

"Ain't it, though. The cops told me he had bills on him. Some guy owed him. I figured maybe that was it and maybe I could collect."

"Joe had a hundred coming from us. On him he had eleven bucks and short change. You could try his mother. He had one."

"Rather not go that route."

"No, I didn't think so." Peterson looked at his feet again. A body went by on a gurney. "Now it's just a possibility, you might not be interested, but here's what I was thinking . . . You say you know Eddie Mikenas?"

"I been in the same bars." The gurney hung a right.

"So maybe you could sort of hang around, help us find him. Maybe he knows something about Joe's murder."

"Why would he?"

Peterson shrugged. "It's a possibility." It was a funny kind of shrug, a hitch in one shoulder. "From what I understand, Eddie runs with a pretty fast crowd. Who knows what was going on?"

The black guy came out of cold storage, tossed a knowing smile Charley's way and said "Life," before sauntering off, whistling a tune. Charley watched his back, then turned to Peterson: "I ain't an informer."

"You don't have to be. You could just hang around."

"Thought you said Joe's info wasn't all that much?"

"It wasn't, but my office would like to find the guy who did him. It's bad PR if word gets out we can't protect our own. Think of it as a Christmas present for Joe. Better than the one he got."

Charley shook his head. "No, I don't think so. I don't think I could do that."

"Go against your religion?"

"Goes against something."

"Give it some thought. I'm sure my boss would cover your loss and more besides." He took out his wallet again and handed Charley a business card—palm-sized with cozy black letters—with his name and phone number on it.

Charley's eyes got wide again. "You guys got cards?"

"Just like salesmen." Peterson's grin and wink were as wicked as the night.

4

A Life

More people die, Charley had read somewhere, at three in the morning than at any other time, that loneliest of hours when the heart murmurs, questioning its reasons for continuing.

Charley arrived home just as a distant clock chimed the mood. The good sea scents had been replaced by a carrion drift, the waves slapped against the shore in melancholy excursions, and the seagulls no longer shadowed the moon in their timeless, wheeling patterns.

Charley wearily climbed stairs that seemed twice their height. Ali was waiting inside his apartment, a blink of neon eyes in the darkness. Charley turned on a lamp by the door. The apartment was small; if he stretched, even the cat crowded him. The furnishings weren't much, a couch, a couple of chairs, a Murphy bed, and tacked to a wall a 1974 fight card poster of Charley looking lean and tough in red Everlast gloves and trunks. In a corner, jazz was waiting to jump. On the couch, there was a paperback of Raymond Chandler's

The Long Goodbye and a pocket dictionary; not that he abused it, but Charley believed in bettering yourself.

His kidneys were aching, a fighter's lingering disease. Charley got a jug of cranberry juice from the fridge and drank from the bottle. He stood there in the dark, fighting a depression that was like a hangover and staring out the window at the pier. He'd taken Lisa there on their first date, cotton candy and quips. She'd wanted to ride the carousel, and he'd stood, hands in pockets, watching the painted horses and her glide by, the pure joy of her laughter washing over and warming him. And now he was here alone, the memory heavy on his mood.

The girl next door wasn't helping—she was snorting coke with some guy. Charley could hear them sucking in the snow and giggling. The giggling kept climbing. He knew her bed would be thundering before long. He wondered what had ever happened to sex fueled by old-fashioned booze, wondered, for that matter, what had happened to carousels and laughter, a song lyric if there ever was one.

By the time he'd turned in, with Ali nestled at the foot of the bed, the age-old dance had begun—through the thin walls, he could hear groans and great sweet Jesus gasps. He wondered, no reason why, if Joe ever got laid.

They were building in the next room, the bed bucking as though it were being bludgeoned. He thought of Lisa, of her smile and her bare breasts above him, an easy rhythm, an encompassing gentleness. The image brought back others, and, in spite of himself, he drifted deeper into memory, the fragments of his life passing by in detail and depth . . .

Charley Tone had been born and raised in the barrio of East L.A., the only child of a Mexican father and an Irish mother. The name was pronounced Toe-nay, but from the beginning, in school and in the streets, he was always called Tone, and that's what it became. Other adjustments weren't as easy—his parents were mismatched, as Charley discovered at an early age; their attraction had been physical. After that faded, there was nothing left. His father was a big, blunt man who had come across the border and stayed to sell used cars with little success, a man who thought that to show affection was to show weakness, a barroom brawler capable of striking a woman or child when drunk, which was often. Charley's mother was a woman of some culture, small, pretty and frail, a hoarder of worries and stresses and nervous tics, who felt she deserved more than life had given her. From his old man, Charley got his muscle. From his mother, he learned to watch the world and his back.

If there was little love at home, certain rituals were still observed. Naturally, with his ancestry, Charley had been raised a Catholic, growing up in a world where prayers had the certainty of truth and the distance of dreams. He could still remember the rich peal of Sunday morning church bells and, less fondly, the Latin drone of the alcoholic priest . . .

Corpus corpore meo . . . Flesh of my flesh . . .

. . . and the gangs. There were more gangs than churches in East L.A.—and there were many churches—gangs with names that reeked of machismo swagger and territorial rights: Chaco, White Fence, Mateo Bombers, City Terrace, Los Vatos Locos . . . Their members wore French pointed-toe shoes, Pendleton wool shirts, zoot-suit overcoats, crotch-crowding pants, and switchblades that leapt to life at a touch. Their pachuco girlfriends flaunted beehive hairdos and sexy twitches, and their fire-engine shiny cars varoomed by with runaway flames painted on their sides and steering wheels wrapped in chains. Charley was too much of a loner to join their ranks, so he had to fight, at school and in the streets, bob, weave, feint, jab, and belt to protect his lunch money and pride. His quick snaking hands and stubbornness earned him a grudging respect: Charley Tone, tough half gringo kid who went to church and said his prayers.

He lost some, although not all, of his faith when, at fifteen, he watched his grandmother waste away from cancer, her own Catholic certainty fading as death drew near. Her body became as dry and as fragile as a summer leaf, and the stench of death hung about her, but she had given him more love than either of his parents, and he stayed by her bed late into more nights than he could remember. When she finally died, they scattered fresh earth over her grave and the alcoholic priest said the prayers for the dead, and Charley cried.

He was sixteen by then. He took his grief out in the gym. Before long, he was spending more time there than in school, punching the heavy bag and jumping rope, sweating out the blues. When he dropped out of school in the eleventh grade, his father shrugged and his mother cried.

The army took him at eighteen—six grueling months of Basic at Fort Ord, another eighteen in Ordnance in Louisiana, where he picked up a brace of boxing medals and learned the many secrets of the ladies of New Orleans. Once out of the service, he turned pro. He never enjoyed fighting much, but it seemed a better living than anything else he could do. He fought with integrity, without shuck, hype, or jive, and with the same quick hands and tenacity of his youth, he won more than he lost. In 1976, he was the ninth-ranked middleweight in the world. He never went any higher. There's a line, no way to cross it, that separates the great fighters from the good ones. The reflexes are a fraction faster, the impulses a little more inspired. Myth to the contrary, a rugged journeyman doesn't swagger in and kayo the champ. He might make it interesting for a while, but that's about all. Charley knew it as well as anybody.

His mother died in 1979, of all her small, accumulated griefs. After that, Charley stopped going to the barrio. His father still lived there, but Charley couldn't forget the bruises, more psychic than physical, his old man had left on his mother. Charley suffered some guilt, even phoned sometimes, but he simply didn't want to see his father; it was one of those things.

Other things were winding down around that time. After nearly twenty years in the ring, he retired, before the nose went north and the words started to slur. Without prospects, he rented an office with what little he had saved and became a bailbondsman, like so many other ex-pugs. His brief and only marriage broke up shortly thereafter, but he kept on going, getting by as best he could,

Charley Tone, tough half gringo who still occasionally went to church and said his prayers.

The passion next door had finished. Somewhere out in the darkness, a seagull screeched and wings beat against the air. A foghorn sang out, blues across the water. He could hear the girl next door snoring softly—small, stifled distractions, like a child's. He thought again of Lisa, who could still make him smile and stir his senses, of a marriage that didn't have time to take. He thought about his future and wondered, the questions assuming shapeless patterns, until sleep took him under her wings for what remained of the night.

5

Marking Time

Charley glanced up at the clock behind his desk. 1:42. Uncoordinated chunks of noise hammered at him from overhead. "Twelfth Street Rag" squealed like the girl with the Minnie Mouse voice. Charley wished he had Southern Comfort in a bag.

Charley's office, even smaller than his apartment, was down near the beach. There was a tap-dance studio upstairs, an English tea shop next door; little old ladies with accents would wander in and ask if he did taxes. It was enough to make you schizzy. Looking for relief, Charley gazed out the window at the Christmas banners hung low and careless over the street. The day was overcast, clouds searching for shelter in a sea of dirty gray. On the sidewalks, citizens apprehensively checked the sky and their pulses.

Charley rubbed his eyes, then he picked up the phone and dialed. The footbeats upstairs were the size of delirium by the time his wife answered.

"Mrs. Tone." Her voice was lived in, a pleasure to the ear; most of her co-workers sounded as programmed as Disneyland guides.

"Lisa, it's Charley. Merry Christmas."

There was a pause that he was afraid would be permanent; he hadn't talked to her in almost a month. In the background, he could hear caroling, muffled laughter, and the strum of an out-of-tune guitar. She worked in a welfare office. Usually when he called he heard screams.

"Merry Christmas, Charley," Lisa said.

"Thought you might be off work by now."

"No, as a matter of fact, we're having a party. The last time I looked, Fran Drucker was doing a striptease on top of Marv Harmon's desk."

"Figures. Where's the clients?"

"Probably vandalizing Reception." Another pause followed, shorter than the first, then she said, "How are you, Charley? How's business?"

"Not so good."

"Bad?"

"Not bad, just not so good." He considered telling her about Joe, but decided against it.

"You doing anything tonight?" he asked, trying to sound nonchalant.

"No. What are you doing tonight, Charley?"

"Not much. Working on it."

"Why don't you drop by, bring Ali?" She was trying hard to be offhand and friendly. Ali was a real concession, since she was allergic to cats. They made her sneeze and say unseemly things.

"You sure you want us to come over?"

Before she could reply, there was a cry of "Look out!" followed by a distinct thud on her end.

Charley said, "Wha—?"

"Fran fell off the desk."

"Oh. She okay?"

"I think so. She's trying to climb back up on it again. She's down to bra and skirt."

"Oh."

"About tonight, of course I'm sure. It's Christmas Eve. I mean, after all, we're separated, not staring at each other over gun sights."

"Give it time."

"Charley . . ." Her voice was clenching.

"Sorry, I didn't mean that."

He didn't. He had said it because he was embarrassed. He really wanted to see her, but calling her was as hard as going ten rounds. His pride had been one of the reasons, maybe the main one, for their splitting up. It was funny. He could see poetry in the moon, but he couldn't bring his wife flowers. Maybe it came from a macho code he knew was ridiculous, or maybe it just came from marrying late. You get set in your ways when you're alone too long. Emotions then are like fighting a southpaw. They can confuse you.

"You still want me to come by?" He tried not to make it sound like a challenge.

Lisa didn't respond. For a moment, he thought she'd put the receiver down, then he heard her voice.

"Around eight?"

"Eight." He could sense her hesitancy.

"Got to go," he said. "Customer just came in."

"Goodbye, Charley."

"Goodbye."

After he'd hung up, Charley looked out the window. The questions from last night were still there, wouldn't leave. His life seemed as empty as the room. A fog bank was rolling up the street; gossamer shreds brushed against his window, then drifted away. He tracked their movement. At that moment, he had a sense of things, of truths he probably couldn't express, yet he had an articulate soul, a little forlorn and foolish at times, but it let him wonder if his malaise wasn't symptomatic of the country; you didn't see too many people happy these days. Maybe everything was too structured, the alternatives too few. He'd grown up in an era when there were still challenges and room to stretch—space hadn't been conquered and you didn't have to cross borders to find a forest. He thought of a movie from that remote time, *Requiem for a Heavyweight.* Anthony Quinn plays an over-the-hill pug who's just been knocked out in L.A. by a young Cassius Clay. His manager, Jackie Gleason, asks him where he is and the fighter, groggy, says, "Pittsburgh and it's raining," the line summing up the despair and frustration of his life.

It was a mood Charley could share. He had become a bailbondsman because he didn't seem to have options. It was either that or collect unemployment and a lousy self-image. He hadn't realized the ramifications of the job; ramifications, that was the word, wasn't it? Bailbonding had nothing to do with justice. It protected the guilty the same as the innocent. You posted bail for guys who were as safe on the streets as runaway trucks. Charley tried to be selective in his clients. It cost him business and he wasn't hacking it financially, wasn't even sure he wanted to. He needed a change, a challenge, nothing more complicated than that.

Peterson's card was on his desk. He picked it up and stared at it. He thought of Joe Torelli, fat and pathetic on a stainless steel tray. He thought of the dead cat, glad he hadn't seen it. For them, life was a carny pinwheel, a flash of glitter never touched.

With the tap-dancers driving hard overhead, Charley picked up the phone and dialed the number on the bright white invitation.

6

A Change

The mood and weather shift abruptly when you leave the fog shrouds of Santa Monica for downtown L.A. Traffic congeals into a clot on the brain, and the air should be tagged with a Surgeon General's warning.

As Charley maneuvered through the late afternoon maze of bleating horns and shouted obscenities, the day hung balanced between menace and beauty—swirling black clouds the color and shape of forest fire smoke under an amber-blue sky.

His slogging engine reminding him of its misery, Charley stopped at St. Timothy's on Pico, to give them both a breather. Taking off his cap, he went inside the empty church. Kneeling at the altar, child-silent and subdued, he said a prayer for Joe and for all fat men and their forlorn dreams. A priest came out of the vestry and Charley asked him to recite a prayer for the dead. The cleric rushed the words and Charley left, feeling neither better nor worse.

The address on Peterson's card was down on Spring Street, one of a welter of modern low-rises—three blocks south, short dog bums slept in their own vomit and briefly found God in a jug of Gallo Gold.

Charley found parking where he could, then he went into Peterson's building, brushing past brisk suits and ties on their way home. The card read Suite 616. Suite 616 wasn't on the directory. Somehow, Charley wasn't surprised. He took the elevator. He was tired of stairs.

Six-sixteen was a pair of double doors, beyond other doors with names, desperate law firms, and a guy who did eyes. Charley skipped the other options and went through the twins. Instead of a hallway, he got a parquet hallway and more closed doors with frosted glass windows. He walked to the only one that showed light.

The door was open, offered a view. Peterson was sitting at a spotless desk that filled the room, cleaning his gun. He was wearing a blue Arrow shirt, shoulder holster, dark blue tie, and darker blue slacks. His outfit from last night—flannel Pendleton, T-shirt and chinos—was draped over the only other chair in the room.

"Saving those for Halloween?"

Peterson looked up and saw Charley gesturing to the dead clothes. The agent fashioned a reasonable smile, said, Have a seat. Charley did. He checked out the walls. Newspaper articles of Bureau exploits were thumbtacked at deranged angles, along with two gaudy posters, one of the Washington Redskins, the other of Madonna, staring down at Charley in wet-lipped invitation. Peterson put aside his service revolver. "Like where I live?"

"Cozy, and not much on advertising."

"Yeah. The main office down in Westwood is a great big white charger of a building, all sleek and shiny, rack-and-pinion steering, four hundred agents, and the Bureau seal right where you can see it in bright red, white, and blue, but here we try to keep a low profile, not to mention overhead. See, we're kind of a satellite station, incognito, undercover as the cops say."

"Uh huh."

Interlocking his fingers, Peterson cracked a knuckle and changed the subject. "After you called, I talked to the boss and he said he thought maybe we could do something for you."

"As simple as that?"

"As simple as that." Peterson pushed away from his desk. "C'mon, I'll take you down to his office."

Charley nodded without enthusiasm. He was beginning to have second thoughts about a change, but he followed Peterson down the hallway. Without the Southern Comfort, the agent's sympathy for Joe was dust in a draft:

"Pretty grubby stuff, dealing with guys like Torelli. You know, I was reading in the paper this morning about how seventy-four percent of the public thinks we're a bunch of first-class S.O.B.'s, on the take and sticking bugs up everybody's ass. *They* should try it awhile on thirty thou a year. Maybe we'd get a little more respect. And you know what the hoods call us?"

"I couldn't guess."

"Feebees," Peterson snorted.

"Something you throw?"

"Not very far. Maybe I should get into something more interesting, like cracking a prost ring or something, you know what I mean?"

"Uh huh."

The hallway ended in a T. At its top, there was a door with RICHARD J. MAYER on the glass. Peterson showed Charley in. Mayer's inner office was behind yet another closed door. His secretary sat guard out front. She looked up from her dogeared copy of *True Romance* and gave Charley, in his faded denim, some heavy disdain. She had movie breasts taxing a sweater a size too small, and too much help about the lips and eyes. One-night stands came off her like cheap perfume.

Peterson eyed her chest. "Know what I mean?" He nudged Charley, gave him a wicked wink. Turning back to the girl, Peterson coughed solemnly and said, "Boss wants to see us, Jennie."

She examined a frayed fingernail, then she pressed an intercom button. "Phil Peterson here to see you with somebody, sir." Her voice was as sexy as wet wax.

"Send the somebody in," the intercom said, with the kind of growl marine sergeants find pleasure in.

Peterson was leaning on Jennie's desk and chatting her up. Her eyes were animated and her back arched. Eyes and back fell when Charley came out. "Your friend's back," she said, picking harshly at a fingernail.

Peterson glanced behind him. "How'd it go?"

"No love lost, but I'm hired." Mayer had been even worse than his voice. Had an Eisenhower cut and looked like he worked out under a sunlamp three days a week. He wasn't someone who made you feel very good about yourself. He was the kind of guy who left you looking for a rusty razor.

"How long you gonna be with us?" Jennie asked, sullen and sighing.

"Two weeks."

She sighed again. "Payroll's to your right."

Peterson walked Charley down. "You know anything about this business, Charley?" he said out in the corridor.

"Babe in the woods."

"I've got to take a piss. Come on along, I'll fill you in. Oh, by the way, I checked on Eddie. No makes."

They ducked into the men's room. Charley hoped it wouldn't start rumors. Peterson went to a urinal and started to relieve himself. Charley checked his mustache for balance in the mirror. It hadn't gotten any better.

"Okay, this is the way it goes, Charley," Peterson was saying over the steam of water. "I'm what you call a street or heavy traffic agent, which means I recruit and work informants, that is, guys who hang around where it counts. Now most these guys, and sometimes they're broads, are the dregs—junkies, whores, pimps—"

"You're doing wonders for my morale, Phil."

"Hell, you know I'm not talking about you." Peterson pulled up his zipper and flushed the toilet. "You're not on payroll as an informer, remember?"

"I know. Maintenance." That was how Mayer wanted it.

Peterson offered Charley a cigarette, taking one for himself when Charley refused.

"Anyway, getting back to my subject," Peterson went on, letting a sink take some of his weight, "once in a while you turn somebody who's a made guy, you know, who has rank in, say, Cosa Nostra. Now you never get them because they're feeling guilty, like maybe they should reform, but because they're greedy—they figure they're going to play both sides, sell info to us on the sly, while at the same time running the same racket they had going before. Now a situation like that, we have to turn our backs and pretend they're outstanding citizens. It's not going by the book, I'll give you that, but it's good business, because these are the guys who can give you God, the big boys, on a silver platter. When you get a guy like that in your file, you pay what the traffic will bear out of slush, goes as high as three, four thou a month, because it's worth every penny, but like I said, most the guys you get aren't like that."

"The dregs."

"Yeah, but you have to use them. You set up meets in inconspicuous places. There's a lot of psychology involved. Sometimes you got to play tough guy, sometimes you hold their hand. You try to figure out when they're giving you the con, but even when they're not, you're probably wasting your fucking time, since most of what they feed you ain't worth the price of admission. Still, you hang in there, hoping for that one bit of fact you don't already know—who's making book or shylocking, who's trying to muscle in where, who's been ground into tomato soup cans. Right now, things are a little slow. Just three or four guys I'm working, haven't been in L.A. that long, I transferred from D.C., three months. Had a real good stable back East, but now—." Peterson's funny hitch of a shrug made an appearance.

"Why'd you change coasts?"

"Got bored. Figured I'd get a tan and see if the broads out here all fuck like bunnies like they say. Anyway, that help you out about the job?"

"Very educational, but how does it work with me?"

"Nothing to it. I'll be your contact. Because you're only doing this in your spare time, the ground rules are simple. You got anything to report, you call me here at the office or at home. You still got my card?"

Charley gave it to him. Peterson scribbled his home phone number on the back and returned the card to Charley.

"If I'm out both places, leave a number and a time with Jennie where I can reach you. If things start to get sticky and you want to cover your tracks, we'll set up someplace to meet."

"Long as it ain't a laundry."

Peterson's chuckle died fast. "One more thing. I might have to go to D.C. for a few days on another case, interstate transport for the purposes of white slavery. If I do, you can check with Mayer to find out where I can be reached."

"Checking with Mayer, that'll be a real pleasure."

"You'll survive."

"When're you leaving, providing you do?"

"Probably Monday. You need me tomorrow or Sunday, I'm here at the office."

"On Christmas?"

"No rest for the wicked."

"Including Mayer?"

"Especially Mayer. Keeps him away from his wife."

"Lucky her."

Peterson smiled through the smoke from his Old Golds, then he changed subject and inflection.

"Where do you think you'll start?"

"Looking for Eddie?" Charley asked. Peterson nodded. "The Corral?" Charley tried. Peterson nodded again. Charley was on a roll.

"Maybe you'll pick up on something the locals missed. I don't think they're trying all that hard. I was on the blower with that cop I know this afternoon, Valley dick named Martz. He'd been talking to Torelli's mother."

"Anything?"

"Yeah." Peterson turned on a faucet and drowned his cigarette. Charley watched the wet ashes disappear down the drain.

"She thought Joe sold insurance for a living," Peterson said, admiring himself in the mirror while he washed his hands. "She thought all he needed was a nice Italian girl to make his life."

"She might've been right."

"Who knows? Anyway, Martz sounded bored. It's the kind of case that dies in files after a week." He shut off the faucet and reached for a towel. "It's too bad," he said, drying his hands. "You know, Joe was a real slob, but I sort of liked him."

"So did I," Charley agreed, with more sincerity.

Peterson snapped his fingers and abruptly said, "Payroll," as though he'd forgotten.

Out in the corridor, there were only two doors left. Someone had taped a sheet of industrial paper over the frosted glass of the one on the left.

"Nice view," said Charley.

"Computer room. If we need something fast, it should be there. Guy who does the programming is sort of a geek."

They went through the door on the right. Inside, a clerk with a pince-nez and a few nasty habits gave Charley his money, two C's in twenties. It had been a helluva trip.

"You pack?" Peterson asked Charley on the way out.

"Not since the army." Charley didn't care for guns. Most murders were of a moment and guns simplified the impulse.

"You should," Peterson said, before Charley left.

7

Storm Warnings

Charley was out on the street by 5:30. His parking allotment had just expired. A meter maid was writing up a ticket. He tried to talk her out of it, but she was one of those types who couldn't be persuaded with a sledgehammer. She stuck the ticket under a windshield wiper and puttered away in her tiny two-wheel toy.

Calling her something unseemly under his breath, Charley jammed the ticket into his back pocket and climbed into his car, trying to gauge miles and hours. He figured he had time for a little legwork before going to Lisa's. It could've waited until after Christmas, but his pride was riled—he wanted a revelation that would wipe the contempt from Mayer's face—Maintenance, shit! Charley decided that in his next life he'd be a cat. Cats didn't have to be concerned about such things—they led the good life of pig-pure naps and momentary yearning.

Coddling the Packard at fifty over the 134 he ignored the angry horns behind him as he worried and winced over every cough and rattle from under his hood, thankful finally for an offramp.

The Corral was a bar on Lankershim in North Hollywood. The neighborhood had flavor—desperate used-car lots, liquor store windows bristling with iron, cheap dives with hot-pants names and unkept promises.

Charley arrived at 6:35 and parked. The lot was stocked with four-wheel drives and big, brutish Harleys burdened with chrome. Several bikers were slouched by their machines, thumbs welded inside their pants. They wore long crankshaft hair and black suede vests with nothing underneath, and they reeked of cheap cologne and watered whiskey. They tried to stare Charley down as he approached the back of the bar—staring people down was what bikers did for a living.

Charley ignored the hard, set eyes and went inside. Two of the motorcycle crowd were playing pool for quarters under a circle of overhead light. They smashed the balls around the felt with the edgy zeal of fanatics, pausing to sip shots from tiny tumblers smudged with greasy fingerprints. Sauntering past them, Charley entered the main room.

The drink and dance arena was Friday night mobbed, mostly axle and high-beam jocks. It had the mild tension of latent violence that accompanies holidays and after-hours muscle. Half the clientele wore tooled leather boots and dented Stetsons; a few might have gotten as close to a horse as Hollywood Park. There was sawdust on the floor and a few tables scattered around. A corner juke, a monster of an old Wurlitzer, was playing the Eagles' "Heartache Tonight," the music loud enough to discourage conversation, not that there was much. The customers were busy swilling from mugs rimmed with ice. A good ol' gal, all flab and mop-stringy hair, had a laugh that could cut glass. Along with the beef flanking her, she was watching hard-core flickering against the far wall.

Charley walked to the counter and took the only available seat, next to the fat lady. The bartender ignored him briefly, the way bartenders always do, before wandering over. He was balding and forty with hooded eyes and a Cagney sneer. Guys who affected that look usually couldn't punch their way out of polyester. When he spoke, it was the standard question.

"What'll it be?" At least it wasn't out of the side of his mouth.

"You got Primo?" Charley asked.

The bartender's eyes got so narrow you couldn't see any white. "Wha . . . ?"

"My first can of beer in 1967 when I was maybe sixteen. Had a cheap paper label that said 'Fully aged slowly,' and a concave top. It was pretty fucking good stuff. Company went outta business after 'bout a year."

There was a crack against the counter, sharp as a rifle report, two sports playing poker dice for drinks.

"We got Bud, Coors, and Heineken," the bartender said, no ifs, ands, or buts about it.

"Coors," Charley shrugged, "and something palatable to eat." He hadn't had a bite since eleven.

"We got cold roast beef on rye."

"Mustard?"

"We're outta mustard, don't you see the sign?"

"Story of my life, missing the sign."

Shaking his head, the bartender shuffled off to fill his order. Resting an elbow on the counter, Charley turned and watched the home movie with the cowboys. A scared-looking kid was struggling out of a Santa suit. A skinny girl wearing only an elf's droopy cap was helping. The black and white print was so bad it looked like it had been shot underwater. The girl fell backward drowning as she pulled off the boy's pants. The fat lady sat enthralled as a housewife watching her favorite soap. The cowboys were taking it in with patient leers and little enjoyment, coolly sipping their beers and comparing sizes. The Eagles thumped across the room, promising that somebody was gonna hurt someone, 'fore the night was through.

The bartender brought Charley his Coors and a sandwich that tasted as stale as it looked.

"Excuse me," Charley said, as he gave him a twenty. "You know a guy named Joe Torelli?"

The bartender turned to the cash register without replying. He brought Charley his change, laying it on the counter.

"Why?" he asked flatly.

"I owed—owe him some money. Figured I might as well pay him."

The bartender's eyes climbed a little. "You lucked out. Joe's dead."

"Dead?" Charley tried to register surprise.

"The cops came in and asked about him last night. Said he was murdered."

"Murdered? No shit!" Sweet Jesus, Charley told himself, I sound like a fool, but the bartender either didn't notice or didn't care.

"No shit. You want to know more, talk to the police, or to her." He cocked his head toward a woman sitting at the far end of the bar.

She was around thirty and black, what used to be called high yaller, coffee stirred with cream. Her hair was cut close, her complexion had a glow, but she just missed being pretty, eyes a shade too small, mouth a shade too big. She was wearing a green cotton dress cut to show strong, smooth breasts. The rest of her was as good, crossed legs shapely in sheer black nylon and braced by high heels. She seemed to be on edge, nothing serious, but it was there. Jiggling one leg, she sat with her lips set in a pout, staring down the barrel of a shot of whiskey. Well, fuck, why not, Charley thought, as he carried his beer high above hostile elbows to the stool beside her.

"Helluva way to be spending Christmas Eve," Charley said. She gave him a glance that didn't really take him in.

Charley said, "I was a friend of Joe Torelli's." She almost noticed him then. It was a start. "I understand you can tell me something about him."

"Understand from who?" She had the big, throaty voice small women sometimes possess, a suggestion of lost echoes.

"The bartender," Charley answered, jerking a thumb back over his shoulder.

"Hmm," she said. She turned away from him, body bent to the counter, skirt hiked high and tight as she contemplated her glass. Then she looked at him with one suspicious eye and said, a concession, "You don't *look* like a cop." Charley took it as a compliment.

"I'm not."

"You sure?" she said, the one eye narrowing.

"Very."

She returned to her drink. "I told them what I know."

"That's an old line."

"And a safe one."

"You told them everything?"

"If you're not a cop, why do you want to know?"

"Like I said, I was a friend of Joe's."

"Maybe."

"Maybe I was a friend of Joe's?"

"Maybe I told the cops everything."

"Do you want to tell me?"

"Why should I?" Her expression didn't change, but her voice was sharp and challenging. A trucker, infected with tattoos, eyed her down and up and evil, saying, "Need any help, lady?"

"Not from you," she shot back. The trucker glowered through a beer-bleary fog, snorted in disgust, and went back to his brew.

"Look," Charley said, keeping his voice down, "you don't want to talk to me, fine. I can understand that. I'd just like to know a few things about last night, that's all."

Cupping the tumbler in her delicate hands, she mulled it over.

"What's your name?" she said.

"Charley."

"Sylvia," she said, without looking at him.

She mulled it over some more, then said, "Okay. Where there's a little more privacy." Charley smiled wearily, felt like he'd just gone ten tough rounds.

Draining her glass, she swung her fine legs off the stool and led him away from the congestion and juke, which had shifted to dirt roads Willie Nelson. Her walk had sex at the hips. Charley followed the rhythm to a lonesome table, where they pulled up chairs opposite each other.

"Why?" she repeated, but without the challenge. Charley kicked a few lies around in his head, but they kept getting up.

"The FBI's paying me to help find the guy who killed him." What the hell, he thought.

She laughed. So did Charley. They both treated it as a joke. Charley shrugged.

"Joe owed me money."

Her laugh dropped to a soft smile. She looked into her drink, as if searching for the hard truths of life, then she said, "Okay. Joe was here last night. I had a few drinks with him right here at this table."

"What was Joe—?"

"To me? An acquaintance, and a customer. Case you haven't guessed, I'm what you call a bar girl . . . a bar girl, not a hooker—there's a difference. If I like a guy, I let him buy me a couple drinks, and sometimes, if I *really* like him, I take him home. Sometimes he leave a little money on the dresser. Sometimes I let him."

"You took Joe home?"

"Once or twice. Not last night. Mostly he liked to talk. He was a lonely kinda guy."

"Ain't we all. So you had a few drinks with Joe . . ."

"And a guy named Eddie, a friend of Joe's."

"Eddie Mikenas?"

She nodded. "Something like that. Now this Eddie, he had more'n a few drinks. Fact, he got downright shitfaced."

"Any reason?"

She snorted. "The best of them. He was scared. It was right there in his eyes. He admitted it. Said he was taking the first flight outta L.A., that they were too close."

"Who's they?" Charley asked, thinking of Mrs. Kravitz's sinister forces.

"He didn't say, but he kept on repeating he'd done a job for them back East and how after it was over, he realized it was too big for him to be messing with. I think he wanted to split before they got the same impression."

"No details about the job, what it involved?"

"Money and power, which tells you nothing, and that something was gonna happen soon, something big and bloody and worth a month of headlines."

"How soon?"

"He didn't say, but according to him, there was some real weird kinks to it—he mumbled some shit which didn't make no kinda sense, about John Wayne and some other jazz."

Charley scratched his scar, tried to keep his tongue out of his cheek. "John Wayne and some other jazz?"

Her lower lip protruded petulantly. "I'm only repeating what the man said." Head down, she ran a finger around the rim of her glass.

"Sorry," Charley said. He realized he was close to losing her.

The lip stayed sulky, but she said, "Don't be sorry. Buy me another drink."

"Which is?"

"Whiskey sour. Don't touch nothing else."

It took some doing, but Charley managed to catch the bartender's attention. He held up one finger and ordered a whiskey sour in a near shout over the noise.

Charley turned back to Sylvia. "He didn't tell you or Joe what he meant by John Wayne? And you said there was some other stuff?"

"No, he didn't. And I was the only one to hear that part of it. Joe, he'd gone off to use the john."

"So you were sitting there alone with this guy you didn't know . . ."

She flashed a crooked smile. "Yeah, it was pretty strange."

"And . . . ?"

"And he's pretty bombed and he's already dropped all this other jazz about a big-time job and getting outta L.A. and I'm thinking this cat's either crazy or he's laying some shit on me I don't want to hear, so I start to get up and excuse myself, in a very ladylike way, and he said, 'If I don't go someplace I'm'—meaning himself—'I'm dead, 'cause I know about John Wayne, Caracas, and the man in the lake.' Just like that, John Wayne, Caracas, whatever the fuck that is . . ."

"Capital of Venezuela. George Foreman knocked out Ken Norton there, title fight, 1974."

"Oh."

"Two rounds. Foreman was very strong. Big as a house."

"Oh."

"Go on with what you were saying. The man in the lake . . ."

"Yeah, well, that was it. I don't know if he even remembered I was there when he said it. The juke was playing Cher, and he had this faraway look in his eyes and his voice was spooky calm, like a dude on death row. Then he sorta smiled to himself and said, "And maybe 'cause I'm Lithuanian," meaning, I guess, maybe he was gonna be dead 'cause of that as well. I think he was joking when he said it, but I couldn't be sure, 'cause his voice, it wasn't much different from when he'd said the rest, and I said, 'Excuse me?' except not the way I'd intended when I'd started to get up, but he didn't look at me, wouldn't. He just sits there staring at his hands, which were shaking. Finally, after a while, he turns around and gives me this real nice smile, innocent and sweet-like, like a kid brother's, and he says sorry, about burdening me, but he was scared, for himself and for his cousin, who was the only other one who knew all this shit."

"He tell you the name of his cousin?"

"No. Anyway, about this time Joe comes back from the john and says he's gonna go do his laundry. He asks Eddie if he needs a ride home, but Eddie says no, he could make it on his own, and I guess he did, which is more'n you can say for Joe." She absently wiped a lipstick smudge from the lip of her glass with her thumb.

"So Joe and Eddie, they showed up at different times?" Before she could answer, Charley added, "It's something I should've brought up before, but I'm new at this sorta thing."

"You're doing OK. Sure you're not a cop?"

Charley's smile was almost comfortable. "Too old."

"Depends on what you're talking about." They both smiled, then she said, "Joe got here a little 'fore eight, his friend a few minutes after. 'Fore he, Eddie, arrived, Joe told me that Eddie had called him early in the day and wanted to know if he wanted to go out for a beer. Eddie told him he'd just gotten back from D.C. and he was uptight and needed to unwind."

"Afterward, who left first?"

"Joe. Eddie sat at the table for a minute or two after Joe was gone, then he got up and thanked me, same real nice smile, for being such a good listener. Said I should forget everything he'd told me 'cause it was all bullshit, it was the booze talking. I think that's how Joe saw it—he was interested, but not so much as he might've been."

"But you didn't think it was the booze?"

She shrugged. "Maybe. He'd sobered up a little by then and he walked out of here straighter'n I would've expected. All I know is what I saw in his eyes. You can fake a lotta things, cumming and religion, but you can't fake scared."

There was a pause. One leg jiggling provocatively, elbows easy on the table, she looked up at Charley with dark expectant eyes, waiting to see if he had any more questions. He stared toward the bar, looking at nothing in particular. Finally, he said, giving it some thought: "Why do you think he told you, somebody he didn't know, all this?"

She shrugged. "Maybe it was building. I just happened to be around when he got rid of it." It was her turn to study the bar. "So was Joe," she said, "around, that is, and he's dead."

She looked at Charley again, hoping for reassurance. He did what he could.

"Don't worry about it. Some geek, some guy flying to Mars

stumbled across Joe and thought he looked like good times, probably some fucking fifteen-year-old with an overload of glands. Homicide's giving Disneyland a run this year."

"Eddie could've killed him, couldn't he? If he was afraid he'd told him too much?"

"Did you go home without company last night?"

"Yes . . . ?"

"So if it was Eddie, why didn't he go after you first? You knew things Joe didn't. He could've waited and followed you."

She shuddered. "Don't say that."

"It wasn't Eddie." Leaning forward, Charley covered her hand with his hand. "It was some street thug, it was a gang initiation, it was a guy in a cape grabbing for kicks, but it wasn't Eddie. Okay?"

Her fingers worried under his palms. Staring hard at her glass, she chewed the blood out of her lower lip, then her body visibly relaxed and her face became composed.

"No. I remember the look in his eyes. It wasn't us he was afraid of. No. It wasn't Eddie."

Charley released her hand and leaned back, letting the chair take the weight of his arm. "Besides, you've told the police all this."

"I told the police that I had a few drinks with Joe and a friend. I tell them more and they ride me."

"Why'd you tell me more?"

"You didn't look like you'd ride. I also got the impression, faint as it might be, you care about Joe dying."

"Yeah," Charley said softly. "Yeah."

He glanced at his watch. It was 7:08. "Finish your drink," he said, motioning to her to stay seated as he got up to leave. He started to take a ten out of his wallet.

"Okay if I leave this?"

"Only if I can take you home." The invitation was open, there was sex in her pocket, and an itch for refuge from the creatures of the night. "You want to come home?" she asked, as much little girl as woman now.

"Yes," Charley said, and he meant it. "But I promised somebody else."

"Sure." Her big voice was lost as she looked somewhere else.

Folding the bill in half, Charley tucked it under her glass. Almost in the same motion, he bent down and gave her a brother's kiss, rosewater gentle, saying thanks as he pulled back, thinking sweet Mary madre de dios, save us all. Mouth twisting up, she gave him a cockeyed smile, followed by a rich, dirty laugh.

"That was out of a bad movie, you know," she said.

"I know. Sometimes life is," he replied, but of course she was right. From his marriage, Charley knew about making the wrong gesture at the right time.

He looked back once as he left the bar. Pausing by the back door, he took in the room. Sylvia had returned to the counter, where she was making eyes at something in rhinestones. The drinkers were drinking, the talkers talking, the juke flashing and belching, and on the screen, two drug-fragged girls writhed, locked on a broken-back bed; everything the way it was meant to be.

Standing there, outlined dark as grief in the doorway, he knew that he'd been tossed a two-bit gig no one else wanted—the police didn't care who killed Joe, the FBI really didn't either, for dead men were too much part of their daily routine, as expendable as the fliers that died on their desks. Charley wondered how much *he* really cared; maybe he really was only doing this because he needed a change and a new transmission. And, at the end of it, all he was probably going to find was that Joe was just another random victim, another name to fill the O.B.'s, and what he'd just heard from the girl was nothing more than a replay of a juicer's crazy jag. He would put it to rest for now, through Christmas and the weekend; then, starting Monday, he'd do what he could. In two weeks he'd collect what they owed him and return to his tap-dancers and little old ladies, and none of it would have mattered, so it was difficult for him to understand the feeling in his stomach, the same jumpy butterfly wings he'd have before a fight; as hard to understand as his belief, gut down as it might be, that John Wayne, Caracas, and the man in the lake had meaning, and that Joe had died for Eddie Mikenas's sins.

8

Lisa

The dirt and dust this day had been particularly wicked, clinging to corners and surfaces. Squatting down, she gave the coffee table a final, forceful spray from the can of Lemon Pledge, rubbed the wax briskly into a gleam, wiped her forehead with the back of her arm, muttered a silent curse, pushed herself up, and collapsed on the couch. She had been cleaning house for three hours straight—come rain, shine, overtime, or divorce, Lisa Tone still kept things in order.

Arms drooped over spraddled legs, she looked at herself in the living room mirror. Even in what she referred to as her domestic uniform—jeans, sandals, blue work shirt with the sleeves rolled up, red bandana tied loosely around her head, she was a handsome woman. Her features were regular, too much so for her own tastes—quick hazel eyes, pert *Good Housekeeping* nose, under a mantle of straight auburn hair. The only flaw in her face was a mole on her left cheek; she liked it very much. Her figure was good, kept trim by riding an Exercycle seven vigorous miles a day. She was thirty, and at times like these, bones and joints drumming dully from an orgy of mopping, vacuuming and dusting, she noticed every year.

She had been born Lisa Fischer in a Brentwood high-rise. As far back as she could remember, she and her parents were at odds. They were into acquisition and tight dogma. She preferred books and fringe causes. Torn cardigan and placards and collective anger became her theme. Her relationships mirrored her rebellion, yet none every quite worked out. At twenty-nine, she wondered if her emotional life was destined to consist of small sinecures of love, as abbreviated as an auto warranty. She thought about children; sometimes she wanted them, sometimes she didn't. Looking for substitutes, she collected objects—knickknacks and antique rugs when she could afford them—like a neutered cat who carries around socks to replace the kittens she'll never have. Then, she met Charley . . .

. . . completely by chance, of course. She'd been prowling through B. Dalton for the latest P. D. James when she'd literally bumped into him in her distraction. They had exchanged a few apologetic words, one of Charley's grammatically incorrect, before going their separate ways. A few days later, she casually returned to the bookstore and he was there. They talked a little longer this time, then went for coffee, sitting in the Topanga mall, watching awkward pirouettes and spills in the indoor ice rink and ignoring the Muzak. They didn't have much in common, but she liked him, liked his offbeat humor and the easy, interested way he listened, unlike so many men who merely tolerated what a woman had to say. And she quickly realized that, if she was the brighter of the two, it wasn't by much, despite his lax grammar and the disparity in their educations.

They began dating. At first, it bothered her that he was eight years older, for she was enough of a feminist to believe in at least approximate equality in all things. Eight years is a big difference, Charley, she'd say. Only with dogs and cats, he'd reply, and she'd grin, for in those days he had always been able to make her smile. The boxing bothered her more, not because she thought he should be a doctor or a lawyer, but because of the brutality of it; to Lisa, a fist in the face seemed the ultimate form of regression. Charley simply told her it was a living and, at his age, one he wouldn't be making much longer. She tried to understand, perhaps even did, and they became lovers. Seven weeks after they met, they took the midnight flight to Tahoe on impulse and were married. Naturally, her parents immediately disowned her.

The first few months were good. They rented the modest two-bedroom home she still occupied in Sherman Oaks, moving in with a grab bag of mutual furnishings and Ali. Lisa made her adjustments, stifling her allergy to cats and even going to one of Charley's fights. She lasted a round and a half of shared pain before rushing out in tears. Afterward, for his few remaining wars, she would wait at home in her bathrobe, chain-smoking and trying not to chew on her nails. When he came home, she would force a calm façade, feed him coffee, and nurse his wounds; only fighters and their wives see the aftereffects: the dehydration, the passing of blood, the pain that lingers.

Together, they watched his career wind down. They talked about his future, never arriving at conclusions; then, abruptly, their relationship no longer seemed to encompass her hopes. She hadn't misread Charley; he *was* kind and concerned, yet he seemed unable to give completely of himself. Probably no one ever could, but she knew she needed more. For her, love came down to nuances, a caress, a word at the right time, the small gestures that were so insignificant, and so important. Not that she considered herself the perfect mate—like Charley, she was too used to living alone. She knew she nagged him about his grammar—which, except for an occasional ain't, really wasn't all that bad—picked at the edges of his nervous habits, and at times could just be downright unreasonable, but, all in all, she felt she put more of an effort into their relationship than he did.

So gradually she withdrew from him, and they moved apart with the aching inevitability of a glacial drift, until one day, after eleven months of marriage, she lit a cigarette, gazed out the window, and said, as calmly as her heart would allow, "Maybe it would be better if we split up, Charley." In retrospect, she realized she was trying to provoke him into an outburst of passion—a profession of undying love would've been nice—but Charley's style in matters of the heart was to go with whatever was the easiest, so he simply reached for his cap and said, Okay. And before she knew it, he'd cluttered the Packard with Ali and his belongings and left, and the worst of it was she knew he wanted to leave no more than she wanted him to, and she felt like grabbing him by the shoulders like a small boy and shaking the emotion out of him, felt like crying out in rage and frustration, damn it, Charley, give!

The doorbell rang. She checked the clock on the wall. It was a quarter past eight. Brushing herself off, she went and opened the front door.

"Merry Christmas," Charley said, handing her a present wrapped sloppily at the ends. It was a long, flat box, just about right for roses.

"Sorry I'm late." he apologized.

"I'm not keeping office hours, Charley. Come in, have a seat." Charley came in. "You didn't bring Ali."

"Got tied up, didn't have a chance to go home and get him."

She set his present down on the piano bench, trying to hide her eagerness to open it.

"Coffee?"

"I could use a cup," he admitted, sitting on the sofa. Cradling his hat in his lap, he leaned back and ran his fingers through his thick hair, taking in the room as she disappeared into the kitchen. The place looked the same—color coordinated, funky, and clean, even the piano. There was a new rug and an old Christmas tree by the front window, pine needles dry, branches drooping.

"Your tree's wilting," Charley said.

"You being symbolic, Charley?" she called back from the other room.

"No, just brutally candid." He flipped open the spiral notepad he'd picked up on his way over and glanced at what he'd jotted down—J. Wayne, Caracas, man/lake, roses?, call Mrs. T. He was about to make another entry when Lisa rejoined him.

"Wilting is what you get for nineteen ninety-five at Ward's," she said, carrying in a sturdy brown mug of strong black brew. She saw the notepad. "What's that?" A kid was throwing dreams at a rainbow on the front.

"Just business." Charley tucked the sky back inside his jacket. He didn't particularly want to tell her what he'd gotten involved in, especially since he didn't particularly know himself. "Thanks," he said instead, taking the cup and sliding a coaster within easy access. He glanced at her through the steam the coffee was giving off. She looked good, all firm, solid lines and scent of Lemon Pledge. He felt like kissing her. He hoped it wasn't the wax. Maybe it was the steam. Blowing it away from the mug's lip, he searched for safer ground.

"They bring them, the trees, in from Big Bear. Already dying by the time they reach L.A."

"Wilting," she echoed, sitting on the piano bench; safer ground was distance.

"You still playing?" He gestured to the piano with his cup.

"Never seem to have the time." There was a pause like lost music. She tried on a cheerful face. "Well, how've you been?"

"Okay. You?"

"Okay." It didn't fit.

The silence took its place. Lisa sat stiffly on the edge of the bench, as though posing for a portrait. She wished Charley would say or do something. For a moment, when she'd handed him the coffee, she'd thought he was going to kiss her. Maybe it was just the steam.

The pause was becoming a modern play. As usual, she'd have to take the initiative, before they both turned to stone.

"I got something for you too, Charley." Springing to her feet, she crouched by the tree and snatched an immaculately wrapped present away from its peers.

"You didn't have to."

"Neither did you," she smiled. "Open it."

"It's not Christmas."

"Don't worry about it."

Charley carefully tore through the paper until he reached Raymond Chandler's *Farewell, My Lovely* in hardback, magenta jacket, blunt black lettering.

"It's a first edition, not quite mint condition, which would've cost an arm and a leg, and no irony intended by the title," Lisa volunteered, returning to the bench.

"It's nice. It really is," Charley said.

"There's something in the back."

He turned there. A sealed cellophane bag containing indeterminate brown shavings was taped inside.

"Grass?"

"Catnip, for Ali."

"I'll probably get busted on the ride home," Charley said with a mild grimace as he set the book down. They both smiled slightly. "Ali'll appreciate it. We both do." The smiles remained. Maybe, Lisa thought, he'd kiss her after she opened the flowers, sweep her into his arms as in a bad Gothic romance; somehow bad Gothic seemed nice at the moment.

"Can I open mine?" she exclaimed, with a child's sudden enthusiasm.

"Be my guest. It's not much," he added, but by then she had the paper on the floor and was sliding off the lid.

"They're beaut—" She stopped in mid-word, staring down at a shiny new car vacuum, complete with detachable rubber hose and unnecessary instructions.

"Like I said, it's not much. I would've got you something better, but I've been a little light and I figured you could use something practical."

"Yes, thank you, Charley." Putting the lid back on, she tried to hide her disappointment, but she couldn't avoid a drop of sourness, like a slice of lemon in milk. "I can always use something else to clean with."

"I guess I could've picked up something more personal."

"Don't apologize, Charley." Eyes downcast, she bit her lower lip. They both turned to stone. Charley stared where the moon didn't shine.

"That's a nice rug. New?"

"And don't try to be polite." She knew he thought rugs were for beating.

"You would rather I'd brought roses."

"No," she started to lie, then she blurted out, "Charley, you know why we broke up? It was because you never brought me flowers!"

"Does this face look like flowers?" He jerked a thumb at his cauliflower features.

"You know what I mean. It's not the flowers, it's the feeling behind it." She was close to crying, a fact that surprised her. She kept back the tears.

"You want some tissue?"

"No."

"I thought—"

"No."

They took turns staring at their own feet, alternating with quick glances at each other. A dog barked belligerently outside. "Shut up," Lisa snapped in response without raising her voice.

"I'm sorry," Charley said, after a while.

"Really?" She sounded like she didn't believe him.

"Yeah. Really." Anguish stalked his face. He gestured helplessly with one hand. "I . . ."

"Yes, Charley?" She waited hopefully, but he hovered over then backed away from his feelings. "I'm sorry," was all he could dumbly repeat. Looking away, he dug at the tissue under his eye.

"Don't—" she began.

He finished for her. "Scratch at my scar."

He sipped at his cooling coffee while she sat, gazing at the floor, vacuum hose dangling like some obscenely wondrous but limp phallus from under the half-open lid on her lap. The dog barked again. People were singing carols somewhere down the street.

"Charley? Do you want to spend the night?"

The question shook both of them. Lisa recovered before he did. "On the couch, I mean. After all, it *is* Christmas tomorrow."

Charley sensed he would have spent it in her bed if he'd brought her goddamn roses.

"You think it's a good idea?" he said.

"No, probably not," she said to herself.

"Maybe I should go home, feed the cat."

"Maybe you should."

Picking up his cap, he got to his feet. "Tuna."

"Hmm?"

"He's been craving tuna."

"Oh."

"Thanks for the book."

"It was eighteen fifty. Less than the tree. Good emotion goes cheap these days."

"Ain't that the truth."

They both managed to smile as he stood by the door, and something like romance passed briefly between them.

"Charley?"

"Yeah?"

"Nothing." She smiled ruefully. "Nothing. Have a good Christmas."

"You too."

He hesitated then closed the door behind him, leaving as quietly as he had two months ago, the same rage and frustration tearing at Lisa with the finality of a broken warranty.

9

Season to Be

The Packard complained. Charley ignored it. He glanced up at the sky as he drove; he couldn't find the moon. It was just as well.

Cruising in a vacuum of traffic down Ventura, he thought of lingering macho codes, of living alone too long, and of another deep-rooted reason for backing away from the reconciliation he couldn't admit he wanted more than anything else; the memory of his parents' marriage was like chewing gravel, nothing to do with him and Lisa, but it was there. Maybe if he could express it . . . He had come close tonight but hadn't cut it, maybe he never could. The realization unsettled and confused him and, detouring to Lankershim, he returned to the Corral, vaguely hoping to find Sylvia and a little creature comfort for the night.

It was going on midnight by the time he arrived, the bar as dead as a hangover. The juke was silent, the porno screen rolled up, the pool table fixed in harsh, Gestapo white light. Only the fat lady and the Cagney clone bartender were left. The bartender was lazily mopping the floor. The fat lady was scrunched up over her tenth beer, seeing how many angels she could count on the head of a Michelob Light.

Hands down in his pockets, Charley casually asked about Sylvia. The bartender shoved the mop past his feet and said that she'd gone home with some guy, tossing in with a sneer that the guy was very big.

Charley ordered a cold shower. The bartender told him to pour his own, that it was on the house. The fat lady looked up, eyed Charley hungrily, saw no possibility for hope, and returned to her task. The clock struck twelve. Slumped over their thoughts, Charley and the fat lady welcomed in Christmas at opposite ends of the counter. Outside, an ambulance pitched past with a high sense of urgency.

"World's a carnival," Charley muttered to his glass and to the universe in general. The bartender glanced over, sighed, and continued to push his mop.

Christmas day didn't start out any better.

Charley got home from the Corral around 1:00 A.M. Locking his car against whatever, he jogged alone along the boardwalk. After three desultory blocks, he stopped, kicked at the sand, swore at the sky, and walked back to his apartment. Once inside, he found that Ali shared his funk. Trying to improve their mood, Charley opened presents. Besides the Chandler, he had six cards, a cologne set of dubious masculinity from a maiden aunt in Belfast, a fat tie he'd never wear from a cousin in Philly, and a year's subscription to *Ring* magazine from his ex-manager, no return address. Muttering "You better like it," Charley gave Ali a cotton Mickey Mouse with an overwrought grin, pipestem arms, and legs spread as invitingly as a hooker's on a businessman's holiday. Ali sniffed the toy, shook his hind legs in disgust, and stalked off to the kitchen where he inhaled Lisa's catnip in less time than the telling. Shouting, Charley called him an ungrateful parasite, and they kept their distance.

Charley turned in at twenty to two. Unable to sleep, with his kidneys aching, he swilled cranberry juice and read sixty pages of *Farewell, My Lovely*, while Ali menaced gulls from the window. The book—which had characters with forties names like Red and Velma and a six-five hulk called Moose Malloy—seemed to be about corruption, messy murders, and long-lost loves. Before it got any better, Charley marked his place and put it aside. Looking for something constructive to do, he checked the phone directory to see if there was a listing for an Eddie Mikenas, which, of course, there wasn't. Around this time, which was too damn late, the girl next door came home to party. At the first sign of activity, Charley pounded fiercely on the wall, cracking plaster and bruising his hand, but reducing the Migrant Angel-Dust Maniac and whoever she was with to a thimble of a worried murmur.

Content, Charley slept eight good hours. He woke with his alarm at eleven, feeling like he could punch holes in brick.

After making his peace with Ali—tuna with mayonnaise on the side—he drove to his office, looking forward to the New Year with hope and to the end of the holidays with a vengeance. When he arrived, the sun was sweeping the sky clean and the birds were singing in anticipation of fat, sluggish worms. Pulling up his blinds, Charley kicked back in his chair, feet up on his desk, and took in the heat from above. Suitably refreshed by the sun, he mapped out his agenda for the day, which began with a call.

* * *

There were four Torellis in the book. Joe's mother was the third Charley tried. There was a lot of Joe in her voice, Old World Italian breaking under its own weight. Charley expressed his sympathy, cleared his throat, hemmed and hawed through her grief. He asked a few apologetic questions, didn't expect answers. She surprised him. When he hung up, he was as pleased with himself as a baton twirler. Driving downtown, he guessed Peterson would be too.

10

Tiny Tim

"Phil's not here." Jennie sighed. "He flew to Washington this morning. He'll be gone a week."

"Thought he wasn't going till Monday."

"Guess he changed his mind."

She looked like she regretted it even more than Charley—her eyes and mouth were sagging and the deep sex in her throat had risen to its natural state, mousy. *True Romance* was swimming in the trash.

"I'm paying for my sins," Charley told himself.

"Huh?"

"Nothing. I was just doing some penance."

She let the remark pass and said, "He got a gun for you. It's in his office." Charley grunted.

Mayer's voice flared over the intercom, a few general insults only sailors should know, then fell silent.

"Do you want to see him?" Jennie asked Charley.

"It'll wait."

"I think he's mad because his wife gave him bellbottoms. I think he feels threatened."

"Especially if they have buttons."

As Charley started to leave, he heard a lament.

"It never started."

Charley turned.

"Christmas," Jennie explained.

"Ain't that the truth," Charley said, on his way to see the computer's geek.

Someone had emphatically printed HUMBUG! across the industrial paper that blanketed the geek's window. Charley rapped on the door and waited, whistling "Jingle Bells."

After a five count, he heard footsteps approaching from inside. After another five count, he heard the squeal of Scotch tape being stripped. A hand rose darkly on the other side of the frosted glass and drew back the BUG. A head and torso appeared, pressed against the window. Although its features were obscured, the head, which hit Charley just above the chin, seemed to be trying to peer out. Charley wondered if he should've brought live meat.

After a moment, the BUG rejoined the HUM and the footsteps padded away. Charley knocked again, with greater vigor. He shifted to "The Twelve Days of Christmas" while he waited.

The footsteps came back. The door opened a crack, revealing sloppy mouth, pug nose, and maybe there were eyes behind the thick bifocals. The glasses squinted, as if adjusting from darkness to light. Although the mouth resembled something you see chickens in and the lips barely moved, the voice was much more normal than Charley expected, a little crotchety and vague, but functional.

"You're off-key."

"Yeah, but I play a mean comb."

The corners of the mouth and eyes crinkled into a mild smile. The door opened another inch.

"Who are you?"

"Charley Tone. I'm on the payroll."

The voice thought it over. "On the payroll . . . Undercover?"

"Close enough."

The eyes sized up Charley's denims without making any judgments. The door opened just enough to let Charley in.

The room was a cave of contemporary parts—OCR's, Vanier graphics, a jazzy computer, and magnetic disks. Printouts curled to the floor from a desk. A wastebasket was upside down. A chipped mug with a coffee drool squatted on the wastebasket's top. On the wall, there was an empty coffeepot on a shelf and a geometric painting of a woman down on all fours, all square planes.

After a while, the geek introduced himself. "Jerome Haines," he said, offering a child's hand. He was wearing a wrinkled white shirt dirty around the collar and light slacks with a Yuban stain on one knee.

"Guess you thought I look a little strange, with what I got on," Charley said.

"Not really. Somebody came in the other day wearing a sheet." Turning from Charley, Haines removed a trayful of printouts. "Hmm hmm, hmm hmm, hmm," he mused, scanning the pages. "Child's play." Crumpling the pages into a cockeyed ball, he strode to the desk.

"I was just feeding Tiny Tim his daily ration of crosswords."

"Tiny Tim?"

"The computer," Haines explained. He tried to stuff the ball someplace tidy; the ball bounced off the top of the wastebasket. Haines didn't seem to notice.

"What do you need?" he asked, bracing against the desk with one hand to keep his balance as he straightened up.

Charley took his notepad out of his jacket and showed Haines the name Mrs. Torelli had given him. Karl Vaitonis was Eddie Mikenas's cousin in D.C.; if you went by Sylvia, he was the only one besides Eddie who knew what Eddie was doing back East. Eddie was always bragging on him, which Joe's mother didn't like. Hate, Charley guessed, was as good a reason as any for remembering somebody.

"Wanted to see if you got anything on him," Charley told Haines.

Haines peered across Charley's arm at the name. "Why do you think we might?"

"Just winging it. Think it might be my lucky day."

"I see . . . common fallacy, belief in luck." Taking the notepad, he went over to the keyboard and pressed a button. The screen lit up, an empty green pasture, but not a tranquil one; the light was that of aliens staring. Haines pecked out a four-digit code on the keyboard. In response, WHAT DO YOU WANT?—a nice reasonable question—appeared in small, focused white letters across the flat green. Haines replied by typing the name Charley had given him.

"Vaitonis . . ." Haines said, glancing down at the notepad. "Slavic, I would guess. Baltic Sea, possibly."

"Not lately," Charley said.

Haines finished typing. Charley watched the video scanner from over his shoulder. After a few seconds, more small, white letters formed on the screen:

KARL VAITONIS . . . 743971687 . . .

"What's it mean?"

"That any information we have on your friend is in the Bureau's Computer Systems division in Washington. If you'll excuse me . . ."

Returning to the desk, Haines picked up the phone and dialed seven digits. Half sitting on the desk's blotter, he said, "This is substation forty-one. Bill Roberts, please." Waiting to be put through, he entertained Charley. "Roberts is the head of data processing at our main office. He has a direct terminal line to Washington."

Haines's attention returned to the phone. "Bill, this is Jerome Haines . . . Fine, humbug to you too. The reason I'm calling, could you check something with God for me? Hmm, hmm . . . see what he has on a Karl Vaitonis. First name, K-A-R-L, last, V-A-I-T-O-N-I-S . . . Okay, thanks, Bill."

Haines hung up and faced Charley. "Shouldn't be more than five minutes. Have a seat. Do you want any coffee?"

"Ah, there ain't any," Charley reminded him as he straddled

Tiny Tim's chair. The guy wasn't a geek, he was a kick, a walk through a lab where the tubes keep breaking.

Haines craned his neck toward the shelf. "Seems you're right." He blushed, genuinely surprised. "Just as well. I make very bad coffee." He looked troubled. "Someone died once shortly after I'd served them. I *think* it was something else that killed him."

"Changing the subject, I don't know I understand all that about Tiny Tim and God?"

"Oh, yes." Haines moved into more comfortable territory. "You see, Tim's a third-string Xerox, sixty-five K's, which means he only holds around sixty-five thousand bytes, or bits of current information. He's a little fellow, mostly a cataloger of names, letting us know if we have somebody on file somewhere else. Somewhere else is generally God in Washington, a monster IBM containing five hundred million bytes—fills half a room five times the size of this one."

"He ever make mistakes?" Charley secretly hoped God did.

"Oh, occasionally you get a speck of dust on a disk, which can cause all kinds of problems, but errors are pretty rare, unless, of course, there's sabotage. For instance, about a year ago, God started going haywire. Seems someone had tapped into—'accessed' in computer jargon—God's brain. During a two week period, over fifteen million bytes were lost."

"Who was doing it? The devil?"

"Sounds pretty sinister, doesn't it. Our glorious Bureau thought so, imagining a brilliant coup by some element of organized crime. Well, finally, after nearly a month of chaos and short tempers, they discovered the bad guys. The oldest was thirteen. Seems that a group of very ingenious kids had managed to hook their school's terminal up to the Bureau's office, then, by trial and error, pushed out the right combinations to link up with God. Some good guesswork after that got them the code password to control the old boy."

"Cute."

"That time, but actually computer crime is rapidly becoming a major national nuisance. It's a lot simpler than people realize. All you need to embezzle a few million dollars from a bank is a cheap home processor, a phone, and a few basic skills that, as you've seen, a bright schoolboy could acquire. There are risks, of course, with prison as a consequence if your game is discovered, but the potential rewards are more than appealing. I have to admit, I've been tempted once or twice myself. I'm certain that with a little effort, I could electronically transfer enough funds to set myself up for life on some desert island, all nice and cozy with my own private library—not everybody's idea of paradise, perhaps, but one that would suit me perfectly."

Charley smiled to himself. Haines wasn't such a stereotype after all, or maybe he was: We all have our corrupt fantasies—they're just sorted out into different packages.

"Coffee?" Haines asked. "Ah, yes, there isn't any," he recalled. Charley was glad Haines didn't smoke—he would have set them both on fire. Haines whistled softly while they waited for the phone to ring, something that bore no relationship to any recognizable tune. He couldn't whistle a lick; the attempt produced light puckering sounds, with an occasional involuntary hiss thrown in.

Just as Charley was wondering if he should turn on Tiny Tim to provide some suitable accompaniment, the phone nipped at Haines's elbow.

Sheltering the receiver between shoulder and ear, Haines sat on the edge of the desk, jotting down the information Bill Roberts was giving him on the back of a printout. Charley's curiosity was as offhand as Haines's whistling. He anticipated nothing special, a little biographical detailing at best.

Concluding the one-sided conversation with a "Thanks, Bill," Haines replaced the receiver.

"How's God?" Charley felt he should know.

"Frazzled."

Haines studied his notes, then he walked over and handed the printout to Charley without comment or apparent interest, before busying himself with mag cards.

Charley scanned his scrawl. Haines had divided the information into three short sections, separated by two looping lines. The first section was mildly interesting. It read:

KARL VAITONIS A/K/A JAMIE LOWELL, RALPH ORR . . . AGE 32 . . . 5′11″ . . . 140 POUNDS . . . MARITAL STATUS DIVORCED . . . WORK HISTORY MECHANIC SPORADIC . . . PRISON RECORD ATTICA '77–'79 EXTORTION RAHWAY '83–'85 EMBEZZLEMENT.

The second section was more than mildly interesting. It read: DECEASED 12/21/89 . . . METHOD GARROTING.

But it was the last part that stirred Charley's blood. It was, like anticipation, a feeling he'd had before in the ring, a raw nervous surge when he didn't know how things were going to come out. If he ever enjoyed fighting, it was at those moments when everything hinged on an unexpected move. Boxing then could be like a game of chess, one of jarring blood and bone, sure, but with riffs of strategy and surprise.

The third section wasn't a message from the stars but it was close: IDIOSYNCRASIES HANDS SEVERED AND QUARTER PLACED OVER VICTIM'S EYE.

11

Passage

Charley couldn't concentrate; the buttoned-down stewardesses were forcing joy on both sides of the aisle, and even from tourist, the flick, a bad comedy, was too loud.

Sighing, Charley dogeared *Farewell, My Lovely* and gazed out the window. The 727 appeared perfectly still, as if suspended by wires in an amusement park ride. When you live in L.A., umblemished blue skies and satin-white clouds never seem to exist beyond movie sets, but now Colorado was very real twenty thousand feet below. The Dolores River stretched like a jagged scar across the face of the snowbound land; buttes and mesas were bruises. Charley tried to appreciate the scenery but he never enjoyed flying, with or without laugh tracks. If his feet weren't on the ground or his own hands tight to a wheel, he didn't feel right. The funny thing was, he didn't fear collisions or rude weather, but passages like this, through drowsy postcard skies, where his imagination had time to paint pictures of an engine suddenly coughing up black blood and the huge, unnatural steel bird shrieking to a bad end below.

Charley had, of course, brought this misery upon himself. After saying goodbye to the geek, he had dropped in on Mayer. Jennie had warned him that her boss was in a life-menacing mood. Seems he had just been on the blower with Martz, the Valley homicide dick, kicking Joe around. Their conversation hadn't been sweet. The shouts Jennie heard had colored the walls blue. So, Charley said, maybe I'll cheer the bastard up, but Mayer hadn't been impressed—coins and hands, what the hell, maybe Joe and Karl Vaitonis had offended the same wise guys somehow, the kind of punks who make their bones with lug wrenches. Mayer was enjoying himself, muscling Charley with his knowledge, then all of a sudden he'd started staring through the smoke from his cigarette; the next thing Charley knew, he had a round-trip and expenses. Charley knew Mayer wasn't just being nice, and, packing, he'd come up with an explanation. Mayer was sending him because of Belmonte and the banderillas.

When he was young, Charley had a great-uncle crazy for bullfights. He would tell the boy blood and sand stories, most of which Charley immediately forgot, but he remembered one: in the twenties, there were two class matadors in Spain, Belmonte and Joselito. Their rivalry was bitter and equal, except for the placing of banderillas, the short, pointed sticks used to goad the poor bull. Joselito had mastered the skill, Belmonte couldn't because of slow feet. To offset Joselito's advantage, Belmonte used a gifted employee named Maera. Maera could place banderillas as well as Joselito, and Belmonte would dress him in the saddest suit of lights he could find, so it would seem that a mere peon was as good as the great Joselito.

Charley guessed that something similar had happened this morning; the call Jennie overheard had triggered a load of competitive steam in Mayer. The detective had probably ridiculed his interest in a killing as lightweight as Joe's. With his sense of priorities and hard values, Mayer would have secretly agreed, but it must have rankled. Then Charley had come in with a few things that might or might not be something. So, Mayer must have thought, why not send him to Washington? If, by chance, he stumbled across anything, the pros—say, Peterson—could take over. In any event, Mayer could call Martz and very nicely point out that one of the FBI's peons had accomplished more than the whole frigging LAPD, a skirmish won in the ongoing war between bureaucracies. After working all this out, Charley had smiled and said to himself, you're getting pretty sly in your old age, Charley Tone. Either that, and he'd smiled again, or you're full of shit.

No matter what, he was on his way to Washington. After leaving the FBI offices, he had made the necessary provisions before his 4:40 flight from LAX. First, he had, for a percentage, temporarily turned his business over to a moonlighting bondsman, known as Weird Arthur because of various disturbing rumors about his more intimate proclivities.

Next, he'd called Lisa and asked if she'd mind boarding Ali and the Packard for a few days. He could have stuck Ali in a kennel, but last night had stirred too many old feelings and it was a convenient excuse for seeing her again. She had agreed to nursemaid car and cat, even driven him to the airport, brushing off his apologies for bothering her on Christmas Day. On the way, snuffling and sneezing and wheezing with Ali perched on the seat behind her, she simply said, You owe me one, Charley Tone, you owe me one, saying it in such a way that he knew he didn't. He liked her for that, as well as for the way she'd asked him where he was going only once and not again after he'd vaguely replied, Somewhere on business. So he *did* owe her, owed her an explanation and some time when he got back.

He suddenly felt very tired. Down below, the open land had given way to the map relief of some unknown city. Sighing, he found his place in *Farewell, My Lovely.* He was at a part where the cracking wise shamus gets drugged and thumped off Sunset, a location Charley knew well. He tried a few paragraphs and gave up. The desperate laughter from the screen was lulling in a strange sort of way. Rubbing his eyes, he adjusted his seat, leaned back, pushed his cap down over his forehead, and, before a dozen sheep had crowded over the fence, he was lost to the world.

Slumber on a plane is like no other kind of sleep. The senses ease into the droning rhythm of the engines so that no matter how many hours you doze, you feel that no time has passed and that you're exactly where you were before when you wake.

It was night when a fasten-seat belts voice returned Charley to the world. Blinking owlishly, he looked out the window. Five thousand feet below, the capital's veins ran in black cobweb arteries; the spine was the Potomac, curving up the west side of the city. To the north, mountains spread dim and low across the horizon, like the backs of sinister beasts of burden.

The 727 was homing in on Washington National. The runway seemed to rise up to meet the plane. Where touched by light, the strip looked like burnished brass. Jumbo jets stood in pledge of allegiance rows. Others lay in playground disarray.

Charley fastened his seat belt as the plane veered, looped, and slowed into its landing pattern. Flaps lowered without sound. Wheels drew down from its belly like prosthetic legs and hit the ground with fluid precision as the 727 jutted and screeched to a stop. It was 11:47, Eastern Standard Time. Christmas was almost over. He had survived.

A blast of Arctic air swept over Charley as he disembarked, and he slipped into the peacoat he'd brought for the weather, the big, wide-shouldered jacket giving him a bully's bulk. The airfield illumination was mixed and aquatic; still searchlight pools and control tower glints, like midnight sun off deep water.

The terminal had the same shambling mood that all terminals, train, bus, or plane, have at night, a sense of activity but none of urgency or even interest from those who pass through. Disembodied loudspeaker voices heralded arrivals and departures with the enthusiasm of blind corner beggars. Charley wondered if this form of catatonia didn't have to do with our means of transportation; when men relied on horses, there must have been an exaltation of energy, a feeling of communion with their animals, of flesh and blood and the slick high heat of flanks. Traveling by machines produced only a dreary desire to get from one place to another as quickly as possible.

Once outside the terminal, a babe in sable stole Charley's cab but he borrowed another, told the hack the Three Seasons. Overhead, a 747 turned its nose to the sky and headed for the moon.

The driver was hunched and sad, with a face like dirty canvas and dandruff on his collar. They rode in silence, crossing over Rochambeau Bridge and the black-bracelet expanse of the Potomac and into the city, where strings of Christmas lights sparkled like gems. There had been recent snow, but the sidewalks and brick and stone buildings were clean—only some slush in the streets and an occasional daring thread of white on an overhanging branch remained. There were few cars and fewer pedestrians, and the night air had the clarity of stillness. The cab's tires squished over the pavement, the sound vulnerable and remote.

Charley had never been to Washington before and finally he asked the driver what there was to see. As he had to a thousand others, the cabbie described it glumly but well. He told Charley how it was a funny place, not quite like any other, about how its hundred square miles were purchased by George Washington and friends over a tankard of ale, which was just about right, for Washingtonians liked their liquor as much as their gossip. He told Charley how in the early years Pennsylvania Avenue, where the White House and government buildings gang up, was rich with ruts deep enough to hold robbers, of which there were many, and how the robbers were still there, only now they wore suits. He told him it was a city of parks and trees and monuments to everything, and of the former the Mall was the biggest, where two hundred years ago they used to have slave pens, but where now you find folk music, soul food, ethnic crafts, and outdoor skating in black and white and name your colors. He talked of how it was a city of rich and poor, mostly the latter, and the rich congregate in Georgetown and Cleveland Park and Arlington, and go for their fun to the Foxtrappe, the Guards, and Nathan's, and the poor live in the black and Latin slums of Adams-Morgan and Meridian Hill and Edgewood, and go nowhere, and how, if you ain't either one, you take the tours and dine and dance and gawk at Fran O'Brian's or Archibald's or the Florida Avenue Grill, and if you like your sports, there's the Redskins for football, the Bullets for basketball, the Caps for hockey, but it's never been the same since the Senators left, and if you're looking for whores, there's Logan's Circle, and if you're looking for limp-wristed boys, there's Pier 9, and if you're looking for God, he left on the 519 for Boston in the summer of '47, and by then they were near Charley's destination, and the driver swung a crisp left onto a boulevard that spelled squalid.

The Three Seasons, flaking brownstone and ten stories, was at the end of the block. As Charley got out of the cab with his suitcase, the driver leaned across the seat and said, "You gonna work the docks outta Chesapeake Bay?"

Charley nodded gravely. "Merchant marine. How'd you guess?"

"You got the look," the cabbie said knowingly.

"So I've heard," Charley replied, and he went into the hotel whistling a maritime ditty.

The interior went with the neighborhood—lobby and stairway looked frayed and soiled. So did the potted plants. So did the staff. Still, there were a few virtues: Victorian mirrors with gold in their glass and a big chandelier that shed forties lighting; Raymond Chandler would have sighed.

Buoyed by such faint cheer, Charley went to the front desk, where he asked which season was missing while he signed in. The clerk, who wore a rug and was a fool for hate, didn't laugh. Charley suspected he hadn't since Lincoln was shot. The clerk perused Charley's signature for errors, then dourly informed him that maid service was once a day at eleven sharp and that sliding down the banisters and jumping out of windows were prohibited. Charley told him that left very little in life to enjoy. The clerk made a face that broke glass and handed him a big bronze latchkey for 409 at arm's length. A vicious-looking bellboy with acne and his fly half undone wandered over to take his suitcase. Charley said he'd carry it himself. He walked across the lobby, neatly sidestepping the devious foot the bellboy stuck out, and rode up to his room. The wood-paneled elevator was foreign to modern society. Instead of a five-dollar hum, he could hear the cables fighting, and opening, the doors gave him time to get out.

Four-oh-nine was without explanation five doors down. Once inside, Charley shrugged off his coat and suitcase. Like the lobby, the room was out of the forties—lavender and porcelain and the smell of jasmine. Thumbtacked to the wall, an ivory scroll read SO SAITH THE LORD. God must have had a laconic day.

It was past Charley's bedtime. Stripping down to shorts and T-shirt, he climbed under the covers. Pillow and sheets were as stiff as boards. Before he'd left L.A. he had called Sylvia to see how she was. She was okay, but she'd had a few ugly dreams. Now, lying in the darkness, Charley let his imagination invade her sleep, saw her sweat bright beneath a lover. When the man got up, he shed her body the way a snake sheds a dead skin. Charley kept staring into the darkness, until her nightmares became his own.

12

Sister

Sunlight slipped past the drawn curtains of flimsy lace and stroked Charley's stubble. He had slept the sleep of the dead, and he woke with a roll. Picking himself up off the floor, he carried the phone into the john. A Coke ad flattered the space over the toilet, a doll in Gay Nineties bonnet and frill. She was holding the product. The bottle looked like a cock. Charley turned the poster to the wall.

Sitting on the open seat, he dialed the Park Central Hotel. Switchboard answered. He could tell it was a ritzy establishment by her affected timbre—arched *e*'s and bottomless *h*'s. He asked for Phil Peterson. Switchboard put him through, but there was no answer.

The operator asked if he desired to leave a name and number. Charley said no, he was going to be out himself; he'd call back, God and Chesapeake-Potomac telephone permitting.

After hanging up, he shaved, dressed, and finished unpacking, including the Chandler; he'd left his dictionary at home; he figured he'd learn enough new words as it was in Washington, such as platitudes, graft, and something for kissing babies. The gun Peterson had left for him was at the bottom of the suitcase, a blue-black .38 with the dull gleam of lethal function. It felt as cold as a whore's embrace. Still, as his mother had once said, you take love where you find it, and Charley tucked the gun and the ammo that came with it in his coat pocket.

At a Hertz within walking distance, Charley paid for three days in advance on a '76 apple-red Camaro that smelled of stale cigar and crankshaft oil. He drove half a block, double parked, and locked the gun and ammo in the glove compartment. Then he went and found the First Precinct.

The station house was scary for a Sunday. Hookers were hipshot and hostile waiting to be booked. A guy was arguing a ticket for parking on a meter maid. A cat in early halfway house had seen God on Constitution with his thing hanging out. The phones were killing themselves, jumping off the desks. There was a black sergeant who looked like he was there to help. Charley walked over and leaned easy as can be on his counter.

"Don't lean, man," the sergeant snapped. He had a potbelly, a steamrolled uniform, and a knife in his voice. Charley returned his arms to his sides.

"What the fuck you want?"

"To fucking see about a guy who got iced, name of Karl Vaitonis." Charley could talk tough too.

"You related?"

"Do I look like I'm in mourning?"

The sergeant tried to forget that Charley was there. He shuffled papers. He yawned. Seeing that Charley wasn't about to go away, he got up and trundled down a corridor; despite his pressed pants, he had a saggy ass that yearned for low places. After a while, he returned with a suit-and-tie cop, so tough-looking that he should've had calluses for whiskers.

Charley put out his hand. "Charley Tone."

"Pete Reiser, Homicide." His handshake was firm, his voice like sandpaper. "Tone?" he said.

"I know. Sounds like a rock band."

"You've been asked that before."

"More than I can count."

"Why're you interested in Karl Vaitonis?"

Charley showed Reiser a card they'd given him in payroll. Reiser looked down, then up.

"Maintenance?"

"You know how it is. Undercover."

Reiser hinted at a smile. He waved Charley along to his office. The sergeant looked disgusted and said, "Federal Bureau of fucking Investigation my fucking motha's ass," with a mean dog snarl.

"What do you want to know about Vaitonis?" Reiser asked, once he and Charley were settled in.

"Whatever you can tell me."

"What I can tell you is an old lady was walking her schnauzer by an alley. She saw a foot sticking out from under an old newspaper behind a garbage can. She took a closer look and found the rest of him. It was not a very dainty killing. His face and the backs of his hands had cigarette burns, indicating that somebody had tried to get him to tell them something. There were twenty-six burns, indicating he was either unwilling or didn't have the answers to their questions. Finally, he or they, whoever did it, wrapped a piece of wire around his neck and pulled—the wire was embedded clear to the jugular, meaning whoever killed him was very, very strong. Then, after he was dead, they cut off his hands at the wrists and placed them over his lap, like they were folded. Then they put a 1964 tin alloy quarter over his eye, the left one. Like I said, not a very dainty killing. You want to see pictures? I've got glossies in the file."

"No, thanks."

"The old lady was so shook they had to take her to the hospital in the same ambulance they hauled Vaitonis off in. I don't know what happened to the schnauzer."

"Distemper?"

"I wouldn't doubt it."

"Any suspects? For Vaitonis, not the dog."

"None. No leads, witnesses, nothing."

"One of those cases you bury after a week."

"Give it two," Reiser said, smiling for the second time.

"Did he have any friends or relatives I could talk to?"

"His friends, they're in prison—he'd only been out a month, unemployed. He had a sister. She picked up his belongings."

"Can you tell me where she lives?"

"We took her statement. She doesn't know shit."

"I ain't doing nothing else."

"Suit yourself." Reiser picked up a pencil and wrote down her name, Janice Vaitonis, and address on a memo pad. He tore off the sheet and handed it to Charley. Despite his bricklayer appearance, he had beautiful penmanship, flowing letters with rainbow flourishes.

"I won awards for that in grammar school," he said proudly, reading Charley's mind.

"I can tell." Folding the sheet in half, Charley tucked it into his wallet, next to a twenty. "You know if she works?"

"Secretary for Comsat-Communications. Not much on looks, but I'd lay odds she gives great head because she knows she has to, to get by."

"Something I'll ask."

Reiser drummed the pencil against the side of his desk, seemed to be running a few rainbows through his mind.

"Nice hair though," he said. "Long, blond, kind of silky . . ." He smiled up at Charley, a gold filling gleaming in the overhead light. "Maybe I'll give her a call."

"Happy times," Charley said, his eyes on the detective's wedding band.

Reiser coughed uncomfortably and dropped a hand over his ring finger. "Anything else?"

"Nothing. You've been very helpful." Charley got up and headed for the open door.

"Hey," Reiser called after him. Charley turned.

"Nothing personal, but why'd they send you for something like this?"

"Because of a guy named Maera, who could place banderillas."

13

Carnival

There was a pay phone in a '76 station a block from the precinct. The vandals had worked the booth over pretty good; the glass was gone everywhere you looked, the directory ripped from its moorings. On a panel of glass that was still around, someone had painted SANTA SUCKS in red. Underneath, someone else had scrawled in black felt tip, *His place or mine?* The booth's door had been removed, probably to save it from too much love. The phone, scarred by penknife squiggles and chewing gum that stuck like cement, swallowed two of Charley's dimes without so much as a dial tone. Swearing, he pounded on the box with the heel of his hand. Despite the noise level, the gas jockeys paid not the slightest bit of attention; they were busy cracking wise over Pepsis in the can.

After half a minute of abuse, the coin return perversely spit out four dimes, a nickel, and two quarters, both tin alloy. Pocketing his profit, Charley inserted half the dimes. This time supply followed demand and the Park Central switchboard put through his call to Room 307. Peterson's roughed-up tenor answered after two and a half rings. Peterson said, "So?" Charley said, "How's the white slavery racket?" An astonished pause and some reckless switchboard interference ensued.

"Charley?" Peterson said, after switchboard despaired. "You sound close. Where the hell are you?"

"Here in Washington. Mayer didn't let you know?"

"Does he ever? What are you doing here?"

Charley told him in detail. Peterson tossed in an occasional "uh-huh." After Charley finished, there was nothing but silence.

"Phil? You still there?"

"Still here." He sounded distracted.

"Well, what do you think?"

"I don't know. I guess I thought you were going to try and find Eddie."

"It went in a different direction."

"Hey, don't get me wrong. I think you've done a helluva job. A helluva job . . ." The distracted quality hadn't gone away. "What did you say the sister's name was?"

"Janice. Vaitonis, like her brother." Peterson asked for the address. Charley gave it to him, then said, "Figured maybe I'd go talk to her after she gets off work tonight."

"Huh? Oh, no, look—let it go until tomorrow. I'll have some free time then. We'll both go see her. Okay?"

"Uh . . ."

"I'll pick you up in the morning, say around ten."

Charley hesitated, then agreed.

Peterson remembered his manners. "Oh, by the way . . . how was your Christmas?"

"Don't ask."

After getting off the phone, Charley returned to the Camaro, got inside, and rolled down the window, trying to chase the stench of stale cigar. He sat with arms draped over the wheel, not too pleased with himself or the conversation. Like Mayer, Peterson's response to his efforts had been lukewarm at best. Maybe murders with hacked-off hands and quarters over snuffed-out eyes were fashionable these days, common as hooker boots or designer jeans. Or maybe Peterson downplayed his joy over what Charley had found because he planned to take over the investigation himself; he'd call Charley at ten and say, hey, look, I stopped by this Vaitonis chick's pad last night and Jesus she gives great head and you ought to try her yourself before we put you out to pasture, which is just around the corner. Another possibility, and a good one, was that the case's only importance was to keep intact the Bureau's street image as guardian of its sources, and only solving the Torelli killing really mattered for that.

Charley spent fifteen glum minutes in this sort of speculation before deciding to go for a drive. The afternoon was good for loosening if not freeing the spirit—air cold but clean, sun dull but there. Keeping the window down, he cruised the predictable sights, taking in the Mall, the Justice Department, the Washington Monument, the White House, Lafayette Square, the State Department, JFK Center for the Performing Arts, the U.S. Naval Observatory, the National Zoological Park, and the city in general. There was a lot to see, some of it too modern for his tastes, buildings so geometric in their design that they strung out the nerves. Others had the grace of tradition, seemed as lived-in as old leather. Charley liked the parks best. They had space and curves that connected, with ice-rich streams, and trees—oak, walnut, hickory, elm, maple, pine—and plants—magnolia, rhododendron, laurel, box bushes, privet hedges, holly, roses—that would be a flowering of color in the spring. And then there were the people . . . There were people everywhere, sex was close to everybody's pocket. The sidewalks kept giving off nerves, the citizens were edgy with knives in their eyes for the tourists who kept swinging in on Nikon chains.

Around five, Charley joined the visitors and their enemies on foot. Without a camera, he mingled safely and well. He finished off the day at the Tomb of the Unknown Soldier, munching a foot-long hot dog and sort of wondering who the dogface was—was he white, black, yellow, brown, or a mix of the above? Maybe it was even one of his great-uncles—not the nut who loved bulls, but a proud cat who had lost his head during Blackjack's push through the Argonne. Charley decided it wasn't him in the tomb, for this particular relative had always had lousy luck; chances were he had been mistaken for a Kraut and down-and-dirty dumped in some part of France that was forever a cow pasture.

Along about six, Charley could see that musing wasn't making him feel any better. He had some anger working, leaning toward Phil and Mayer. Maintenance, that was how they saw him, keep you sweeping, then leave you hanging in the air. Fuck it, he said to his face in the car mirror, fuck it, he said as he drove to her apartment.

She lived on a street of high-rise horrors painted art deco colors of vomit green, jaundice yellow, and infant-ass pink. Janice Vaitonis's was a bilious blue on a corner, six stories dedicated to the proposition that American architecture was on its last legs.

Seven o'clock arrived with Charley. Darkness worried the sky. The city, distant and close, had that fine early evening slur of casual noise. Charley found a space down the block, parked, and got out. It was getting cold and he shrugged into his peacoat. A mounted policeman coaxed his horse between the parked cars and slow traffic, the chestnut's careful hoofs clattering lightly, the breaths of man and beast forming white, smoky clouds. The cop had a good-natured, ruddy face and he gave Charley a tip of his nightstick as he passed by. Charley returned his smile as he walked down the sidewalk with a sailor's rolling gait. Merchant marine, he thought, smiling to himself.

Outside the blue building there was a ragged old lady—had a white cane and black glasses and a body that was losing and a face that was curdled milk. Kept a shepherd in one hand, a Santa bell in the other, and a tin of pencils at her feet. She rang the bell with Salvation Army fervor at Charley's approach and he dropped a quarter into her cup. She listened and scowled when she didn't hear another. The shepherd sniffed Charley's pants, caught the faint scent of cat, and growled, tail bushed, ears tight to the skull. A friend in every port, Charley thought, as he hurried into the building.

The lobby was flashy, with two Hollywood cupids embracing in a fountain. Charley walked to where you rode and pushed up. While he waited, he mentally hummed "Night Train" and scanned a wall, where fliers announced thinly disguised orgies with the sort of multiple exclamation points favored by religion.

The elevator doors opened and closed in Charley's face, just gave him time to jump inside. He managed to avoid mutilation as he got off at the right floor—1012 was the number in Reiser's flowing hand. No light flowed from beneath Janice's door. Charley twisted an imitation-gold chime, shaped like a teardrop. A two-note melody he didn't know came back. He tried the chime again. The melody was in a rut. He was about to leave when he noticed the marks.

He might never have seen them if the paint hadn't been so thin. Crouching down, he studied the key slot. The edges were scratched, looked like someone had tried to force the door with something that didn't fit.

Getting up slowly, he took off his cap and rubbed one eye with the back of his hand. He checked the corridor. No one there. He knew his imagination was raising monsters out of a little wear and tear. He had neither reason nor right to open the door . . .

The latch moved without resistance as his hand carefully turned the knob. Replacing his cap, he stood motionless for a good twenty seconds, a tight, scabrous feeling scraping his insides. He had a vague desire for the gun in the glove compartment, even considered going to get it. Instead, ever so quietly, he nudged the door, which swung inward with the smallest of snicks, like the turning of a page. Arm extended, he stopped the door when it was halfway open and peered beyond it.

There was a smudge of light coming from somewhere, just enough to keep the apartment from total darkness, an impression of carpet and little else. He could hear a soft gurgling, spasms of sound at three-second intervals, like the breath leaving a man dying underwater. There was no indication of anything to fear, but some responses are ingrained, as impossible to control as a hiccup or a strong sneeze or the pounding of your heart when you step into a dark room where something might be wrong. Taking a deep breath, Charley slipped inside and carefully closed the door behind him, listening until the latch had returned to its slot before he released the knob.

The entryway was narrow, widening quickly into the living room. Although the drapes at the far end were drawn, the lights from the city showed through, providing a faint, shifting illumination; he could make out the dark hulking shapes of furniture, couch, table, lazy man's chairs, and a dead Christmas tree in a corner. A section of wall angled off to Charley's right, leading to the kitchen. To his left, just past the foyer, a patch of light fell into the living room from a hallway.

Just beyond the light a good-sized aquarium glowed against the living room wall. Air filter bubbles, the source of the soft gurgling, troubled the surface of the water but not the half dozen large, tropical fish—rainbow colors meandering in silky patterns without purpose. A black fantail circled, watching Charley with steady cartoon eyes.

He walked cautiously toward the light from the hallway. The carpet was up to his ankles, built for exclamation point fucking. Except for the fish tank murmurs and his cushioned footsteps, the silence couldn't be touched. He wasn't sure why he was moving slyly or what he expected to find. He knew he should call out the girl's name, knew she could be there somewhere beyond the corridor of light, knew there were any number of ordinary reasons why she hadn't answered the doorbell, just as the nicks on the keyhole were bad nerves. Still he didn't call out and he continued to move like a soldier lost on the wrong side of the lines. Circumspectly, that was a good word—nice, secret ring to it; that was how he was moving, circumspectly.

He reached the doorway, braced against the living room wall, paused, then sidled into the hall, quick iridescent shimmer of scales curving away from his elbow as he brushed past the tank. The aisle of carpeting was brief; Carl Lewis could've broadjumped it with ease. There was an open door halfway down, another open door a few feet more. The first room was dark; the light came from the second—he could see a section of bright bathroom mirror and white wall. He covered the dozen feet to the first room with the same care as before. Shuffling steps, images of British spy cunning and old-age coupling. Shuffling.

Bracing again against the wall, he leaned a little forward and peered into the room; dim shapes, then more dim shapes, that was all. Twisting one arm around the corner of the doorway, he found the light and, as soft as love, switched it on. The sudden brightness jumped him and he shielded his eyes.

The room wouldn't have been much. Too pretty wallpaper with cherubs embracing like the cupids in the lobby. Jungle gym waterbed wrapped in a pale green spread. A Snoopy, ragged at the ears, propped against a pillow. Books on a dustbound shelf, the Kama Sutra and a taste for Judith Krantz and Rosemary Rogers. Everything the way you'd expect except for what was at Charley's feet.

The boxes were department store cardboard with interlocking flaps. There were four of them. All had been ripped open with prejudice. Their contents, Karl Vaitonis's belongings, were thick across the floor. Someone had been searching for something, but something seemed to be nothing—J. C. Penney threads, leather shaving kit, a hand job supply of girlie mags. There was a clothes closet beyond the mess, two angel white doors on mischievous rollers. The left side was open, waiting. Stepping over polyester, Charley walked to it. Brushing aside skirts and blouses, he could see where the cartons had been stacked, a dust-free square in a corner. He opened the other door and slid its hangers over, half expecting to find a body—soft silky hair and bulging eyes amazed at the severed hands folded neat across her lap—was greeted instead by mothballs and space.

Leaving the bedroom light on, he returned to the hallway with more assurance—somebody had been here, gone through Karl's possessions—okay, ransacked—but left.

He glanced casually into the bathroom, caught the outdoors scent of Lysol and perfume redolent of bubble bath, saw in a quick second the familiar design of tile, sink, medicine cabinet, toilet, and tub.

He started to turn out the light, then his eyes swept back to the tub and he saw her, long peroxide hair down against the porcelain, blond on white, saw the upslanted knees, the sex of her submerged beneath the water and an O.D. of bubble bath suds, cool rich smell of gardenia lingering sweetly.

For an instant, Charley thought against reason that he had walked in on her soaking the nine-to-five blues away, and he started to say sorry, didn't want to accept what he was seeing, even though he saw the blood welling in the tub beneath her hair. He tried to say he was sorry, mouth working like a sick dog's, even though he saw the pink shine in the suds by her head and the broken-off manicured nail, as bright as the blood, on the rug; then what he was seeing slapped him hard and he pulled her from the water. The small, wet body was surprisingly heavy and he grunted from the effort.

The scent of gardenia thick in his nostrils, he stretched her out on the floor. Down beside her, Charley was calm now, a fighter's instinct; put flesh and blood before him and he could act, no matter how horrifying the image. Lifting her boneless white hand, he checked for what he knew wouldn't be there, a pulse, before lowering the hand with a sigh.

She was dead, of course, either from drowning or the blow to her head; beneath the sodden strands of hair, her right temple was swollen and still seeping blood. He gingerly wiped the suds from her face. Above a beard of blue bubbles, her eyes stared at him with the same cold, agate indifference as those of the fish. Reiser had been right. She wasn't much on looks, but even in death, her mouth hinted at pleasure given.

She hadn't been dead long; the water in the tub was just starting to cool. Charley clocked possibilities; she had come home from work—and maybe dinner because of the hour—bone tired and drawn a bath. She had used the john, reading to pass the time—a copy of *Scruples* was on the lid—until the tub was full. Then she'd undressed—her clothes were on the doorknob—and settled in for some comfort. Her killer had either been in the apartment and hidden when she arrived or come in later. She probably didn't hear him until he reached the bathroom and struck her down. Might have done it quick or he could have told her to keep quiet and she'd freaked. Same result. Charley must have arrived not long after the guy left.

He could hear the water from the aquarium. It reminded him of the bubbling of blood. His hands were supporting her head. He lowered it gently to the rug, as if she could still be hurt. There was gore on his hands from the seepage. He got up and ran water over his hands in the sink, pink-red rivulets disappearing down the drain. He avoided looking at himself in the mirror. He glanced down at the girl. Her eyes stared up past him, locked in sudden horror. They must have looked like that when she'd seen her killer—a final instant of comprehension then a blinding white flash of pain that had frozen her heart forever.

Died for Eddie Mikenas's sins . . .

He left the bathroom to find a phone. He would have to call the police. Some of the explaining would be difficult, but he'd manage.

At the end of the hallway, he stopped short, certain someone was in the other room. The presence was like the whisper of a ghost over a grave. He felt a cold tingling along the back of his neck, but he stayed calm, listening for . . .

. . . A door opening. Whoever had killed the girl was slipping out. Something in Charley said stay back, let him go, but something stronger drove him into the darkness.

The man was by the half open front door, his thick back to Charley, dressed all in black, pullover, slacks, ski mask, and gloves. He turned toward Charley in slow motion, lazily bringing up the long, satiny black barrel with the silencer tube. The gun slowed Charley, held him like eyes. Snap out of it, damn it, react, Charley told himself, and somehow he did, did the only thing he could, threw himself away from the gun, diving toward the darkness to cut the legs out from under an invisible runner.

Black angels were doing riffs—a short flaring of light and a low whump and the sharp crack of glass exploding—and he was aware of falling below the light, of the floor hard and sudden against arm and side, and of a door slamming, a glimpse of black cloth and steel vanishing with it. His ears were ringing. He could hear footsteps somewhere, couldn't tell if they were coming or going. He pushed himself to his feet, not so easy. He stood, maybe swaying, his breathing hoarse. Something was stirring within him—he could feel bugs jumping beneath the skin. He felt for permanent pain, decided he would live, but something else had shattered—glass, scales, clear green water, and rainbow coral were alive on the floor, the fish thrashing desperately against the carpet, flashes of black, ivory, and gold under the light dying from the hallway. And something was stirring within Charley, driving him toward the door, the fantail's cold, dull eyes following his feet.

Open the door, a voice, remote yet urgent, was saying, open the door, and he did, caught the closing stairway door down a corridor that seemed too short. He heard another door opening to his right and spun toward the sound as though he had a gun, saw something in terrycloth, all flab and baldness and fright, staring at Charley, but Charley was no longer there, Charley was chasing black angels, chasing the barrel of a gun, and something was certain within him, fierce and angry and thrashing, then he was through the exit, gathering himself, listening, pressing down the anger, pressing down the thing within him. Stay calm, he told himself. Stay with it but make it like a fight, keep your wits, think about what you're doing, no good the other way. He listened, could hear confused voices from where he'd been, could hear but not see the killer, could make out his footbeats clanging hard down the metal stairs. Charley tracked their path. The stairs fell at angles, a sense of corrugated iron, thin railing and tight, flanking walls.

His hand skimming the rail, he started down the stairs, careful to stay far enough back to allow room for retreat in case the man should come back. He counted the floors as he ran . . . seven, six, five . . . The man's padded soles clattered like tin below, seemed echoes of his own. Once he saw a huge shadow weaving down the wall and he hung back, then he was running again . . . three, two . . . He heard a door bang shut . . . one . . .

At the bottom, it was small and cold. He stopped to catch his breath, chest rising and falling as he listened to the hard footsteps going away outside. Options, think of options—he could keep after the man, see where he went, maybe glimpse a license plate before he was gone, but it was too damned risky . . .

Charley went out the door, the bitter night air and street noises stinging him with a cold shower rush. The stocky black-shrouded figure was running around the corner of the building. Ten stories up, a woman leaned from a window and screamed. She was trying to say something, but the words couldn't thread their way to meaning through her anguish. She was doubled over, arms pressed tight against her stomach, holding in the horror of what she'd seen. She continued to scream, deep short cries, as Charley looked around the corner.

The man was running down the sidewalk. He ran like somebody who'd lost the knack, body straining for balance, yet he was gathering speed as he sprinted toward where Charley had parked. Charley wondered why he hadn't stripped off the mask and looked to get lost in a crowd. He couldn't see the gun, but the killer's right arm was hidden, pressed against the front of his sweater. There were no more than a dozen people on the block, eight or nine on foot, three cars. One of the autos and all of the pedestrians had stopped; the other two cars had slowed, their drivers watching the guy in black like witnesses to an accident who are unsure of their roles. Ten floors up the woman had stopped screaming.

Yeah, sure, Charley swore to himself, and he kept on going, past the blind lady huddled under the entry archway, trembling with fear. She had lost her dark glasses and she stared at Charley with eyes as good as his. The shepherd was dancing to the action, moving back and forth, great happy tongue lolling, metronome tail pacing his rhythm.

The guy with the gun was turning, wheeling toward Charley. A big black lady in clumpy wool shrieked, an operatic blast to shatter glass, as the killer took on a cop's firing crouch, weapon braced by both hands, gloves sleek as sealskin, grimy brown sneakers spread wide, and Charley ducked, the way he'd bob under a punch, behind the high back fins of a lowdown Chevy. Hunched down by the trunk, he listened to the flat whump, heard the bullet strike close before whining away; he could see the hate it left, could make out his face foggy in the gleaming maroon metal, and he lifted his head a little to see a little more, and the man was still there, steady in the same stance, the eyes behind the mask wide and wild. The eyes caught Charley's cap above the trunk and a dancing yellow flame spun from the long black barrel, which bucked up under the revolver's kick. The bullet struck the chrome of the Chevy's side mirror, the sound like crowbars fighting. Severed at the base, the mirror cartwheeled indolently through the air.

Keep low, Charley told himself, and he did, waiting until he could hear the guy moving again; the slap of soft rubber on cement was sharp, clean, close to pleasant. His hands felt cold. Clap hands, Charley, he said to himself without knowing why. Getting to his feet, he did once without knowing why, the crack of palms loud in his ears, then, staying close to and behind a string of parked cars, he doggedly moved forward. He was aware of the bystanders on both sides of the street. Some had flattened themselves against the sidewalk, including the fat lady who continued to shriek. Others stood stock-still, gazing dumb as dogs; maybe it was that the gun made so little noise that it didn't seem real, maybe they saw it as a movie, but they seemed blind to any personal danger. A hook of a smile even crossed one man's paunchy face.

Intent on his pursuit, to Charley they were as real as store dummies, or where there was movement they seemed formaldehyde figures floating through water, their motions loose and far away. They were without context and he ignored them. He was counting steps to the Camaro, the way he had stairs, focusing on the .38 in the glove compartment.

Up ahead, fatigue was setting in—Charley could hear the man's hitching, labored breathing, his knees lifting lower and lower as they pumped, his body starting to lurch. Charley's own pace was steady, his wind good. Pausing to catch his breath, the man spun around and fired once more. Ducking a little late behind a four-wheel drive, Charley heard a whiplash crack as the bullet went by, and he realized the movies lie, that it's a rare piece of luck to cut down a moving target with anything you can hold in your hand, and Charley kept on, clap hands, closing on the Camaro, fumbling for his keys, sex in his pocket, there he goes, there, a car just missing, fright flick face behind glass.

Charley found the keys, jabbed at the keyhole, got it, only two tries, flung open the door, leaned in, glove compartment, there, sick strong odor of chamois and oiled steel. Stretched over the seat, he snapped open the cylinder, forced a fat copper shell into a chamber that seemed too small. Options, Charley, options, but not the car, too many places a man could slip into.

The man was turning again, it was all one motion, whirling and sighting and firing, the bullet starring the windshield as Charley dove down behind the dash. The game had become a nursery rhyme: the big bad man turns and shoots and Charley ducks. Inhaling the residue of musty cigar, he stared at the spent shell, dumb as a first date on the seat beside him, options, reach across yourself, open the fucking door. Another bullet smacked into the windshield to let him know he hadn't been forgotten as he slithered across the seat. He hit the sidewalk rolling, the guy in black going too, crashing into a pretty girl scrambling, the impact as audible as an exhalation in the ear. The man kept his balance, kept on going, but the girl dropped hard, her face smashing and contorting against the pavement like a child's face pressed against a window. Bracing herself on her hands and knees, lips puffed, bleeding, teeth smeared red, she gazed at Charley with a shy, dazed smile, as if she'd just committed an unpardonable social gaffe.

Lying on his stomach, Charley sighted on the back of the black sweater, snub-nosed revolver at the end of outstretched arms, the anger stirring within him. Tightening his grip, he pulled back the hammer. His finger touched the trigger but

Jesus, there're people, I could

and the guy was gone, high-rise granite where he'd been, and Charley was going too, nickel for speed, everything was a riff, his feet were throbbing, take a rest, Charley, blisters there to haunt him. He could hear the man's thick breathing and feet, thudding more than slapping now, tap-dancing

Clap hands, Charley.

and snapping open the cylinder, he jammed two more shells home, counted to three and spun around a corner, gun poised.

The man was on the move, winging it behind a city bus just starting, rear doors closing, the killer reaching like a drunk desperate for a lift, leaping inside, as Charley once more failed to fire.

Charley was running again, arms flailing, instinct pushing aside sense, sprinting, hard nickel's ride, but the bus was short-changing him, gathering steam in a winnowing of gears, and he stayed with it, knees driving up toward his chest, and through the windows, under the bunched advertisements and harsh light, the black mask bobbing down the aisle, and the driver, white and old, starting to turn his head back—everything had happened so fast that the driver's eyes, soft behind thick glasses, were only now beginning to widen into shock.

Feet jarring beneath him, Charley pounded on the doors with the butt, the barrel, of the gun, the glass showing its surprise. He heard a voice, his own, far away yelling, and the driver was still turning, a slow-moving old guy, turning toward the crazy-quilt nightmare stumbling toward him like some jazz baby terrorist, and his brain wasn't buying, for he touched a lever, a reflex for what was maybe Charley's request, and the back doors parted, even as he slammed on the brakes, and Charley jumped inside.

Charley reached for a railing, missed, nothing to stop him. The floor rushed at him, his knee caught pain, so did his head. The world swung around then swung back. He saw the gun near his nose, saw the elusive dark shape, butterfly wings, disappearing through doors—the angle was wrong, everything was too far above him. He realized his face was pressed to the floor. Doesn't belong there, maybe, he dreamily thought.

He couldn't understand why the driver was staring at him, or was it at his hand? Maybe he wanted his fare. The old man was dancing light and cloudy eyes, staring, staring at what I'm holding, what the fuck and Charley started down, started toward the poor old guy with his arms outstretched, going to tell him it was all right. His head was ringing, couldn't understand why the driver was backing away, sweet Jesus, out the front doors, made no sense, going where the other guy had gone, and *that* man was dangerous, not Charley, who loved cats and who still occasionally said his prayers. And Charley followed, trying to explain, only it wasn't working, for the driver was

See the funny man run

staggering away, and sweet Jesus again, stumbling blind to the quick lights of a car, and there were brakes and a thud and a uniform rolling from sight under a wall of wheels, thick glasses splintering on the pavement. And Charley couldn't understand, everything was happening with too much speed, a bad drug trip on roller skates; sister can you spare a dime, more than you can pay to look through the screen, at the guy in black all played out, running so silly like he was staggering through wet sand

See the funny man

and the funny man was waving and shouting and Charley smiled dumb as two dogs and started to wave back, only the funny man wasn't waving for him—he was gesturing with his gun and yelling at some guy in a truck, a big shiny pretty slow-moving diesel pregnant with gas, and Charley couldn't hear what he was saying but the diesel was braking, tires sparking, and the trucker was bailing out the shotgun side, so the funny man must have said something not so nice, not so nice at all, and Charley was trying to imagine what it could have been, was very curious about the whole thing, and in that instant, the world snapped back.

He wondered how much time had passed, probably only seconds, since belting his head on the floor had tossed his brains. Through the bus's plexiglass he could see the killer climbing jimquick into the cab of the diesel. Still sleepwalking, Charley told himself, it didn't make any kinda sense, then it did—the truck was muscle for bullying through traffic, was safe as a church, bullets would be fuel for a six-block blast, a nice, clean logic that Charley could share, for his own head felt like nitro.

Options, think of options . . . Here you are trapped inside a bus, no idea how to spring the doors, something to write home about in itself, and you're watching this fucking crazy person pulling away in a dead-drift of black exhaust, so what do you do, wave goodbye? No, goddamn, you get behind the wheel, jazz the ignition, shove the shift into first, clutch and stomp on the pedal, and don't forget to put on your hero's cap.

The bus dug it, too much to ask, but there it was, lugging and straining, but they were going. "They" was right—Charley had company. Saw him for the first time in the rearview mirror. Black kid in his teens, with the wise glint of a hundred bop wars in his eyes, sitting ten rows back, a class act in rags. Looked at Charley with cool, for he came from a place where kinks were as common as a Saturday night stagger. Charley felt he should say something reassuring, took a second look, decided it should be the other way around, and kept on going.

Up ahead, the diesel swung wide onto New Hampshire—a big, broad, slash of a street. Charley followed, working against the big wheel, clutching and shifting down, the gears wrenching in pain under his unpracticed hand. He could hear the killer laying grief on his horn, great bleating blasts forcing traffic out of his lane, the cars scurrying like bugs for cover. Yeah, sure, Charley said, clearing a path with his own horn. He was keeping a good pace behind, holding the needle steady at forty, go faster you invite mayhem. Dinosaurs, that's what we got, Charley told himself, big bucks on a tear, no limits.

Headlights slashed Charley's face, chased his sweat. Startled faces shot by from the sidewalks. He felt a tingling along his spine, noticed his knuckles flat and white against the wheel. He could hear the wail of a siren, a stoned baby, then another, closer, coming up fast on his right—spinning blue strobes and squad car steel streaking in proud on two wheels.

Charley felt cheated; it was his chase, not theirs. Got downright indignant about it as he watched the black-and-white draw level with the diesel's cab, watched the cop riding shotgun whip down his window and motion hard to pull over. The cop couldn't make out the mask, it was cave dark in the cab, or maybe he didn't know the guy had a gun, for he didn't draw his own heat. He just kept signing to the curb with a beefy arm. Charley could see his mouth working in tight, angry sets. The truck slowed; to everyone's surprise the guy was obeying, then he wasn't—the long, black barrel snaked through the cab window, lifting its striking head as lazily as it had in the girl's apartment, and Charley could see something of the eyes, had seen them somewhere before, and then the barrel showed light and a vivid dark hole appeared in the angry cop's throat. For a split second, the cop remained frozen in surprise, a fine red mist lingering in the air, then, clutching at his jugular, he fell back loose across his partner's lap.

The car was going to dance with Charley, came out of control at him with 3-D thrust. Too quick to count, Charley caught details; the dead cop's thick arm out the window swinging against the door, his partner's panicked eyes as his hands fought the wheel, the mist of blood settling on the windscreen. For that brief moment, Charley watched as if it didn't involve him, then he jerked the steering hard to the right and the dazzling, gyrating lights and steel and chrome danced past, found other partners, shy fenders and doors, did them dirt, before dropping from exhaustion. In the mirror, Charley saw the crumpled car; its hood was gone, so were half its parts, but the strobes and siren wouldn't give up. Charley glanced in the mirror at the boy. He was the same as before, all cool observation, just a hint of concern tracing through his eyes. Yeah, sure, Charley said, and he kept on going. He could feel the blood pumping through his veins, coursing through his body. Words raced through his mind—pawn moves, blood and bone, what a world.

Seeing heavier traffic now. Big city colors. Bright stabs of light. Hospital to the right. Blacked-out buildings to the left, high-gloss steel, distanced like paintings. Through the screen, bright octane silver splintering into flame, all in the head, what was real, diesel swooping around cars, swooping around cars into the wrong lane—oh yeah, no rules to this game—jamming traffic, jamming the goddamn world, black angel riffs, the hog agony of brakes, locked horns and screams as sharp as glass across the throat. Bad notes and good. Jesus, my head hurts . . .

Clap hands, Charley

Bad notes and . . .

"Gonna fuckin' walk next time," the boy swore behind him, bringing Charley back. Said it without humor, said it flat and with awe in his low cool voice for the pagan gods who'd taken over the night, turning it into the wildest of carnival rides. Charley glanced in the mirror, caught a fragment of his own face, eyes staring but steady. He glanced down at his hands, still there, tight and spread on the wheel. Staying with it, cool and objective now, oh yeah.

He was turning up ahead—fleeting red glint of brake lights—the killer was swinging a fierce left onto Pennsylvania. Charley followed, forced the wheel in a direction it didn't want to go, double-clutching while he did it; gearstick slippery with sweat under his hand, left foot braking, right foot pumping twice in a tap-dancer's spasm.

Pennsylvania Avenue.

More dark buildings and darker shapes, no definition. High-strung sentry fence to the left, spokes like knives. White House ahead to the right, no time for awe. Trees and curvy lawns, boss man's home beyond. Park coming up on. Trees and statues and lawns, lawns as smooth as dark ice. Shadows falling into other shadows. Beautiful park, beautiful and still as night. In East L.A. they had parks like scabs . . . What did it matter . . . ?

Charley shook his head fiercely, cleared his vision, looked straight ahead. Traffic was thinning. The killer was hitting his horn in short, sharp blasts like punches. With room to maneuver the diesel was gathering steam. It had too much power for the bus, simple as that, it had too much power. Charley felt a light, helpless sensation rising in his chest as he watched the truck, giant wheels blurring, start to pull away. Losing him, Charley said under his breath. Losing him. He pressed the pedal to the floor, kept it there, the whine of the engine rising in his ears, but the distance kept on growing. Losing him, Charley said once more, then he saw the apparition.

The mounted policeman was walking his horse across Pennsylvania toward the park. For a brief second, Charley thought he was the cop he'd seen before, but the man was too small, the horse too dark. They were right in the path of the speeding truck, there quick as a phantom, no time to slam your horn. Charley caught a camera shutter shot of white wide eyes and shiny horse hide, polished by high beams.

Blinded, the animal went high in terror, its rider wrenching the reins to control it. Head and body twisting as it fought the pressure, the horse, still all huge white eyes, went down whinnying—the cry cutting through engines—with the cop somewhere underneath, an arm reaching for air from under a flank, and the truck turned tricks, wheels jumping off the ground, peeling wicked curled rubber. Charley saw the black gloves losing control as the great silver beast knifed toward the trees and the dark ice grass and the statues, high-chinned heroes. The diesel took out Duportail, sliced off Rochambeau's brave right arm, caused Liberty to tremble and Lafayette to bend his knees, but the heroes fought back, sent the truck sliding, stealing a base, across the lake of perfect lawn, and Charley braked hard, a final anguish of gears, and braced for the explosion . . .

14

Roller Coaster

. . . *which didn't come.*

Charley lifted his head cautiously over the wheel—the diesel was down on its side a nice distance away, cozy with Andrew Jackson. Lazy hands of amber flame were reaching up from under the hood, gesturing expressively to the surrounding darkness. The hands were a ballet that quickened and grew, embracing the cab, light dancing to its own heat. The sight was sweet, all pretty parts, then the explosion came, seemed to spread from all sides, dazzling the sky as it shot up two hundred feet.

The diesel came apart, a fierce shedding of steel. Dangling rubber, a tire came at the bus through the charged air. Charley dropped, belly to the floor, eye to eye with the thrust of the gearshift. He thought of the fish tank shattering, the wet thrashing of scales and the glassy accusing eye of the black fantail following him.

Something hard thudded into the bus, which shuddered. He could hear things landing on the street, clanging, then nothing.

He waited.

He waited until the silence was secure, then he glanced back at the boy, who was slowly getting up from behind his seat. Charley pulled himself gingerly up by the steering wheel and stared outside. A light went on in a White House window.

The remains of the truck were burning like a reminder of war. One of its wheels lay ten feet from the bus. Sirens, heat to equal the diesel's own, lashed out from other streets. Charley watched the candy-colored horse, velvet flanks solid with sweat, trot riderless by, hoofs easy on the pavement. Charley stared at the park and the guy should've been a cinder but there he was, free of the flames, and Charley said fuck it to all the dirty angels of the night, sweet Jesus, then he kicked open the doors, was out in the darkness, where Rochambeau offered him a stump.

He had his second wind, ran in a very fast jog, arms up loose by his hips. Felt like he was in training, humming away the miles. He tried a bar of *"Night Train,"* but lost the tune, settled for small, chuffing sounds as he went into the park. Smoke, gray and acrid, drifted toward him, stinging his eyes. He looked up—the hands of flame were gentle again, waving like a friend. The grass was short and damp, the fire stayed close to the snarled metal, but Charley angled away, where there'd been one explosion, there could be two. He ran past the statue of Jackson, singed but still astride his horse. He could hear sirens and the soft whirr of a helicopter in the distance. More music.

Clap hands, Charley

He had gained ground. Reduced to a stumbling trot, the killer was only a football field ahead. Closing, Charley asked himself a question, why keep risking a bullet? Couldn't come up with an answer, so he kept on going.

He heard footsteps behind him. Slowing, he turned his head and saw the black kid.

"Get the hell back!" Charley yelled. Maybe the boy stopped before Charley turned back to a bullet. The familiar sound jumped at Charley's head then jumped by. The man resumed running. Sighting on his back, Charley braced his gun hand with his left palm. Helluva sensation, too much power, and Charley took a while to squeeze the trigger, remembered to do it with love. He felt the blue-black handle buck against the heel of his hand and had a sense of heat in front of his face. Saffron flame flashed from the snub barrel and he heard a loud thump; up close, the report of the revolver was the sound of one man whacking another on the back with a heavy, open hand.

Somehow, he expected the man to drop from his bullet, but he just kept going. Charley aimed a hair in front, allowed for the guy's momentum; his second bullet had no more effect than the first. He had no idea if he'd even come close.

The man was out of the park now, there were buildings and lights where he was going. Charley tried to pick his thoughts.

And where the fuck had he seen those eyes . . . ?

Lose or kill Charley, the guy's chances were pretty damn good. Charley tugged on his hero's cap, glanced at his watch. Just after nine. Most of the stores would be closed, but there'd still be people on the streets. People could be hostages, crowds a place to get lost. Charley felt the ground change, cement replacing grass. He was on a walkway. He shook his arms lightly to relax. He jogged past a park bench with ALICE LOVES MARY carved into a slat. Yeah, sure, Charley said, and he kept on going. He heard rotors overhead, looked up and saw a helicopter skimming low, searchbeam skating over the green ice, busy insect blades scraping air. The noise faded as the chopper canted deeper into the park, heading toward the burning wreckage, where apple-shiny fire engines and cop cars were converging to add to the blaze of color and light.

The killer was going where Charley didn't want him to go. Pushing, he halved the distance between them, the cement stabbing at his soles. Dark walls and roofs loomed large, city sounds gathered.

Keep him in sight, that was all that mattered, then he was gone—he was there, then he wasn't, disappearing by magic between two buildings big as bullies and then Charley was there himself, so suddenly he had to remind himself to stop. He hunkered behind a corner, back favoring a wall. His breathing deepened. Five more shells in his pocket, maybe a lucky number; the snick of cartridge into chamber was awfully loud. A big cop bullhorn was hot somewhere, doing a job, pushing people off the streets. Horns and voices clashed. Back in the park, he could hear police dogs barking, harsh and eager. He thought of the German shepherd and the blind lady who wasn't and the fear in her eyes

Clap hands

and he peered around the corner with one careful eye, saw an angle of shadowed alley. A Gestapo glare fell halfway down from a fanlight. There was a dirty dumpster underneath the dirty light. There was dirty writing on the bin, dirty writing on the walls, none of it spoke of love, and a pair of clean fire exit doors with pushbar handles were just beyond. He could see a street at the end of the alley. Cars were crawling. The bullhorn and quick cop hands were telling them things. A guy leaned out of his Dodge, trying to catch the action. A siren shoved him back. The siren was coming fast, maybe running to a rumor. Charley wondered if they'd cordoned off the street, wondered where the man they were all looking for was, wondered, without hope, if God was in his heaven.

The snap of the cylinder warned him and he pulled back. There was a flash and low whump from behind the dumpster. He heard the ping of the bullet at it struck the edge of the wall, saw a spray of concrete and felt needles in his eye. Wincing, he swiped at the pain with his arm. Concrete mites clung to his sleeve. The eye was burning, water cozy with the sweat that already lived there. His mouth had the hot, dry taste of sickness. The siren was making demands. He felt like he was in the ring, waiting for the bell. Bells, story of my life—church steeples peals, the timekeeper's hammer and gong. "Between rounds" drifted through his mind; you got a minute to rest and then . . .

His head hurt, forceps stricture, where he'd hit it on the bus. So did his knee, but it hadn't tightened up and the throbbing you could live with. The siren was getting louder and the chopper had returned to circle overhead. It occurred to Charley that the cops might shoot him instead of the other man. Options, Charley, options. Ducking into the alley seemed deranged at best. The bullhorn bass was somewhere to the north, the dogs to the south. The siren kept drawing closer, shrieking in his ears. He swiped at the damaged eye again. Through a haze he saw the black kid coming from the park, jogging toward Charley yardbird loose—maybe he'd just wait for him and . . .

And then he heard the slap of feet running away from the dumpster. The siren had taken part of his head; Charley swung what was left around the corner of the wall, saw a squad car, blue dome spinning, streak the alley; in that fraction, the cops saw the killer, the killer saw the cops, no love lost. The black-and-white braked hard, the killer scampered back to the bin and Charley decided to crash the party, two shots joined, his and the bad guy's, both too fast to find their targets

Clap hands

as Charley ducked back behind the wall. The dogs were closing somewhere to the south, the chopper was swooping in from the east, the big bullhorn voice had taken the 519 to Boston and the black boy had gone God knows where, and up above, the moon was oblivious to it all, and behind the wall, Charley tensed—something tightening within him—sweat-laced muscles cording in his jaw and neck, and even as he started into the alley once more he heard a whump and a clang as the funny wild elusive guy shot the lock off fire exit doors, an alarm even wilder erupting as he crashed through them, and Charley was sprinting toward the light

Clap hands

sprinting toward the light, pounding feet and cop static off somewhere, something fierce and angry and thrashing within him as he drove a linesman's shoulder into the doors, jarring joints and teeth, and he was falling through the doors, landing hard on his bad knee, the pain telling, only he didn't notice, falling into a smear of empty department store, and he pushed off his good leg to his feet, felt his knee buckle, felt himself falling again, heard a bullet sing by, and from his knees beside a rack of bright cottons he saw through his good eye the desperate figure all in black aim with deliberation from somewhere up above, the sleek black silent familiar barrel leveling down, and expecting his bullet, Charley fired a final time, a single instinctive defensive shot without the hope of hitting home.

The man dropped leadenly without drama or flair.

Charley blinked and wiped the perspiration from his eyes. The man was lying at the top of an escalator sixty feet away. He was on his side, facing Charley. The long black barrel lay beneath him. The hazel-green eyes were closed. The escalator was as motionless as the man.

Charley lowered his gun, dragged himself up with a hand from the clothes rack. He felt the savage energy leaving his body, felt the pain spreading in its place, but it didn't matter. Favoring his leg, he hobbled toward the escalator. The alarm was ringing like old grief in his ears. It didn't matter. Someone shouted "Freeze!"—a movie echo behind him.

Without turning, he stopped, let the gun fall to the floor and placed his hands over his head, for it didn't matter. He heard low cop voices prodding someone else, glimpsed a black man in janitor denim doing their bidding. Charley felt hands giving orders that his body obeyed as he was frisked. He heard the escalator come to life as maintenance sprang it, its soft purr muscled aside by the alarm.

A voice was telling him to turn around. The cop looked sixteen, had a mustache thin as a razor and groping, kid-clumsy hands. Seemed pleased with himself as he frisked Charley again.

The black kid appeared through the double doors. His eyes danced with excitement and he looked at Charley with cool admiration and the shared smile of survivors. Charley wanted to tell him that it didn't matter, that it wasn't such a good thing to kill a man, but he knew the boy wouldn't understand—he'd take this night back to the ghetto and turn it into legend, his own part growing until it became myth, or worse, TV. Charley gazed sadly at him, then the boy was gone, pushed back and blotted out by others, some official, some not.

The purring stopped. The young cop walked over to the laundry sack lump at the bottom of the shiny steel stairs.

A hand at Charley's elbow started to guide him away. Turning to the escalator, he hesitated before yielding to its pressure. His bullet had struck the killer in the chest. Blood was pooling, a shallow lake settling over the floor. Careful not to soil his shoes, which were polished to mirrors, the young cop crouched and checked for a pulse that wasn't there. Then he stripped off the mask, drawing back the coarse black cloth delicately, the way you might silk.

There shouldn't have been any surprises left, but the night had kept the worst for last.

The face underneath the mask was that of a young JFK.

15

The Price of Admission

"Got any Murine?"

Charley's request came too high and almost had a quaver. The cop with the sandpaper voice opened a drawer and tossed him a bottle of Visine. Charley tipped his head back; he had trouble coaxing the drops into his bloodshot left eye. He felt like something left in a dumpster.

They had brought him straight from the department store to the precinct house, before the onslaught of reporters showed. During the ride they'd asked him little and he'd answered less, volunteering only that the dead man was an FBI agent named Peterson. Reiser had been waiting for Charley in his office, watching TV—a newshawk with coke-bright eyes was selling the night's spree. A zoom lens was sniffing out blood.

Reiser turned off the TV. Charley tossed the Visine back to the detective, who showed good hands.

"Coffee?" Reiser asked. Charley shook off the offer.

"How's the knee?"

Charley was resting his leg on a chair that the black sergeant had grudgingly provided for his ease. He leaned forward and tried to massage out the knots.

"Day or two, it'll be okay."

"Good, because the chair stays. Think you can remain in one piece long enough to answer some questions?"

"Depends on what you're asking."

"Start with the obvious—what happened? Make it simple and we'll get to the details later."

Charley grimaced and wiggled his toes for sympathy. "I went to Janice Vaitonis's apartment to talk and I found her dead. The guy who killed her, Phil Peterson, was still around. There was a chase. The action got what you could call complicated."

"Well, that's simple, all right." Reiser drummed a pencil, fast as hummingbird wings, against the side of the desk. "You're not a cop. Why go after him?"

Charley shrugged. "Seemed like the thing to do."

"You always do things on impulse?" No challenge to the question, just curiosity.

"I admit it's a bad habit."

Reiser tossed this between his fingers for a moment.

"Okay, there was a chase and a little damage to some citizens, which we won't go into right now, and you finally caught up." He pinched the bridge of his nose and studied Charley suspiciously. "That was a helluva shot for an amateur."

Charley sighed and rubbed his leg again. "I was down on both knees under a rack of Hawaiian prints with my head spinning and one eye that could see maybe the tip of my nose. I aimed with all the talent of a drunk falling down a flight of stairs. If you want to call that a helluva shot, that's your fucking privilege."

Reiser was thinking about what to call it when a scrawny cop with a chicken neck stuck his head through the door. "What do we do about the reporters?"

"Shoot them," Reiser answered, with a straight face. The scrawny cop swallowed—Adam's apple dipsy-doing—and did a double take. Reiser shooed him out the door, gulped the coffee on his desk, and belched without apology before getting back to Charley.

"I'll say this—you gave Washington one sprightly circus. Best fucking spectacle we've had since the peace march of 'seventy-two. Even Dan Quayle woke up."

"Do I get the movie rights?"

"They'd never make it and, by the way, do you have to be so flip, because it's starting to rub off."

Charley answered rapidly and with some emotion. "No, I don't have to, but it helps. It helps keep my stomach from turning more ways than it already is. It helps me forget that I'm gonna have trouble sleeping for a while. It helps me pretend maybe none of this happened and maybe I didn't really kill nobody. I don't like drugs and I don't see nothing to drink, so unless you got something better, why don't you let me deal with this in my own way, which believe me ain't easy no matter how I cut it."

Reiser's face showed heat and he leaned forward in his chair. The phone cut in before he could get evil. The call took five minutes, brought Reiser down. Charley's eyes skated around the room while Reiser said yes, sir into the receiver. After he hung up, he looked at Charley the way a parent might at an unwanted child.

"That was my boss. He just got through talking about this with Pat Hanlon, the associate director of the FBI. The Bureau had some requests. They asked that not only should you be kept clear of reporters, but that no one should know you were even involved. Hanlon suggested we tell the press we have no idea why Peterson offed Ms. Vaitonis. He also suggested we issue a statement to the effect that Peterson himself was killed by one of our own undercover agents, whose street activities would be jeopardized by revealing his identity. In return, he promised us future favors, which is an old story with not always a happy ending."

"Do you know why he was suggesting all this?"

"I didn't ask, but unless you have an itch to play hero, that's what my boss wants and that's the way we'll do it."

"I think what Mr. Hanlon proposed would be very nice."

"I was afraid you might. There was one thing more—Hanlon wants to see you, say tomorrow afternoon at one in Franklin Park, corner of Fourteenth and K. I'll give you directions."

Charley scratched his scar. "You got any idea why, except maybe Mr. Hanlon ain't playing with a full deck?"

Reiser shrugged, a slur in one shoulder. "The Bureau works in mysterious ways. Now can we finish the fuck up, because I'm damned tired, my wife's home in bed with the flu, and I feel a headache that'll last at least a month coming on, and it's not even New Year's."

Charley's complete statement, taken down in shorthand by Reiser in the privacy of his office, consumed an hour and four aspirins. By the time they were finished, Ballistics and Forensics had determined that Peterson's gun, a .32, had accounted for both the dead cop and the Vaitonis girl; traces of her hair and blood were on the butt of the revolver.

At 11:04 Reiser drained the dregs of his coffee, scribbled directions to Franklin Park on the back of a used robin's-egg blue envelope, his penmanship no longer so fine, and asked Charley if he knew his way home. Charley said maybe. They scrounged up his pea coat, which had been removed from the bus, but not his gun, which he didn't want anyway.

By 11:15, when Charley and Reiser slipped out a back door, the chief of police had issued a statement reflecting Pat Hanlon's scenario. Naturally the press wasn't satisfied and throughout the city, editors were already beginning the self-righteous process of indignation and innuendo regarding police procedure and responsibility, a protest as old as society itself.

None of this concerned Charley as Reiser drove him to the Camaro. During the ride, Charley politely asked about the night's casualties. Reiser told him there were four dead; the Vaitonis girl, Peterson, the cop, who was a rookie named Jerry Czyck, and a not so elderly gentleman who'd suffered a stroke during the excitement. Besides the fatalities, there had, in the various collisions, been enough broken bones, contusions, lacerations, and traumas to keep three hospitals happy for a year. The bus driver had two shattered legs and a concussion. Czyck's partner had multiple fractures and a septum that had settled somewhere south of his nose. The policeman who had gone down under his mount escaped with bruises, a cracked rib, and a yen for armored trucks. The horse was last seen somewhere in Texas.

The detective finished the toll around the time they reached Janice Vaitonis's block. Although the CRIME SCENE signs and arc lights were up, the street was relatively deserted—only the lab techs were still prowling the sidewalks and gutters, scrounging for spent casings and latent blood. They had been here for over two hours and had the lazy, sated eyes of tomcats after a three-day orgy. Somebody from Ballistics had found one of the pretty girl's teeth. He was holding it up to the light, checking for cavities. The blind lady was back on the corner, having recovered her dark glasses and nerve. She shook her bell fiercely at the techs, who ignored her. The shepherd lay beside her, menacing anyone who passed by. Reiser took in the scene, went uh-huh, uh-huh, and stopped at the end of the block. The Camaro had aged ten years. The starring of the windshield was impressive.

Reiser asked Charley if he'd done that, looked disappointed when he said he hadn't. There was a parking ticket nestled under a wiper. Charley said, "Shit." Reiser said nothing. Instead, he delicately removed the ticket with the tips of two fingers and just as delicatedly tore it into shreds. Charley said he hoped his wife was feeling better. Reiser said he wished he had another wife, then he said goodbye.

Charley got into the Camaro. He sat slumped, arms flat against the wheel. The techs had plucked the cartridge from the seat and dusted the dash for prints; two days from now, they'd probably bust the smoker of stale cigars and throw away the key. Charley held his hands up in front of him and stared at his fingers. The tips smelled of cordite. Ash-gray specks of gunpowder were under his nails. It reminded him of when he was a kid and his mother would look there for dirt. It made him fell like going home and washing his hands, slap of too much soap and water.

He caught his reflection in the rearview mirror. He seemed to be the same person he'd been four hours back. Glancing up at the faceless moon, he adjusted the mirror and switched on the ignition.

He got back to the Three Seasons at 11:55. Everything was normal; the desk jockey was spraying Black Flag into the potted plants. The vicious-looking bellhop was sniggering and playing with himself.

Up in his room, Charley felt like calling Lisa, but what would he say? Hi, babe, how's it going and by the way, I just killed a guy and half a city? So instead he threw up into the john. Then he washed his hands with prejudice, scrubbing out the cordite and the gunpowder under his nails. Then he took a cruel hot shower. Then he turned in.

Lying in bed, he bounced the night off the walls. Reiser was right, you couldn't film it, too fucking implausible, but then so was life: Dolly Parton gets thin, a pope gets gassed, Christ turns into a skyscraper to rap with a guy named Oral. Back in the ghetto, the black boy's story didn't have a prayer.

After a while, Charley went to sleep. After a while, Sylvia slipped into his dreams. She was reckless on a high stool, her back to Charley, tossing down whiskey sours. When she turned she was laughing, but her face was something found in blood-snarled alleys, something like a claw, or the hollowed-out stare of a splintered skull.

16

Eyes and the Dispenser of Coins

The slender blond man deftly removed the lens from his left eye, imagining how a quarter would look over it; he found no amusement in the conjecture.

As he washed the lens, he studied his face in the bathroom mirror, the way a man does just after shaving. He appeared younger than his forty-five years. His light hair was styled but short, his complexion fair, his expression as impersonal and perfectly pressed as the gray tailored suit he wore. His smooth face looked like it had never known a five o'clock shadow. He gazed at his vivid blue eyes. The odd thing was, his face was softer, more human, with lenses. It was as if they masked his soul. Naked, his eyes were cold and unyielding, like gems without the sparkle. Renaud had called them snail's eyes and he, Lawrence Dake, objective in all things, had to admit the description was accurate.

The doorbell, a rich cathedral chime, rang from a long ways off. Tipping his head back, he returned the lens to his eye. He delayed going to the door, straightening his tie with unnecessary care. As infrequent as they might be, he never relished meetings with Renaud. It wasn't that he was afraid of him—others infinitely were—but the man made him uneasy, a rare response since there were very few things, maybe charity and love, that unnerved him.

Fortified by a deep breath, he closed his lens case and went to answer the door. It was a long walk, for his house was immense, all cherrywood, Regency, and inlaid marble. Although he took his time, he knew the doorbell wouldn't ring again.

Taking another deep breath, Dake opened the front door. Renaud looked the same as always, open smile, dark wind-swept hair, clothes causal to the point of negligence, a technicolor memory, Burt Lancaster at thirty-four, the face so accessible that, paradoxically, it was more a camouflage than Dake's own. You never knew what was brewing behind the dancing eyes and grin, never could quite grasp his mood, for his expression didn't vary. He had never seen Renaud kill, but he suspected his eyes glittered with the same conviviality as they did over a drink, a joke, or an assignation.

"Hello, Lawrence," Renaud said. His voice, which harbored a French accent, was resonant and reassuring, like the brace of good wine.

"Come in," Dake said reluctantly. Unlike Renaud, he rarely used first names, and his intonation, although imbued with the cool assurance of professional occupations, seemed reedy and small by comparison. Renaud wiped his feet vigorously on the mat, the gesture closer to defiant mockery than courtesy, like a dog leaving his mark. Dake showed him into the living room, where he motioned to a sofa. Renaud spread out comfortably, long arms taking up the backrest. Dake took a chair opposite him, sitting self-consciously, back stiff, arms rigid at his sides. Renaud smiled at him and looked around, amusement working the corners of his eyes and mouth as he gazed at the lighted fountain that was the centerpiece of the room. Dake knew he considered his lifestyle ostentatious, that Renaud preferred to live like a prole.

"How was your Christmas?" Renaud asked.

"Fine," Dake replied.

Leaning forward, Renaud picked up a framed photograph from the glass coffee table in front of him. Blonde, bronze-tanned, and youthful in tennis chic, Dake's wife was as suitable a party decoration as a man could desire.

"She looks better all the time," Renaud said, looking down at the gloss. "She win any more trophies?" The hint of mockery hadn't gone away.

"A few."

"She on the courts today?"

"Yes." They both knew that Dake had made sure she wouldn't be home while Renaud was there.

"How're the kids?" Renaud sounded as though he really cared.

"Still away at college. Drink?"

"No, I don't think so," Renaud said agreeably. He returned the picture to the table, setting it in precisely the same position as he had found it.

"What did you want to see me about, Lawrence?" Again, they both knew why he was here.

"The way you're conducting business."

"Oh?" Exaggerated incredulity and the same amusement.

"I certainly can't complain about the results—"

Renaud cut him off. "He."

"Excuse me?"

"You should have said *he* can't complain about the results, that is, unless this is your show now?"

Dake felt his face flush. Naturally, Renaud would call him on that, for there was only one man in the world Renaud was loyal to, and that allegiance was cast in marble.

"You know what—" Dake began defensively.

"This isn't your show now, is it, Lawrence?"

"No, of course not."

"Go on. I didn't mean to interrupt."

"I started to say you know what I meant."

"I was just being exact."

Dake concealed his irritation. "Whatever. Anyway, *he* felt, as anyone would, that your methods left something to be desired."

"Regarding Vaitonis and Torelli."

"Yes. Perhaps I—he can understand killing one time in an unusual way, to satisfy some personal whim—" He stopped as Renaud slung one leg over the arm of the couch. "Please don't."

Renaud stared at him innocently. "Please don't what?"

Dake tensed, watched the ease of the water in the fountain.

"Excuse me, please don't what?"

"Nothing." Dake looked over at him. Renaud smiled and removed his leg from the sofa arm, picked up where they'd left off.

"The severed hands and the coins over their eyes, you mean."

Dake looked for composure in the fountain. "Yes. I'm sure you're aware of the potential problem with identical murders." For a moment, the mild activity of the water seemed the soft roil of blood.

"They weren't identical. I used a knife on one and garroted the other."

Dake didn't reply; the conversation was becoming as unreal as etiquette. Perhaps if he didn't respond, Renaud would stop trying to goad him. "Leaving a trademark could allow people to connect the two killings," he heard himself say. Of course Renaud knew that. He wondered if he hadn't left the hands and coins out of curiosity, to see if anyone did actually make the connection. Or possibly, with his affinity for painting, he liked the visual effect, seeing it as a grotesque parody of Dali or some other flaming surrealist. No matter what, the fact was that Renaud had always, like the song, done things his way. Lately, however, the tendency had become pronounced and disturbingly bizarre.

"It's adolescent," Dake added, as much to himself as to the other man.

"I agree," Renaud said pleasantly. "It's a form of regression. I've been going in reverse, trying to turn back the years. I suppose eventually I'll end up an embryo like the star child in *2001*."

"Be serious."

"I am."

Existentialism was another of Renaud's new toys. It was ironic. Renaud's definition of a lawyer was someone who, if you asked him the time, would build you a watch, a tendency Renaud shared himself.

"Just out of curiosity, can you tell me why you killed them in that manner?" Dake asked. Blood seemed safer ground.

Renaud answered without irony. "For my pleasure and for the resonance."

"Pleasure and resonance aren't professional."

"But they're my way."

Yes, of course. Play a derelict, stage a scene, the French were always big on neo-Greek farce. The trouble was, Renaud's little dramas were better than anyone else's. If his imagination caused him to do things that involved unnecessary risk, like a schoolboy daring traffic on his bike, then it also allowed him to find and eliminate people no one else could touch. To keep Renaud, at least for the time being, was simply and undeniably pragmatic.

Dake shifted subjects. He always saved the most significant matters for last; his form of drama. In this particular instance, he had another reason as well; he hated dead-ends.

"You said on the phone there was nothing new on Eddie. Can you fill me in on the details? What about the girl, what was her name . . . ?"

"Sylvia. Old-fashioned tag for a very hip lady."

"Sylvia. What about what she said regarding him leaving the country?"

Renaud looked down and studied a protruding knuckle. "I checked the Los Angeles airports, even those outside, but no luck. He undoubtedly used cash-and-carry ID and passport."

"But you're certain he left the country?"

"I wouldn't have come back from L.A. if I wasn't. It was the only sensible thing for him to do at that point. He'd been staying in a neon dive on Ventura . . ."

Dake looked startled. "How do you know that?"

Renaud's smile was indulgent. "Because, as trite as it might sound, it's my job to know. I found a phone number in Torelli's wallet. It was scribbled on a napkin, the kind they use in bars and, of course, a bar was where Eddie and Torelli had just been, according to Peterson. That was something about him last night, wasn't it?"

Dake didn't know where he was going. He hoped his wife wouldn't come home early.

"Peterson and his little jaunt through downtown Washington," Renaud explained.

Jaunts were existential. "Yes, something," Dake said.

"Short, jazzed-up journey. Urban picaresque."

Dake said, "Yes." He was afraid Renaud would want to discuss the FBI agent's motivations, was relieved when Renaud resumed his narrative instead.

"As I was saying, there was the impression of a glass still on the napkin—the ring hadn't faded yet—so I figured it was from the bar where Torelli had been earlier in the evening. So the odds were pretty good that Eddie had written his number down and given it to Joe. Of course, it could have been the girl's number, but then I didn't know that Eddie had talked to anyone besides Joe until the following night when I went to the bar. Anyway, I called the number from a pay phone and got a motel manager. Knowing that Eddie moved around a great deal, I figured the odds were even better that he was staying there. I asked how much the rooms were and got the address—I didn't want to ask if our friend was in residence and run the risk of the manager mentioning my call to Eddie before I got there. Anyway, as it turned out, it didn't matter. He'd packed and left—he was registered under his own name—left five minutes before I arrived, good luck for him, bad for us. The manager showed me his room as a prospective tenant. There were two phone numbers crumpled up on scratch paper in the wastebasket—it was a good night for numbers—one was for LAX, the other for the Burbank airport. So, as you can see, it's reasonable to assume that Eddie took the first flight, convenient or otherwise, for parts unknown."

Dake sighed wearily and ran a hand down his face, his features suddenly old and drawn under the pressure of his hand. "The thing I don't understand," he said, staring at Renaud, "is why he panicked. He did his job, turned over the tape, and we paid him. Why in God's name did he tell first his cousin, then this Joe Torelli about it?"

"He was oral compulsive?"

Dake wanted to say something nasty but Renaud waved him off.

"No, I know, be serious." He mulled it over for a moment, idly rearranging the blond stunner on the table. "My guess is that in hiring him, we were too concerned about technique and not enough about temperament. Eddie had all the skills, but he never handled anything this big before. Obviously, he didn't have the nerves for it." Renaud looked down at his feet. He snorted to himself. "It's funny. I wonder why Victor approved him in the first place. He always used to consider things like emotional makeup."

Dake quickly changed the subject. "What do you think Eddie will do now?"

"I imagine, given the opportunity, he'll hole up for a while. Then he'll do one of two things—he'll either disappear altogether, assume a new name and life in some small corner of the world, or he'll go to the authorities and bury all of us."

Renaud presented the second option like a man who could take poison with pleasure. Dake, who had naturally already considered both possibilities himself, felt no compulsion to share his derangement.

"What are the chances of finding him first?" he asked.

A faint smile remained on Renaud's face. "They exist."

"If he goes into hiding," Dake suggested hopefully, "he might have to make use of underworld contacts, and our grapevine is pretty good in a number of countries."

"So we might get lucky. Of course, he is a loner, so we can't count on too much in that direction. If we could somehow isolate the city he's in, I imagine I could find him, being a somewhat solitary guy myself. We're a peculiar breed, you know, us loners—all of us seek the same kind of caves and cubbyholes."

They had something resembling a dialogue going. Dake went with the mood. "A favor. If you find him, no more severed hands and coins?"

Renaud's smile broadened. "Not much left in life to enjoy."

"And another favor? Kill him quickly without risk, providing there's nothing he can tell us that we don't already know."

Renaud nodded compliantly. "As I'd already planned."

"By the way," Dake said, relaxing a little in his chair, "you haven't told me what you did with the girl . . . Sylvia?"

Renaud nodded again. "Sylvia. I don't think you'd like the details. They might spoil your breakfast. All you have to know is that it was different and no one will ever find the remains, unless they're talented with sieves."

Sieves. Well, that was fresh. "Good," Dake said.

Renaud yawned elaborately. "Anything else?"

"I don't think so. You'll keep working full time trying to locate Eddie?"

"Of course," Renaud replied. "It's funny, isn't it . . ."

"What's that?"

"The kind of games we play."

Dake managed a weak smile in response. Still, he felt better about things, and he got to his feet with Renaud, ready to play considerate host.

"That's all right, I'll show myself out," Renaud said, waving him back down. Dake started to object, then stayed in his seat as Renaud went to the door. Opening it, Renaud paused and half turned, profiled against the light spilling in from outside.

"Something I've been meaning to bring up," he said without inflection, eyes to the floor. "I'd like to see Victor."

Dake felt the blood draining from his face, felt the tension entering his back once more, but he kept his voice steady. "You will, when he's better."

He was certain he'd kept his equilibrium, his sang-froid, as Renaud would say, but he didn't care for the way the Frenchman was examining his face, like a coroner before dissection—the brown eyes had lost their laughter and the easy features were rigid.

Renaud studied him for what seemed an existential moment, then the hard, set lines relaxed into the familiar, toothy grin. "Soon, Lawrence, soon," he murmured, his inflection still a mystery, then he was gone.

Dake waited until he heard Renaud's car pull away, waited until the whine of the engine faded and vanished, leaving a silence so complete that it seemed Renaud had never been there. Only then did he push himself carefully out of the velour folds of his chair. He walked to the cherrywood bar beside the fountain with deliberation, as though he were wading through treacherous water. Once there, he poured twice his normal dose of Scotch and half the soda. Then he took the long trek to the rear of the house. The liquid in his hand looked like a clear crystal lake when the sun first finds it, and he thought of the man who was there, and then he thought of Renaud, and he drank as he walked. The booze tasted bitter but he kept on drinking, and because it was preferable to thinking about Renaud, he tracked back over his life.

He had been born into borderline poverty, a fact he was neither proud nor ashamed of; born Larry—the Lawrence came much later. His mother, a face from a cameo locket, had died of a disease of the heart when he was two, leaving him to be raised by his father—a musician, a dreamer, a borrower, but never a possessor of grandiose visions. They existed on welfare and on tomorrows and, for a while, like his old man, he sought refuge from their second-hand lives in art. As a boy he assiduously studied piano, had fantasies of Carnegie Hall glory, fireworks on an endless string. Yet something had been missing, something intangible and elusive that would always deprive him of the possibility of greatness. In his scrupulous manner he sifted it out. He had technique but no real passion, the poetry of expression.

The discovery was a brief disappointment but no more than that. While his father slipped deeper into the morass of the dogday blues, theme without variation, the boy steadied his own life. With the same precision he had brought to the keyboard, he mapped out his future. Lacking poetry and passion, he would substitute prosaic success. Seeing that the world ran on a certain glibness, that the profound ones like his father were sucked under by their fatal refusal to compromise, he clinically charted professions. Medicine came to mind first, then law. The latter was the most reasonable choice, an area where logic could be showcased into wealth. With that in mind, he fought his way through Harvard on grades and determination, then passed the bar with ease. His career followed naturally after that, shifting gradually into greater degrees of prosperity. He married; sired two proper sons—both now safely ensconced in the social whirl of Colgate—then divorced and remarried. With his current wife he shared a modicum of scheduled affection, a leisure world of saunas and sunny boredom. He knew of worse unions.

Yet, as his creature comforts continued to grow, so did his unrest. Something troubled the substance of his life, something elusive and intangible, and as before, he sifted it out. He had what he wanted but needed something more, an excitement, an edge, a theme with variation. He sought solutions, found none, watched his world turn gradually gray, then one day he flew south, met Victor, and found what he was searching for . . .

He realized he was at the back of the house, in a room without furnishing or purpose. He looked down at the glass in his hand. It was empty. Stooping, he set it carefully down on the floor before pushing back the Oriental rug that covered the trapdoor. Grasping the brass handle, he lifted the heavy wood frame with effort, lowering it over him as he descended.

The darkness swallowed him momentarily before his hand located the switch; row upon row of phallic glass rose phantasmagorically toward him in the shadowed light, as he went down the ten firm steps leading to the wine cellar. The dank space had the heavy odor of fermentation and old wood, an animal musk mingling of life and decay. Resting in oak racks, the bottles, opaque greens, whites, ambers, and browns—Margaux, Spätlese, Montrachet—were locust-thick with dust. He promised himself he would open the finest vintage when all of this was over, but he had come here now for what was concealed in a corner. No one else even knew the wall safe existed—if all the circuits of his brain should suddenly short, the contents would remain inside until the house rotted to a skeleton of splinters and rust.

Striking a match, his hand found the combination lock . . . twice left to 7, right to 24, back once more to 9 . . . As the last tumbler softly clicked, he opened the door and peered into the black interior. For a moment, he imagined against reason that the tape was gone and his heart lost a beat as he thrust the tiny flame deeper into the vault; along with the log of his calls to Panama and Ghana, the reel of magnetic ribbon was there, of course, bringing back images of the starless, wind-whipped night and the meeting in the abandoned tenement. There had been no possibility that the tape wouldn't be where he had put it, but then enough had gone wrong the last few days that he needed the reassurance of seeing and touching it.

All of their luck hadn't been bad of course; if Karl Vaitonis, currying favor and money, hadn't come to them with what Eddie had told him, they might never have had the opportunity to stop the information from spreading. So there had been deaths, all of them necessary, and undoubtedly there would be others and who knew where it would end, all because a wireman's nerves had strayed. And that was the crux of it, what Renaud had said about temperament. You could take an idea, a scheme as smooth as a soft hand over velvet skin, and something intangible could turn that unblemished beauty into a ragged, desperate whore scrambling to survive. Emotion was what he, Dake, had overlooked. No matter how perfect the circle of a plot, men still had to work its wheel and men were fallible, given to sudden fears; it made them unpredictable, like Eddie, like Peterson, and yes, like Paul Renaud. Yet it was far from hopeless. Kill Eddie and things would be all right. Then he would take human frailty into account in the future, be more cautious, make no more mistakes. Kill Eddie and his worries would be over, for Eddie was the key, a living, breathing tape that must be erased. All they had to do was find him, somewhere in the world.

As Dake closed the safe, he noticed that his hands were trembling slightly. Perhaps he was becoming more human himself. He found no pleasure in the thought as he trudged back up the stairs and turned out the light.

17

Pigeons

Charley woke with a slow sun at nine. It took him a little time to remember where he was, Washington, December 28. Five days ago he'd been sitting in his office talking to Joe. Five days ago he'd wanted a change in his life. He'd gotten it.

Pushing the sheets aside, he sat on the edge of the bed and checked for damage, gingerly fingering his forehead. There was a bitch of a lump, but not enough to warrant ice. Rolling up his pajama leg, he examined his knee. It was a not so pretty purple, and stiff, but alive. He felt like the morning after a fight—the aches and bruises were still there, but the worst was over. Mornings were always better, even if

Jesus, but I killed a man

Charley pushed himself off the bed and away from the memory. He dressed, Levis, sneakers and denim jacket, and went outside to run. Exercise was therapy. Something to live by. The day was as crisp as corn flakes. The slush in the streets had melted to pools of slickness. The sky was clear, the clouds cushions of snow. He jogged at double time, breathing in great chunks of cool air. People stared at him, double takes; nobody ran in D.C. unless it was away from something; well, what the fuck, that was what he was doing.

He was feeling pretty good by the time he stopped at a greasy spoon, where he ordered a ham and egg special from a waitress who was all bony angles and dentures. The coffee was death, but the food was fair. Someone had left the *Post* on the counter. He read the story while he ate. There was a main-event photo of the burning diesel—snaking flames and the blanket spray of firefighter hoses. The article below gave the sequence of the pursuit. There were a number of eyewitness quotes. One lady, a Mrs. Renate Fairchild—who suffered a bloody lip and two black eyes when "trampled" by the alleged killer—said she knew the man chasing him was a "police officer" all along. She could tell by the way he handled a gun and by the "determined hateful look" in his eyes.

They had Bush's reaction on page 2, underneath a late-night snap of the president and Barbara. They were standing on the White House lawn in matching silk robes. George looked properly pissed and put out, with a patch of banty rooster hair jutting out from his head. His wife looked like she always did, like she lived in a bubble. Bush was quoted as saying he had it on reliable authority that the killing spree was part of a Cuban plot. The president, however, denied reports that a surface-to-air missile had been fired, adding that, besides, it had fallen harmlessly in Havana.

Charley folded the paper and left it on the counter with a quarter tip. Legitimized in black and white, he found it difficult to believe he'd had any part in it. Maybe it really had been an undercover cop who shot Phil Peterson.

Jogging back to his hotel, he shaved and showered, then phoned his Santa Monica base collect to see how business was going. He had a little time to kill before his one o'clock appointment and it seemed better to stay busy, keep things normal. It was only when weird Arthur accepted the call and asked what the hell he was doing—did he know how much this was costing him?—that Charley realized he wasn't all there. Of course, it was true that wall-eyed, bald Arthur had the hots for money—he was the sort of guy who'd sell kerosene to a firebug and hold the matches if the price was right—so a certain amount of hysteria over long-distance expenditures was to be expected. At least he was doing Charley some good at the office. He'd come up with a felon, a two-time loser, and a safecracker rabid on bennies. His only complaint was that "these old dames speaking some language no normal person never heard" kept wandering in and asking if he did taxes. Charley guessed Arthur held their hands and said fuck, yes.

After breaking the connection with Arthur, Charley drove to Franklin Park, with Reiser's map on the dash to guide him. He covered the five miles with a few concerns, decided Pat Hanlon was either a sly as sin leprechaun or a mad sex computer, a box with live wires well hung from steel loins. Well, it was a way to pass the time.

The park was pretty; two toned shades of green, with sandboxes and sparrows haggling over the price of a worm. After parking, Charley cut across the grass, served a forced smile to a six-year-old kid with angel food eyes and a red nymphet mouth. Hip to false gestures, the girl scurried to the safety of mom. An ogre a day keeps little girls, keeps little girls, nosed through Charley's head, a stick-freak's nursery riff. No, he definitely wasn't all right yet, but he was trying.

The associate director of the FBI was hunkered down on a bench, feeding a frenzy of pigeons from a brown paper bag. He was decked out in brown patent leather shoes and something that wasn't quite a trenchcoat. A porkpie hat was too small on his head. The hair underneath was red that showed gray and the skin was fair. He was as Irish as Paddy but the sly blue eyes were the only leprechaun part of him, for he looked to go over six feet and two twenty. You would have called him uncle and out of shape until you noticed that the creases of his coat were from muscle, not slack.

Hanlon wasn't alone on the bench. A guy with even more creases in his trench sat at the opposite end, arms folded across his chest. Had brass-shiny skin, a flat nose, full lips, the face you saw on a buffalo nickel, wore his hair in a style you don't see these days, parted in the middle and slicked. A toothpick leaned from the corner of his mouth, which frowned at the pigeons, who, heads bobbing, glass button eyes glazed, charged his toes.

"Only damned birds in the world look stuffed and mounted while they're still alive," Pat Hanlon said. He had an easy baritone that carried its masculinity without effort. "Don't see Geraldine," he added with concern. "Hope she's all right. She's been looking a little long in the feathers."

"Maybe a sparrow got her," the buffalo nickel said with a grunt. "Neighborhood's got some pretty tough ones around." The gravel in his voice came from either cancer, whiskey, or nature. Charley had an idea they were his kind of people.

Hanlon saw they had company. "Tone?" he asked. Charley nodded. Hanlon leaned forward, introduced himself and shook hands.

"K.C. Jones," his friend said, putting out a hand that dwarfed Charley's.

"K.C. for Kansas City?"

"K.C. for Kripple Creek, South Dakota. Oglala Sioux, Crazy Horse's people, by way of the Black Hills."

"Charley Tone, Mexican-Irish, by way of the barrio," Charley said, shaking the numbness out of his fingers. K.C. and Hanlon exchanged smiles—Charley was their kind of people as well.

"Have a seat, Charley," Hanlon said. Charley did, between them. They could have been three strangers waiting for a bus.

Hanlon tossed breadcrumbs at his feet. "Damn good fighter," he said to K.C., then to Charley, "Who ever hit you the hardest?"

"IRS, then a guy named Turner."

"Summer of 'eighty-three, wasn't it?"

"You remember?" Charley was surprised and a little pleased.

"Sure do. Saw it on TV." Hanlon seemed to be addressing K.C. again: "It was in the Garden. Turner was an up and coming kid with speed and style and the kind of cockiness being twenty brings. Nine rounds, Charley's in there trying, but the kid's too fast and it must've been pushing a hundred degrees . . ."

A hundred and ten under the lights, Charley thought, for he remembered it too, remembered being drenched in his own sweat and the water they sloshed over him between rounds and the Vaseline crowding his eyes and the taste of blood in his mouth.

". . . Charley's got one eye that's a slit and another that's heading that way fast and midway through the tenth Turner decks him with a beaut of a combination, six punches with the poetry of a young Ali. Charley gets up at seven but he's hurt and Turner knows it—he's grinning and dancing, enjoying himself, and the crowd's chanting Turner, Turner, Turner, looking for the kill. Charley's by the ropes, where he should be covering up and trying to survive, but instead he's moving forward and he feints with his left, the kid's too confident and he goes for it, and Charley nails him with a terrific right over the top and Turner's eyes go flying up so you could see nothing but white and suddenly the grin's gone and Charley doubled off the left, follows with a right, then another left, and the crowd's chanting Charley, Charley, Charley as Turner goes down and stays. Helluva fight," Hanlon finished, shaking his head.

"Got lucky," Charley said, meaning it.

Hanlon grinned. "Yeah, same way you got lucky when you shot Phil Peterson."

"Wondering when you'd get to that."

"Like you're wondering why I asked you to meet me here."

"Among other things."

"I'll get to the other things in a minute." Hanlon took off his hat, wiped his brow with his sleeve and gestured south.

"See that building over there, the big, ugly six-story mother? I got an office on the fifth floor with three intercoms, two secretaries and my own bar, and most the time I'd rather be down here feeding the fucking birds."

Charley understood. "Okay."

"I asked you here to compare notes. Let me give it to you from our side first—last night around ten, Matthew Byrne, maybe you've heard of him, the director of the FBI, he phones to tell me the chief of police had just called with this cockamamie story about one of our own going batshit before being killed by some pug. Since not having to dig in the dirt is one of the privileges of being top dog, and since I've always been closer to the dirt than Matt, he asked me to pick up the pieces. I did a little fast checking and decided this could be fairly complicated and that other lives might be in danger, yours included."

"Which explains why you wanted to keep me outta the headlines."

"Wouldn't want you on my conscience. You Catholic, Charley?"

Charley let his shoulders rise and fall. "Hanging on."

"Remember the stuff when you were a kid, with the wafers and . . . never mind. Where were we?"

"Pickin' up pieces," K.C. said.

"Which is what I've spent more hours than I'd care to count doing since last night—phone calls, leafing through files, trying to sort things out."

"You talk to a guy named Mayer?"

Hanlon's eyes twinkled. "This morning. Lovely man. I had the distinct impression he thought you should be shot. Anyway, he filled in some gaps, if that's what you want to call them, Caracas, John Wayne, the man in the lake. Needless to say, I can't make jackshit out of any of that, but I think I can figure out some of the rest. Want to hear how I see it?"

"Could I stop you?"

"Only if you doubled off the left. Just a minute, I've got some notes." Handing the paper bag to K.C., he took a spiral notepad out of his coat.

"You use one of those too?" Charley said.

"Down to the cardboard." Hanlon flipped to a page coffee stained for easy reference.

"How about starting with Peterson?" Charley requested.

The twinkle left Hanlon's eyes. "As good a place as any," he said flatly, lowering the pad. He spoke without referring to his notes. "Phil grew up here in Washington. He joined the Bureau in 'eighty-three. Had a good, solid record, although maybe he was a little impulsive, which I guess you'd know."

"You called him Phil. You knew him?"

Hanlon nodded. "He worked under me in Heavy Traffic, before I got kicked upstairs a couple years back. Unlike K.C. here, he wasn't your typical street agent. He came from tenth generation Eastern upper crust, not much money, but tons of tradition. Went to all the right schools, shit, he went to Princeton. Had a father who blew his brains out, which might explain something, although I'm not sure what. Anyway, you would've expected him, with his background, to take a cushier job."

"Street agents don't got it easy," K.C. said, scattering crumbs around his feet.

"Different breed," Hanlon said.

"Don't get invited to no penguin suit parties."

"Or opera boxes on the cuff."

"Or dames with diamonds down to their toes."

"You're sort of like a homicide cop," Hanlon embellished to Charley. "There's a lot of easy and sudden violence, especially sudden. It gives you a different view of things."

"Cynical?" Charley tried.

"I'd like to think balanced," Hanlon answered with a faint smile. "You travel around in a world where the edges are creased, it makes it damn hard to give life a Madison Avenue gloss, to get snowed by all the pretty platitudes."

He paused, watching the pigeons feed like sharks, then added, "Of course, the flip side is that it's easy to get turned, to end up taking what you can get wherever you can get it. You see guys who should've had their plugs pulled living high on the hog, you figure why not me? You work heavy traffic long enough, it's a thin line between balanced, and yeah, you had the right word, cynical."

"That what happened to Peterson?"

Hanlon shrugged. "He wouldn't be the first to work both sides. Odds are somebody was greasing him to keep them posted, to let them know when and where the heat was coming."

"So how do Eddie and Joe and the rest tie in?"

"Okay," Hamlon said, looking down at his notes, "I could be dead wrong, but here's how I see it. Let's say for the sake of saying it that some people, some underworld types, have a job they want done here in D.C., something that needs a good wireman. Now maybe they're the people paying Phil off, maybe not, but no matter what, he hears they're looking for a class act from out of town—if there was trouble, a local guy would be too easy to trace—he hears that and that they're willing to pad everyone involved for services rendered. So Phil thinks of Joe's friend Eddie, who according to our grapevine is one of the best, even though he's never been rapped. So these underworld types, they fly Eddie in and he performs, only he doesn't go straight home like a good boy after he's finished—he tells cousin Karl what he's gone and done, who knows why. You still with me, Charley?"

"Me and the pigeons."

"Had a feeling you would be," Hanlon said, the twinkle back in his eyes. "Okay, somehow Eddie's employers discover his little transgression and they kill the cousin. Then they go after Eddie, who's back in L.A. by now. The only problem is they don't know where exactly, since he's got this lousy habit of not staying in one place long enough to hang his hat. So they have Peterson set up a meet with Torelli, hoping Joe might be able to steer them to Eddie. Now there's no way of knowing if Phil found out where he was, but he must've learned that Eddie told Joe and a roller named Sylvia a few things they shouldn't know. So after leaving the laundry, Peterson places a call to the underworld types and they go and slaughter your friend, leaving, and I don't have the answer to this one either, Charley, the same souvenirs they'd left on the cousin."

"Maybe Peterson killed Joe," Charley suggested.

Halon shook his head and checked his notes. "According to a homicide cop named Martz who questioned him, he had a late dinner date with Mayer's secretary—the girl and witnesses confirmed it—at the time Torelli was getting himself killed. How am I doing. Rambling?"

"You couldn't tell it by me," Charley admitted. "What about Sylvia?"

"Missing, according to the L.A.P.D., since Sunday."

Charley bit his lower lip and nodded thoughtfully; somehow, he wasn't surprised.

"Okay," he said, "Joe's butchered, which is where I come in. Peterson recruits me because he thinks there's an outside chance I might stumble across Eddie and get back to him. Then he could've made another call and Eddie ends up with his hands cute over his lap and a nice shiny new quarter over one eye, which maybe is how it is anyway. So I come across Sylvia—"

K.C. cut in, joined the dance. "A question. Ain't Peterson takin' a pretty big risk bringin' you in?"

Hanlon's turn. "You mean instead of just looking for Eddie himself?"

"Yeah, that's what I mean."

Hanlon weighed it. A sparrow darted in and stole a crumb. The pigeons tucked their chins into their chests and cooed in righteous indignation.

"Maybe, but not so much," Hanlon said. "It was a good gamble, a street agent's move. With Torelli dead, Peterson knows Eddie's going to have his suspicions about who set Joe up, that he's going to make damn sure Phil doesn't get within eyeshot of him. Then, you got to consider, Peterson has to see to it that he doesn't start Mayer wondering by spending too much time scrounging around for Eddie, who's pretty low on Mayer's priority list. So bringin' Charley in is a good way of shortening the odds. Sure, if Charley finds Eddie, it's going to look a little funny if Eddie gets knocked off before we can haul him in, but no one can prove squat. Besides, Peterson could've always covered himself by saying, Jesus, we tried, but the other team got to him first, maybe even make it look like Charley was someway involved. Make sense?"

K.C. nibbled on his lower lip, then nodded. "Okay. So where were we?"

"Charley with Sylvia."

"Who tells me a few things, but before I can get back to Peterson, he's sent here on another case."

"Peterson *requested* another case," Hanlon said. "My guess is he wanted to check in with the people he was working for."

"Who're probably based here."

"Who're probably based here, and get a better feel for what was coming down on their end."

K.C. still had questions. "Think he'd go to the fuckin' trouble?"

"If he was getting nervous, damn right I think he would. Things were getting dicey, maybe out of hand, and his prints were places."

Charley scratched his scar. "So when I show up and call him about the sister, he gets scared and decides to see if there was anything at her place, a note with a name, a letter from Eddie, that could cause grief. He goes up, breaks in, does a job on her brother's things, she shows before he's finished. He hides, she takes some comfort, he comes out and that's that."

K.C. kept pushing. "Why not just slip the fuck out when she's in the fuckin' water?"

Charley shrugged. "Who knows? Maybe that's what he had in mind, why he took the pullover along—yank on the mask and get out fast if he's discovered. Only, put yourself in his place. He's down there in the dark, listening to the water run, and he thinks why not, why not kill her? Maybe he figures Karl told her something and something means it's safer to cave her skull in."

"And he does, which is where you come in again," Hanlon said.

Charley grimaced. "Yeah. That's where I come in again."

And Jesus her hand white and boneless in mine and all that followed, all the dead and dying eyes . . .

The three men gave silence some time. Ignored by K.C., the pigeons had deserted their bench.

"*Was* there anything in her apartment?" Charley tried, mostly on himself.

"No," Hanlon told him. "K.C. went through Vaitonis's stash at precinct this morning."

K.C. coughed. "Real royal cover-up, ain't it?"

Hanlon said, "Wouldn't be the first."

Charley said, "Maybe they cut it." The other tossed him questions with their eyes. "I mean, maybe they killed everybody who knows."

K.C. said, "Except themselves."

"There's Eddie, maybe," Charley added.

Hanlon squinted up at the sun, removed the porkpie, shielded his eyes with the same hand, and wiped the sweat-shine from his brow.

"Mayer ran a computer check on the L.A. air traffic," he said, replacing his hat, "but there was no Eddie Mikenas on the manifests. Not that that means squat. For a guy in Eddie's line, dummied passports and ID are about as hard to come by as Kleenex. Say he's on skates, hiding out in the sticks overseas, it's really pretty simple—either we find him, they do, or nobody does."

K.C. nodded slowly, accepting the logic.

"Who has the best shot?" Charley asked.

"Eddie," Hanlon said. "Still, there're a helluva lot of people here and in Europe who work both sides. Like Torelli, they sell trade, sometimes two or three times. If one of them came across Eddie and knew he was worth moving, he'd decide where the percentage was, telling us or them."

"Which still leaves us with tryin' to find a guy that might already be pushing daisies," K.C. complained.

Charley was blunt. "You got anything better?"

Hanlon and K.C. exchanged sorry smiles. "No, we don't, Charley," Hanlon admitted.

"So where do we start?" K.C. asked his boss.

"With Caracas. Maybe the Venezuelan consulate on Massachusetts can tell us something. Maybe some guy in Caracas is known as the John Wayne of the country. Maybe the man in the lake means something. Maybe none of it means shit. Hell, I don't know."

"Venezuelan consulate," K.C. confirmed with a high sign.

Charley coughed and said, "Mind if I tag along?"

K.C. and Hanlon stared at him.

"Why?"

"Come this far, I'm interested, that's all," Charley shrugged. A pigeon pecked his ankle, not quite drawing blood. K.C. and Hanlon exchanged looks. They were in a rut.

"He's earned it," K.C. suggested.

"Yeah, but I don't know," Hanlon said, making a face.

"You speak Spanish, K.C.?" Charley asked. K.C. shook his head.

"Well, I do, which might come in handy. Besides, you want to keep me outta the headlines."

"That a threat?" Hanlon asked amiably.

"Just thinking." Charley turned to K.C. "We could take my car."

Hanlon gave K.C. a good smile. "You see why he beat Turner?"

K.C. gave the brown bag back to Hanlon. "Where you parked?" he said to Charley. Charley showed him with a thumb. K.C. caught a stagger of gray wings in the sky as he and Charley started toward the Camaro. "Geraldine's back," he said over his shoulder.

Hanlon chuckled contentedly as the pigeon landed, shaking her ragged, tick-ridden feathers. Charley glanced back once as he walked. Hanlon was slumped forward on the bench tossing crumbs in Geraldine's direction, trying to beat the rush of button-down birds who flocked in a rage of ground-born wings to deprive the old girl of what little life offered her.

18

The Price of Tarot and Gas

*"Did you know Peterson?" Charley asked, immediately regret*ting the question.

"Enough to say hi in hallways, that's 'bout it," K.C. replied. "We worked diff'rent parts of the city."

The exchange hovered, waited for a continuation, found none. The memory of the man made them both uncomfortable. K.C. shifted topics and mood.

"You smoke cigars?" he said, holding his nose as he rolled down the window to let in some fresh air.

"They guy who rented it before me did Castro imitations."

K.C.'s laugh was a snort. He returned to the map, napkin-stretched across his lap. They were cruising down K Street, with Charley behind the wheel.

"Turn left here, I think," K.C. ventured, then an instant later, "No, damn, keep goin' straight."

Charley jerked the wheel back to the right. "You live here or don't you?" he asked, perplexed, as he leveled off.

"Yeah, but fuck, I ain't never been shit on directions. Besides, it's harder'n hell to see 'round this sonabitch," he said, touching a bullet hole in the windshield with the spatulate tip of his index finger. "Coulda been your head," he added as a casual afterthought, then, as another afterthought, "Excuse all the swearin'. I don't believe in a man swearin' more'n he has to, but the only thing I hate worse'n maps are poodles."

Charley squinted at him out of the corner of one cautious eye. "Poodles?"

K.C. nodded earnestly. "Poodles are enough to turn you into a fuckin' sailor."

"How you feel about cats?"

"Cats are okay, long as you don't turn your back on 'em."

Charley quickly switched to the weather and the price of gas. After three missed turns and enough cursing by K.C. to turn an old salt blue, they realized they were going in circles. Massachusetts was a myth. It's a state not a street, Charley said. Shit, no. There, K.C. said, pointing. There.

They were driving. K.C. was behind the wheel.

"Adams-Morgan around Argonne, right?" he said with wary hope.

"Had an uncle killed there," Charley said, studying the map.

"Huh?"

They never had found Massachusetts, but at the corner of Columbia, a kid on skates had helped. Told them where the Venezuelans usually lived. Now all they had to do was find

Adams-Morgan. K.C. wasn't looking too confident. He stuck a toothpick in his mouth and made conversation to hide the fact. It beat maiming pedestrians.

"I notice all the Mex fighters cross themselves 'fore a fight. Must've helped you, havin' that kinda faith."

"'Specially when you're spitting up blood between rounds."

"I useta box a little, Golden Gloves stuff, that kinda crap. Only trouble was, I'd get these fuckin' nosebleeds all the fuckin' time. It got to where a guy just hadda look at my nose and it'd start gushin'."

"Where'd you fight? Here in D.C.?" Adams-Morgan. Maybe it was in another state.

"Naw. Back home in South Dakota." Talking seemed to help.

"You really Sioux?" Maybe it was a state of mind.

"Full blooded, if you'll excuse the expression. My full name is K.C. Jones Wicasta Tuwe Tuktekten Hinhpayapi Cantanhan, which means somethin' like Man Who Falls Out of Trees Occasionally. I grew up on the Pine Ridge reservation, which explains why I'm not the brightest guy in the world. See, the Indian Affairs agents, they run the res schools and their idea of an education is teachin' us to grunt and shuffle. Guess I was luckier'n a lotta my friends, though. Most of 'em ended up in front of the tube and a bottle in a fuckin' shack."

"How'd you land with the FBI?"

"After the navy, stared datin' this gal that worked in Minneapolis–St. Paul. I was layin' brick at the time and she figured I should be doin' better, so she talked me into takin' the test. I flunked it two times, quicker'n you can say shit. I never would've taken it a third 'cept she was so good in the sack."

"What happened to the girl?"

"I married her." He winced at the memory as he braked for a red light. "Where the fuck are we?" Panic was returning to his voice. Charley tried to ease it away.

"Getting close. Take a left at the next light."

"You hitched?" K.C. asked, nursing the accelerator as the signal changed.

"Separated."

"How long?"

"Two months."

"How you feel 'bout it?"

"Shitty."

"That's too bad," K.C. said, shaking his head in commiseration.

Charley noticed he wasn't wearing a wedding band. "You still married?" he asked.

"No. We was together, if that's what you wanta call it, five years, then she falls for a fuckin' contractor. He was in cement, looked sorta like a poodle. I thought 'bout beatin' the crap outta him, but decided it was easier to get a lawyer, even though they're all fuckers."

"Like poodles."

"Like poodles. That's when I transferred out here, after the divorce. Wasn't long 'fore Pat Hanlon took me under his wing, sorta like the pigeons. His wife, she died a year back. He tries to pretend it don't bother him a lot still, you know, he jokes and smiles, but sometimes you see it in his eyes. They get real sad when he don't think nobody's lookin'." K.C.'s own eyes turned mournful. "It was cancer, a real shame. They'd been married better'n twenty years. She was a damn fine woman and he's a damn good man. Where . . ."

"A left," Charley said.

They were driving. Gremlins were breaking the compass's arm and face. Black angels were skating over the glass. K.C. was still behind the wheel.

"I think we're the fuck in Virginia," he said, his knuckles turning white.

"A right," Charley said, then, "There's a space." They parked between two bumpers on Argonne and got out.

There weren't any signs telling them exactly where to go, so they stood around taking in the scene. With its cobweb windshield, the Camaro fit in fine—the local wheels were punched-out Chevies and Fords, more rust than paint, and holed mufflers. Black-lung exhaust danced with the sweet odors of home-cooked sweat—garbanzos, ajicos, tamales, tortillas—from the tenements that lined both sides of the street, dull brick buildings left to the weather. A daisy in a pot was doing hard time on a sill. Donna Summers was escaping from a Chevy radio, belting "Thank God It's Friday," only no one was listening. Dirty writing was scrawled on sidewalks and walls, confessions of undying love and *chinga tu madres,* for the street belonged to the kids, also doing hard time, splay-legged on steps, leaning against railings. Even the games, stickball and hopscotch, had a yardbird beat. They lived five to a room in scarred, dirty rentals, where rats as big as kittens prowled midnight floors and sex was two shadows angry on the wall. They would be wise in the wrong ways by ten, the girls knocked up at thirteen, and maybe, just maybe if they were lucky, they would drift away, leaving nothing behind but time and space and memories as empty as yesterday's dreams.

Charley let the atmosphere and a little nostalgia play over him, then he and K.C. strolled to a stoop where a chica in Goodwill cotton sat dragging bitterly on a cigarette. She told them to go fuck themselves before they could get out a smile.

Things got better. Charley asked an old lady sweeping the steps a few questions. Yes, she was Venezuelan she replied in wary Spanish; she had a face seen in old tintypes, and a voice that harbored even older fears. No, she told them, she knew nothing of lakes or John Wayne, had never seen either, but if there was anyone who might, it was Señor Suarez, who lived next door. He was from Caracas and had known *familias muy importantes*, very important people there, but no, he wasn't home now, but yes they could find him that evening at Los Trucos on Calvert, where the old people went to dance, although, *madre de Dios*, she would never go there herself. Charley thanked her and asked if she knew where they could get a good meal. Anywhere but here, she wistfully replied, anywhere but here.

* * *

They ate in a drive-by with a fierce red, white, and blue sign. The waitresses were dray horses, the burgers juice-sloppy and maybe cooked. K.C. inhaled three Relish Delights and an order of fries out in the Camaro. Picking at the edges, Charley asked him if he'd ever killed a man. K.C. carefully wiped his mouth and said that when he was in the fucking navy doing his fucking time, his tug had chased a VC junk in the Gulf, big eight-inch guns tossing prayers at little dark sinners in black p.j.'s, but, *madre de Dios*, they'd missed. 'Course, he'd also busted a couple jaws and an arm, all in the line of Bureau duty, but no, he'd never snuffed nobody. Lucky you, Charley said ruefully. Lucky you.

They reached Calvert by seven. The street wasn't the best—the stores were brick tombs, the sidewalks grew glass. Los Trucos was down the block. It resembled a warehouse and seemed to sag. The club's name was in scared neon, the L and the C were out, the other letters weak; management was either saving on electricity or trying for mystique. The front door was wedged open and a tango floated through Charley's open window, mixing nicely with the ghosts of cigars.

"Jeez. Didn't know they played music like that anymore," K.C. said.

"They don't," Charley told him.

With nothing better to do, K.C. parked at the curb and they went inside.

Inside, they were playing a tango, but it could have been a convalescent home; except for the sloe-eyed girl behind the register, everyone in the place seemed past retirement or much else.

There was an unassuming bar without a mirror against one wall. No one was at the counter except the bartender, who was polishing glasses with his profession's practiced nonchalance. A few couples sat hunched at tables around the dance floor. Each table had a rose-colored cloth, green flower vases, and candles. A few of the candles even showed a flame.

A corner was reserved for shadow and a mariachi band in loose green jackets and black slacks. They played like sick dogs. Out on the shiny dance floor, a half dozen couples stayed in step. The arc lights overhead were cruel, accenting wrinkles and crimped eyes and tears of sweat. The women wore too much blue eye shadow, rouge, and powder. You could find the same faces in open coffins. The men postured stiffly in an imitation of masculine pride, leading their partners through joyless, barely remembered motions. Like the kids in the streets, they were doing time.

Charley turned from the dancers and said, "Buenas tardes, Señorita," to the sloe-eyed girl. She had a hook nose, bright olive skin, and a stare that could level your soul.

"Buenas tardes, Señor," she said, not meaning it. "Dos billetes por el baile?" The sharply stressed words—rolling *y*'s that were *l*'s and flat, hard syllables—unfolded fast.

"No, ahora no," Charley replied. "Ando buscando un amigo, un Señor Suarez."

"Está atras, en la cuarta puerta, diciendole a un tonto la buena ventura con las cartas," she told him, brushing a strand of perfect black hair from her brow.

"Muchas gracias," Charley said, touching the brim of his cap.

"De nada," she said, touching nothing.

Charley ambled toward the back of the club, where the diners slouched in soft focus. K.C. trailed just behind, two left feet looking for relief. The band had shifted to a waltz. It sounded like the tango. The three surviving couples on the dance floor were locked in rigor mortis.

"Favor," K.C. whispered in Charley's ear as they skirted the action. "Next one, see if she talks our lingo. It'd save some grief."

"Fair enough."

"Well?" K.C. said impatiently. "You gonna lead?"

"She said Suarez was in a room in the back."

"Doing what?"

"He tells fortunes."

K.C.'s face tried on a few colors. "That's great," he said. "Maybe it fits. We're lookin' for somethin' that probably don't exist, so we go to a guy with a fuckin' crystal ball."

"Cards."

"Huh?"

"He reads cards."

"Well, that's sure as shit's better, now ain't it."

They went into a short, undernourished corridor, pale walls in need of paint, four doors in need of something. One of the doors said Señoritas. A toilet threw up and a crickety old gentleman came out and menaced them with a cane before falling down.

"Hope that ain't him," K.C. whispered in an aside.

Charley said, "Happy times." He led K.C. to a door that wasn't; a tawdry purple curtain. They parted it.

The room was about the size of Charley's office. The table in the center was a clone of those in the dance hall, rose cloth and candle; only the flowers were missing. An empty water tumbler and an open bottle of Blue Nun rested in their place, the wine releasing a sweet aroma. Hanging from a ceiling chain, a bulb barely bothered the table, muted by a pink shade with painted green parrots in profile.

The man sitting at the table was a pair of hands dealing out Tarot cards with a blackjack dealer's slick grace. The circle of light from the overhead lamp extended only to the edges of the cloth, leaving the rest of the room and the man shadowed. The hands would appear magically from the darkness, flicking out large, glossy double images of kings and queens, knights and slaves, and a skeleton with a stoned leer. The hands should have had a concert pianist's slender, sculpted beauty—would have, if it hadn't been for the fact that the wrists were grotesquely deformed, angled in and locked, the bones pushing against the skin.

"Señor Suarez?" Charley said, his mind on the wrists.

The hands stopped moving with the suddenness of surprise.

"Sì," came back from the darkness. Although the bottle was nearly as drained as the glass, the voice was cold sober.

"Habla ingles?" Charley asked.

"Yes. You're here to have your fortunes told?" Charley's request had thrown him, but not that far. His voice was soft, his English at home.

"Not exactly," Charley replied. "We'd like to ask you a few questions."

"Police?"

"Not—"

"FBI." K.C. apparently didn't care for charades.

Suarez showed no surprise. He simply nodded, bent forward, and carefully poured the remainder of the wine into the glass. Then he motioned to two chairs against the wall. Charley and K.C. unfolded the chairs and sat opposite Suarez, who was now within the circle of light. Even seated you could see he was small. He was wearing the sorry green and black of the band. The sleeves of his jacket showed too much soiled white cuff without links. He was about forty and they hadn't been easy years. His skin was dead and gray, his cheeks sunken, his eyes razor scratches behind cut-rate shades. A pair of crutches held up a wall near the table.

"I'd offer you a drink," Suarez said, "but I only have one glass and one fading bottle."

K.C. seemed to decide he'd shown too much muscle. "You really tell fortunes?" he soft-pedaled.

Suarez shrugged. "I play in the band sometimes, run errands for the owner, and yes, I tell fortunes."

"To the old folks?"

Suarez's smile was dry. "They're the only ones who listen. I tell them that their children love them, that God notices their prayers, that they have done good in their lives and will continue to do so. Mostly lies, but it makes them happy."

Charley wanted to know what happiness cost. Suarez told him two bucks. K.C. wanted to know if the price was better in Caracas, couldn't help himself, asked if he'd also told lies there, but Suarez didn't miss a beat:

"No, the truth," he said, "at least what I saw, in my limited way, as the truth." He idly turned over a card, twisting his arm to compensate for his wrist. "I can't understand why your agency would be interested in my whimsical little history, but then I'm sure you'll tell me."

Because we're going on a wing and a prayer, Charley felt like saying. Instead, he said, "A lady next door to where you live . . ."

"Mrs. Reyes?" Suarez asked confidently.

Charley nodded. "She told us you knew some important people in Caracas."

"Señora Reyes thinks that anybody who doesn't dig ditches or paper walls for a living is important. I was an instructor at the Universidad Central de Venezuela. Economics."

"You left that for this?" K.C. said with cartoon amazement.

"I didn't have a great deal of choice."

"Why?"

Suarez sighed and leaned back, the hands disappearing at his sides. "Let me explain about my country," he said, his voice sliding into shadow as he made his speech. "Until 1958, it was a dictatorship where the people, almost all poor, lived in fear of a tyrant's whim and the SN, his secret police. Now both dictatorship and SN are gone and we elect a president every five years and call our government a democracy, but things really haven't changed—it's still a fat, corrupt land for the few in power, where the ugliness and poverty have simply assumed more discreet forms, and one day, last March, I made a terrible mistake by saying all this and more. I said that the government was covertly controlled by a military junta and American oil, that the poor wouldn't inherit the earth as long as God had a whip in his hand, epaulets on his sleeve, and Exxon at his back—in other words, I said what I believed, which wouldn't have been so bad if I had expressed it in the privacy of my own home, over a bottle or to my wife. Unfortunately, I stated it during a class, a moment of careless passion and rhetoric I immediately regretted, but it was too late, as it always is in my country."

He paused long enough to drain the glass. Replacing the tumbler on the table, he left one hand beside it, as if to spell out what he was about to say.

"One of my students," he said, and his sigh was something that lived in his voice, "was a police spy. They came for me in the middle of the night, soft boots and a light knock on the door. The secret police now go under the quaint name of DISIP—Directorate of Intelligence and Prevention Services. They are large men who wear trim uniforms and pleasant faces. They politely ask you questions you have no answers for. They took me to a room with no light and blood on the walls. Soon the blood was my own. They broke both my wrists as irreparably as bone can be broken, and that was the best of it. After five memorable hours they took me home and dumped me on my front porch. I was alive but not by much. I knew that in a day, a week, a month, they'd come back and finish what they'd begun. Fortunately, I had friends, I still somehow had friends. They smuggled me out of the country within twenty-four hours. What you see now represents nearly a year of rehabilitation and I still can't walk two feet without every muscle in my body crying. I don't know what you want from me, but I can assure you that after that night, nothing holds any terror for me anymore."

They could hear music. A toilet flushed. Suarez was leaning forward, elbows on the table, watching Charley and K.C. The gray in his face seemed to have deepened. Charley thought of his grandmother dying, her eyes staring hard at the ceiling. He wished Suarez would settle back into darkness, but he remained in the light, dark eyes watching, waiting.

"We ain't in the same business," K.C. said. His short cough was uneasy.

"Aren't you?" Suarez's smile was faint but secure. K.C. was sweating. Charley knew how he felt. Guys with brains, they could bloody you faster'n bruisers.

Charley wasn't just along for the ride. "What we want, John Wayne or the man in the lake mean anything to you?" Charley didn't expect squat.

Suarez's gaze stayed steady, then he looked up at the ceiling. "A shame there isn't more to drink." He leaned back into shadow with the casualness of a cat escaping the sun. "Yes. It means something to me."

And prayers could sometimes fly. "Tell us," Charley heard himself say. "Please."

19

Riffs

Lisa lowered the receiver with a small sigh of pain. A snake was working its way up to her chest. She'd had a bad day. The date with Marv started it. They'd gone out and looked at antique rugs. After a while, Lisa wanted to say rugs are for beating. Marv worked in her office and was about as exciting as a stroll through your own living room. At least with Charley, you didn't know what to expect, as the call had proved.

Ali mewled. Turning, she saw him hunched and dreary and staring out the bay window, a scruffy Christ waiting for his cross. Hanging up the phone, Lisa went over and scratched his ear. "You miss Charley too, don't you," she said. Ali's purr died in his throat.

Lisa had almost hung up when she answered the phone, there was that much deep breathing; sex came off like heat through the wires. Then the man told her he was a friend of Charley's, name of Arthur. Arthur had a habit of repeating himself— "I was sitting here doing this old broad's taxes, doing them, you know"—but after a while Lisa had gotten the drift. Arthur had talked to Charley and didn't think he sounded right; trouble kept sneaking into the pauses. Arthur wanted to know if Lisa knew anything 'bout anything? Not much, Lisa had told him, not much. People were for beating.

The night wasn't getting any shorter, her chest still felt tight. She needed a change. First, she went and turned the water on in the tub. Then she poured herself a stiff drink and carried it back to the bathroom, along with a pack and a saucer for an ashtray. Then she undressed, budding stretch marks of belly and breasts unnoticed in the mirror. Naked, arms dangling on knees, she sat on the rim of the tub while the water ran, keeping her mind free until the tub was full. Only then, after easing into the heat and lighting a cigarette, did she try conclusions, tracing recent memory.

Charley had been on edge on the ride to the airport, not much, but it was there. At the time, she'd consigned his mood to his hatred of flying, but now, after her conversation with Arthur, there were other things. Why hadn't he let her know where he was staying? And why go to Washington in the first place? A few days on business, he'd told her, but what kind of business? And why not board Ali if it was just for a few days? The questions had the pressure of pain.

By eleven, she'd finished her gin and tonic and half a pack. She took a second drink to bed to ease her senses into sleep. Head back against a pillow, glass cupped in both hands, she watched Ali playing at the foot of the covers, jabbing at imaginary threads. Soon the threads dimmed into webs of darkness, and she dreamed of softly spinning patterns—circling, spiraling games that searched for a source and a name—called tracking Charley.

Matthew Byrne dipped the silver spoon into the china bowl and carefully tasted the lobster bisque, anticipating the worst.

"How is it?" Hanlon asked from across the table.

"Adequate," Byrne's voice had the quality of self-assurance that only old money can bring—condescension thinly concealed by good breeding, judgments formed from on high.

He and Hanlon were eating lunch in the Potomac. The director of the FBI was having soup, cascading salad, and wine with enough breath to fill an oxygen tank. Hanlon was having lemon meringue and stale coffee. The Potomac was one of the newer and posher bistros on 8th, near Ford's Theatre, where Lincoln had been shot. Its pretensions were apparent in the antebellum decor and in a smugness that filtered down as far as the cooks; orders were returned only at the risk of an arsenic revenge. Hanlon preferred the joints along Calvert and Lanier, where the flies were winning the war against the waiters and you didn't need a Ph.D. to read the menu. Byrne wouldn't be caught dead in dives like that. Hanlon couldn't come alive anywhere else.

Of course, their backgrounds were different. Hanlon was Bethel, PA, shanty Irish; Byrne was Virginia patrician. Hanlon's old man had stoked steel mill fires; Byrne's had bred horses and manners. With his cool, corporate appearance, Byrne even looked different; Hanlon usually looked like he'd been sleeping in parks. Everything considered, however, Hanlon decided that Byrne could have turned out worse. Minorities excepted, Matthew didn't seem to feel superior to other people. He just wasn't comfortable with them, including, or rather especially, his own wife. When he talked about others, it was always from an emotional distance, as though he were observing them from across a crowded room.

Lowering his spoon, Byrne dabbed at his mouth with an embroidered napkin and said, "This fellow who shot the agent . . . what's his name?"

"Charley Tone," Hanlon said, cutting through crust.

"Charley Tone. Strange name."

So's Matthew Byrne—it was always Matthew, never Matt—Hanlon felt like saying.

"I believe it's Mexican."

Byrne's grimace was that of a man brushing a gnat away from his face; in his world, Mexicans trimmed the hedges, swept out the stables, and said sir with lowered heads.

"You say he's a fighter?" he asked without interest.

"In the ring and out."

"I think I prefer horses."

"Least you don't have to shoot fighters when they fall down."

Byrne didn't smile. He didn't have a sense of humor, but he didn't resent those who did. He'd politely wait out a joke, then return to the matter at hand.

"Let's see, where were we? Special Agent Jones and Tone went to the night club where they talked to a Mr. Suarez, who told them

John Wayne was the nickname for a Venezuelan businessman named Victor Cedillo."

"Oil millionaire, got the name 'cause he was a freak for westerns, but there's a kicker."

"I assumed there would be."

"Cedillo is dead."

"Dead." Byrne's inflection showed little life.

"According to Suarez."

"That does complicate things, doesn't it?"

"Well, let's say it makes for more confusion."

"Death frequently does," Byrne countered, accidentally cracking a joke. "What did he die of?"

"Of a plane crash. He was out of favor with the current government, so he skipped the country, destination unknown, before gentlemen in jackboots came to his door. Trouble was his private jet flamed out in a Dominican Republic lake, which is maybe where the man in the lake comes in."

"Interesting," Byrne commented in such a way to let him know it really wasn't. "This is also according to Mr. Suarez?"

Hanlon nodded. "Not exactly gospel, but it's what we've got."

"Along with the vague hearsay statement by a wireman named Eddie that 'something big and bloody and worth a month of headlines' was going to happen soon."

Hanlon nodded again. "Going to come down, yes, sir."

"I hate street idioms."

"Yes, sir."

Byrne studied the ceiling fixtures for stability. "Do you think, given the information we have, that this matter is worth pursuing? We could simply turn it over to the police."

"Well, we don't have enough bodies for genocide yet, but there does seem to be a trend."

Without replying, or even indicating that he had heard, Byrne raised a discreet hand. Their waiter, who was obviously wearing makeup, came over with the bill.

"You could feed half of India for that," Hanlon volunteered, glancing at the amount. The waiter and Byrne studiously ignored the remark.

"You want me to leave the tip?" Hanlon asked.

"I've already added it in." Byrne paid the waiter, who thanked him in French.

"Reminds me of my date for the senior prom," Hanlon said, watching the man's snug cheeks leave.

"So you think we should keep the file open?"

Hanlon hesitated. He really wasn't sure. "For the time being. I thought I would keep Jones on it. He could report directly to me. Maybe Charley Tone could help him out."

"Tone isn't an agent."

"No, but he's cheap."

Byrne sighed and frowned. His lips were thin to the point of extinction; scrub them and they'd disappear, Hanlon thought. Byrne's lack of enthusiasm for Hanlon's enterprise was apparent, but it wasn't worth spoiling his afternoon by belaboring the point.

"Very well," he agreed. "Let me know if anything of consequence turns up."

"Instantly."

"Longer than that, I hope." Byrne delicately jabbed at the corners of his mouth with his napkin. "You'll have to excuse me," he said, getting to his feet. "I have a call coming in this afternoon from the vice president."

"Last I heard he was lost in Zaire on a handshaking tour. Something about natives and a cooking pot."

"His flight arrived from Africa this morning."

"With or without him?" Hanlon asked.

"What time will you be back at the office?"

"One-thirty."

"Sharp."

"I'll wind my watch."

Byrne couldn't tell if he was being mocked. It was something outside his experience. He stared at Hanlon, then left without figuring it out.

Hanlon remained at the table after Byrne was gone. He knew

he'd pushed it with his boss by being too flip, but he couldn't always control himself. Part of the reason was Ann. After her death, everything had acquired an edge. Pain was how you bought love. Yet Ann wasn't all of it. Much of his mood had to do with the new breed in the Bureau. He'd labored twenty hard years to reach where he was and he'd cared about such neglected things as ideals—justice, fair play, the rights of the individual. The new men were different, showed, beyond lip service, no such concerns. Buttoned down and interchangeable, they never made mistakes, for they operated without passion or regret. In a world given over to fast food and fast entertainment, where values weren't rules to live by, but fads, he supposed it was only natural that the neat, faceless order would take over. One day, one of them would sit in Hanlon's chair, and the transfer of power would be executed with all the ceremony of the insertion of a tape cassette, and, like the men themselves, that bothered him. They troubled him in a different way than Byrne; Byrne had acquired his post through social connections and was dry as old leaves, but at least he wasn't one of the new elite, who were as incomprehensible to Hanlon as nuclear war, unisex, and electronic games, and whom he resented with a fierce and frequently irrational passion. It affected his work. Maybe that's why he fed the pigeons. Like them, he was just going through the motions, although he lacked their advantage of being too dumb to know it.

A simper of matronly revelry from the next table broke his mood. He glanced at his watch. It was a quarter past one. If he left now, he could just make it back by one-thirty sharp. He started to get up, then stopped. Settling back, he waved the waiter over and ordered another cup of coffee.

It was twilight. The sky was red and gray, a confederacy of colors. Charley sat alone on the bench, feeding the pigeons. He watched a girl wearing harlequin glasses and little else roller-skate past an old man limping along with a cane. Something of life and death there, Charley thought. He gazed up at the sky, wondered about Geraldine. Maybe a sparrow got her. Pretty tough ones in this neighborhood. He watched sleek wings hurry across the horizon.

The dark sun set, leaving neither warmth nor glow.

20

Night Moves

Lisa turned on her brights, opening the web of fog and darkness; the headlights fell in gossamer shreds, like luminous spider legs.

Rolling her window up against the chill, she threaded her way down the one-way street leading to the beach and boardwalk. Parking was succinct, a high-beam slice of vanishing curb. Easing into reverse, she squeezed between a VW and a Porsche, wedged her wheels tight, yanked on the emergency and switched off the ignition. It was seven o'clock and felt like midnight.

Getting out of her car, Lisa paused beside the door, hoping to hear a carousel song, but the pier was dark, the arcades closed. The heavy air settled and shifted around her, gray giving way to gray, and she hugged her coat to her body as she walked to the yellow slatboard building and went inside.

They were making love in an upstairs apartment. Lisa could hear a bed creaking overhead. The rhythm was deliberate, a deceptive lack of tension. She thought of her nights with Charley as she walked to the manager's apartment, where television voices rose and fell on the other side, like spirits from the dead. There wasn't a doorbell. Lisa knocked tentatively, then harder. A dog barked from inside, part defiant yap, part question mark. The TV lowered to a hush. Weightless footsteps came to the door. Lisa sensed the person behind it, waiting. She knocked again, gently.

"Who is it?" The voice was frail and frightened.

"Mrs. Kravitz?"

There was the same sense of waiting, then the voice said, "Yes?"

"Mrs. Kravitz, it's Lisa Tone, Charley's wife. Could I talk to you?"

The door opened two inches, as far as chain and bolt would allow. Two wary, ancient eyes filled the negligible space.

"Charley's wife?"

"Yes."

"He's not here."

"I know. That's what I wanted to talk to you about."

There was a final hesitation before a hand, as fragile as parchment, slid the chain out of its slot and the door opened halfway.

"Come in," Mrs. Kravitz said.

Feeling furtive, Lisa slipped through the gap. Mrs. Kravitz quickly closed the door behind her, bolting it. She was wearing a flowered cotton housecoat, with nothing apparent underneath.

"There was somebody a little while ago, outside," she said. "I think Max scared them away." Old and scabrous, the chihuahua didn't look like it could scare an arthritic mouse. From a corner nest of cotton pillows, it eyed Lisa with the dead weight of suspicion.

Mrs. Kravitz motioned to a couch with the same floral pattern as her housecoat. As Lisa sat, she took in the room, which was thick with antimacassars and dated photos, stern Talmudic men wearing yarmulkes and knee-length beards; their women wore their hair back in tight buns and had on dresses that allowed no flesh. The pictures reminded Lisa of family album portraits of her great-grandparents, who were Orthodox to the point of perpetual melancholy.

"You want some tea?" Mrs. Kravitz asked. "I have water boiling."

"No, thank you. I didn't interrupt your dinner?"

Mrs. Kravitz made a self-deprecatory gesture. "Old ladies don't eat, they kvetch." She settled into a cushioned rocking chair and said out of left field, "So, you're Jewish."

"Yes." Lisa wondered if it was that obvious.

"Charley told me. He talk about you sometimes. I think he miss you, but he don't want to admit it."

Caught off guard, Lisa blushed, but she was secretly pleased. To cover her embarrassment, she glanced away from Mrs. Kravitz to the TV. With the sound off, the images seemed incomplete, a jacket without pockets. They were showing a freeway accident. A pretty, coiffed anchorwoman was facing the camera with a mike, earnestly selling blood.

"There was a murder-suicide a half hour ago," Mrs. Kravitz told her, gazing at the display of metal and bodies. "A mother shot her daughter, then she used the same gun to kill herself."

"It happens," Lisa said, at a loss for a response.

"All the time anymore. The worst was in the capital, you couldn't have missed it. Buses, trucks, explosions . . . terrible." Mrs. Kravitz shook her head and rocked lightly back and forth, savoring the memory, then said, "You want to talk about Charley?"

"If you don't mi—" The high, keening whistle of a kettle cut in from the kitchen.

"Excuse me," Mrs. Kravitz said, smoothing her housecoat as she got to her feet. "You sure you won't have some?"

"No, really."

Mrs. Kravitz shrugged and went to the adjoining room in short, wooden steps. When she returned, she carried a photograph along with her tea. The picture had a cardboard base and was dark with age. She handed it to Lisa.

"I was a beautiful woman once. You would never know it now."

Lisa looked at the face. The young woman was plain, with neurotic eyes and smile.

"Yes, you were," Lisa said, handing the picture back.

Shaking her head sorrowfully, Mrs. Kravitz put the picture down and sat in her chair, cradling saucer and cup in her lap.

"Sad how people get old," she said.

"Yes . . . About Charley . . . ?"

Mrs. Kravitz sipped gently at the lip of her cup. The rising steam brought a slight flush to her cheeks. She faced the flickering screen images again before she spoke. "I knew he was in trouble that night when the police came." Her voice was distant.

Lisa felt as if someone had punched her in the chest. "When the police came . . . ?" she repeated, keeping her voice steady.

Mrs. Kravitz rocked indolently in her chair, the delicate creaking reminiscent of the rhythm of the bed upstairs. "A week ago. Two nice young men, goyim, but very polite. They go and talk to Charley, then they leave. After a while, he goes out. I ask him what's the matter, Charley? He tells me a friend of his has just got killed." She paused for emphasis, fixed Lisa with an exact eye. "Murdered."

Lisa sat staring at the TV, dumb as dog biscuits, as Charley would say. A few ugly images crossed her mind, filled the pockets on the screen; Charley on the edge, a child's matinee memory of suicide cliffs and wave-lashed rocks below.

"Do you know his friend's name?" Lisa said. At that moment, she knew she wouldn't rest until she found her husband.

"I have it right here." Mrs. Kravitz dug a news clipping out of a drawer; her apartment was a museum of hiding places. Lisa mentally noted Joe's full name and read the single column. The details of the killing, severed hands and a quarter over one eye, did nothing to reassure her. She had hoped for a simple mugging.

"Did you ever meet Joe Torelli?" she asked, returning the clipping.

"Only on the news. It was the feature story on Channel Nine." Mrs. Kravitz scrupulously refolded the article—stiff fingers prolonging the task—tucked it in the drawer, and glanced at the television. An agitated young man was engaging in various histrionics in front of a meteorological map. Mrs. Kravitz frowned.

"Weather. I hate it. They all got attitudes. Especially that one."

She switched off the TV. The weatherman smiled, then vanished. As if on cue, Max sighed and went to sleep. Lisa felt it was time she made her own exit, but she had a final question:

"Did Charley tell you where he was going?"

"He don't tell me nothing, except he's going away for a few days. I ask him, Charley, does this have something to do with your friend and what happened? He tell me no, but I don't believe him." She looked at Lisa craftily. "You know something about this?" Her eyes were so alert that she seemed to have shed thirty years, seemed almost her memory of herself.

"Less than you, I'm afraid," Lisa told her.

Old again, Mrs. Kravitz nodded with fatigue and retreated to the sanctuary of her chair. She rocked briefly in the room of antimacassars and fading light, her thoughts elsewhere, then she said, "It's funny . . . Me and Charley, we don't always agree, and Max hates that cat of his, but, you know, I feel better, safer when he's around."

"So do I," Lisa said. "So do I."

It was past eight when Lisa got home. From the lawn next door, her neighbor, divorced, drunk, and predatory, asked if she wanted to come on by for a drink. Without breaking stride, she shook her head and left him standing there, swaying, cocktail glass in hand, stuporous and mildly belligerent and wondering where he'd gone wrong.

Once inside the house, Lisa fed Ali, then she called Information and requested the police precinct for crimes committed in Sepulveda. The operator gave her a number that turned out to be wrong, but they referred her to the West Valley station. She asked for Homicide. A flagged cop voice inquired if she had one to report, was noticeably relieved when she said she hadn't.

After half a minute on hold, another, deeper voice came on the line and identified itself as Detective Brooks. She asked him for information on the Torelli killing, told him she was a relative. Brooks said she'd have to talk to the detective assigned to the case, a Sergeant Martz, who wouldn't be in until the morning. She asked Brooks if he could help. He assured her he couldn't. She had him spell the sergeant's name, thanked him, and hung up, experiencing the same infuriating, mounting frustration she had felt before with Charley, only now the feeling had a new edge, as exact as a curettage, an emotive incision called fear.

21

Morning Dreams

"Some people pop pills, I do toothpicks. Want one?"

"What colors you got?"

"Let's see . . . green, purple, red, pink, yellow . . . all outta blue."

"How about a red? Reminds me of roses. Reminds me of Lisa."

"Your wife?"

"Barely."

Charley took a shiny red from K.C. and probed the pain in a lower incisor. They were driving north on Connecticut with Charley behind the wheel, and the mood around them was high. It was the morning of the 29th, getting toward New Year's, and outside the liquor stores, the citizens were queuing up for the annual debauch. Couple of days at midnight, there would be confetti and sloppy kisses. In the morning, there would be bodies on the floor.

K.C. had his own reasons for feeling good. He had put in a call to the Venezuelan consulate, got a real sweet gal on the line, honey of a voice. She'd done some checking and, surprise, found something in the files about Victor Cedillo, a visual aid, which suited K.C.'s nonreading tendencies just fine. So without asking more questions, he went to Charley's hotel, dragged him screaming out of bed and shoved him under the shower; dressing he let Charley do by himself. Then, being reasonably responsible adults, they returned the Camaro to Hertz, where they shrugged the shattered windshield off to routine urban kicks, before renting an '88 blue and white Buick Cutlass at the Bureau's expense.

The car was a working slob's dream. The heater avoided cremation, the wipers snicked briskly without mutilating the glass, and not a trace of stale tobacco clung to the seats. As content as a hen on her nest, K.C. reclined against cool vinyl, tucked a bit of purple heaven into the corner of his mouth, and beamed at the bright, clean day.

As for Charley, he wasn't feeling too bad himself, if you didn't count the toothache and the guilt that nipped at his face. It was the guilt that K.C. caught as he stuck the toothpicks back in his pocket.

"What's the matter?"

"Nothing."

"Tooth?"

"Nothing." There was a dull crack. "Broke your toothpick," Charley said, swinging a left onto Massachusetts; the street really did exist.

"Ain't gonna worry me."

Charley stopped for a red light. Squinting up at the signal, he said, "I was thinking about my wife . . ."

"Who reminds you of roses."

"Yeah, and how maybe I should've told her a few things before I left L.A."

"You got a lot to add since."

"Ain't that the truth."

"So why didn't you tell her?"

"Because I'm a stubborn son of a bitch," Charley answered without pride as the light changed.

"Believe it," K.C. agreed with a smile.

"I had a dream about her last night. It was damned nice, sort of soft and gentle. Bothered the shit outta me."

K.C. flushed the plastic container from his pocket and selected a pale pink. "Me, I don't have much time to dream," he said, " 'cause I got insomnia sometimes, like every other night. Do have this one dream though, 'bout these naked Indian maidens—least I think they're Indian, 'cause they got skin like mine and straight black hair that hangs down to their butts and tomahawks tattooed on their tits. In the dream, there's 'round five or six of 'em, not sure which, and they do a little dance, somethin' between rain ceremony and break."

"Trade you a few of my dreams for yours."

"Yeah, well that's all right, 'cause they don't put out, even though I haveta admit' I wake up half the time with wet jockeys."

They drove on in silence for a moment; then K.C. said, warming to his subject because he was feeling expansive, "You know, the Sioux got this belief you can dream yourself into the real world. Don't look at me so sorry, let me finish. Like I might've mentioned before, and like you might've noticed, I ain't the smartest guy in the world, but I had an uncle who was, and he explained it to me. He had M.S., so he had a lotta time to work these things out. He said people who know somethin' 'bout the center of the earth, like the Sioux, could make some pretty terrific things happen by doing, ah, somethin' to their dreams . . ."

"Interpret?"

"That's it, interpret. That's what Sittin' Bull went and done durin' the Moon of Makin' Fat, when the Hunkpapas danced and opened their fuckin' veins to the sun. Sittin' Bull, he had this dream that when he looked up into the sky, he saw soldiers fallin' like fuckin' grasshoppers with their heads down and their hats fallin' off. See, he seen all those soldiers droppin' right into the Indian camp. So that's how come he knew, when the bluebellies came to the Little Big Horn, that he was supposed to fight 'em, and that's how come he was able to kick Custer's ass. Course we ain't done so good since, maybe 'cause of the res and TV, but it makes you think sometimes.

Now this guy Cedillo, they called him John Wayne, which you gotta admit is sorta like Custer, so the way I see it, all this crap with Eddie and the spics means that maybe my dreams 'bout the girls are meant to show me that the Indians, at least this one anyway, are gonna rise up and stomp some cowboy butts again. Maybe it means we're gonna solve this fuckin' case and I won't haveta feed the pigeons and play straight man no more, not that I'm complainin', you understand."

Although he could have used an hour, Charley took half a minute to digest this before suggesting, "Maybe it just means you're going to get laid."

K.C. considered it. "Well, now that wouldn't be so bad neither."

At that instant the Venezuelan consulate loomed up ahead like a concrete calvary fort or, more accurately, a contemporary nightmare.

22

All God's Children

The sweet gal with the honey voice had told K.C. to meet her in the annex in room 107. It was down a corridor of mild neglect and just past an open door tagged Janitorial Supplies.

"Want a mop?" Charley asked innocently as he and K.C. strolled by.

"Story of my life," K.C. said, opening the door to 107.

One-oh-seven had the bent of a freight elevator and not much more breadth. The walls were acoustic tile, the floors beat up lineoleum, the lighting insecure. Fold-out chairs were stacked against a wall. A big glass-framed, dusty photo was balanced between two of the stacks. The guy in the picture had oily, slicked-back hair and a huge handlebar mustache. He was posed ramrod straight, chest thrust out, hands planted like anchors on his hips. The angle of the picture made it look like he was lecturing a groundhog. Charley wondered, didn't give much of a damn, who he was.

The rest of the furnishings didn't need explaining. Cans of film jazzed up shelves on a wall. A hard-riding Latino with rolled-up sleeves and a padded crotch was next to a small projector, trying to make time with a very pretty girl and plainly making her nervous. K.C. cleared his throat, catching the man by surprise. "Mierda!" the man swore, knocking a canister to the floor with a clatter. Relief was in the girl's walk as she hurried over to welcome Charley and K.C.

"Mary Conde," she said, putting out a slender hand. She was wearing a black cotton skirt and a pink ruffled blouse. The body underneath looked good. So did her smile. You could paint it on a billboard. Charley shook her hand and mumbled his name. Over her shoulder, he could see the operator tossing knives his way as he stooped to recover the can.

Mary apologized to the room. "I'm so sorry, but this is the best I could do on short notice."

"Do just fine," K.C. said, giving her his best grin, which wasn't very good.

"Who's that?" Charley pointed to the picture between the stacks.

"The last president of Venezuela."

"Uh-huh."

Mary's smile fell to something faint and dubious. K.C. hurried to her rescue. "You said you got some flicks that might help us?"

"Flicks?"

Charley hipped her. "Movies."

"Oh, yes, on Señor Cedillo. Won't you have a seat, please?" Sounds like a Disney guide, Charley thought, as they pulled up chairs, Mary in the middle—there was music to her voice but it was the melody of an instructional tape—this is the way we swallow our food. He also noticed that the sweet-sincere smile appeared a little too fast, and there were filaments of steel in the ever so eager to assist eyes. K.C., however, seemed unaware of her flaws; he sat moony eyed, which was to be expected since, as Charley knew, infatuation, not love, is blind.

"One of our staff mentioned that we had this in our archives," Mary was saying. "These films are intended for educational use, to provide young people in America with a better understanding of what life in Venezuela is like. Whenever a school wishes, we make our films available to them, except on Sundays and after five, of course. Unfortunately, we do not seem to receive too many requests from your institutions of learning."

"When was the last time you had a request?" K.C. asked, trying to sound interested.

"Nineteen seventy-nine, I believe." She cocked her head back toward the projector. "We can begin, please."

The guy with the padded crotch switched off the overheads and started the machine. The stream of light hit Charley in the back of the head. Pushing his cap down over his forehead, he slouched, folded his arms tight across his chest and stretched out his legs. Maybe they'd serve popcorn.

A white frame overwhelmed the white screen, scratched with scars that looked like lint. The screen remained blank for a long time. Mary filled in with babble.

"Since there was not time for us to edit this film, as I'm sure you understand, we will have to wait until we get to the segments with Señor Cedillo. However, I think you will find what precedes to be very informational."

"Happy times," Charley said.

"Excuse me, please?"

Before Charley could fake an apology, a harsh, pushy male voice erupted from the projector, snapping everyone to attention. "Buenos dias, muchachos y muchachas," the voice blared, accompanied by travelogue music that managed to be both festive and depressing.

"If it was intended for American kids, why ain't it in English?" Charley asked, with impeccable logic.

"This is a very good question." Mary seemed nervous, wouldn't look at him.

The operator lowered the volume, but the noise level stayed reckless as MODERN VENEZUELA jerked onto the screen, steadying at a punch-drunk angle. Charley slumped down again as a whitewashed tour of the country began, with Mary translating the voice-over into English. For some reason, she didn't have the operator further drop the sound—Charley wondered if she was hard of hearing—so that she frequently seemed to be at odds with the native description, like a debate between foreigners unfamiliar with each other's tongue. As if in confirmation, the narrator's voice would rise here and there, as though he'd taken offense at something she'd said. As for Mary, she would race through unnecessary depictions at times, then just sit during other sections, staring at the pretty pictures on the screen, as if she didn't have the faintest what they meant.

K.C. and Charley learned more than they would have liked. Most of the footage was the sort of sleeping pill propaganda issued at taxpayers' expense by every government large and small; substitute another language, and you could be in Des Moines or Leningrad.

Some of the material, however, was of passing interest. They were told that Venezuela was the sixth largest country in South America, about the size of Texas and Oklahoma combined, with a population of over fourteen million, of which seventy percent were mestizo, twenty percent white, the rest mulatto, black, and Indian. They discovered that because of oil it was the richest state on the continent, and that in darker times there had been dictators, but, of course, that was a thing of the past, for now it was a democracy, just like America. They learned that it had the world's highest cable car and waterfall, and perfect freeways and beaches and a thousand rivers that jazzed the terrain. They saw Caracas, with its skyscrapers, dreamy climate, and narrow, sloping streets; and the Orinoco rain forests where the locals still hunted with bow and arrow; and the undulating, wild west plains of Illanos, with its cattle herds, jaguars, snakes, and cruel sun; and Maracaibo, where flamingos, Arab traders, and U.S. oil executives roamed; and Margarita Island, where Christopher Columbus fished for pearls. The camera skimmed like a bird over the water, and through it all, through all the pretty pictures, Charley kept thinking of what Suarez had said—that it was a fat, corrupt land with the ugliness concealed, and even here, in an occasional shot that someone had failed to edit out, he could see glimpses of the dark, fierce underbelly of the nation. Once, the camera darted past a courtyard wall pocked by bullet holes; another time, a background image of a peasant giving the government filmmakers the finger, and finally a faint pool of blood in a cobblestone square, residue and emblem of urban despair. Mary would titter nervously at such moments and utter something profoundly inadequate.

They endured twenty dead-blood minutes, stifling a dozen yawns; even Mary seemed to be dying. Charley was bending over, trying to rub a little circulation back in his leg, when K.C. suddenly said in a near shout, "Who the fuck's that?"

By the time Charley's head shot up, the scene had shifted to rice paddies.

"Oh, yes, I'm sorry," Mary said, reviving. "That was Señor Cedillo."

"Would you run that again?" Charley requested politely.

The operator swore under his breath and rewound the reel several frames. Scrubbed kids praying in pews appeared briefly; then a conference room gathering filled the screen in dirty black and white, a dozen guys in stand-out suits. They were hanging around a long polished table at what was obviously the finish of a business confab; there were a lot of quick smiles and handshakes and half glances at the camera. The lighting and camera work were particularly bad, the movements jerky and rapid, like a Sly Stallone film.

"Yes, this is it," Mary said dreamily, gazing at the jumpy images. "The narrator's saying here we have a meeting of the board of directors of La Combinación, Venezuela's second-largest banking firm. Venezuela's banks are managed according to the most modern techniques, providing their customers, both rich and poor, with the best possible services available."

The camera singled out a lean, fit-looking Latino of sixty, with direct features, hawk nose, and a mantle of fine white hair just right.

"Here we have La Combinación's chairman of the board," Mary translated, "Señor Victor Cedillo, who, despite his great and varied success, remains a dedicated public servant, never forgetting his humble origins."

Charley leaned forward and studied the man. Oblivious to the camera, which caught him mostly in profile, Cedillo had the total self-assurance of someone long familiar with the ways, means, and benefits of power. Charley noticed the way his colleagues gave him just a shade more room than anyone else, no brushing of elbows or any of the small, tactile gestures of men in close quarters; it reminded Charley of the way animals set up rank. Cedillo's eyes alone would have been enough to put him on top; a clean, rich brown, they were hard and hungry, yet compassion and humor lived there as well.

After half a minute, the scene shifted to the paddies and stooped peasants smiling up from their labor.

"That it?" K.C. said.

"Not quite," Mary replied.

Suddenly, the rows of rice and farmers were replaced by half a dozen guys burning energy down the marble steps of an official-looking building.

"Señor Cedillo leaving the National Pantheon," Mary translated, while the operator muttered something like "Shitty job of editing" in Spanish.

Cedillo was in the center of the wedge, dwarfed by the big, hard men flanking him.

Charley said, "Looks like bodyguards." K.C. agreed.

"A man of Señor Cedillo's stature needs protection," Mary volunteered, hands folded primly in her lap.

"Needed. He's dead," Charley said flatly.

"Oh." Mary's sweet eyes were on vacation.

They watched as Cedillo and his goons—suits and ties aside, that's what they were—got into a block-long limo, fenders like a roller ride. The most formidable of the muscle, the only gringo among them, opened the door for his boss. The camera isolated him in a good, close shot before he climbed in behind the chairman of the board; he had a nice, cheerful grin, with an excess of teeth.

"Looks sorta like Burt Lancaster," K.C. suggested.

"Yeah," Charley said, but he wasn't really listening. He was watching a pair of legs—they'd never stop shows, only this one—standing near the shiny black car door. The rest of the man was north, leaving only the bottoms of a pair of dark slacks and wine-red oxfords with buckles over the top, and, as he got into the car, a glimpse, as shy as a maiden's ankle, of a saffron-yellow knit sock with an embroidered stirrup on the side. The shoes and sock brought back some vague, recent memory, as exact as déjà vu, stayed with Charley an instant; then he focused on the screen again and realized he was in a Maracaibo museum.

The documentary meandered for five more minutes, winding down to an abrupt fade-out of lint-streaked white. The operator switched the projector off and the lights on.

K.C. blinked, adjusting to the glare, stretched and said, weakly, "Interestin'." Planting his monster hands on his knees, he added, trying to look happy, "What next?"

"That's all we have," Mary said.

"That's all?"

Mary jiggled a crossed leg and petulantly pushed a strand of errant hair back from her forehead. "You should have told me he was dead."

"See, I figured it would fuck your enthusiasm," K.C. explained.

The leg kept jiggling. "I thought you were looking for someone who was alive. I thought that seeing him would help."

"Well, yeah, I suppose that's somethin'." K.C. was trying on a few colors again, his face had a range. "At least we know what the guy looks . . . looked like."

"Nothing else on him at all?" Charley asked Mary. "No newspaper teasers, government reports?"

Mary lifted and dropped her slim, lovely shoulders in an exaggerated shrug. Charley had the impression that, at this point, she'd respond in the same way to any question he'd ask—Do you douche? Is your mother albino? Avoiding redundancy, he made his exit with a "Thanks for your time" and graced her second shrug with a sweatbox smile.

For a change, K.C. wasn't falling over his feet. Charley glanced back and saw the poor slob spoon-feeding his brand of sweetness to the princess. Mary had cheered up, was playing coy—she knew the game.

The operator wasn't so happy; he was tossing more knives, his eyes bled brightness.

Charley waited patiently by the door until K.C. joined him, grinning wall to wall.

"Got her number," K.C. said.

Charley said, "All God's chillen got wings."

23

Needlepoint

There are travelogues then there are travelogues, as Big Bill or Henry, give 'em a pint, would let you know, and there are some that ain't so pretty, luv, just take your thumb and run it down a few cities where the continental underworld grapevine roams.

In Seville, glutted with bull rings and God's chimes, information is passed with grace and awe, a sense of death and heaven as one. In Marseilles, with its sinister, night-spun alleys and carrion scents from the sea, secrets are sold with a wary desperation and a dagger fleshing out your side. In Milan, that center of art and beauty, the word is given with elegance and over wine; in politic, cloud-heavy Frankfurt, with a slogan in the rain; in open, meadowed Amsterdam, with sunny nonchalance; and in eclectic London, where the criminal types swing in Soho, it's done with a quick, grimy grin and a lowlife quip.

There was a time when Soho was a call to the hunt, before the Great Fire, you know the one, luv, made sport of Shaftsbury and Charing Cross, and sometimes it seems the flames are still chasing, for the devil turns tunes on every corner where the sun and the hawkers prey, and when it gets dark the neons come out and so does the sleaze and the smoke, limey and strip if you please, and the G-string lot, they flaunt in garters and orange-ringed eyes, but they're as cold as Brighton clams—touching makes the flesh grow fallow—but the three-quid whores, bless their stained hearts, give value for the snaps they hang in their windows, glossies of cleavage and come hither under two hundred crimson volts.

Fat, florid, and forty, Henry Sykes lived just down the street from love on Shepherd, where the byways are gutted cobblestone, the buildings bunched without easement, and the gas lamps go back to Dickens. When the fog rolls in, the residents, who work with their hands when they work, say that the bloody uptown toffs are pushing their frigging soup south. As remote from Whitehall protocol as the Casbah, you live by your wits here, lad, or you don't live at all. On Shepherd at night, the pimps and strong arm flex and slouch in dour doorways, marking their time, and the pubs are full, the pockets empty, and the soul's a smirk.

Poor Henry, he'd slogged it all in the district, working the con and the cly and the dustman's game. The best had been in '79, when he'd done the tickets for Big Bill Durkin for six and five, before the booze and bad nerves brought him down. Since then, Henry scrapes by, living off the National Relief and his dear old mum, not to mention an occasional piece of murging, a bit of the old hand out. No doubt about it though, his luck'd been running ragged, it had; why just last week, he'd dropped six and ten on the nags on St. Nick's, old Henry who used to be able to tab 'em with the best.

So Henry, he was looking for a bit of a change in the old fortune the morning of the twenty-sixth, sitting in Danny La Rue's over a penny pint, when who should drop by but Alf the Weasel. Bought Henry a round and gave him a gander at this glossy he did—gnashy-looking, knockabout lad with black, snaggly hair and big, jittery eyes. The Weasel, he slaps Henry on the back and says, Henry, mate, they're looking for this here bloke they are, and it's a pretty penny they'll pay to the stout lad that finds him—course Henry knew you never asked who *they* were or how much; you just understood they'd give you enough to keep the kitty warm if you could do them their turn. Give a shout if you should happen to set sight on the lovely little nipper, the Weasel he says. That I will, Alf, that I will, Henry he replies.

And if that weren't enough, but what should happen the following day while poor Henry's scrounging bangers and fritters on Berwick for dear old mum, when who should stroll on over but Sergeant John Clive Baker himself, of Her Majesty's finest, big as six snakes and twice as mean. Sidles up to Henry he does and whispers, all nice and cozy, Henry, old son, give an eye to this here bloke, and damned if it ain't a snap of the lad with the gnarly hair and squirrelly eyes he's showing him on the sly. So Henry he nods uh-huh, uh-huh, and says all cool and easy, what's the silly sod gone and done, mate? John Clive he says, no questions asked, but this much I'll tell you, it's the bleedin' Bureau of Federal Investigation itself that's doing the looking, and if you should happen to spot him and give us a holler, why then perhaps I'll find it in my heart to give old Judge Cranbell the wink when you go afore him on the tenth for putting the snatch on poor decrepit Mrs. Latimer's purse. So Henry, still having a mite of the brains the tipply has left him, he says, I see this coshy boy, which I doubt that I will, I'll be sure to give you a holler, John Clive sir, and the Sergeant, just before he goes, he says, that's a good fellow, he does, and he touches the brim of his cap with his great bloody stick, just like Henry was a proper gent and all.

Now Henry, he gets a bit of the giggles after John Clive's gone, oh, a fine lovely case it was, hiccups down to his toes, 'cause he knows there's no more chance of him seeing the lad than of finding the old needle in a haystack or of putting a stitch and nine to the stars, so imagine his surprise four days later when, browsing among the cabbage, who should he see but our darlin' boy, big as life he is by the whelks, and all clotted with fright and little naggly twitches. So Henry, calm as can be, he pays for his cabbage and ambles on home where dear old mum, dry as burnt toast, is tucked in front of the telly as always, and Henry, he goes into his room and has another lovely chuckle over the turn of the wheel—he sits there on his bed, with the knockers and gams on the walls all around, trying to decide who to tell, the crushers or the coves. There's good and bad to both—the coves would pay more, but the crushers could keep his poor nobbly hide out of the nick for the favor. Henry, he sits there for five and twenty trying to work it through, but it's tougher'n touting the nags when the mud's settled in, so he goes out and takes a stroll, the fog tugging at his sleeves as persistent as can be, but the walking don't help, so he leaves it to chance—got a 25-pence piece in his pocket he has, with Queen Lizzie on the front and a Gibraltar monkey on the back, and he plucks it out and balances it on the black half-moon nail of his thumb, then he flips it into the horrible cold damp air—the bleeding Queen comes up it's the crushers, the chimp, it's the coves—and he's standing there in the great dirty gray soup drowning, watching the coin twisting and turning, end over end, and it seems to be hanging up there forever it does, and poor Henry, he's hoping it don't stray off to the sun, because then he never could decide, and he's waiting, getting all chilled and clammy, his fat man's sweat sloshing through his pockets, and then he sees it, a shimmer of bright, clear silver tumbling down, tumbling down . . .

24

Thimble

Lisa's left thumb was sore. She'd torn the nail wrestling with a desk drawer immediately after arriving at work. By ten o'clock, when the cuticle had turned an irrevocable burnished black, she'd handled a bellicose absent father, a hysterical mother with a rampant brood, a deep breather, and seventeen other calls of varying length and urgency. She had also managed, with practiced haste and expediency, to slip in three calls of her own to Sergeant Martz at the West Valley station. Each time she'd been put on hold, then transferred, then told he wasn't there.

On her fourth attempt, the pattern changed and he came on the line, a raw, seared voice with nerve ends for inflection. When she asked about Joe Torelli, he told her, politely but adamantly, that he could tell her nothing over the phone. She inquired, just as politely and firmly, if he could be more open in his office. After a pause so extended that she thought he'd hung up, he told her that would depend. It was with so fragile a prospect that she'd taken an early lunch break and driven from Canoga Park to Van Nuys.

Van Nuys Boulevard had a flavor. From when she was young, Lisa remembered the taste. On humid evenings, packs of giggling girls and prole cars prowl, teasing cock, and the boys, also in packs, rev their souped-up engines in response, and everything jams into six miles of horns, whoops, and KROC sounds, and the cops swoop where they can like frazzled hawks, the bile climbing in their throats, their lives reduced to a muttered curse, and one day they'll explode in a flailing, club-swinging frenzy that will make Chicago '68 look like your niece's slumber party, but until that day, tempers will continue to rise like steam on a window and the ritual will remain, as primitive and as relentless as a Cro-Magnon hunt.

Lisa arrived at eleven, long before the ceremony. Sergeant Martz's office was three short floors up, across from a brick church, next to the county courthouse. His door was wedged open with a rubber stopper and the remote, restless odor of brewing coffee wafted out into the hallway like the morning news.

"Smells good," Lisa said, sticking her head in the doorway.

"One of the few pleasures I have left," Martz replied with rueful joy. He was a compact, well-knit man in a compact, well-knit office, with a Corning electric coffeepot making delicious, sly noises nearby. Martz had thin hair and fat eyes and a tie that needed knotting. Straightening the latter, he asked Lisa how he could help her.

"I'm Lisa Tone. I talked to you on the phone about Joe Torelli."

"I remember. Have a seat." He waited until she'd settled into a piece of functional wicker, then stated as fact, "You're not a relative, are you."

Lisa's blush was loud enough to provoke a bull. "How'd you know?"

"Lucky guess." He eased back in his swivel chair. "As straight and simple as possible, why do you want to know about him?"

Lisa's response was as subtle as her blush; her emotion came through like steam rising. "Because he was a friend of my husband's, who I think might be in trouble because of him and that doesn't make me feel happy."

Martz scratched behind his ear and acknowledged, "That's straight and simple. You know for a fact that your husband's in trouble because of him and if he is, I'd be interested in knowing how."

"It's part supposition, part intuition." In two concise minutes, she ran through what little she knew. Martz listened with an occasional, patient nod, as though he were waiting out KROC sounds. After she was finished, he said, "Well, I'd like to help you, but the trouble is, there's a lid on this case."

"As far as I'm concerned, lids are something you put on pots and pans. I don't know what that means."

Martz grinned. "It means that I'm under orders to keep my big mouth shut about the deceased." The Corning pot perked with a sound like the earth stirring. "Coffee?" Martz suggested.

"No, thanks."

Martz got up and filled a mug for himself with a connoisseur's care.

"I don't mean to be persistent," Lisa said after he'd returned to his seat, "but is anyone in particular giving you these orders?"

"I'm not allowed to say." Sipping, he gave her a small, embarrassed glance and a helpless shrug over the rim of his mug. He obviously wanted to help, felt bad because he couldn't, although Lisa noticed that his blush lacked the authority of her own.

"Then I'm wasting my time . . . ?"

"Afraid so. Sure you won't try the coffee? It's damn good, if I do say so myself."

Declining, she shook her head and looked down, took in her knees, then she lifted her eyes to his in a final, faint hope. When he shrugged helplessly again, she tucked her leather purse under her arm, smoothed her skirt with an absent caress, and got up to leave.

"Mrs. Tone?" Martz said, when she was halfway out the door. She turned toward him.

"2614 Main Street. Sixth floor. Go to your right after you get off the elevator. And if anybody asks, your husband told you."

Lisa had a good memory for numbers, but he'd taken her by surprise. "26 . . . ?" she said.

". . . 14 Main."

"Sixth floor. To my right. Can you tell me what's there?"

"I'm not—"

"—allowed to say," she finished for him. "Fair enough. Am I allowed to thank you, Sergeant?"

He gave her a good grin. "One of the rare pleasures I have left, getting thanked. Feel free."

"Thanks. And Sergeant, can I ask you one more question?"

"That depends."

"Why'd you change your mind?"

Martz took a solid draw on his mug before replying. "That address I just gave you . . ."

"Yes?"

"Let's say I don't like somebody who lives there."

She nodded and started out the door.

"How about half a cup?" he tried hopefully.

"Another time."

"You won't be sorry."

They exchanged the nice, knowing smiles of strangers who liked each other, but knew they would never meet again.

After she was gone, Martz listened to her high heels vanish in a series of precise clicks down the hallway. Turning to the window, he sighed. Outside somewhere, engines were stirring, gathering a mean life of their own. Outside somewhere, beyond the brick church, knives were appearing like magic from boots and pockets and belts, and the only angels were the legends on the backs of blood-dyed denim. By the end of the day, if it was like all the rest, there would be nineteen cases of aggravated assault and two and a half murders in his district, but for this brief moment, he was content.

"God bless us all," he said to no one in particular, as the steam from the mug rose and soothed his spent, creased, enduring face.

The button was bait, too tempting to ignore. Easing forward on the edge of her seat, Jennie pushed it warily, as though it might spring teeth. The lady's voice escaped through the box, sounding strained from the effort:

". . . I don't understand. I don't understand the secrecy, I don't understand any of this, but I do know that I don't like being bullied because of some perverse, ugly game you're playing. The last I knew, Charley was a bailbondsman and now suddenly he seems to be working for you, which makes me question his sanity, but skip that—all I know is that I seem to have missed something of more than passing interest that's happened to him in the last week, and I'd like to know what. Now you tell me—is that so damn difficult to understand?"

It was a good speech, banked by energy and emotion. Nice try, but it won't work, Jennie told herself. She switched off the intercom before Mayer colored the walls blue. She thought how pleasant it might be to punch him in the mouth.

After a few seconds, Lisa came out close to crying; the sounds were still all KROC. She brushed past Jerome Haines's arrival and attempt at a smile. Haines watched her disappear rapidly down the corridor, then he ambled over to where Jennie was painting her nails garish.

"What happened? You malfunction?" she asked coolly, finishing one nail and moving to another.

"Came to borrow some cigarettes."

"Top left drawer."

"Thanks. What was that all about?" he asked, as he leaned across her desk and fished out a pack of Winston Lights. Computer slag drooled from the pocket of his work smock. Yuban had invaded a sleeve.

"She wanted to find out what's going on with her old man."

"Did she?"

Jennie froze him with a stare. "Get serious." She wore so much makeup, she looked like she had been punched about the eyes.

"You missed a spot, right there . . ."

"Thanks." Jennie daubed the pink out of a corner; it was Russia invading Poland.

"What else did you hear?"

"Oh, lots," she said coyly, as she continued to exaggerate her nails. "Why?"

"Because I think it's a shame she's upset," he said quite seriously, adjusting his bifocals and drawing himself up to Napoleon's height.

"Why do you care?"

"Because I'm a romantic."

"A romantic." Jennie didn't quite laugh.

"How about dinner after work?" Conversation was making him bold.

"You aren't my type."

"Try me."

She sized him up head to toe as professionally as a meat factory inspector. "After work," she shrugged. She held up five fingers, admired their luster. "Funny. Here I figured you were only turned on by things with wires and lights and funny little squeaks."

"I am," Haines said, lighting a cigarette and a smile that was a sin.

25

Dancing

At exactly 8:12 P.M. *Washington time, during a Brooke* Shields pitch for Calvin Klein, image and memory met, sized each other up, decided they liked what they saw, and waltzed off together arm in arm.

After dropping K.C. off, Charley had picked up a take-out order of egg roll and sweet and sour at a joint called Moon Palace; then he'd returned to the Three Seasons. Reaching his room, he'd tossed coat and cap onto the bed, yanked off his shoes, checked his feet for gangrene, switched on the TV and settled in for the main event from the Garden. The fight was slow, a pale, slick kid and a PR with a boxcar left, so Charley casually read *Farewell, My Lovely*. He lay on the board of a bed flipping pages, wiggling his toes, munching gobs of pork skewered on one of K.C.'s toothpicks and, every now and then, glancing up to see whose blood was on the floor.

By 8:12, when NBC broke for commercials, the canvas was a mess, the kid was reeling toward the green room, and Charley was just getting to the egg roll. He sat there, watching Brooke wiggle her delicious ass and mouth heavy-duty bull, when déjà vu came winging in and landed in his lap. It almost made him smile.

His first stop was Los Trucos, where he learned that Suarez had taken the night off. Next, he drove to Argonne Place, arriving at 8:47. The night was bitter, the moon vacationing in Des Moines.

Parking the Cutlass, he doused lights and heater and got out. The girl who'd told him to go fuck himself was sitting legs open on the steps, dragging to kill on a Pall Mall. He asked if she knew what apartment Señor Suarez lived in. She told him, with a fine gutter flair, to go fuck himself again. Charley suggested in passing that, if he could do that, he'd never get out of bed, then he went next door.

The walls and floors were a bug green, the plaster crawling. A stench clung to a corner, either Brylcream or cum. There wasn't a directory. There weren't even numbers. Television mirth bounced behind each door. The laughter had all the joy of beggars lost in a canyon. Charley knocked awhile, and a woman came out nursing a baby. She had track marks on her arms and the baby had fast-dying eyes. It wasn't easy, but she pointed Charley in the right direction.

Charley went and rapped on Suarez's door. He waited some more; then the door opened a foot. Charley stuck his own in and said, can we talk? Suarez said, I thought we already had. Charley said, not enough.

The apartment was seedy, but not without a certain charm. The furniture was scarce, the posters on the walls French and a Mayan frieze. A TV with a Salvation Army tag was on low to a game show; the animation on the screen was the size of delirium. The only other lighting came from a candle that looked like it came from the club.

"What do you do? Carry your atmosphere with you?" Charley said. He was being arch. So was Suarez.

"Like it? I had a Home Sweet Home sign over there, where the mantelpiece would be, but the resident vandals got it last week in the monthly pillage."

Suarez flicked on a table lamp. Charley noticed the pain in his face and his acceptance of it as, with effort, he hobbled to the TV on one crutch and switched it off.

"I would've figured you to be in here reading something heavy or at least watching Buckley."

"I like game shows," Suarez said without shame. "They lull my mind, something devoutly to be wished." He indicated a chair that was leaking fabric. "Have a seat, but be careful. There's a spring waiting to blossom."

Charley sat and found it. He hoped it wouldn't start rumors.

"Don't you ever take off your hat?"

"No."

"Not even during—?"

"Not even then."

Suarez sat opposite him on a couch. Rescuing a deck of Tarot cards from the sofa's arm, he said, "I would offer you a drink, but it's been a slow week at the club—too many of the old people dying off—so I'm forced, rather bitterly, to stay sober. You wouldn't happen to have any glue?"

"Just questions."

"Without your friend?"

"I thought about bringing him along, but decided against it."

"May I ask why?"

"I figured you might cut the bull if I promised he wouldn't be hanging around later, asking the same questions harder and longer."

"And why would he be doing that, my friend?" Suarez kept the cards busy between his ruined hands. Charley kept his voice soft for effect.

"He would if I told him you and Victor Cedillo had traveled in the same circles."

Suarez's shuffle was as smooth as before. He was good, but not quite good enough. His narrow, blood-bright eyes remained steady behind light shades, but he couldn't hide the color deserting his face.

"You're confused. I already explained that my knowledge of Señor Cedillo was secondhand."

"I know, just like Rose, but then why turn white?"

"Perhaps I faint easily. What makes you think I lied?"

"Pretty pictures. Always easier'n words. There's a piece of bad propaganda over at the Venezuelan consulate, but at least it's in color. There's a shot of Cedillo and his goons getting into a limo and there's this pair of feet by the limo door. Took me a while to place them. The oxfords had more of a gleam and the socks were a little cleaner, but I kinda doubt that there're too many pairs of yellow knits with embroidered stirrups back home."

Suarez glanced self-consciously down at his feet. "Tan loafers and blue cotton."

"Not last night."

Suarez's mouth creased into his thin smile. "You really would have Mr. Jones pay me a visit?"

"Just as soon as I could find a phone."

The slender smile lost focus as Suarez leaned back against the couch. "A terrible mistake—stirrups certainly weren't my style." He ran a hand wearily down his face, looked at Charley from over his fingers, and said, "Now, you'll have to bear with me, I'm a little slow tonight, what with being deprived of my daily ration of Blue Nun, so let's take this very carefully . . . As far as I can tell, you're offering to strike a bargain?"

"You've very quick."

"You forget, my field's economics. Now, as far as I can tell, in exchange for any additional facts I might be able to give you, you'll do your best to keep Mr. Jones and his employers from paying some very unpleasant and possibly habitual visits, the kind of interviews that, as you might have guessed, I tried to avoid by not telling you, the other night, of my involvement with Cedillo. Is that correct?"

"In too many words, yeah, that's correct."

"As I said, I'm a little slow tonight. Now, I have another, shorter question. If I tell you anything, how do I know you won't go directly to the FBI and tell them who you got your information from?"

"I know this sounds like a movie, but you'll have to trust me."

"Why should I?"

"Simple logic. I could've brought my friends, could call them right now, but I won't, because I'm not a government servant, I'm only temporary help, maintenance. I don't have to tell anybody nothing I don't want to. You trust me to keep you out of it and I will."

It was one of Charley's better speeches, made with sincerity and conviction, but Suarez didn't respond. Instead, he carefully took off his glasses, pinched the bridge of his nose, and closed his eyes. He sat lost within himself, glasses dangling from one hand. Finally, without opening his eyes, he said, "I don't see that what I could tell you would help that much." For a moment, the only sound was the muffled laughter from next door, then Suarez painstakingly put his glasses back on. Sighing deeply, a sigh past decorum or grace, he reached under the couch and dragged out an untapped bottle of Blue Nun. When he spoke, his voice was husky and drawn with fatigue:

"If you would be so kind, there's a corkscrew and two glasses on the kitchen sink."

"One glass will do."

"That's right, you're on the job."

"Temporary."

"Or something."

"Thought you were outta booze," Charley remarked, as he went into the kitchen to fetch.

"I keep a spare bottle for emergencies," Suarez called after him. "I didn't think tonight would be one." His irony had a few shades.

"One never knows," Charley said without irony, as he returned with a rusty corkscrew and a plain, long stemmed glass. "Want me to open it?"

"No, I need the exercise." Taking the opener from Charley, Suarez slowly drew the cork out of the bottle, the effort required evident in his face.

"In Venezuela, I had three sets of tumblers, Swedish cut glass," he said wistfully, as he filled the J.C. Penney reject to the brim.

"Times change."

"Yes, don't they."

Suarez took a bracing sip of the pale wine. He sighed again, this time with satisfaction.

"Better than game shows?" said Charley.

"Much." His voice was sharper, his color better. "Where do you want me to begin?"

"Where the truth stopped," Charley said, taking out pad and pen.

"That's a question that's baffled philosophers for centuries, my friend."

Suarez took another sip, crossed his ankles, leaned back, glass in hand, and draped his arms, loose at the elbows, over the back of the sofa. TV happiness bookended them from the adjoining apartments, but the sounds seemed remote. The dry air in the room was still, the candle's teardrop flame steady as prolonged sin. The light from the candle held Suarez evenly, underscoring the deep, hard lines in his face, reminded Charley of the portraits by some Dutch painter Lisa had taken him to see. Shadows within shadows, she'd called them, and that was the way Suarez looked now.

"Let's see . . . To start with, I *was* a professor of Economics at Universidad Central, with some reputation in my field. I had a wife whom other men envied, children who respected me, and a home which was unpretentious but paid for. It was a good life, a life of adequacies and small but affirming pleasures."

He paused for a stronger draw of Blue Nun, wiping the liquid from his lips. He studied the damp hand for a few seconds, staring at the deformed wrist, wondering if it had a future.

"A good life," he said, the candle's light in his eyes, "and then, then one day I came home to find my wife packing. I asked what the matter was and she said, quite simply, that she was leaving me. I went through the standard expressions of bewilderment and shock, but it was useless. She'd fallen in love with another man, or rather, or so I liked to believe, with his money and power, both of which he had in excess. Anyway, to make a short story even shorter, she left and took the children with her—God knows I was in no shape to nurture them without her. Up until then I had been a teetotaler, something of a prude you might even say, but the sudden exit of my family and the reason for it gave me a different perspective on things. I started drinking, heavily. I also started fantasizing about money, about how my life might have taken a different turn if I had had it. One day, while in my cups, I explained all of this to a colleague in a vague, rambling way. He understood. He told me he knew of an acquaintance of an acquaintance who was looking for men with my sort of expertise, however besotted it might be at the moment. He told me this acquaintance of an acquaintance paid exceptionally well for services rendered. I asked why he didn't take advantage of such largess himself? He explained that shady ventures and risk were involved, elements that didn't appeal to his conservative nature. Shady ventures and risk, however, sounded good to me at the time, so my colleague arranged an introduction with this twice-removed man."

"Let me guess. It was Victor Cedillo."

Suarez smiled. "You're very quick."

"Comes from slipping punches. Go on."

"I was taken to a villa that would not have shamed a Roman emperor, where I met this highly persuasive fellow I had known by name only. Over brunch of caviar and champagne, he told me that despite all evidence of elegance and reassuring success, he had a problem. The problem was the new government, which wasn't too sympathetic—something to do with his past involvement with the wife of a general. Victor felt that in time they, including the cuckolded officer, might be maneuvered into seeing the virtues of coming to terms with a man of his wealth and experience, but he wanted to prepare for any contingency. In other words, he knew that there was a very real possibility that he would have to get out of the country with exceptional speed."

"I don't see how your, ah, expertise enters into this?"

"I was getting to that. Unlike the government, protecting his fortune wasn't a problem. He had already taken the precaution of converting most of his assets into cash, which in turn he had transferred to Swiss banks, accounts with numbers but no names, arranged through intermediaries. That part was easy. What he was concerned about was what he would do if he was forced to leave Venezuela. Consider the situation—he would have to remain in hiding for as long as he current government was in power, since they would surely try to find and kill him. Yet, at the same time, he was too used to the mechanics of power himself to give up its manipulation. So he had what you would call a scheme—"

Suarez stopped to fortify himself with wine. He let the liquid settle into his throat before continuing.

"—a financial arrangement he required assistance for. He needed someone to help him work out the ramifications and nuances."

"Which is where you came in."

"More or less."

"What was the scheme?"

"A simple concept really, as the best ones always are." Suarez took another sip of wine. "Myth to the contrary, organized crime is not a monolithic organization with vast central resources. It's a large number of individual syndicates which are often at odds. Victor's concept was to take advantage of this weakness, the fact that these syndicates are frequently short of working capital. He wanted to set up an underworld bank, with branches in unregulated tax-free countries such as Panama and several of the African nations. These branches—which would naturally have the standard legitimate fronts, a mere formality to arrange—they would make loans to various criminal organizations for whatever projects the syndicates needed financing for, all at large interest rates, of course. Victor's own capital was to have formed the foundation for this covert lending institution. In addition, he hoped to attract investors. With his connections in the international business community and with the amount of potential profit involved, I'm certain that this too would have been a mere formality."

Suarez took time to stare down at his glass.

"And that was his scheme?"

"Yes, that was his scheme." Suarez didn't look up.

"Cute." Well, maybe more than that.

"And feasible. Victor had already made contact with someone here in America, a seven-figure-a-year lawyer with strong political ties and influence and, even more important, a clean public slate."

An attorney. It made sense. Staring down people was what lawyers did for a living.

"So you provided the financial knowledge and he provided the legal," Charley said. Suarez nodded.

"Does this seven-figure-a-year stud have a name?"

"No. Don't forget, I was simply an employee hired for a

specific task. It would have been foolish to tell me anything more than I needed to know."

"Very foolish," Charley agreed. Shifting, he moved away from the intimacy of the chair's spring. "Now that this is turning into a sociable evening, tell me about Victor."

"The personal touch?"

"A hang-up I have."

Suarez cradled the glass between his hands and looked almost happy.

"Let me see," he began, "how can I do this without sounding like an infatuated schoolboy—not that I thought he walked on water, far from that. He was a robber baron, a consummate high-stakes thief, but he was more than that, much more. He was dynamic yet intimate, aggressive yet reticent, vicious yet kind, a self-made man from peasant stock. There could be a hundred people in a room, yet he would convince you that you were the only one who mattered, which I suppose goes a long ways toward explaining his success with the fairer sex. He was well past sixty, yet he still loved many women and just as many loved him. In short, to *sound* like an infatuated schoolboy, he was something we don't have much of in the world anymore—he was a romantic."

"Liked John Wayne."

"Yes, but not because of all that bluff, macho posturing, but because Wayne represented a tradition where values were basic and right and wrong possessed a clarity lacking in contemporary society. In private life, Wayne exaggerated these mores into the biases of a right-wing ideologue, but up there on the screen, he was Arthurian in his purity of purpose." Suarez shrugged, as if to apologize for the hyperbole. "At least that's how Victor explained it."

"That's very nice," Charley said, scratching his scar, "but first you tell me he's some kinda high-rolling hood planning to bankroll whatever cute little vices organized crime desires, now you're saying he was out there riding on a white charger."

Suarez shrugged again. "You wanted to know about him. All I mean is, he was a complex person."

"Okay, so he was a complex person, so before I get smitten

myself, there's somebody else I'm curious about. That piece of bad propaganda I mentioned—there was this guy, one of the muscle, who looked outta place. Anglo, and had a good grin."

"Paul Renaud. French. He was more than a bodyguard, he was Victor's enforcer and guardian angel, always there in the background. What I know about him is sketchy, a few offhand remarks. I understand that he had been a mercenary for the wrong side in the seventies, during one of those nasty little South American flare-ups we call a revolution. Renaud was captured, sentenced to a firing squad. Victor was in attendance the day he was to be shot. He'd witness executions sometimes, to see how the victims stood up to it, I suppose."

"Part of his romantic code." Charley was thinking of the dirty, bullet-pocked walls in the film.

"Something like that. Anyway, when Renaud was led out with the others, Victor interceded and asked that he be spared. Perhaps he saw something in him that could be of use, or perhaps he simply liked the way he faced death. Victor had a great deal of persuasion with the regime then in power and Renaud was pardoned, quite literally into Victor's hands. Like his benefactor, Renaud was a complex man, bright, with some talent as an artist. I also had the impression that if anyone had so much as nudged Victor off balance, Renaud would have killed them on the spot, and without a change of expression on that smiling, cheerful face."

"Okay, I'll take your word for it. Let's get back to Cedillo. He had this plan in case he ever had to get outta the country . . ."

"Which, of course, he did. A week before it happened, he realized he wouldn't be able to come to terms with the government, that his position was untenable and he would have to leave Venezuela. He sent Renaud to Washington to meet with the lawyer and make arrangements. Victor was supposed to join them a few days later, flying to America under a false name and passport, only he thought he had a little more time. Two days before the final arrangements were made, his enemies came after him—the secret police would have surprised him if not for the fact he still had friends who warned him, allowing him to escape in the middle of the night. I, unfortunately, didn't inspire such loyalty. The official thugs paid their three A.M. visit, demanding to know where Victor was hiding."

"How'd they know you were cozy with him?"

"They had their informants, like any other government."

"Right."

"Well, as you can see, they all but amputated my hands when I swore I didn't know where he was, which I didn't. After they'd gone, I lurched to the bathroom where, after vomiting, I washed and staunched the blood as best I could. Suddenly the phone rang. I considered not answering, wasn't even sure I could, after what they'd done to my wrists, but finally I did, and with a great deal more pain. It was the ex-colleague who'd introduced me to Victor. I told him, very shakily, what had happened. He said that Victor was absurdly safe in the attic of the mistress of the minister of finance—who just happened to be Victor's mistress as well. My colleague told me that Victor was going to be smuggled from the country the following night. There was a plane waiting to fly him out. He also told me there would be another plane leaving at the same time, carrying others in the same delicate position as myself. He asked if I would like to be on it. Now, for all I knew, my friend was a police spy playing the sort of sadistic games they enjoy, but my options were limited. I said yes, and he gave me a time and a location. I informed him that I would be lucky to be able to stagger across a room. He volunteered to help, said he felt responsible for the fix I was in. He said if I could make it to my back yard tomorrow, where there were a few shadows and trees, he would pick me up after dark and hide me in the trunk of his car. The following night, I did and he did. Somehow, we managed to make it to this rutted field on the outskirts of the jungle without being followed or without my suffocating. It was all comic drama, but it didn't seem funny at the time, it still doesn't now . . . There was an ancient DC-4 waiting, engines already drumming when we arrived. My friend helped me aboard and said goodbye. I often wondered what happened to him."

Suarez paused to drink a little wine.

"When was this, that you left?"

"In April. This last April."

There wasn't much wine left in the glass. The fatigue was coming through Suarez's voice again. Charley watched the candlelight detail his ravaged features as he spoke in a flat but wistful monotone.

"So here I was, half dead, surrounded by strange, anxious faces. As the plane took off, barely clearing the trees, one of the few men I knew came over and told me what had hastily been worked out. Our plane and Victor's were to travel low over the Caribbean, avoiding known air routes. Our coordinates were set so that the two planes would meet once we were across the border and over the ocean. Although we were then to fly in tandem, there would be no radio communication between the planes. Too much risk of discovery. The plan was simply to go in a straight line to the Florida coast—we had enough fuel to make it without stopping—and land in Key West. Our pilot assured us there wouldn't be any problems. He had flown in shipments of cocaine from Bogotá in exactly that manner on a number of occasions, as had Victor's pilot. Renaud would be there waiting, with transport to take us out and with new identities. Once safely inland, Victor would set up shop in some chunk of secluded grandeur near Washington, D.C., where the lawyer was, and everyone would do their part and be rich and happy. It sounded very simple, but I think I'm safe in saying that not one of us on that plane believed we would ever get out of Venezuela alive." He tilted his head lazily toward Charley and said, "Am I boring you?"

"Not yet."

Balancing the glass in his lap, Suarez leaned back against the couch, letting the memories pace his mood.

"The night was clear when we started, nothing but black empty sky. No one spoke. There seemed to be this shared premonition that something would swoop down on us from out of the sky, like an angry hawk, at any moment. There was a fly, fat, with ragged wings, on a sideboard. It didn't move. It just remained there, waiting. I don't know why, but I couldn't take my eyes off it.

I kept staring at this obscene, bloated speck on the wall, kept staring for what seemed hours, though it must have been only minutes; then suddenly I heard an excited murmur and a stirring all around me. I looked out the window in the direction the others were pointing and saw the lights from Victor's plane. There were smiles now and some conversation—it had more to do with Victor than with being out of Venezuela. We traveled side by side, lights from an occasional village below us, my attention still drawn to the fly. Then we were past the border, out over the Caribbean, nothing but our own lights in sight. In his exhilaration, the man beside me shook my hand and congratulated me, as if I had somehow personally obtained our freedom. I smiled, painfully disengaging my hand, and congratulated him too. It was that kind of moment. Even my physical pain seemed less. Everything was going well. The moon looked as firm as an anchor and the stars were out. Ignoring the fly, I watched the stars and the moon, and of course, the lights from Victor's plane, the time passing quickly now, until word came back from the cockpit that the Dominican Republic was just up ahead, with Florida only a couple of hours beyond. Yes, things were going well, very well." Suarez smiled ruefully, ran his thumb down his glass. "And then . . . and then it all changed, all started to go bad."

He glanced up at Charley, stared at him as though he were a fly on a wall; then looking away, he went on:

"It began innocently enough, as we started over the island, with clouds, a few at first, then more, passing over the moon, and then, then there was lightning, very distant, then big slow thunder. At first it was almost soothing, knowing you're safe in this smooth, steady machine. You could see the rain, soft and misting, falling around but not touching you; then suddenly it changed. Suddenly, in a matter of seconds, it seemed like some giant hand had ripped the sky in half, and all you could see were sheets of water and flashes of lightning bright as day, and everyone got quiet again, and people were looking to the side, to the lights from Victor's plane—it was as if he were all right, we would be too. For a moment, the storm slackened. Both planes were flying low to avoid the worst of it, and up ahead I could see a lake, a dark lake, dark and glistening, with the vague shapes of trees all around it, and the silhouette of a church off to one side. For an instant, it was all so clear as we started across the water, Victor's plane maybe two hundred yards to the right, then the storm hit twice as hard as before. All you could hear was the crash of wind and rain and thunder and the bells—you see, I swore I could hear the church bells ringing, and maybe they were, from the storm. The plane was trembling, coming apart. The man nearest me was wringing his hands and praying "Madre de Dios, madre de Dios, madre de Dios," and there was an explosion of lightning and I looked up ahead and saw the belfry falling, and I looked to my left, to where the fly had been, and it was no longer there, and I looked to my right, saw the lights from Victor's plane, saw them steady through the rain; then they were gone—they were there, then suddenly they were gone—and I looked down and saw something flash far below, a brief flaring of bright light near the water . . . not lightning . . . Then all I could see was darkness and the rain."

He raised the glass but seemed to lack the strength to get it to his lips. His hand and the glass sank back to his lap and he sat with his head down. His voice had risen in energy and passion as he relived the storm. Now it was subdued:

"There was nothing we could do, of course, except try to survive ourselves. The storm let up as abruptly as it had started and we were all right. There was a small airstrip not far from the lake. Our pilot radioed ahead and told them a plane was down. By the time we landed, they'd already sent out a rescue party—two helicopters, led by a young American, a Peace Corps volunteer. Very brave, don't you think, considering the conditions? Anyway, they gave us coffee and cigarettes, also American, inside a bungalow. We waited there over an hour, then one of the helicopters returned and the American—I never found out his name—told us what had happened. They'd found three survivors clinging to a section of wing, badly injured, but Victor was the worst; the other two had kept him from drowning. The helicopter's lights caught them down there in the water, too weak to even wave. The American said it was hard, hedgy work—the rain was coming down heavily again and the wind was whipping the choppers around—but they managed to get them out of the water and to the nearest hospital. Naturally, all of us at the bungalow wanted to go there right away. We managed to round up three jeeps. I rode in one with the American driving, a nice, sincere boy, one of your strong, quiet ones. Victor would have liked him. It was still raining—I thought it would never stop that night—but it was softer, the drops padding lightly on the jeep's canvas top." Suarez paused to sigh. "So wet, cold, and shivering, we got to the hospital, a small, concrete building in a small, concrete town called Neiba, where a doctor told us Victor was in surgery. Both his legs were broken, he had three fractured ribs, multiple lacerations, and they were operating to remove a hematoma on the brain."

"Blood clot," Charley said, remembering the condition as a boxer's risk.

"Yes. The surgery took three hours, during which other doctors set my shattered wrists, and we could see the rain outside the whole time. Then a doctor came out of post-op, still wearing his gown and gloves, and said Victor would live—he'd have to be under intensive care for a while, but he'd live. It was two in the morning by then, and his people, myself included, were in a state of nervous shock, besides which I was so weak from the beating by the police that I could hardly stand. I certainly wasn't able to think. I told the others I couldn't wait it out until Victor healed—what if the police had agents in the Dominican Republic? What if they came for us? You see, the memory of the beating was too fresh. I told Victor's people I would fly to America. I had my own passport and could legally enter the country. I would fly to America and let them know where I was and wait for them to contact me. They agreed. After all, Victor's plan was still operative after he recovered. Two days later, I landed in Washington and found the most inconspicuous place I could, right here. I sent a cablegram to the hotel where the others were staying in Neiba and I waited, but I never received a message of any kind, never heard a word."

He glanced down at his empty glass. "I seem to have finished this."

Suarez appeared exhausted—it had been a long trip—and Charley let him rest before he said, "That was over a year ago?" Surarez nodded. "And as far as you know, Cedillo could be dead or living in America?"

"Or on that small, dismal island." Like his nod, Suarez's shrug was mechanical, on hinges.

"And that's everything you know?"

"Everything."

Charley stared at the silent TV. They were fighting World War II. An American kid was about to be ambushed by a German who needed a shave.

"One thing. How do I know you're telling the truth? I mean, that was a very nice story, very vivid, but how do I know you didn't make it all up? You lied before."

Suarez smiled. "I suppose you have to trust me."

Charley put notepad and pen away and said softly, "A very nice story," as he got to his feet.

"Before you leave, *por favor*, one thing?" On the screen, the German made a mistake and the kid shot him.

"What's that?" The German dropped from high up, arms stretched out, his helmet falling before him.

"Let me read your fortune?" and behind the shades, just before Suarez shifted back into shadow, Charley caught something like mischief and a lasting irony, while black angels danced off the light from his glass.

Lying in bed, arms for a cradle, Charley stared at the ceiling. The cards had been pretty, knights with swords, a pageboy holding a cup, a hand holding the sun. Reading them was ritual—the same way a fighter crosses himself in his corner or wears the frayed trunks he won in last June—and Suarez had had a little magic in the way he turned them. You could almost believe the words, wheel of fortune, wheel of life, only the last had come up a skeleton hanging, and no one had to tell Charley what that meant.

On the wall, something was crawling, so saith the Lord, sweet Jesus, what a week, what a life.

A week ago, he'd been sweating his mustache and a sick car. Now he'd killed a guy, almost got killed himself, still could for that matter, and all for a few C-notes and expenses. Only don't bullshit yourself, he thought. If it'd just been for casual repairs, he'd have walked away from the whole damn mess in a blink. No, it really was because of poor, fat Joe Torelli and maybe the dead cat that he'd gotten involved. And—don't kid yourself, Charley—for the riffs, that good, raw rush of being on the edge, and for the questions.

Something big was going to happen soon. Soon could be a month from today or five minutes ago; it was all in the cards Eddie held, and Eddie seemed to have fallen off the face of the earth. Finding him wouldn't be easy, none of it would, but Charley would see it through, out of old and new rituals, until he had final answers to questions that didn't even concern him. He would stay with it, no matter what it might bring, for he still was what he'd always been, Charley Tone, tough half gringo kid, who occasionally went to church and said his very necessary prayers.

26

Fog

Eddie Mikenas drew back the flimsy curtain and looked out the window. A fog blessed by the blind was rolling in, veiling South London.

There was a cockroach on the ledge, trying to get in out of the cold. The dirty gray bug reminded him of where he'd been ten days ago, reminded him of where he'd learned mortal fear. They had paid him five, he had a little over three left, yet some things never changed, never would . . . Nobody loves a Lithuanian.

A kettle whined. Closing the curtain, he went into the kitchen to nurse it. The flat was small, even smaller than the one in D.C.; he had to watch his elbows. Turning off the burner, he poured a cup. Tea had never been his style, but there was a dampness that lived in the walls, and he needed proof against the chill. Holding his hand over the top to keep in the heat, he carried the cup to the flat's only chair and sat, letting the steam warm his face.

Nobody loves a Lithuanian, his father had told him when he was a boy. Lithuanians were the hod carriers, garbage slingers, cesspool cleaners, shit shovelers, bearers of slime and sludge, and general all-around niggers of Eastern Europe, maybe of all the world; even Poles got more respect. If you were Lithuanian, you either groveled or did things a little better than anyone else, so lacking size and strength, Eddie had learned to perform one highly specialized task inconspicuously well: to snoop, wire, bug, and tap—to plant a transmitter so small and secure that God and a host of angels couldn't find it.

A copy of the *L.A. Times* was folded on an arm of the chair. He had picked up the paper after arriving in London under the name Ted Edwards; Ted Edwards, that was as clean as they come. He'd rented the Soho flat on Christmas Eve, only gone out once since, to join the crowds in Trafalgar Square on Christmas Day. Bundled in topcoats and wool, the people around him had been happy, cozy and warm in the glow of the season. Smiling, they stared up at the Square's Christmas tree, floodlit by a fountain, gold branches gleaming, lights like rainbows remembered from childhood; staring at a star as bright as a neon sun at the top, reaching toward the sky and the steeple towering like God behind it. Standing there with the night all about, hunched and frightened and shivering in tight leather, Eddie had looked at the people and looked at the tree. Oh yeah, it's Christmas, he'd bitterly thought. Oh yeah.

The warmth from the steam was fading. He opened the paper, stared through the story again. Joe was dead, so was Janice. So was Phil Peterson; what the fuck, they were doing their own. He wondered about Karl. Karl had a mouth, was probably shut by now.

Putting the paper aside, Eddie gulped his tea, but the chill wouldn't leave him. His joints, bones, the very roots of his soul ached. He wondered if he was getting arthritis, wondered if he was getting old. A man could waste away in here, turn to rust. He needed to get out. He needed to breathe. Going to the closet, he took out his dark leather jacket and his dark leather cap. What remained of his payoff was in the lining of the hat. Glancing once around the room for invisible enemies, he removed three ten-pound notes for his wallet. Then he buttoned his jacket with the care of an old man. Before going out the door, he returned to the window and drew back the curtain; the cockroach had fallen off the ledge, was lost somewhere in the fog.

He tried not to think about it as he left.

The bars were on Frith. A local had told him Shelley and Marx and Mozart had once lived on the street. That didn't mean squat to Eddie. It was like looking at a star at the top of a tree.

Songless, Eddie moved onto Frith. From a few blocks away, he could hear hard voices hawking their wares. Although it was midday, the gas lamps were lit, leaving ghosts on the cobblestones. Skirting their light, he walked with a brisk, furtive stride, eyes haunted and alert under the low brim of the cap, listening to his own footsteps on the sidewalk as he went past brownstone shops and low-light windows of lousy repute. He had a funny habit with fog, brushed at it with his hands, as though he could push the soup aside and clear a path. He realized his hands were working just that way now, and he stuffed them into his narrow pockets, pausing only to pull his collar up tight to his neck.

Not that he had to worry about drawing a crowd. Frith was close to deserted, except for the cries of the hucksters and the herds of cats; moggies the limeys called them; that was about right. When he'd gotten out of L.A., Eddie had considered burying himself in some hamlet, but he figured the smaller the place, the more conspicuous he'd be. Here in Soho, live and let live, that's what they believed.

A sudden explosion came close to giving him doubts. For an instant, he glanced from side to side, hands groping the fog, looking for a place to hide. Then he heard laughter and a mechanical growl as a boy and a girl on a motorbike appeared out of the haze—happiness, then a burst of colors—and Eddie realized that what he'd heard was the bike being kicked to life. Nerves not worth a tic, he thought, as he watched them pass, the girl clinging as only youth can to her man's waist, before they again became one with the fog. Jamming his hands into his coat pockets, Eddie headed for Strip Row. The neons were off but a few places were open, and Eddie suddenly felt fine, full of cautious hope as he shrugged off the chill and slipped into the nearest door.

The place was called the Prime Rib but looked more like leftovers. The chairs were turned down on the tables, the lighting was grim. A handyman as dusky as a chimney sweep was mopping the floor, which was lacquered, but not lately. There was an empty orchestra pit and an empty stage; the strippers were just snaps on a wall.

All the business was at the bar. There were three customers—a leprechaun with darting eyes and a sly brogue, a hunchback in a dusty mackintosh, and an off-duty stripper with skin the color of disease. The leprechaun and the hunchback were at the far end of the counter solemnly trashing an absent pal over pints. The stripper was nearer the door, sipping a Pink Lady.

"Poor old sod, he's got himself a sense of justice and it's killing him," the hunchback was saying, as Eddie slid onto a stool two seats from the girl, who ignored him. The bartender was sitting as well, watching heedless soccer players on the telly. His eyes stayed on the screen as Eddie ordered a Watney's. Stupid fucking game, Eddie thought, running and kicking and tripping. The bartender brought him a glass. He had a walrus mustache and black bands coiled around his white sleeves. Eddie paid him a pound and he returned to his perch; from his face Eddie couldn't tell if the right side was ahead.

Eddie had the glass to his lips when he heard the front door open. Looking over his shoulder, he saw two men silhouetted there, the fog muddied and mysterious and unsettled behind them. After a second or so, they ambled over to a table, righted two chairs, and sat twenty feet from the bar. They were both young, one dark, the other blond, well-built in a lean, supple way, limbs that knew no limits. They were a pair in dungarees, tennies, and cheap wool sweaters, their hair mod long. The blond asked the bartender who was winning before ordering two Becks. Looked like the rest of the footloose types around South London—no jobs, no prospects, just wearing down the sidewalks.

Eddie turned to the girl. She was twenty pushing forty, dark cat eyes made darker by blue liner and lashes that weren't her own. Her eyes were puffy, the makeup yesterday's. She was wearing a Japanese print kimono open over black leotards and a white sweater, round where her breasts filled it. She looked mean and used, a boot to the groin, Eddie knew the dance. Sipping his beer, he imagined her twisting to his own dirty beat.

"Hi, how're you doing?" Eddie hoped he sounded like he enjoyed being under a heel.

The girl stared at him, shrugged, and returned to her drink. Jesus, but you got a lousy way with women, Eddie thought. He sat glumly drawing on the beer.

"There's purity in dishonor, there is," the hunchback was saying, "or some such rot."

Eddie tried again. "Name's Ted. Friends call me Teddy, like in bear." She didn't even turn this time. He knew he should let it go, but the beer was getting to him. He never could drink; he'd get sloshed on just the fumes, then he'd talk too much, like in the Corral.

"Missed *your* name." He hadn't had a woman in a month. His cock was as hard as it was ever going to be. The girl jiggled one crossed leg in irritation, held her dainty glass up before her curled mouth, and said, "Princess Di."

The leprechaun peered around the high shoulder of his chum and chortled at Eddie—he even laughed with a brogue—his eyes round and alive with sport.

Eddie flared before he could stop himself. "Shut up."

The stripper smirked at him, pursed her lips in a silent "ohh" of burlesque fright. The leprechaun and the hunchback exchanged chummy smiles. The chimney sweep had disappeared behind a curtain. The barkeep couldn't care less.

"Was it me he was talking to?" the leprechaun said in mock astonishment.

"I believe that it was," the hunchback replied.

"Just mind your own fucking business," Eddie snapped.

"A tongue he has," the leprechaun said to his friend, as the girl rolled hers over her upper lip, licking away a glimmer of crystal booze.

"That he has," the hunchback answered.

"I'm warning you." Eddie couldn't seem to keep quiet. "Keep your goddamn mouth shut," he threatened, his voice rising. They were all staring at him now, the bartender glowering as he sat with his beefy hands planted on his hips, the TV dance of high-stockinged legs and careening ball above him.

The hunchback said, "A twit he is."

"A wee mon," the leprechaun agreed.

"Wee cheeky bugger, that's got it, mate," the girl added, tauntingly.

"Just fucking shuddup!" Eddie shouted, springing to his feet, his small fists clenched. He was sweating, shaking out his fear, thinking, shit, I'm gonna get stomped but shit, I can't stop myself, and it was the goddamndest thing, but his hard-on was even stronger than before—it was as if all his anger and frustration had focused there, and he started toward the leprechaun even though he glimpsed, as if in slow motion, the bartender leaving his stool and moving his way, then Eddie heard a voice to his right, soft and solicitous, and what the voice said drained him of all fury and lust, shriveling him, and his priorities became what they should have been all along, a wee mon's instinct for survival.

"Hard times, Eddie?" the blond in the turtleneck said. He was much stronger than Eddie and maybe that made him careless as he gripped him by the shoulder, or perhaps it was the strength of desperation that allowed Eddie to break free, slithering, scrabbling away. The astonishment on the faces of the blond and his companion was real, and before they knew it, Eddie was out the door, leaving behind a swirl of fog, but the shock only lasted a drummer's lost beat, for Kevin, the blond, and his partner, Steven, were trained to react. Sprinting to the open door, they dashed out into the dankness, chased by a leprechaun's careless laughter.

Kevin was in the lead and he spotted Eddie up ahead, legs pumping frantically, half obscured by the shrouded air; Eddie seemed to have no feet, only arms and knees lifting out of the heavy fog lying flat on the street. Kevin had played right wing for Leeds and, vaguely aware of Steven's steps pounding behind him, he closed smoothly on the wiry apparition. He stayed steady on his target, watched as it swam into then out of a pool of street light, running like an old film—Chaplin, awkward yet balanced, hands strangely paving the way—as Eddie ducked into an alley, charging past the startled faces, as fixed yet as suggestive as a painting, of two urchins scrounging. Kevin kept closing, closing until he could smell the sweat of Eddie's fear, the black leather jacket and drenched black hair focused even in the fog, and he reached out, reached out until he was almost touching him, one more second and he would have him in his grasp, and then he felt a jarring pain as his leg struck metal and he went down hard with a curse.

For an instant, when Kevin fell over the garbage can, Steven didn't know what to do; he had relied on his partner's speed and agility, but had no confidence in his own. Then he drove himself on, chasing the sound of Eddie rather than the sight of him. He ran like a larger version of his prey, with a labored, clumping lack of grace. He felt his chest constricting, his breath shortening, his gasps matching Eddie's. He stayed behind their harsh wheeze, out of the alley onto Dean Street.

A motorbike grumbled past, headlamp carving a shaky route, hand-held radio blaring punk. Steven could hear the hawkers from Berwick: "Whelks and vinegar, luv, toffee and eels, duck . . ." They seemed nearer, Eddie farther. Steven tried to quicken his pace. Double time, he told himself, like in the bloody army, but he seemed to be losing speed rather than gaining. A sudden fear seized him, became a conviction—Eddie was going to get away, they had him, but he was going to get away, and then it'd be back to the pavement and counting moggies for him and his mate Kevin. He recalled a wildlife documentary he'd seen, flash-juttering images of a hawk pursuing a ground squirrel. The sleek, lethal bird would draw close in a flurry of extended wings and claws, yet the rodent always seemed to just escape, scurrying on tiny, knotted feet into a burrow, and that was what Eddie was going to do, slip sly as could be into some dark cubbyhole. Steven was convinced of it—nothing to be done, lad, might as well pack it in—so it came as a complete surprise when he saw the black back appear out of the mist before him, and he gleefully threw himself through the air in a flying tackle, one that would have done Kevin proud. He felt his hard arms grasp flesh, and even the fierce asphalt felt fine as he brought Eddie down.

"I'm Teddy Edwards," Eddie cried out in a scream of unreasoning, final despair.

"And I'm the bloody Pope, mate," Steven retorted as he resoundingly knocked Eddie cold.

It was four in the afternoon when Chief Inspector Clarence Brown left the room where Eddie was cloistered.

As he walked down the familiar tidy corridors of New Scotland Yard, he carried a cup of tea on a saucer, for he was a man who measured his life in precisely observed rituals. Impeccably dressed, with a temperament as unruffled as dogma, he paused every two dozen steps for a scrupulous sip of Black China. To each bright brisk secretary who bustled past, he gave a nod and an indulgent smile, and his pace remained unhurried as he went by the room where Kevin dourly squatted, nursing his sprained ankle in a bucket of Epsom salts and tepid water, and where Steven sat beside him, reading the *Daily Express* in quiet, gloating triumph.

Outside, the sparrows were singing hosannas to the glories of Whitehall tradition, and Chief Inspector Brown's pace remained constant as he entered his office of immaculate conception. Placing the saucer and cup in their designated location on the left hand corner of his desk, next to the fading photograph of his wife of thirty unmemorable years, he calmly picked up the phone and, in refined, courteous Oxfordian inflections, asked to be put through to the headquarters of the Federal Bureau of Investigation in Washington, D.C.

Under ordinary circumstances, Jack Slater wouldn't have received the call—he was only a special agent with short seniority—but the honchos, Byrne, Hanlon, et al, were in a meeting solving the state of the nation or the equivalent. Slater knew nothing about Eddie Mikenas or the Bureau's interest. So, when the call came through, he should have put Brown on hold, hustled up two flights of stairs and interrupted the confab. At the very least, he should have checked with Files to see why Eddie deserved so much love.

Two things stopped him from doing either. He avoided the

former because upper echelon gatherings were sacrosanct, not to be disturbed under penalty of instant dismemberment. He didn't do the latter because of a personal flaw, a fear of others considering him a flunky, incapable of handling matters of even minor shrift. So when Brown told him they had this chap Mikenas, whom he understood the Bureau had expressed some regard for, Jack Slater said, with all the authority he could muster, Fine, ship him back. Brown informed him, University modulations intact, that presented no forseeable problems. After the necessary paper-noodling, double stamped, they would have him on wings by evening our time, early afternoon yours, along with the tape of the brief and incomplete interrogation they had already, quite correctly, subjected him to, God and the ghost of Labour bless us all. Brown then inquired, because it was only proper to do so, more hosannas sung, which the Bureau preferred, a commercial or a private plane? Slater hesitated, kicked the question around for ten seconds; the Bureau's budget was tight this year, Scotland Yard would bill them for private. Commercial, put him on commercial, Jack Slater said.

It was his final mistake of the day, one that would send him to an early retirement and others to even earlier graves.

Thirty-six hundred and seventy-four miles from FBI headquarters and just down the road from New Scotland Yard, Paul Renaud gazed at the posters of the pneumatic girls and yawned.

He casually scanned the rest of Henry's bedroom; single window so dirty it needed no shade, fading dresser and mirror, skeleton umbrella leaning against a skeleton chair, sagging bed covered with a rumpled eiderdown, numbing dampness that seemed to seep through walls and floor. Renaud was convinced that a London flat in winter was worse than the deadliest of Medieval racks.

Glancing almost indifferently at Henry, who was sitting on the edge of the bed, he straddled the chair, facing him. Renaud's overcoat was unbuttoned and as sorry as the bed, hanging loose at his sides, and his face was seamed with fatigue, but his voice remained pleasant:

"Now, Henry," he began with unctuous charm, dangling his broad forearms over the top of the chair, "I've had a long trip from the States, not to mention some other fairly taxing rides lately, and I'm not as patient as I'm accustomed to being, so I'd appreciate it if you'd speak plainly with me."

"Don't know what you're talking about, guv," Henry replied, none too brave; perspiration shone on him wherever you looked, and a nervous tic worked the corner of one eye.

Renaud's manner and inflection stayed relaxed. There was no need to worry about interruptions. Henry's mother had just dottered off to do the shopping, which would take her the better part of the year.

"Well, Henry, I think you know. I came all this way to have a chat with one Eddie Mikenas, and since I've been deprived of the privilege, Big Bill Durkin says I might as well talk to you."

"Nothing I can tell you, you don't already know, guv."

"I know that, Henry, but I would just like to clear up a few things, for my own satisfaction."

"Whatever I can do, mate." The tic was a bug trying to get out from under Henry's skin. There hadn't been even the suggestion of a threat from the big man—sweet Mary, the size of him—but Henry felt himself squirming, legs jittering and damp beneath his trousers.

"Good." Renaud's eyes showed the pleasure of two friends exchanging confidences. "Now, the way I understand it, Big Bill asked you for this favor . . ."

"And I done you the turn, now didn't I?"

The Frenchman's nod was slow, had the languor of a dream. "Which you were well paid for. That's not the problem," he said, picking idly at a tooth with a fingernail. "The problem is you went to the police as well, didn't you now?"

Henry felt his face flush, his hands go cold. "No, it weren't like that at all, guv. See, I admit I couldn't make up me mind after I come across the lad, so I tossed twenty five pence to decide, see, and it come up the monkey, and off to Big Bill I go."

Renaud repeated his lazy nod. "Then the police."

"Not me, guv. It was luck, old dame fortune, that brought the crushers to him." Henry sensed he was a parody of Soho's worst parts.

"Paul," Renaud said. Henry's eyes glazed over. "The name's Paul, not guv."

Henry nodded dreamily. The bug had climbed up his head, turned itself into a nail.

"Now," Renaud went on, "it would be better if you admitted it, because Big Bill's man in the Yard says you were the one who told them, and if you don't tell me the truth, I can make things very sad for you. You believe that, don't you, Henry?" Henry nodded, just as dreamily as before; sad was the dole and a bad day at the track. "Good," Renaud said with infinite patience and care.

There were voices and mad laughter from the street. Renaud glanced through the window, glimpsed phantoms in the fog. He waited until they passed.

"Now you went to Big Bill, then you went to the police. That was what happened, wasn't it, Henry?"

"I . . ."

"Wasn't it?"

The nail was doing a turn, making him bleed, only the blood was sweat running into his eyes; he could hardly see, and he was going to piss himself. He tensed to keep it in.

"See, it was the fog," he heard himself whine. "I lost the bleeding coin in the fog."

"So you got greedy and decided to collect twice."

"I . . ."

"Didn't you?" There was no menace to the voice.

Henry stared past him at his own reflection in the dresser mirror. It wasn't his face and he turned to the wall, where a girl with red hair smiled at him from Rio. The pressure in his crotch was becoming a flame.

"Didn't you?"

"No . . ."

"Didn't you."

Sad was making the wrong choice. "I did it for me poor old mum." Henry realized he was crying, wringing his hands like the ladies in the soaps. It was funny, blood and nails and a turn. He wanted to laugh. Instead, he looked up at Renaud. "Me old Mum . . ." he pleaded, very softly. It was low-rent drama.

Renaud smiled with compassion. "I'm sure you did." Bracing his hands on his knees, he got to his feet. "I'll be going now. Thank you, Henry."

"Going . . .?" Henry looked at him warily. Blood and nails and the telly; it was supposed to end on a cross.

"Going," Renaud assured him.

Henry felt the relief wash over him, or was it his bladder; his leg was warm and wet. It was funny, a turn, and he laughed.

"You want what the Yard give me, it's right here in the top drawer." Eager to please, another role.

"That won't be necessary, Henry. Would you mind seeing me out?"

"Sure thing, guv . . ." Renaud wagged an admonishing finger. Funny, Henry thought. "Paul," he said, as he hurried to open the bedroom door for his guest.

The knife moved with such speed that Henry didn't know what it was until it entered him, puncturing the left lung with a mild sweetness, the sound as soft as a kiss. Henry's mouth reached high drama; as he stared down, nails were a lovely red spreading over his hands as they clutched at the blade, one fat finger idly fondling the hasp. He reached out with a hand, had a point to make; love was sad.

Renaud followed him down, only freeing the knife after Henry's body touched the carpet. He drew the blade out gently, the mild sweetness repeated, as though in postcoital release, the carefree, posed faces promising perpetual ecstasy above him.

Renaud studied the dead face. It reminded him of the man he'd killed in the tunnel, the shock in the eyes reflecting a life of small betrayals and, for an instant, he felt truly sorry for them both, wished it could have been another way, then his compassion slipped away with the ease of life itself.

Straightening up, he removed a broad white handkerchief from his back pocket and scrupulously wiped the blade clean, before discarding the scarlet-ribboned cloth in the wastebasket beside Henry's bed. He gazed at the knife. The weapon was handcrafted steel, sharp enough to halve a dove's feather in midair, or sever a hand if the man possessed the necessary brute strength. There would be no such refinements this time; he had killed Henry the way he had talked to him, lovingly, like a priest giving benediction.

Returning the knife to its home inside his coat, he delicately skirted the body and walked to the mirror, where he studied himself in the glass, checking for Henry's blood, but it was all on the floor. Slipping on a pair of brown kid gloves, perfect complements to the skin, he opened the top dresser drawer, pushed aside a clutter of tipster sheets, and removed half the amount Henry had been paid for his services. The rest he left for poor old mum. It was the least he could do. Then he left the chill of the flat, closing first the bedroom door, then the front door behind him.

Walking down the short, depressing corridor, he regarded the problem of Eddie. Others, with their conventional methods, would have considered it cause for despair; Eddie was in the exceptionally firm grip of Scotland Yard, sequestered and watched with typical British bulldog zeal. Yet Renaud was certain he could find a solution, a faith almost religious in its conviction. Durkin's man had told him that Eddie would be leaving Heathrow on Flight 109 at 6:30 P.M., and, in fact, the manner in which he had killed Henry had given him an idea.

The fog was lifting as he went outside, and he stepped into the cold, clearing air with a smile, ready for the night.

27

Pacemaker

By the time Eddie arrived at Heathrow, the evening fog was a kitten's purr, sweet and low.

He was accompanied by a pair of cuties, Reg and Jer. The two detectives were dressed like Thatcher groupies. Eddie himself was wearing fifties JD—black leather, jeans, sneakers, and fucked-up hair. He was handcuffed to Jer, the shackles hidden beneath Jer's coat, which was draped over his and Eddie's arm. Eddie wondered why they needed the cuffs. Even without, his chances of escaping were worse than none.

Both his guards went around six solid feet. Jer had a skinny white face and knuckles flat from working out on flesh. Reg's knuckles were smooth, but wrecking balls would bounce off him. He had freckly skin, ghoul eyes, and a tony toupee that didn't fit. Neither he nor Jer had much to say. They didn't seem to like Eddie, didn't seem to much like each other.

"Bleeding hot in here," Jer observed, as they waited for their flight.

"Too many bleeding people," Reg grunted.

"Foreigners," Jer added with disdain. Eddie longed for the easy wit of Steven, who had regaled him with stories of fond encounters between Sussex farmers and their sheep.

The P.A. system called their number and they fell in line. Except for a giant bulging with acromegaly and a kraut in hiking boots who kept taking snaps of passing stewardii, the passengers were predictable: vacationing families, suits and ties returning to the States, and a rock group with flames on their sides. If there were any terrorists, they were being discreet.

Metal detection was brief, delayed only by a flaky lady in tweeds with a death grip on a medallion of Princess Di. The scanning was all pro; even a black-cassocked priest with a pacemaker card and a cane had to surrender his cross and take a frisk. "That's all right. I'm from New York," they heard him say. For a cripple, the priest was a card.

They had tourist in the Delta wide-body. Jer took a window seat, pulling Eddie in beside him. Reg sat across the aisle, next to the flake. She was in a snit, which suited Reg just fine.

Eddie shifted his wrist, trying to relieve the pressure of the handcuffs. "How about taking these off?" he asked Jer. Jer and Reg exchanged looks.

"Nowhere he can go," Reg shrugged.

Jer agreed. "Nowhere."

Reaching into his doubleknits, he removed a key and unlocked the cuffs, tucking them neatly under his folded coat. "If you have to use the loo," he said, "one of us will have to accompany you."

"And hold it for me?" Eddie cracked. Neither Jer nor Reg smiled. Coughing self-consciously, Eddie leaned over and checked Jer's watch. It was 6:30 P.M. London time, 1:30 in the afternoon back home.

"How long before we get to D.C.?" Eddie asked, making conversation.

"Seven and a half hours, including a stopover in Boston," Jer told him, checking out the civilians.

"You couldn't get nothing straight through?"

"Not on short notice." With a motion of his head, Jer indicated the giant. "That one, Reg. Don't like the eyes."

"Stare through walls they could," Reg agreed, nodding sagely. "Noticed him in line."

"Best keep an eye on him," Jer said. Reg nodded wisely again.

"Looks sorta like Frankenstein," Eddie volunteered.

"Jer corrected him. Frankenstein's monster. Frankenstein was the scientist."

"Oh," said Eddie.

"I happen to be a student of the cinema in my spare time."

"Fucking A."

"Pretty big sod." Reg had his black eyes on the priest ten rows up. Looked to be in his fifties and wasted, a sport of disease.

Eddie kept the jokes coming. "Maybe he'll bless the pilot."

"Looks like an actor," Jer said. "Yank."

Reg said, "Who?"

"It will come to me in a while," Jer said, with a twitch of irritation. Reg shrugged and opened a book.

As if he knew they were talking about him, the priest glanced back and gave Eddie a lazy, benevolent smile. A few rows back, a little girl comforted her doll: there, there, there.

"The evening wasn't exactly what I'd expected. I take her for a nightcap—that's what they call highway robbery here in D.C.—at Raphael's, and everything's goin' perfect. She has that good smile goin', and I even manage a foxtrot without breakin' none of her toes. So I suggest 'nother cheaper nightcap back at my place and she's more'n willin'."

"Fucking A," Charley said. He and K.C. were walking down a corridor where the sun didn't shine.

"Like I said, everythin' was perfect. We had ourselves 'nother drink and 'fore you knew it I had her in the sack, maybe on it, only she ain't smilin' so much by now, in fact I kinda hadda force her a little, though not very much, you understand, and not very far, 'cause she says I was too big, you know, down there, not to mention smellin' like a buffalo. So when she says that, I tell her I'd managed real nice without havin' that problem before . . ."

"Too big, or the part about the buffalo?" The call had come in half an hour ago. Hanlon wanted to see them. It was important.

". . . then she goes and changes the subject on me, says I went and deceived her—here she figured special agents was somethin' like congressmen and made as much bread or thereabouts, which she says obviously ain't true since my apartment looks like urban renewal. So I says—we're still on the bed now, but she's tryin' to get off—I says, lady, you deceived nobody but yourself, which was true, gospel. Then she leaves throwin' shit, some on my head. I figure maybe she gets dressed in the elevator or in the back of some asshole congressman's Jag. Afternoon, Mrs. Ryder." Mrs. Ryder, who belonged in Salem torching witches, shoved them through an open door.

Hanlon's office had style, redwood paneling and big dual windows with J. Edgar Hoover thumbtacked to a wall, a dart in his fish-dumb right eye. Hanlon was seated in a leather swivel chair behind four Anacins on a Kleenex, a fading glass of 7-Up, and a travel brochure—sailboats high on champagne waves.

"Catching cold?" K.C. asked as Hanlon blew his nose.

"Last guy I knew who had a cold is dead," Charley said.

"Nice," Hanlon snuffled. He flicked a wise dart, blinded Hoover. "They're bringing Eddie in at nine-oh-two. You're picking him up."

"Jesus!" Charley and K.C. said. "Where?"

"Dulles, one-oh-nine from London. He said a few things, Scotland Yard got it on tape."

Charley checked his watch. It was going on four. "You coming with us? Gesundheit."

"Excuse me, no, I got other business. One more thin—" Hanlon blew his nose. "Thing I've been meaning to bring up—you ever get your gun back, Charley?"

"Hell, no. Let the cops give it to Goodwill."

"You really should have a gun."

"Why? So I can mug little old ladies or trash the city again?"

"Pat's right."

"Why?"

"See that he gets a gun, K.C."

"Cold's gone to your brain."

"I got a spare," K.C. said. "Now that that's settled—"

"No, it ain't."

"—what're we doing for the next few hours?"

Hanlon squinted foggily. "You ever play doctor?"

"In shifts," Charley said, heading out the door for more 7-Up.

The giant with acromegaly made his move at 6:02 EST, just before they reached Boston.

Unfolding in sections from his seat, he rose, face knotted, one mottled paw over his stomach, as if ready to fast-draw. Ponds of sweat filled his forehead.

"Jer . . ." Reg whispered in warning, letting his own hand drift toward his shoulder holster.

"I see him," Jer replied sotto voce, his flat, heavy hand closing into a fist.

They waited expectantly, counting seconds in heartbeats and the huge man's footsteps. Eddie remained calm; he was sound asleep.

The man kept drawing closer. Reg gripped the familiar steel inside his jacket. Time seemed stillborn . . .

The giant strode past them with a pained sigh. Reg and Jer's heads turned as though on hinges, tracking, doing their job. The giant lurched to the serving counter directly behind them, leaned on a stewardess, toweled the sweat from his forehead with his sleeve, grimaced, and said basso profundo, "Got any dramamine?" The stewardess picked herself up and gave him two pills and a tank of water. He washed them down, thanked her, and belched, sending minor tremors throughout the plane. Eddie, sleep-drugged, slurred, "Take it off, take it *all* off, there, there, there . . ."

The priest was hobbling down the aisle. Reg and Jer stared in stony embarrassment, watching him come toward them. The clergyman moved laboriously, his heavy upper body pressing down; his cane was bent, had bumps. They were watching a Dickens short.

"You don't suppose, Reg?" Jer whispered. He needed a threat.

"No, Jer," Reg softly but emphatically replied.

"No, I suppose not." Jer sighed; his fist unraveled.

The priest smiled and nodded politely as he limped past. Jer

The air had a bite but the crowd was mellow, exchanging pleasantries and small confidences. An elderly gentleman in topcoat, bowler, and scarf, was showing snaps of his grandchildren to a freak with long scraggly blond hair and beard. The kid, who had flames painted on his sides, was nodding a little too politely and saying, "Real cute, sir." A few feet away, three toddlers—the oldest no more than five—in hooded parkas were huddled around their mother, munching vendor hotdogs, the sick drunk odor of pork and processed relish thick about them. Nearby, an Air Canada jet slowly sidled for takeoff with a great grinding of gears and pneumatic wheels.

K.C. looked at Charley and tapped his own wrist. "Three minutes," Charley told him. He noticed the children's mother strain slightly forward; looking up in the same direction, Charley saw the pinprick lights and dim shape of the 747 approaching.

Eddie leaned across Jer and glanced down at Dulles. He could see jumbo jets jockeying for position on the ground, their high-beams dueling. A DC-10 lifted toward Eddie, a heft of fusilage and canted wings angling away darkly to the right.

Eddie watched the plane's guide lights wink into the void; then he settled back in his seat. There was a sense of casual preparation around him, people stretching, books being closed, small talk. The rock band stirred eagerly, dreaming of strobe-lit mobs and one-night stands. Even the airsick giant seemed content.

A stewardess was working her way down the aisle, straightening a false eyelash and seatbeats. She had cropped blond hair, upturned nose and breasts, and a receptive Fly Me expression. If Eddie couldn't do that, at least he could engage in a mild flirtation, something to brush back the sour memory of the Soho stripper. Straightening his collar and running a smoothing hand through his hair, he confidently awaited her approach.

Charley took in the runway, where a ground crew prepared for the 747's arrival, refueling and de-icing trucks still and shadowed, while motorized carts cut through blades of light. The mechanics, with their khaki uniforms and rakish caps and the easy energy they brought to their work, reminded him of guys he'd known in the army, a confidence bred by a knowledge of parts and a religion of hands. Behind them, the control tower glowed, a cathedral of glass, where unheard voices coolly brought in Eddie's flight.

Charley turned his gaze to the people around him. The elderly gentleman was closing his wallet. The freak was jittering loosely up and down, his hands jammed into his changeless pockets. K.C. had taken his box of toothpicks out of his coat.

Charley looked up and saw the plane, high beams hard on the darkness, drifting toward him in a steady, seemingly motionless glide, its landing flaps and wheels lowering. It was coming down so nice. Could have been an angel looking to soothe. Watching, the smallest of the toddlers had a slash of mustard across his mouth, like a wound. The mustard made him look obscene, a dirty dwarf-clown, a blemish on the beauty surrounding him. All eyes and fat lips, he stared up at Charley, bringing back the girl in the park with the nymphet's mouth. For no real reason, Charley expected him to turn and run away, then the boy's mother squatted beside him, opening her purse for a Kleenex to wipe the mustard off.

Overhead, the plane drew closer, its lights reaching for the lights from the field.

Jer gazed absently at the lights below. Ever since Boston, he'd been trying to put a name to the face, and now it came to him. Turning from the window, he leaned across Eddie and said to Reg, "Burt Lancaster, that's who." Reg nodded, didn't have the foggiest what he was talking about. Jer leaned back smugly and cracked his knuckles.

Eddie couldn't care less, he had his eye on the blonde. As she paused beside him, he gave her his best smile and wink. "Nice night," he said, cool sex in his voice. With a look that could carve granite, she stared right through him and pivoted. His smile faded as her bright white heels clicked back up the aisle. Should've been a nun, he thought angrily, should've been a goddamn fucking nun, then the corners of his mouth creased into another kind of smile, firm and ironic and absolute in its knowledge.

Nobody loves a . . .

From the ground the flash seemed Fourth of July, bright flaring of light in the Bible-black sky. The air shuddered, and there was a sound so low it seemed an echo.

The world's a carnival; God's parting the heavens and giving us a show, Charley thought. He watched in awe as the back of the 747 broke apart. Dark, torn metal began to appear out of the white light, falling, tumbling down. He thought of the diesel in the ice-green park, shedding steel and flame, but this seemed slower, so much slower. He heard screams, but like the spectacle above him, they were without context and faceless, a shape of dark sounds gathering about him.

He stared at the sky; the resplendence was waning, but he could still see the fusilage of the 747 leaning against what was left of the light. The plane seemed to be trying to steady itself, a stagger of wings, like a wounded bird—or was it an angel? For a moment, it hung fire, then it plunged down in a rush; for an instant, he saw dark, doll figures behind the stretch of lighted windows, silhouetted like passengers on a passing train, thought he saw Eddie clawing at glass; then the plane bellied into the ground. Flaring into even greater brilliance, it sheared the wing off a stationery jet, the wing catapulting after the cone of metal like a graceless child pursuing its parent. He watched as the fusilage quivered abruptly to a stop far away, so very far away. There was no explosion, only a billowing wreath of orange-red conflagration and the blackening steel skeleton entombed within the flames. A man, just one, burst clear, a scarecrow of fire waving his arms, flailing against the heat. He seemed to be imploring Charley; he was so far away, yet he seemed to be pleading with Charley to help, and Charley watched mesmerized as the man briefly ran without reason or direction until he dropped to the tarmac and lay still, the flames consuming him.

The faces around Charley slipped in and out of focus, steadied, and held. They seemed actors in a drama he wasn't part of.

His eyes wild and gleaming, K.C. was softly repeating, "Jesus, Jesus," like a lobotomized priest. The toothpick container was in his palm. He had snapped it in two. His thick fingers were kneading the shards of plastic and colored wood. The elderly man had buried his face in his hands. His wallet lay open at his feet. The freak was staring at the burning hulk; his hands were still deep in his pockets, but he stood glazed and stone-still, sweat glistening on his forehead. The children were bunched around their mother, who was crying, the kind of sustained, wracking sobs that can't be shut off. The oldest was whimpering against the woman's leg, confused, almost understanding. The youngest still had mustard on his lips. He looked up at his mother, wondering what was wrong. And only then did Charley consciously know; only then, with the screams and the ambulances and the fire engines locked around him, did he accept what had happened, and he turned to the turnbuckle fence and punched it as hard as he could, just once, leaving a memory of bright blood on the metal.

Much later—Charley didn't know how long, because time had lost all meaning—after the flames had been hosed down to an occasional shred of smoke, K.C. found him alone and leaning against the fence. He was staring through the arc lamps and TV minicams and shiny apple-red fire engines that ringed the scene.

Under the glare of the artificial light, teams of firemen in yellow tunics and airport personnel in gray prowled, grimly rummaging through the debris and carnage and gathering remains; a charred arm here, a leg there. Looking like fetal sacs, a long line of translucent body bags rested near the foam-coated skeleton of the 747. A score of paramedics were loading the bodies into ambulances, serving no purpose beyond the bearing of corpses. They handled their burdens quickly and at arm's length, as if each cadaver might spring up and touch them with the contagion of death.

Not far from Charley, a fireman removed his hat, bent over,

vomited, then glanced up shyly as though it mattered if anyone noticed. Charley didn't. He was gazing at a plastic cup lying on the runway near the wrung neck of a steel guitar and the spike of a bright white high-heel. The cup bothered him. Although charred, it was uncracked and upright, as if waiting for a martini.

"Charley?" K.C. said softly. Charley didn't turn. K.C. joined him beside the fence. "All those people," K.C. said, shaking his head. He stared at the runway with Charley.

"Hanlon's here."

"Where?" Charley's voice was faraway, his eyes on the cup.

"Inside."

"What's he doing?"

"Drinking."

"What else."

"Yeah. What else."

They went into the terminal, past the cameras and hysteria and the reporters shoving mikes like punches at anyone who had anything to say.

They found Hanlon at the counter of a deserted bar. His coat was open, dangling at his sides. His head was down and he was on this third scotch, straight. "How're you, Charley?" he asked, his voice sober, but raw and weak. His shoulders were sagging, his eyes rimmed red, either from the booze, the cold, or crying, Charley didn't know which.

Without replying, Charley eased onto the stool beside him. K.C. sat on the other side of his boss. Charley gazed at his own dark reflection in the gleam of the counter-length mirror; his features were set, his eyes somewhere else. He glanced up at the overhead TV. The screen was blank, avoiding the news.

"What'll you have?" the bartender asked without interest.

"Primo and 1967," Charley said. The bartender raised his brows. "Coors," Charley said. K.C. had the same. They sat in silence, brooding over their drinks. The light in the room was the light of a fire in a cave.

"Shit," K.C. said to himself. It was about the best thing that could have been said at that moment.

There was another pause. Hanlon took off his hat, ran a hand through his thinning red hair. "How do you feel about getting drunk?"

Charley studied his bruised knuckles. "They don't have Primo."

"We can go to my place, see what I've got."

K.C. shrugged, heavy muscles taxing his coat. Charley did the same.

"Good idea," Charley said.

"Yeah," K.C. said. Hanlon simply finished his scotch.

As they got up to leave, a reporter with short, bandy legs hurried by on his way to a phone. His face was flushed and he looked as happy as a groupie at a concert for the Grateful Dead.

"Shit," K.C. muttered, watching.

"Yeah," Hanlon said. "Yeah."

Somewhere someone was crying and a camera bulb flashed, bright as a new day.

28

Fathers and Sons

Renaud lay naked to the waist on the king-sized bed, forearm across his forehead, letting the smoke from his cigarette settle around his fatigued face.

Glancing down at his chest, he idly fingered the dry blood beneath his right shoulder. He wondered, with mild curiosity, what Eddie was thinking at the instant of the explosion—wished he could have seen the brief terror in his face, but such small pleasures had, of course, been denied him. Having arrived at Dulles, minus cassock and makeup, on an LC-10 less than an hour ago, he had, nevertheless, heard the news, witnessed the emotion and media hype. Passing through the terminal, he had learned that there had been no survivors. The information came as no surprise. When he was involved, there never were.

Taking a lethargic drag on the cigarette, he let his gaze wander across the half-dark room. Deep in D.C.'s Meridian Hill ghetto, the cupboard apartment was bare, except for the books—Sartre, Camus, Genêt—and the oil paintings, his own. The pictures numbered an even dozen, some inhabiting the walls, others a corner. They were of people he'd known, all dead, except for one. The earliest, a sketch of his mother dating back fifteen years, was macabre, the features distended and deranged, the whole as starkly brutal as the slash of a knife mired in midnight. Yet with each new effort there had been a softening of texture and line, so that the last, a nearly completed self-portrait, was gentle; as his method of killing throughout the years became increasingly grotesque, his canvases grew more benign. It was as though he were working toward some final completion, a private canonization and catharsis through public horror and neglect. Considering his origins, somehow it was apt.

Tossed between Germany and France, Alsace-Lorraine is a volleyball, not a country, a circumstance that makes for schizophrenia and a high suicide rate. Paul Renaud was born there in 1955, in the town of Kaysersberg, the birthplace of Albert Schweitzer. Paul's father was an artisan, a fair crafter of wood, his mother a farm girl, as sturdy as the soil that nurtured her. What love he received came from her; affection was never part of his father's nature. In school, Paul made friends easily with his agreeable smile and manner, and lost them as quickly with a temper as sudden and brief as a summer storm. His formative years were channeled and predictable, rituals within ritual. Then at the age of fourteen his life turned around: his parents were brutally murdered.

His memory of the event was vague even in its immediate

aftermath. He had come home early from school with a pounding headache. The day was hot, increasing the pressure, pistons through the brain. As he started through the door of their modest house, he thought he heard his mother's voice calling his name, a distant pleading, echoes from a cave, but that couldn't have been, for when he entered, both his parents were lying dead on the living room floor, dressed in blood. Someone or something had gone berserk with his father's ax, which rested nearby, the handle broken off at the blade, the scene one of cleaved flesh and exposed bone, red on white, a sense of meat carved and haphazardly discarded. There was gore and membrane on the walls, on the furniture, and on the family cat, which had shredded the curtains in its attempts to escape. Both of Paul's parents had soiled themselves in their terror, the stench oppressive in the still, fetid heat of the room. Besides their mutilation, his father had been decapitated—his head was in a corner, one blank fisheye staring at his son—and his mother's hands had been severed at the wrists.

Paul had stood in the doorway, swaying in shock, oblivious to the doglike growl of the cat low under the kitchen stove. He remembered thinking it wasn't decent about his mother's hands, recalled gently lifting her arms onto her grisly lap and placing her hands against the bloody cartilage and tendons of her wrists, as if to restore them to their proper place. He remembered her blood on his own hands, recalled washing then, cleansing himself, the act another ritual, like baptism or absolution. And that was all he remembered until much later, when men in crisp, laundered white drew softer white over the bodies, and the police asked their sympathetic yet suspicious questions, questions that lingered until they lost their purpose in repetition.

The maniac who killed his parents was never caught, but that didn't really seem to matter, for Paul discovered then that he was different from others; in the days that followed he felt no real grief, experienced a vague disquietude at best. Accepting what had occurred, he resumed his life, making the necessary adjustments. He lived for a while with an aunt—dourness enforced by peasant piety—doing the labor on her farm and increasing his already remarkable strength. Then, at the age of nineteen, he simply left one night without a note or a goodbye. Traveling as far as an upraised thumb would take him, he ended up in the province of Champagne, where he found employment in the dank stone vaults of the winery of Moêt et Chandon, near the desolate World War I battlefields of Soissons and Verdun. His job was to clean the twenty-thousand-gallon vats. Under cloistered light, he would squeeze through the large bungholes at the bottom of the barrels and shovel out the sediment within. He enjoyed the work, felt a strange, existential euphoria in the solitary hours spent ringed by fermentation and forty-year-old oak. Yet, after a year, he moved on once more, restless and with a compulsion to find his destiny.

He discovered it in Marseilles through a middle-aged Dutchman named Hans Enklaar. Enklaar was a freebooter, adventurer, and thief, with a gift for painting. Taking the boy under his worldly wing, he became more of a father to him than his own had ever been. Through him, Paul learned how to handle what Enklaar considered the essentials of life: women, an easel, and a gun. Each had their element of art, each their degree of danger, even when merely psychic.

For a while, they played the Marseilles underworld circuit as freelance muscle; the money was minimal, the experience a lesson. In midnight excursions, Enklaar taught him the nuances of manipulation and quiet persuasion or, when that failed, the expediency of cutting a man's throat so fast he wouldn't know he was bleeding before he was dead. Paul developed his own talents along the way—his offhand if caustic charm, a knack for languages, and the quick-study ability to duplicate any accent. And of course there was the strength, always the incredible, natural strength, a sledgeweight presence behind the ingratiating grin.

Through Enklaar's guidance, Paul moved from adolescence to manhood in a matter of months. He complemented and abetted the older man as well, and they soon saw the world through a mercenary's sights: the Congo, Costa Rica, Iraq, Ireland, Thailand. It was in the last that Enklaar was killed, strafed by a friendly Phantom 140 on a day of rest.

With his death, Paul grieved for the first time in his life. For a while, he hired out for high-risk assignments, courting a death that never quite found him. It was one such commission that brought him to Venezuela, fighting for a side that couldn't win. He was captured, sentenced to die, saved by a whispered word from a man he had never seen. Enklaar had been dead for four years and Renaud needed another loyalty, something visceral and absolute, and he found it in his savior, Victor Cedillo, the man they called—with respect, not ridicule—John Wayne.

Paul became devoted to him, spent his days and most of his nights in his service, his spare time in reading, for books became a sudden passion; women were an occasional pleasure, to be used and abandoned as readily as his smile. The years gathered and faded like seasons, grew secure and predictable; then it all shattered.

In many ways, the memory of that dark, desperate time was as blurred as when he'd stumbled through the blood-rich room decades ago: the growing certainty of exile, the preliminary plans, the flight to America, the final preparations with Dake for Victor's arrival . . . Then word of the plane crash reached him.

His first response was despair and the desire to fly immediately to Victor's side, but Dake advised against it. His logic was irreproachable; Victor would need Paul here, an anchor for his future plans when he was well enough to make the trip. Paul had reluctantly agreed, but not without consequences, for his second impulse had been savage. Fueled by frustration and anger, he had gone out and murdered a man, a homosexual who'd bought him drinks in a bar. He had killed him by painful degrees in the man's own home, intricate torture to no purpose except his own satisfaction, the homicide and method catharsis for his fury.

Afterwards, sated, he measured his days out in insignificant ceremonies, anticipating news from a distant island. Word had finally come in the person of one of Victor's bodyguards, who told him they'd smuggled Victor in two weeks earlier. Controlling his anger over not being notified in advance, Paul quizzed the courier gently, the way he later would Henry. Although he never touched him, the man, his voice thick with fear, had told him where Victor was.

Even then Paul hadn't gone to him, for word came from Dake that their mutual boss, still not fully recovered, wished to be left alone until their "scheme"—God, what a cheap, trite word that was, lawyer's jargon—was completed. So, out of his respect for his mentor's privacy, Paul had waited, doing the gruesome work that was asked of him, executing it, as always, efficiently and well, but, as always, waiting . . .

He stared at the ceiling, following the plumes of smoke. He thought of the hours spent in the gloomy recesses of the winery when he was young. It seemed that his life hadn't really changed all that much since then; he was still slipping into remote, dark places—some of the soul—cleaning out sediment, only now the dregs wore clothes.

Lowering his cigarette, he glanced at his watch on the nightstand—10:47. In just over twenty-four hours it would be finished. He had waited so long, he could wait that much longer. It was what was expected of him, what Victor would want.

For a moment he continued to track the smoke, then a cryptic smile, thin but resolute, formed on his face. Snubbing out the cigarette, he reached for his coat.

He would wait no longer.

29

Chorus

They drove in two cars, Charley and K.C. trailing Hanlon's Datsun in the rented Buick. From his speed—30, hands never leaving the hub—Charley guessed that the liquor was dragging on Hanlon.

Neither Charley nor K.C. spoke during the forty-minute ride from Dulles. Charley fiddled with the radio, searching for music and avoiding the news. K.C. sat lumped on the passenger side. He had carried out his drink when they'd left the terminal—simply walked away from the bar with it—and now he hunched deadweight beside Charley, the tumbler cupped invisible and forgotten between his big hands. Finally, he drained what liquor was left and placed it on the dash, like a man ordering another shot.

The glass remained there briefly, vibrating with a light rattle. It reminded Charley of the cocktail glass upright on the runway. Reaching across K.C., he took the tumbler and placed it delicately on the floorboard by his feet. Up ahead, Hanlon turned into his circular driveway and parked. With a low sigh, Charley swung in behind him.

Where Hanlon lived was nice, trees and lights, a neighborhood missing crime or even raised voices. The houses showed something of New England, bay windows, gabled roofs, wide white clapboards and brick chimneys, snugness contained within size. There wasn't a FOR SALE sign on the block.

Fumbling for his keys, Hanlon unlocked the front door and

ushered in his guests. The interior was expensive without being showy. The living room ceiling was cathedral, the walls white and barely adorned, the floor lacquered hardwood and sort of covered by shag rugs. The furniture—sofa, divan, chairs—was in matching deep browns, an impression of rich soil uprooted from the earth. A Steinway piano squatted against the far wall. Sheet music was open on the rack, but the keys were coated with dust. A short stairway, curved not winding, led up to bedrooms and darkness. Although far from unkempt, there was a sense of mild neglect, that peculiar and subtle quality of a man living without a woman's touch. Yet, paradoxically, there was also a feminine aura to the shadings of the home, a presence that lingered as stubbornly as smoke in damp air.

"Nice place," Charley said soft and sincere, as he removed his cap.

"Yeah, nice place," Hanlon echoed; then his voice became brisk and conversational as he took his guests' coats and hung them in the hallway closet.

"Picked it up for twenty-seven five back in 1953 with a VA loan right after Korea. Ann—my wife—Ann and I lived here ever since. Raised a relationship through two second mortgages, three major recessions, and six shitty presidents. Make yourselves comfortable."

Charley sat on the sofa while K.C. filled an armchair. "Any kids?" Charley asked as Hanlon crossed to a liquor cabinet of hand-tooled wood.

"No, we couldn't have any," Hanlon said without explanation.

As Hanlon squatted down to open the cabinet, Charley noticed a photo of a woman on the piano. Good-looking lady, dark hair just starting to show gray, eyes strong and the color of cactus, bedrock resilience and dignity, the kind of woman who would leave her imprint on a home or a life. Charley didn't have to ask Hanlon if it was his wife.

"What'll you have?" Hanlon asked. "We got Jack Daniel's, J and B, Johnny Walker, and Fundador. No Primo," he shrugged.

"J and B straight," Charley requested.

K.C. said, "The same."

Hanlon brought them each their own bottle and glass before retreating to the piano bench with a fifth of Fundador and a tumbler. Sitting sideways, head bent, he pecked out two soft notes on the keyboard, said, "You could've been a star, Charley, name up in headlines," stretched out the irony like a song. "Regret it?"

Charley shook his head as he poured himself a little poison. "I've been there before. Sometimes you end up in the loss column. Like now."

No one had anything to say. They sat dogging the blues, each huddled with the booze and his own thoughts. A hallway clock ponderously struck eleven. Charley waited out the chimes then said sadly to himself, "Pittsburgh and it's raining."

Hanlon let a note hang, glanced up. K.C. just kept drinking.

"It's a movie," Charley explained. "*Requiem for a Heavyweight.* Anthony Quinn's in the dressing room with Gleason and Wynn. He's just gotten the shit kicked outta him by Cassius Clay in L.A.—"

"Before he was Ali?"

"—before he was Ali, and Gleason, he asks him, Quinn, where he is, to see if he's all right, you know, and he says he's in Pittsburgh and it's raining. That's the way I feel right now."

Hanlon understood. Tight-lipped, he nodded. He glanced at K.C. The big Indian with the buffalo nickel face was staring into space, eyes unfocused, clenching and unclenching one fist. The huge hand kept opening and closing; pillows could live in there, Charley thought.

"You okay, K.C.?" Charley asked.

K.C. didn't look his way; his eyes stayed on the walls. When he spoke, his husky voice was lined with bitterness, adding to its rawness. "How the fuck did they get a bomb on the goddamn plane? How the fuck did they even know Eddie was on it?"

"Doesn't matter much now, does it?" Hanlon said, adding his own bitterness to K.C.'s.

"Yes, it does! Yes, it goddamn does!" The anger came off him hard—hard and a little comic, the way it always does with a big man. "Too many people dead and it should be finished but it's not, 'cause Eddie coulda told us what we needed to know to stop it and Eddie's dead. We were that close, and Eddie's dead and now all we can do is sit on our fuckin' hands and wait."

As close as a flaring of white brilliance in the sky, Charley thought. As close . . .

"It's over," Hanlon was saying, bringing K. C. down. "Nothing we can do about it. Get drunk, K.C. It'll look better in the morning."

"All those people," K.C. mumbled, staring.

"Get drunk, K.C.," Hanlon insisted. "If you were Irish you'd know that when people die you get drunk and try to forget." As if determined to practice what he was preaching, he took a long pull from the bottle, ignoring the glass. K.C. did the same. Charley refilled his own empty tumbler, taking his time.

"What the hell are they doing?" he wondered out loud. "What the hell are they doing that so many people have to die?" He sounded like a child, maybe a little comic too, but Hanlon wasn't noticing.

"I don't know," Hanlon told him. "I don't know, but I'll tell you this—no matter what, the world won't end because of it. That's what all the bad movies want you to believe—there's this plot and the world's going to come crashing down unless somebody stops it, but it wouldn't work that way. Bush and Gorbachev and all the rest could be goddamned raving but the world's not going to blow because of it . . . One man's not going to be able to push the button because there's too much backup since Hitler and Hiroshima. No, what we got going is a moral slide since Watergate and maybe before, a great, big fucking slide toward cynicism. You can see it in the faces of the people all around you, smirks instead of smiles, indifference instead of concern, and maybe that's worse, maybe that's worse than the fucking bomb. You know what I mean? You know what I'm driving at?"

Charley said, "Most."

K.C. said, "Some."

"Fuck it," Hanlon threw in, taking another swig. "Don't know if I know myself."

"Get drunk, Pat," K.C. said. "Get drunk."

Hanlon smiled, a whiskey-shiny grin. "Working on it. Damned if I'm not working on it."

They all were. It was serious drinking, no dainty fingertip sips, but hard heavy chug-a-lugging, 80-proof purgation. The others blurred momentarily for Charley, not much, but enough to let him know the liquor was reaching him.

"What do you think of death, Charley?" Hanlon said, almost defiant, comic.

Not much, Charley felt like saying. Instead he said, "Helluva time to ask."

"No better one," Hanlon said.

Charley snorted and blinked. "What do I think? That it wouldn't be so bad if there was no dying involved."

"Jesus," K.C. swore. "And they say *Indians* can't drink."

"No, listen. I wasn't trying to be funny, not now. I was being serious. I mean if it, dying, was a place you could go visit for a while, say a week—"

"A day."

"Fifteen or twenty minutes?"

"—that you could go visit for a rest then come back all nice and refreshed, then it might be okay."

"Sioux believe in an afterlife," K.C. volunteered.

"What about you, Pat? What do you believe?"

"I'm Catholic," Hanlon said, as if that explained it all.

"Me. I'm not so sure," Charley admitted. "Wish I knew but I ain't so sure." The room was warm, getting warmer, but he shivered. He felt like it was raining outside—the sky through the window was clear but he felt like it was raining, and he hugged himself, bracing against the cold. "I want my wife back," he said abruptly and with emotion.

"So do I, Charley," Hanlon said. "So do I." His small eyes were vibrant—sparks of blue fire set against the deepening flush of his face—but they weren't alive, were instead the desperation of a drowning man. They held Charley briefly, then, looking away, Hanlon hurried to another subject:

"Read something a while back, about transplants, replacement parts. Read about how maybe someday nobody'll have to die."

Charley coughed. "Get pretty crowded."

"Think I'd start with my face," K.C. said.

"What part?"

"The whole fuckin' thing. What was that 'bout Pittsburgh . . . ?" K.C. slurred, spilling half his drink. He had a stupid grin on his face and his eyes were glass tombs. Jesus, but he's sloshed, Charley was thinking. Probably dreaming of maidens with tomahawks tattooed on their tits. Jesus, but what a sight, Charley thought, laughing uncontrollably, the tears rushing to his eyes.

I want . . .

"Spilled it." K.C. grinned at him with a small boy's mischief, wrinkling his nose.

Blinking, Charley looked from him to Hanlon, who was going his own way, catching a different rhythm.

"Better if you can choose your way of dying," Hanlon was saying. "Knew this guy once, friend of a friend of a friend, worth a million, all the goddamn money in the goddamn world. You know what he'd do for kicks? You know what he'd do? He'd fly to the lake, to Tahoe, play the nickel slots—you know, the ones if three bars come up it pays you seven fifty, three genies it's fifty bucks. Seems this guy, the millionaire, had a dicky heart. Said the rush he got from hitting the bars was better'n a shot of nitro. Did this for years. So what happens? What happens is one day he's pulling a handle and the genies come up. Never happened before and he starts grabbing at his chest, has a coronary, big as a building. Killed him on the spot, but that's all right, because he was doing what he wanted and it was quick. Like the people on the plane, at least it was quick. Not like Ann, not like her . . ."

Charley and K.C. were very still now, listening as Hanlon worked it out.

". . . had a good woman and twenty years," he was saying, "and one day she comes home from shopping feeling weak, nothing serious, just a little weak, and then, a couple days later, it happens again . . . so I take her to the doctor, thinking maybe she has a touch of flu, that's all, a touch of flu, and they run some tests, and a little while after that, they say she has cancer, just like that, she has cancer . . . so you go with her for treatment, hoping, chemo and all the rest, and the doctor's telling you to have faith, and all the time her face keeps turning this pale, sick blue, and she keeps getting thinner, the skin drawing tighter and tighter against the bone, and all the while she's fighting it, quietly, but fighting it the way she always has everything she's had to fight, only this time she doesn't win. Only this time she goes to sleep one night and she doesn't wake up . . ."

The silence in the room was a wall without breach. Charley wished the clock would chime to break it. Hanlon was crying. He wasn't sobbing and the expression on his face hadn't changed, but the tears were running down his cheeks.

"All those people," he said, continuing to cry. "All those people . . ."

It was eleven, a sweet, sad hour, by the time Charley and K.C. slurred their fond, sloppy farewells and left Pat Hanlon alone with his bleary grief.

K.C. was drunk and Charley, high but functioning, drove him home, doing his damndest to sort out his companion's scrambled directions and to keep his mind off Hanlon and his dead wife. K.C. mumbled a Sioux death chant—Hey-yah, Hey-yah, Hey-yah—during the ride and fell out of the car onto his fanny when they reached his building. Charley got him to his feet, no small task, and helped him inside.

The apartment ran to formica and vinyl and pop magazines, and there was broken glass in a dust pan resting against a wall, compliments of sweet Mary. K.C.'s size 14's were dragging by the time they reached the bedroom, where Charley dropped him on the bed, breaking a spring.

"Ain't too big," K.C. swore, his head a Raggedy Andy.

"Pittsburgh," Charley said as he exited, trailed by a shuddering snore.

* * *

Charley got back to the Three Seasons just before midnight, hurting the fender behind him as he parked. Yeah, sure, he said once and, before he got out of the car, he looked in the rearview mirror, expecting John Wayne over his shoulder.

As he walked, kept a pretty straight line to the entrance, a stone loony in caddy castoffs and a Ben Hogan cap asked if he knew the color of rain and that Tinker Bell flew over the hotel every night twelve sharp? Wouldn't be at all surprised, Charley replied as he brushed past. Wouldn't be at all surprised.

Safe in his room, Charley stored holster and gun in a dresser drawer, company for his socks. He gingerly undressed, took care not to trip over his feet. Down to his shorts, he crawled under the covers and flipped open *Farewell, My Lovely.* He read three pages before skipping close to the end, stopping at the place where Moose Malloy gets shot. He studied the territory twice, wincing each time as the bullets entered the big man's body, then he put the book aside.

He lay there in bed with the light still on, sorting out things. He thought of storms and explosions and planes, and of cards with a skeleton's smirk, and he decided maybe he'd go by thumb if he ever got back to L.A. Then he thought of other things, of empty, silent rooms and tears running down a strong man's face, and then he thought of Lisa and his heart ached—he'd never have put it that way, but his heart ached. He thought of the way her weight shifted against him in the night, and how the light fell across her face at dawn, and the more he remembered, the firmer his resolve that it was time for long overdue affirmations. It wasn't the booze, it was simply that during the last week, with life a balancing act on wet wire, he had come to a few facts—that stubbornness and macho pride were the route to loneliness, and that if he loved Lisa and wanted her, waiting wasn't the way to show it. And with that in mind, he picked up the phone and called information for L.A. The operator was as helpful as an ulcer, but he wouldn't let her off the line until she'd found what he was looking for. The only florist shop still open was in Beverly Hills. They wouldn't be able to deliver until the following morning, and they charged an arm and a leg, but under the circumstances it was worth twice the price. He dictated the note, told them to make sure they got it right because it was important, then he told them to bill it to his office, Charley Tone, Bailbondsman, and not to let a guy who sounded like a deep breather dissuade them.

Replacing the receiver, Charley snuggled under the covers and turned off the lamp. He was asleep inside a minute, a smile secure on his face.

Somewhere, not so far away, a clock chimed twelve and Tinker Bell flew overhead, scattering moondust and clouds.

A hundred miles away, his mood fathoms removed from Charley's, Paul Renaud pulled to a stop in the soft, ashen dirt and turned off the ignition, which fluttered and died. He sat staring at the wheel. His respect for Cedillo was such that, despite his earlier resolve that evening, he had found the most trivial of excuses for delay—an unwanted meal, an hour dissolved in a bar—before driving to his destination. Even now, he had to force himself to thrust open the door.

He was free of the car now, moving toward the house. The night was impossibly cold and his breath clotted the air. He could hear the low, nocturnal sounds of animal life rising in fits and starts from the woods. A wind knifed in from off the lake, threatening to turn into something spectral and fierce.

As he approached the lights falling snow-soft from the windows, the hesitancy left his long stride; his pace became rapid, a quickening that remained constant as he hurried up the steps, past the guard who sat bewildered as Renaud went through the door.

The men inside were big, built for confrontation, but trying to stop him would have been like trying to hold back time, and they meekly pointed up the stairs when he asked, his voice soft but banked by invisible fires, where Victor was. Subdued, they watched as he went up the stairs, climbing toward the TV murmurs and glaze of blue-white light coming from beneath the closed door. They waited while he hurried down the dark hallway and entered the room, the door snicking shut behind him. They waited the better part of an hour until the door opened and Renaud came out. They watched as he strode down the stairs and past them, thick arms swinging at his sides, liquid brown eyes inflamed as he went out into the cold, cutting night.

No one spoke even after they heard the car's engine recede into the wind and the darkness. Finally, one man, bolder than the rest, reached for the phone to call Dake, for he should know that Renaud had been there, but then the man remembered the coiled fury in Renaud's body and face, and he replaced the receiver as gently as he would a bomb.

Alone in his study, Lawrence Dake stared out the window, watching the star-glimmer of a jet track across the sky.

Renaud had gone too far—it was a bad joke, a vaudeville routine, over a hundred dead; he would have to be eliminated after this was over, it was as simple as that. He had done what the moment required, in fact had no other choice, but his style was too far removed from Dake's own; for if he saw his own role as preclusive, darkening cellar secrets, keeping out the light, then with the Frenchman there was always the impulse toward conflagration, something that burned deep within, like Greek drama, shadow yearning to become flame.

Still, his scheme was intact. His first impulse, when he'd caught the news, was to get drunk and call the whole business off. Then, as always, reason had taken over. The crash had brought headlines, but nothing could be proved, probably not even known. Planes went down. Such things happened, were part of the contemporary landscape. Except to the relatives, the deaths were only numbers, newsprint, math. Public horror over the mutilation of a child was greater; sometimes more really was less. It would pass.

His hands and mind steady, Dake gazed up at the sky. The jet seemed to be where it had been before, motionless as a still life, a paradox, traveling imperceptibly through the night.

Urban picaresque.

30

Flowers

Charley woke at nine with visions of black cats and fairies dancing through his sleep-jammed head. He'd dreamed that he was a patient in a psychiatrist's high-rise, a little couch and comfort in hazy technicolor. Ali was the shrink. He was seven feet tall and decked out in purple gabardine, with pink sneakers, the laces untied, on his paws. Moose Malloy was his receptionist and even bigger; he was wearing ballet tights with a tutu over the tattoos on his biker thighs. Moose had a real sweet smile, but he was leaking blood through the tights and both his hands were off at the wrists. Ali didn't seem to notice. Sitting jack-high in a designer chair and stroking his whiskers, he kept telling Charley in la-di-da English that he should've sent Lisa tiger lilies 'stead of roses. Charley kept saying yeah, sure, and watching the blood seep through the soft black nylon. It was a helluva good dream to wake up from.

Sitting up in bed, Charley rattled his head to make sure it was still there. He had a deadweight ache migrating from his left temple to the bridge of his nose, but there were no other signs of permanent damage. Reaching across the pain, he picked up the bedside phone and called room service, asking for aspirin and something to chase it with. The bell captain, who had a fake high-bred accent, inquired if the gentleman was feeling indisposed? Only when it rains, Charley told him, urging him to hurry.

Charley passed the time by doing situps; he didn't particularly feel like jogging around the bed. He was on 139 when there was a cautious rap at the door. Charley said Come in and a kid with curly hair and acne that looked contagious sidled inside, hefting soda and two Bayers on a chipped tray. The kid appeared to be scared, nervously watching Charley as he finished his head to toes. As he reached 150, Charley told him there was a buck in change in his pants hanging there on the knob, take it, don't be shy. Blushing through his patchwork skin, the kid fished out four quarters, keeping one fright-flick eye on Charley the whole time and quickly exiting with a squeaky thanks. Charley hit 157 and stopped, pulling at his sweat-soaked T-shirt. Gulping down the Bayers, he fell back on the bed and went back to sleep, praying for no REMs.

Five minutes later, the phone rang. Charley stirred and pressed the receiver almost to his ear. It was the front desk. They wanted to know if the gentleman would be staying with them much longer? Charley said the gentleman doubted it. Front desk sounded relieved.

Five minutes later, the phone rang again and Charley answered. It was getting to be a habit.

"They found the tape Eddie made in London," K.C.'s voice said. He sounded sober if dreary.

"Which means?"

"Probably nothin'. It was in this cop's briefcase and the explosion blew it out and damaged it some, but the case took most the blast. The lab boys are workin' on it now. They figure to get it pieced together by ten. Figured you might like to listen in."

"Yeah, I might."

"Okay, Hanlon's office, see you there at ten. Nobody expects much, but you never know."

"Never know," Charley said. "How's your head?"

"The one on my shoulders or the one up there on the ceiling?"

"Sorry I asked."

Charley hung up. As he got up to shave, shower, and observe all the niceties of going out into the civilized world, he wondered if Lisa had gotten the flowers yet.

He hoped they hadn't wilted.

Life goes in cycles, Lisa was thinking, just before the phone rang.

It was nine A.M., Pacific Coast time. She was sitting at her desk, adjusting a long-stemmed red rose in a glass jar while she waited for the screams, and her instinct told her things were looking up. The signs were already there, small, totemic blessings. She had spent a miserable day and a half, feeling helpless and depressed after her visit to Mayer's office, a bear of raw nerves clawing at her stomach. Then, last night, the agony in her belly had magically departed and a second miracle occurred; Ali had insinuated his way into her bed and she hadn't sneezed, not once. Maybe, just maybe, she thought, the unexpected boons were symptomatic and *everything* was going to get better.

The flowers had clinched it, arriving from, God forbid, a Beverly Hills florist at 8:45. Looking silly in a paper party hat, Marv had been standing beside her desk, rambling about nothing, when the delivery boy strolled in with the bouquet of American Beauties, petals as fresh as a baby's kiss. "From Charley?" Marv grumped as she read the note; her only response had been to beam and Marv had skulked back to his own desk, angling away from added frustrations.

The note read, "Does this face look like flowers? Love, C." More important than the sentiment and what it meant, Lisa knew he must be all right.

So her mood was as good as it could be without his actually being there when the phone rang. Her instinct told her it was

Charley, and she snatched up the receiver and answered with an eager "Hello?"

"Mrs. Tone?"

"Yes?" Lisa's enthusiasm fell with her face.

"This is Jerome Haines. I met you yesterday in passing at the FBI offices."

"Yes?" She had no idea what to expect, maybe deep breathing.

"Had a hell of a time reaching you, three transfers and fifteen minutes on hold since I got your office number from personnel." Haines paused to catch his breath. "You want to know where your husband is, is that correct?"

Lisa's voice jumped back to life. "Yes. Can you help me?"

"I would have called you last night at home, but I got tied up in, um, a certain intimate situation, tangled, you might say . . ."

"Yes, of course, I understand. But you do know where he is?"

"Well, where he should be. Do you have a pencil handy?"

"Yes," she said, reaching behind her ear.

"He's at the Three Seasons Hotel, Room four-oh-nine, in Washington D.C. The phone number is 546-7371."

"546-7371." She jotted the information down under a Happy Face.

"Area Code two-oh-two. I shouldn't be telling you any of this, but I think your husband's gotten in over his head and I feel you have a right to know."

The claws clutched at her stomach again. "What do you mean, in over his head?" Overhearing, Fran Drucker stared at Lisa curiously. Lisa ignored her.

"Well, I'm not aware of the details," Haines admitted, "but he's temporarily employed by the Bureau on a case of some magnitude, and I believe of some danger, if that isn't too melodramatic."

"*Why* is he involved? How could he . . . ?" It was too melodramatic. So was she.

"Like I said, I don't know the details. I just thought you should know."

"Wait . . . !"

"I am."

"Is that all you can tell me?"

"I'd think it'd be quite enough."

"Yes, yes it is. I'm sorry. Thank you."

"*De nada*, as we used to say at computer school. Goodbye and good luck."

"Goodbye . . ."

Lisa kept the receiver by her ear as her voice trailed off. Fran was glancing at her and whispering to a co-worker, inference reaching for gossip. Lisa didn't notice. Her head was swimming, struggling against crosscurrents—excitement over locating Charley, fear as she realized he really was in danger. It was still too melodramatic. Danger was bad TV.

The phone was drowning in her ear. Breaking the connection, she dialed 9 for an outside line, then 0. When the operator's voice broke in, Lisa read off the number Haines had given her and asked that the call be billed to her home phone. As the operator put the call through, Lisa sat chewing on a fingernail and thinking she'd kill for a cigarette.

The Three Seasons switchboard picked up the call and tried Charley's room. It rang a while before the operator said, bored, I'm sorry but your party doesn't answer. A few more times, just a few more times, Lisa said. Sighing, the operator let it ring a little more before repeating the obvious. Lisa left a message with the front desk, asking that they have Charley call her back, please, please call her back—she could live with bad TV—then she finally hung up.

She sat there, staring through the flowers and note as she sifted options. Instinct and long-distance pleas could take her just so far; bumming a cigarette from Fran, it took her two minutes to make arrangements to board Ali, five to bully and cajole her supervisor into letting her have the rest of the day off—after all, it *was* New Year's Eve—another five to make arrangements with Delta; they had a seat open on a one o'clock flight to Washington, tourist. Telling the dispatcher she'd take the pilot's lap if necessary, she tucked Charley's note into her purse and was heading for the door before the phone had settled into its cradle.

31

Eddie's Last Tape

K.C. was waiting in the corridor when Charley arrived. His face looked like it had gone through receiving, but he was chewing on a burgundy toothpick and his eyes were alert.

"You're feeling better," Charley said as they walked. "And I don't just mean the booze."

K.C. kept his emotions simple. "Yeah. I'd just like to get the bastards responsible, that's all."

"So would I," Charley said. "So would I."

They hustled past Mrs. Ryder and went into Hanlon's office. Hanlon was slouched behind his desk, eyes puffy, cheeks sagging from lack of sleep, a brown ceramic coffee mug loose in one hand. The mug, which had his last name printed in block lettering, was resting on a Sony tape cassette with shiny cream-colored casing. There was an empty spool on one of its two spindles.

"Depressed?" Charley asked, as he took a wing seat.

"Still," Hanlon confirmed. "Sometimes it's *not* better in the morning."

K.C. checked his watch. 10:04. "The tape here?"

"Not yet. Should be any minute. I've also got a call in to Chief Inspector Brown—you know, the guy who interrogated Eddie—to see what he can remember about their conversation. He should've called by now."

"Got you worried?" K.C. asked.

Hanlon grimaced. "Yeah. Too many bodies turning up. I keep thinking his could be another." His grimace deepened. "You got anything for hangovers?"

"Try gargling vinegar under a hot shower," K.C. suggested.

"It also helps if you sing," Charley added.

"Least your cold seems to have gone away."

"Yeah. Least my cold seems to have gone away."

Charley considered another droll remark, but Hanlon seemed to lack even the energy to be amused. For the next seven minutes the associate director pretended to read administrative fliers. K.C. and Charley passed the time by playing darts. Charley won, mostly because K.C. kept hitting the wall.

The tape came in at ten o'clock, delivered by a lab tech with a straight-arrow shirt and face. Hanlon had to sign in triplicate before he'd give up his prize. After the tech was gone, Hanlon got on the intercom and told Mrs. Ryder not to disturb them, that they were going to have an orgy. A chair fell over on her end of the line. Big as a building, Charley remarked, then they got down to business.

The lab techs had looped the magnetic ribbon on a fresh spool. The ribbon itself gave evidence of meticulous surgery, banded, spliced, and coated into a usable consistency. Hanlon placed the tape on the empty spindle and threaded it where it belonged. The only light in the room came from a window behind him, where a pattern of overcast gray leaned through the blinds, creating a melancholy mood. Shadowed, Charley and K.C. watched as Hanlon pushed the Start stud; the sound of the spools turning was that of angel wings fighting. Ten seconds passed before voices filtered through.

"This conversation bugged?" a man said abruptly.

"Very funny, Eddie." Chief Inspector Brown didn't sound amused.

"It helps pass the time."

Charley leaned forward, hands tight over his knees. The lab boys had done a first-rate job. The tape's quality was surprisingly clear, just an occasional tic where it had been spliced. Eddie's voice was a stranger's. Charley had met him once, an intro over brewskies followed by a how-are-things exchange, so he didn't really remember its beats. The voice was flat and nasal, New York street swagger, but without the dems or youses. There was a morbid fascination in listening to a dead man's words and a greater stillness had fallen over the already hushed room.

Charley glanced at his companions. K.C. looked scared, like if he moved he might miss the world. Hanlon sat with a hand pushing up one cheek, his eyes cast down in rapt attention.

They could hear the subtle clash of tea cup and saucer, then Brown saying, "You don't seem too perturbed by your capture, Eddie."

"Could be worse." The shrug was perceptible in Eddie's voice. "I mean there *are* people out there trying to kill me."

"Which is why I don't understand why you simply didn't turn yourself in to the police in the first place?"

"Guess I figured I could have it both ways. You know keep my freedom and stay alive while I was at it. Guess I was wrong."

Brown sipped his tea—a cautious sound—then said, "Now, these people want to kill you because you 'bugged' a conversation, is that correct?" He said "bugged" as if using slang was a knife in his side.

"No, they're trying to kill me 'cause of my running off at the mouth. Bad habit I got when I'm drinkin, 'long with being horny."

"Tell me about the tape, Eddie," Brown said patiently, ignoring his last remark. "What was on it?"

During the pause that followed, K.C. hunched forward. Face still cupped in his hand, Hanlon looked without expression at Charley, who returned his gaze.

"You sending me back to the feds?" Eddie asked.

"They have jurisdiction, yes."

"You send me back, I'll tell 'em then," Eddie told him emphatically. K.C. leaned back. Hanlon looked down again, his face falling into shadow as he reached for a Kleenex.

"Very well," Brown agreed, sipping his tea. "Can you tell me who hired you to record this conversation?"

"Uh-uh. No names, least not the important ones, 'til I get back. That's my ace. I tell you everything, you don't have such good reason to make sure I get home safe. Get my drift?"

"I get your drift, Eddie, but I can assure you that you don't have to be concerned about our providing adequate security."

"Yeah, well, I know how these things work," Eddie said knowingly, shifting in his chair.

"Very well. Could you possibly give me a few unimportant names then? That wouldn't harm your 'insurance,' would it?"

There was a longer pause as Eddie mulled it over. "No. No, I guess not," he finally admitted. "Okay," he said, warming to his subject. "I'll give you the bones of what happened."

"The bones?"

"Yeah, you know, I keep the meat, you get the bones."

"I see."

"Yeah, figured you would. Here's what happened. It's back around the first, and I'm just kinda hanging around, looking for some action, when this feebee named Peterson—"

"Feebee?"

"FBI agent. See, he was working a friend of mine name of Joe."

"Joe?"

"Torelli. He's dead now. Peterson, he was working Joe as an informer, small, diddly-shit stuff, only Joe don't know this Peterson is playing both sides, you know, taking it under the table. Now what happens is, Peterson—who looked kinda like JFK, which I always thought was interesting, really resembled him—Peterson, he hears from this outfit he'd had some dealings with back East. They tell him they're looking for somebody to do some business, real specialty job, and I don't mean blowing joints."

"Bugging?" Brown inquired, cutting off any additional obscene references.

"Yeah, that's right," Eddie said, "a little touch and tickle only they want some guy got miles, see, 'cause the local talent's too easy to trace, so this Peterson, he checks out my rep and he comes on by."

"He knew about you through Joe?"

"Yeah, through Joe. So this Peterson shows one night and tells me about this gig in D.C. which pays five G's, cash and carry, no questions asked."

"So you took it."

"Hell, yes. Five was more'n I'd seen in a month of Sundays. Besides, it gives me a chance to visit my cousin who I grew up with in Queens, but who's now living guess where."

"So you went to Washington."

"Yeah, on the nineteenth. I tell Peterson to pass on what I want waiting when I get there, shit I couldn't take on the plane, you know, a kit, tools of the trade. So I fly to D.C.—it was a Tuesday, I remember—four a half hours and I'm there by five, just in time for tea. It's all been arranged. There's rental wheels, nice clean Cad, but old, you know, nothing that's gonna stand out, and a room at the Park Central. I no sooner get in the phone's climbing the walls. There's this guy, calling from a pay number natch, real deep voice, favoring a frog accent I'd say. No small talk—how was your trip, that sorta crap—he gets right to the point. Gives me an address and a time—that night."

"Cutting it rather thin, wasn't he?"

"Very. The address is for some skid trap on the south side, you know, a bunch of crud waiting on the wrecking ball. I'm to go to this certain one and go up some stairs, go down this hallway, third door on the right, and plant a bug even the fucking Holy Ghost couldn't find. Then I'm to hustle a spot and record this meet that's been set up. Then next day I'm to take what I got down to a locker at Dulles and squirrel the tape. My money's waiting in the one next to it—the keys to both was already in my room, 'long with my ticket for my return flight and the kit I'd requested—then I'm to scoot home and that was it, get out clean and simple."

The tape tracked silence before Brown said, "A question, Eddie. Why do you think they chose a tenement to meet in?"

"Least likely place where they'd be seen." The shrug returned to Eddie's voice. "Guess that was it."

"So you went out there that night . . ."

Eddie's voice dropped a decibel, as though he were reliving the evening. "Yeah. Put on my working clothes, black windbreaker, Levis and tennies and a pack in my pocket, then I drove out round ten. I find the place, just a lotta cruddy buildings falling apart with nobody round to notice. It was real dark, a real mean night, moon like something witches cruise, spooky as jack-all, and the wind's blowing to boot, real vicious sucker. Nothing I hate worse'n wind on a cold shitty night, know what I mean?"

"Perfectly. Go on."

"Yeah, so I park the Caddy 'hind this building where nobody can see it, and I open the truck and get out the kit, then I go up these stairs to this shithole of a room where I look round a little—it's the kinda place that ain't even fit for a fucking cockroach. Oh yeah, I'm saying to myself, I got me in with some real big timers, meeting in a hole ain't even fit for a fucking cockroach. Got myself in with some real fucking loonies, that's what I gone and done, but I got my bread so I'm gonna do the job, right?"

"Right."

"So I look round a little and see right off where I can hook a spike mike outside the window, you know, gouge out a tad a' wood on the frame and doctor it over so's the point of the mike's just tickling the pane, that way you vacuum any noise from inside, nothing spiffy required—no conductive point strips, microcircuits, sonic spectrums, lasers, or infrareds—nothing like that. Easy money, I'm saying to myself, easy as a spic with no switch, oh yeah. I'm beginning to figure Frenchie and his friends ain't too swift. I mean, any amateur coulda swung it, any snotnosed punk knows a reflector from a coil, nothing to it. That's what I'm figuring 'til I hear what I'm bugging, then I knew why they couldn't take no chances on a fuckup, that they hadda have somebody real good. The fuckup, that came later."

Brown tasted his tea again and returned cup to saucer with the mildest of clatters. "All right, Eddie," he said, "Let's continue to do this chronologically."

"How?"

"In the order the event occurred, to avoid the possibility of missing anything. You finished planting the mike at what time?"

"Coupla minutes past eleven."

"And then?"

"And then I hustled my ass over to the building 'cross the street and set up shop and wait."

"Where were you in relationship to the first building?"

"Second floor, eye level with the room 'cross the way. That's the best for acoustics, you know, eye level."

"Could you be seen from across the street?"

"Not if I was careful, which I was. There was boards nailed over what's left of the window of the room I'm in, you know, like an X, so I could kinda peek out when I want, and the room was dark with just enough moon sneaking through so as I could see fuck-all. It was colder'n a witch's tit and the wind's beating on through the boards and I'm sitting dragging on a coffin nail, sitting waiting with nothing to do 'cept read the fucking writing on the wall and smell the piss in a corner. That's what I'm doing, smoking a ciggie and watching the goddamn paint peel—oh yeah, real good times, I tell you—when long 'bout half past eleven this car cozies up to this alley 'cross the street. Liked the way he parked, real sly, sorta like a cat creeping on something all cool and low."

"All right. So this man parks his car. Was he alone?"

"Yeah, just one guy."

"And what happened then?"

"This guy gets outta the car. What do you think, he's there to make out!"

"That's what I'm trying to find out, Eddie, what he's there to do. Did you notice what kind of car it was?"

"Never had no chance, not 'til later. Where he's parked, you can't see squat, yeah, real sly, just like a fucking cat. Never saw *him* neither far as that goes, least so I could say what he looks like. I didn't look out the window 'til after I know he's inside."

"The building across the street?"

"That's the one. Saw the shape of him through a window later, that's all I seen."

"Now you say that he arrived around half past eleven, yet earlier you stated that the meeting wasn't scheduled until twelve, is that correct?"

"Yeah, that's right."

"Then why do you think he was there so prematurely—so early?"

"Probably to check things out, see if he's been set up, but there's no chance of him finding nothing. I take pride in my work. No fucking chance."

"I'm sure there wasn't, Eddie. Now," Brown said with a sigh of accomplishment, "we have one of the participants in our drama on the scene. How long was it before his accomplice arrived?"

"More'n half an hour after the first guy."

"Did you notice the exact time?"

"Twelve-twelve."

Brown hesitated, as though wondering if Eddie had suddenly acquired a stutter; then he confirmed the time. "Twelve minutes past twelve. So he was late."

"Maybe he hit traffic or started to get cold feet or kept plumber's hours."

"And nothing happened between half past eleven and twelve-twelve?"

"Yeah. This goddamn roach crawls outta a busted bulb like some fucking genie. Got almost to the window."

"I mean—"

"Like split pea on my shoe."

"Across—"

"Takes me twenty to clean it off."

"—the street."

"Huh?"

"Nothing between half past eleven and twelve-twelve?"

"Uh-uh. Guess the guy, he just sat waiting like me. Maybe he has more to do to pass the time—the graffiti was better where he was."

"When this second man arrived, was he also alone?"

"Yeah, just like the other one. Only diff'rence was, the blond shows and parks right beneath me. The other guy, he's got more smarts about it, parking off the street, but maybe blondie ain't had too much experience at—"

"Excuse me for interrupting, but you actually saw the second man then?"

"Huh?"

"You said he was a blond, so you must have seen him."

"Sure."

"Why did you take the chance?"

"Meaning what?"

"If I follow your line of reasoning, you made certain the first man was inside the building before you looked outside—to avoid the possibility of having him see you, is that correct?"

"So?"

"Then why take the risk of having the blond chap spot you?"

Eddie answered impatiently, as though the answer was obvious. "'Cause it wouldn't have made no diff'rence if he does since he's the one having the room bugged. I knew it had to be him 'cause the other guy was driving a compact—I could tell by the engine. Blondie's car, it had a big V-eight sound, so I knew."

"I don't understand."

"You know, the frog's friend's supposed to be driving a big old De Soto," Eddie said, the impatience hurrying his words. "That's what he told me."

"But you didn't tell me," Brown reminded him. Charley could hear him muting his irritation.

"Oh, yeah, guess I didn't. Sorry about that. You know, I can't remember jack-all, this ain't a fucking quiz show, 'Price Is Right.' Anyway, it was a real clunker, lousy with dents. Least I'll give the guy that. Knew enough not to drive class out there. Old De Soto, that's what. Black, maybe a real deep brown."

"I see. Now what about the blond fellow? Can you give me a more detailed description."

Eddie hesitated, then tried. "Not young, not old, maybe on the short end of forty. Dressed cheap, but expensive cheap, if you know what I mean, which *wasn't* so smart. Tad on the skinny side like me, with real cold blue eyes, kind you see on TV, you know, the guy pointing the gun, only it's somebody else pulling the trigger."

There was a short but distinct noise from the mike in the interrogation room; the squeak of an electronic mouse.

"What kinda equipment you using?" Eddie said, distracted by the flaw.

"I wouldn't know, Eddie."

"Not the best," Eddie remarked.

"As you were saying, the blond chap . . ."

"Yeah, the blond guy gets outta his car, looks back once over his shoulder—that's how come I seen his face—then he goes 'cross the street and into the other building, so I light my second ciggie, turn on my equipment, put on my phones and listen in."

"Let me interrupt you again for a moment, Eddie, if you don't mind?"

"Not at all."

"This is a very important and private conversation you were about to tape, something I imagine its participants would prefer surrendering to as few ears as possible . . . You look confused."

"Well . . ."

"To get to the point, I assume you were given the privilege of listening in on the off chance that if something of a technical nature went wrong with the bugging, you could correct it. Is that reasonably accurate?"

"Yeah, reasonably so. You been around a little, ain't you?"

"Sometimes I wonder . . . Go on with what you were telling me."

"I'll try and get back in the mood . . . Okay, I got my equipment set up and I'm listening in. After a minute or so I hear the blond go in the room, then there's this pause like he and the other guy don't know what to say, not even Hi, how are you, then they start rapping. They're talking real low, keeping it down like they're afraid of the walls, even though there ain't supposed to be nobody for miles, but that don't make no diff'rence 'cause I'm getting it all." Eddie's voice fell a decibel again. "Colder'n a witch's tit and I'm squatting and listening on this cruddy floor like a spaced-out junkie . . . You got a smoke?" There was a pause—maybe Brown had left the room, maybe he was afraid of the walls—then Eddie explained, "You know, a cigarette."

After several more seconds of silence, Charley could hear the swack of a match being struck.

"Thanks," Eddie said, exhaling.

"You're welcome." Brown returned to his tea, rattled about, before continuing.

"So they talked. Can you tell me, Eddie, as long as we're not using names, what they discussed?"

Eddie took a long unhealthy drag on his cigarette; his voice almost got lost in his lungs.

"Yeah, sure. Why not?" Once into his story, he seemed to be enjoying himself, turning tricks with his knowledge. "The blond guy was buying the other one, simple as that. See, blondie and his friends, they had something big comin' down and he wanted to pay this dude for protection. This other guy could offer that, he's got that kinda muscle."

"The blond chap wanted to pay him for some sort of protection from interference with their plan?"

"That's right, yeah."

"What was their plan?"

"A scheme, that's what blondie called it, a scheme. You're asking a lotta questions, you know that?"

"That's my job, Eddie, to ask a lot of questions."

"What a life, huh? You know, I didn't catch your name?"

"Chief Inspector Brown."

"No, I mean what your friends call you."

"Thomas," Brown said, not very comfortably.

"Thomas. Not Tom?" Eddie considered the name. "Thomas. I can live with it."

"You were saying, about the plan?"

"Yeah, the scheme. They wanted to set up this sorta underworld bank, high-interest loans to the wiseguy crowd. Blondie went into more detail'n that, but that was the gist of it. Cute, huh?"

"Very."

"Oh, yeah, they was real cute, and this guy they're greasing could keep 'em safe from heat like you said, not a hundred percent, you understand, but close enough. Sorta like sweet-rolling a cop to watch out for your turf."

"Is he a cop?"

"No, not exactly, not in the real pure sense."

Whitehall protocol showed a few teeth. "Can you tell me *what* he is?"

"A real son of a bitch," Eddie said without rancor.

"Seriously."

"No." Eddie's refusal was emphatic, no tricks at all.

"Then that was it? That was the extent of what you recorded?"

"Fuck, no. That wasn't the best of it. See, the best was a little detail blondie threw in gratis at the end, something he told the other guy he was gonna have done to insure the success of their little project."

"Which was?"

"Kill somebody. Somebody real big."

"Who?"

"Uh-uh. No names, Thomas."

"Sorry, Eddie. I forgot."

"I'll bet."

"Did this other chap accept this part of blondie's proposal?"

"Well, he didn't seem so happy . . ."

"In the real pure sense."

"In the real pure sense, but yeah, sorta."

"When is this assassination supposed to occur?"

"Tomorrow. New Year's Eve, which is why you'd better get me back home in a hurry."

"Your flight leaves at six-thirty tonight. Let me ask you, Eddie . . . Is that what frightened you so much, that they were going to murder someone important? Is that why you went into hiding?"

More silence, except for the angel glide of the tape, then Eddie carefully replied, "No, it wasn't that so much . . . I mean, you can kill anybody and it ain't that much of a shock no more, not the way the world's been goin' . . . No, that ain't what shook me so much—it was that they weren't playing it straight . . ." He seemed to be fumbling for his thoughts. "See, I done gigs for other guys who weren't exactly pussies, but they played by the rules. And that's what was wrong here, they was already double-crossing their own."

"How?"

"Can't tell you that, I'll tell 'em back in D.C., but that's what got me so scared, shoulda seen my hands. I figured—see look at 'em now, Buddy Rich—I figured a situation like that, everybody's open game."

"Expendable?"

"Yeah, especially the little guys, like me, what I always been. Maybe I was wrong. I mean, I got paid, got back to L.A. . . . What do you think?" He sounded genuinely interested in what the chief inspector thought.

"I don't know," Brown said, removed. "There's one thing that's bothering me, though, Eddie—one thing that is really bothering me. Did the blond chap and the other fellow use each other's names during their conversation?"

"What do you think? No way."

"Did Peterson or the Frenchman tell you who they were?"

"Hell, no."

"Then how did you know? You're telling me you know their names, yet I don't see how you possibly could. Perhaps you won't give me any names because you don't know them yourself—"

"You're trying to trick me."

"No, I'm not Eddie, I'm really not. I just can't see how you could conceivably know their names."

"My cousin," Eddie blurted. "I got the names from my cousin."

"I don't understand. The cousin you wanted to visit while you were in Washington?"

"Yeah. Can we walk this back a little, back to when I finished taping the conversation?"

"Of course."

"Okay, after they finish their business I wait 'til they're gone—I watched 'em leave—then I drive back to my hotel and catch four hours shut-eye. The next morning I go to Dulles like I've been told and I find this locker, number 492, and I lock the tape in it, then I open up the locker next to it—there's a briefcase inside. I take the briefcase to the john, settle all cozy into a stall, and snap it open. There's five G's in hundreds and my ticket back to L.A. My flight's in half an hour and I shoulda just gone to boarding and waited, only I don't, 'cause I'm curious. See, it makes me nervous not knowing who I been playing for after what I just heard up in that shithole of a room. So I find me a phone and call my cousin. I tell him where I am, that I'd love to stop off and see him and the kid sister, but I gotta get back to L.A. He says, Gee that's a shame and what can I do for you then? and I ask him if he still dates this broad—can't recall her name—who works for DMV."

"D.M.V?"

"Department of Motor Vehicles. My cousin, he says, yeah, and what about it? So I ask him to have her check the plates of these two cars, see who they belong to, do it like it's no big deal."

"Which two cars?"

"The fucked-up clunker and the compact, a tan something or other. Like I told you, I looked out the window and saw 'em drive away. The moon was good and I got the numbers."

"Go on."

"Yeah, well, my cousin says okay, he'll be sure to ask and give me a buzz after I get back home. So he does, with the info, only he ain't too eager to hand it over just like that. He wants to know what I'm doing fucking with people like this, then he gives me this song and dance about how he's been on the short end as of late and how about a loan? So I tell him, give me the names and we'll talk. So he does and I say Jesus F. Christ! and he says, yeah, exactly, and what do I say to five big ones to tide him over and I say, here he was supposed to be doing me a favor and I can swing a hundred, and he says, fuck you, Jack! and hangs the fuck up."

Brown took a while, sounded like he was drinking from an empty cup, before saying, "And then you took a flight to London."

"No, then I called Joe Torelli and asked him if he wanted to go get drunk. Then I caught a flight. You know, my cousin and me didn't part the best of friends, but I'm worried about him. Maybe you could find out if he's okay. Everybody I talked to seems to end up dead, even some I didn't, and I got some concern. His name's Karl Vaitonis." Eddie spelled it.

"I'll see what I can find out."

"Thanks, I'd really appreciate that."

"You're welcome."

There was a pause. The conversation seemed to be winding down.

"That good tea?" Eddie asked.

"Very."

"Looks like good tea."

"Do you want some?"

"Yeah, maybe."

"I'll get a cup for you in a minute. There's one thing that's still bothering me though . . ."

"Yeah?"

"I just wish you could give me a name, Eddie. I would feel much better if you could."

"Just one name, huh?"

"Yes, just one name. It would make me feel much more confident that what you've told me is the truth." It was a last-ditch, ploy; the inspector's voice was offhand and without hope, so Eddie's response must have come as a genuine surprise.

"Okay," Eddie said, "one name, Thomas, 'cause you still need the rest."

"I'm listening, Eddie."

"I'll give you blondie's, the lawyer's. He's important, but not so much as the other guy."

"Yes?"

"Well, see like I told you, my cousin, he got the plates through this broad. The one guy's car was registered in his own name, but the shyster's, it wasn't. It was under the name of some kid, which of course blondie wasn't, providing you can count past thirty. So being real clever like I was, not to mention curious, I call up this punk who happens to be in the book. I tell him I'm from Traffic Control, part of a new program trying to give suckers a break before sending them their warrant, that he's got this ticket outstanding from a coupla weeks back, and the punk says that can't be, I don't even *have* the fucking car, I loaned it to my fucking uncle to get it repaired. So I asked him who might your fucking uncle be, and so he tells me."

"Yes?"

"Dake. His name's Lawrence Dake. Could I have a little cream in—"

Charley had become so immersed in the tape that it took him several seconds to realize that Hanlon had shut it off. Charley glanced up; Hanlon's face had paled with the shock of revelation and his gaze had traveled to some distant place.

"Jesus . . ." he muttered under his breath.

Charley and K.C. exchanged glances before turning back to him.

"What is it?" Charley asked. "What's the matter?"

It took Hanlon a moment to focus on Charley, his eyes slow in arriving.

"What is it?" Charley repeated.

"Dake . . ." Hanlon said softly, the wonder and amazement evident in his voice. "Lawrence Dake is Matthew Byrne's best friend."

32

The Country Club Set

Black angels danced on the gray light falling through the blinds; then Hanlon replayed Eddie's last lines to make sure the name was right.

It was. It was also bad TV. You could have walked a mile on the silence before K.C. cleared his throat and showed he could understate.

"Confusing, ain't it?"

Charley looked to Hanlon for clarity. "What do you make of it?"

"That God isn't in his heaven. What the hell can you make of it!" He was playing to the audience; bewilderment was making him dramatic, or maybe it was just that he was Irish.

Charley scratched his scar and said, "This room soundproofed?"

"Like a vault," Hanlon assured him, then he was pacing, doing a turn.

"What the hell can I make of it? Byrne has known Dake for more years than I can count. It's a perfect marriage. Byrne is Southern blueblood, Dake is New England noveau riche, a corporate lawyer who knows all the nasty little legal maneuvers for breaking a fledgling company's back. He and Byrne share three-hundred-dollar wines and two-fifty-a-side golf games. Their wives trade gossip and tennis strokes, their kids have attended the same schools from prep to college. They probably even screw at the same time. If two men ever ran by the same clock, they're it."

"Which means maybe it was Byrne who Dake had the meet with?" K.C.'s assurance didn't carry too far.

"I don't know, but let's try it from there. Say Dake throws out feelers to his friend and finds he's receptive to a little corruption, so they set up a meet to discuss terms. As head of the Bureau, Byrne is in a perfect position to block any large-scale investigative action against Cedillo and company's venture."

"But Byrne is only one man, he ain't the whole Bureau," K.C. objected.

"One man who dictates policy and makes the final decisions as to who we go after and who we don't. For thirty years Hoover pretended there wasn't a Mafia, which is maybe why it's such a going concern today."

"You mean Hoover was on the take?!" K.C. said.

"No, he was just dumb," Hanlon said, staring down the shredded bulldog scowl on the wall.

Charley said, "I still don't see how they'd get all that much benefit by buying off Byrne." It was prime time, fat cats coughing the Fifth into mikes, he wasn't having this conversation, sweet Jesus, but to Hanlon it was kicks, doing his job, he was just warming up:

"Okay, look at it this way, we live in a time and a place where everyone's looking for an edge, right?"

"To smooth things out, right," K.C. agreed.

"No creases," Charley added. He couldn't just sit there looking dumb.

Hanlon nodded. "Now, let's walk it back a little, like Eddie would say. Victor Cedillo has a scheme, according to Suar—" He cut himself short as he glanced at Charley. "Sorry, almost forgot, no names." Charley had promised. "According to somebody, Cedillo has a plan, something worth about the weight of Texas oil, something a little better than Social Security for his retirement years, a bank with no overhead or name, just someplace for wiseguys to go in a pinch. Now, I'm just winging it, but here's how something like that would probably work, according to what somebody told you, Charley—some legit-looking rep of some syndicate jets down to Panama or Africa and meets with some legit-looking rep of Cedillo's at Zaire Greater Enterprises, or whatever, and arranges for a loan for construction, say for gold dredging in Utah. There's a transfer of a cozy three or four mil—the money in fact going for prost, H and C, porn, your sister Bernice, any of your mainstream delights—the loan repayable at interest to beat the prime rate all to hell. You still with me?"

"On roller skates," Charley confirmed. He was starting to enjoy this. K.C. just grunted.

"So it's a damned good plan Cedillo has. Get out of Venezuela and set up shop in the land of hotdogs and sweet opportunity, with Dake running the business side and Renaud handling the muscle, only Cedillo doesn't quite make it. He runs into something he can't control, nature, and ends up all crippled in some rinky-dink town on an island that was just a place to fly over, leaving Dake and Renaud to go solo until he's better."

"Cedillo passes instructions on from his hospital bed in Neiba and they carry them out," Charley said, "getting ready for when their boss can fly to the States."

"Staying away from storms and lakes, only maybe the plane crash has made them all think a little more about how chance can get in the way of the best-laid plans. The way they'd see it, the heat's no threat—anything the cops come across, it's our baby, they'd turn it over to us. So it's the Bureau Cedillo and his friends have to sweat. They'd have to guess how easy it'd be for some junior agent just out of diapers to stumble over their plan, through an informer or say maybe dumb blind luck. So Cedillo figures they need an edge, a wall you can put up in brick. So they think about it, but not very long, because it's not hard to see that they've got their edge right there in their palm, Larry Dake's golfing partner and pal, master of all he surveys, the director of the FBI, Matthew Byrne. Have him on your side and the odds all swing in your favor. I mean, buying a Phil Peterson is nice, but it's squat compared to this. Sooner or later, every important piece of change comes over the director's desk. So say some junior stud stumbles across Cedillo's scheme, like Charley did with somebody. He's not going to get it all at once, just bits and pieces, because Cedillo and company are going to have covered themselves, they're going to have a few layers of insulation."

"No tapes in the Oval Office."

"Dating yourself."

"Tell me."

"No, no tapes in the Oval Office. So what's going to happen is that the kid's going to send word up through the chain of command until it reaches you know who. Now, providing he's on the take, that gives him a chance to sideline the investigation or steer it in the wrong direction, or if it's too far along for that, to let Cedillo know he's got to cover his tracks, try another location, close up shop for a while, or maybe feed us a scapegoat or two. Having the chief on his payroll gives Cedillo options and time, which, like Eddie said, might not be a hundred percent against getting nailed, but it's as close as you can get. And that's just the beginning, just the tip. Have the head of the second most powerful agency in the government—autonomous, answering only to the president and mostly not even then—have him in your pocket, there's no end to the games you both can play—grand scale graft, buying pols by the bushel, scams and schemes and cloak and dagger plots, abuse of power, Jesus, you get the picture, no end to the fun. All you need is imagination and the guts to act it out. Have the director of the FBI on your side and it's like going through hell with six angels and the Holy Ghost riding on your coattails."

Charley was smiling—had to, but so was Hanlon. He also knew it was prime time; he was giving them value, feeding them the big speeches, but damn his Irish soul, it was making sense, only Charley needed more:

"Let's say you're right about Cedillo having Dake buy Matthew Byrne. If they're such pals, why not discuss it over a couple highballs at home? Why drive out, excuse the expression, to hell and back in the middle of the night?"

Hanlon was on a roll. "Okay," he said. "Now I'm still just

"Self-destructive?" Hanlon suggested. "Trying to get caught?"

"Matthew Byrne?!"

"I know, I know. It doesn't add up."

Hanlon sighed. A sparrow fluttered past the window, chasing illusions of sunlight and warmth. Hanlon sighed again. "Lot of questions, with not many hours to find the answers."

"Afternoon soap," Charley said.

"Big screen," said K.C.

"Something big and bloody is going to happen," Hanlon said, "and we're not going to know what until after it's over, maybe not even then." He leaned forward and reached for the phone.

"Who're you calling?"

"Matthew Byrne. See if he has a little time for some friendly conversation."

"Pat?" Charley said.

"Yeah?" Hanlon said, the receiver cocked by his ear.

"You sure your phone's not tapped?"

"Jesus," Hanlon swore as he started to dial. "Don't say that. Not even joking."

"I wasn't."

Puffing insouciantly on his meerschaum pipe, Matthew Byrne opened his brown calf's-leather appointment book and checked his schedule while he waited for Hanlon. The robin's-egg blue pages were filled with precise notations regarding the day's activities: breakfast—freshly squeezed orange juice and half a grapefruit—served by one of his secretaries at nine, a twenty-minute call to his broker at ten, an eleven o'clock reminder to his wife to have the muffler checked on the Jensen, lunch with the vice president at noon, the rest of the upcoming afternoon smothered in a minor budgetary squabble with federal auditors. A typical day.

During the conversation with his broker, between mutually expressed concerns regarding the fate of Dow Jones, the subject of the 747 tragedy had come up. "Unfortunate" was the sum of Byrne's expression of regret. The broker had shortly found a convenient excuse for getting off the phone. The man's reaction didn't come as a shock; Byrne knew that people considered him a cold fish. Perhaps he was. Detachment was as much a part of his makeup as organization.

He had learned both qualities from his father; his father, partriarch and provider but never a friend, a disagreeable presence at the far end of the table, never dad or my old man but always sir, a voice not from the heart but from the geometric prisms of logic. 'Passion is a property of orators and the poor and as such should be distrusted,' his father had pontificated. So be it. Men were to be measured not by their good works but by their success and even by his father's standards, God bless his unlamented soul, Matthew had succeeded. He had observed all the proper ceremonies of his class: Law degree magna cum laude from Harvard, burgeoning Louisville practice, wedlock at twenty-nine to a Radcliffe princess. There was, as to be expected, no passion in their union, but there were, as required, two belated children, both girls and both as insipid and frivolous as their mother.

The family prospered and, much to everyone's relief, didn't settle into the pastoral elegance of Kentucky. Byrne could have lived out his years there in casual repetition, letting the junior partners handle the briefs while he devoted his time to small eccentricities and breeding thoroughbreds, but his ambitions ran to more conspicuous symbols of power. He coveted a site in the public eye and a few hosannas sung, however rotely, in his name. The post of director of the FBI was open. Although he had a background in criminal law, there were far more qualified aspirants, but none as devious. Byrne lobbied, maneuvered, manipulated, and stabbed or patted the right backs, and the president, with his own eye to an election year, anointed him. Naturally, protests and a few flailings of indignation followed in media waves. Byrne ignored them all, secure in his knowledge that he had achieved his proper place, that God was in his gilded heaven.

* * *

The pipe was going out. Byrne tapped a careful ounce of Dunhill Reserve into the pouch. At that moment, his intercom buzzed and a secretary announced Hanlon.

"Send him in," Byrne said, striking a match.

Hanlon entered almost on top of the command. Byrne motioned him to a seat while he breathed life into his pipe.

Settling into elegant leather, Hanlon looked around. No matter how many times he'd been here, he never seemed prepared for the board-room symmetry of Byrne's office, which was half again the size of his own. Everything—chairs, cabinets, pictures—seemed at parallel angles to their twins on the opposite side of the room; not the most pleasant of effects, unless your taste runs to two-way mirrors.

"What is it, Pat?" Byrne said impatiently, as he finally produced an acceptable puff of smoke.

"Nothing much. Just thought I'd see if you needed me for anything this afternoon."

"I would have told you if I had."

"Yeah, I guess you would've. Shame about the 747, all those people."

"Yes, unfortunate. Have you heard Scotland Yard's interrogation of Eddie Mikenas yet?"

"Yeah, as a matter of fact I have."

"Anything of interest?"

"Ah, no, not really."

Byrne grimaced mildly as he cleared the smoke from his lungs. Hanlon was beginning to irritate him. He had a crowded afternoon and evening scheduled, and his assistant was wasting his time with information that could have been communicated much more briefly over the phone. Not only that, but Hanlon was acting like a shy schoolgirl around him, sheepish and evasive, and that irritated him even more.

"Nothing at all of importance on the tape?" Suspicion curled around the question.

"No, not that we didn't already know."

Byrne studied his thumb like a vain woman painting her nails. "Well, it's a strange, unattractive business, one that we'll certainly want to have answers for. Perhaps with this Mikenas's death it's finished. No matter what, I believe it can be put in abeyance until tomorrow."

"Um." Hanlon watched the smoke climb toward the ceiling. "What're you doing for New Year's, Matthew?"

"Why?" Byrne snapped, a little more sharply than he intended. The last thing he wanted was some sort of party invitation.

"Just asking."

Byrne relaxed slightly. "Dinner at home, then Linn and I plan to spend some time with Lawrence Dake and his wife. We have for years. You know that."

"Yeah. Guess I'd forgotten."

Byrne glanced at his wall clock. 11:17. "Is that all?" he asked peremptorily.

"Think so," Hanlon said, rising from the chair. "Have a Happy New Year's, Matthew."

"Thank you. You too." Byrne's voice was distant, his mind somewhere else. In the late morning light, he looked like one of his pictures on the wall.

It was 3:40 by Hanlon's watch. They were scrunched up in his Datsun in underground parking, low-slung concrete for a view. K.C. was worrying a molar with a toothpick in the backseat. Charley was in front, studying his own hands. Hanlon was behind the wheel, searching for answers.

"How long has it been since this all started?" Hanlon wondered. "A week?"

"And a half by my calendar," Charley said.

"Seems longer."

"Much."

Wheels shuddered by overhead, sounded like bricks dancing. After they were gone K.C. said, "What now?"

Hanlon had his answer ready. "Byrne leaves here at five-thirty. I want you to tail him, K.C."

"Just like in the cop shows?"

"Just like that."

"Who do I use for backup?"

"Nobody. You want to try to explain all this in the next hour? Besides, who do you trust?"

"Getting paranoid?"

"Damn right."

"What about you? What're you gonna do?"

"Never thought you'd ask," Hanlon said with some of his old style. "I'm going to drive out to Dake's, confront him with what we have and hope he'll crack and give me what we need to stop whatever's coming down."

"He'll deny everything," Charley said. "We're holding deuces at best."

"Not even that. We've got a dead man's testimony that would stand up in court about as long as the telling. Dake knows that as well as I do, but we've got to try something."

"Do I go along with K. C.?" Charley took it for granted.

"No. You're out of it, Charley. Thanks, and I really mean that because you've done a helluva lot, but you're still a civilian. Odds are it's going to get hedgy tonight and there's going to be some shooting. I know you can handle a gun," Hanlon said, overriding the objection Charley began, "but a couple hundred a week isn't enough to risk getting shot. You're temporary help, remember? Maintenance and after hours. Go home and get some rest, Charley. We'll let you know what happens."

Hanlon had made his speech, kept down its size, but Charley caught the hurt as he avoided Charley's eyes. A bond had formed between the three men in the past few days, the kind soldiers find in war, and now Hanlon was doing what he knew was best, but it wasn't easy.

"That it?" Charley said. "No way I can talk you out of it?"

"Only if you doubled off the left. Besides, I don't know why you'd want to."

"Stubborn."

"I know," Hanlon said affectionately. "Go home, Charley."

"Yeah." Charley opened the car door. "Make sure you let me know."

K.C. said, "Figured you'd fight it harder."

"So did I." Charley shook hands and wished them luck, then he broke away before the emotion had time to take hold. As he strode toward Visitor Parking, he heard Hanlon say to K.C., "You know what I wish? You know what I wish I had time for?"

"Feed the pigeons?"

"You got it. Crazy, hun?"

"You want to hear something crazier? Me too."

Charley almost turned then and went back, to what purpose he didn't know, but instead he kept on walking toward the Buick.

As he passed through the terraced shadows, he heard soft, low laughter behind him, a shared moment he should have been part of but wasn't, and an ache started in the pit of his stomach and worked its way up, leaving his throat dry as dust as he got into the rented car and drove away, the speed gathering like the pounding in his chest.

33

Calls

Charley went past Franklin Park on his way back to the hotel. The day was cold and fading, the benches barren, the pigeons gone.

He told himself, as he inched along with the late afternoon traffic, that he hadn't fought it harder because of Lisa; stack up your priorities like an infant's blocks and it came down to this—stay alive and go home to her and hope she'll still have you. It's nearly finished; you're not paid to take chances—2300 miles back to L.A. and it'll all be a blur, and a bullet knows no distance beyond its own. Stay alive, he told himself as he drove under the gunmetal-gray sky, because the cards all come up skeletons, and it only makes sense. Stay alive, because you already beat one kind of foolish pride when you sent the flowers, and roses are better than a wreath. The answers he gave himself were good ones, as firm as faith, so it was hard to explain the way the ache remained, lingering like memory.

Back at the Three Seasons, the desk clerk told him of Lisa's call and her request for a return. Up in his room, Charley tried; it was 1:30 L.A. time and he phoned her at her office. Fran Drucker took the call and said she'd left hours ago in a hurry and without explanation. Fran added that the flowers were lovely and asked in a half whisper what was going on? Charley thanked her for her time and broke the connection.

He had no better luck trying Lisa at home; he wore out the rug listening to the phone ring. The pacing stayed with him after he hung up. The ache had shifted to the kind of nervous edge that leaves the belly half sick and the back of the neck tight. He had the feeling of being in limbo, of leaving things incomplete.

The light through the fourth-floor window was gloomy, deepening his mood. He drew the curtains and switched on the ceiling fixture, but the grayness kept pushing through. He wanted to get out and run, let the cold air fill his lungs, yet he stayed caged within the room, waiting for the shrillness of the phone, waiting for calls he couldn't afford to miss. At 8:27, after a few hours of trying to watch TV and less of reading Chandler, the phone gave him a break:

"Charley, it's K.C." K.C.'s voice was steady. Charley tried to keep his own in neutral as he sat on a corner of the bed.

"Where are you?"

"Still at headquarters. Somethin' I figured you should know—I called Dake's office a while back, told his secretary I was calling from IRS."

"Why—?"

"You gonna let me explain?"

"Why not."

"I told her there was some discrepancies—looked it up in the dictionary to make sure I had the right word—some discrepancies in Mr. Dake's filings for the last few years, some things we hadda clear up. Told her I needed some info 'bout any trips he might've taken. Don't ask me why, but see I had this hunch there might be somethin' there we could use."

"K.C.?"

"Yeah?"

"Why're you telling me this? I'm out of it, remember?"

"Not as far as I'm concerned. Took me a while to decide, but I figure you got a right to know."

Charley thanked him sincerely. K.C. told him to forget it.

"Okay, now you gotta bear with me. I might go a little slow 'cause I gotta make reference to my notes . . ."

"I'll bear with you. What'd you learn?"

"That Dake had taken a plane to . . . Neiba in April."

"When Cedillo was there?"

"Yeah. Dake was gone a week 'fore coming' back to the States. I asked his secretary—her name's Teresa, real sweet gal by the way—I ask her why her boss was flyin' to the Dominican Republic and she says she don't know the details."

"Nice," Charley said admiringly.

"Yeah, well, I ain't so smart, but there's a few ideas I can come up with when the moon's right."

"Your uncle would be proud."

"Doubt it. Anyway, the part I just told you, that part's good, but you wanta hear the kicker?"

"Wouldn't miss it."

"The kicker is, I say to Teresa, funny place, ain't it, the Dominican Republic, for him to be goin' to outta the blue, and she says . . . no, not really, maybe he had some friends there to visit, and I say like what kinda friends, I don't get it, and she says maybe he made some friends last year, maybe he stopped off there last year on his way back from South America, and I say . . . I still don't get it, and she says, well, when he was a . . . guest lecturer for six months in Venezuela, teachin' law at the . . . Universidad Central."

"Where?!"

"Yeah, that's right, got it all here in my notes."

"Have you told Hanlon?"

"Ain't had a chance. He left for Dake's a coupla hours back."

"Home or office?"

"Home. See, that's what gave me the idea of calling Teresa. Pat, he had already checked with Dake's office—made the call from a pay phone with me standin' there beside him—to see if Dake was there, and she told him he'd gone home for the day."

K.C. paused to catch his breath. "Well, like I said, figured you'd like to know. Now I gotta figure out how to tail Byrne without him knowing. Maybe if I try a disguise. How does a little black mask and Hi-ho Silver sound?"

"Like bad casting. K.C.?"

"Yeah?"

"Good luck."

"You already wished me that."

"I'm doing it again."

"Okay. Be seeing you. Maybe I'll come on by, fill you in after this is finished."

"Yeah, sure."

"Oh, yeah, a coupla things 'fore I go. The girlfriend of Karl Vaitonis, the gal that worked for D.M.V.? We did some checkin', found out who she was, Linda somethin'. Been missin' since last Wednesday. We think she might've turned up on a police blotter though. They fished a still, a Jane Doe, outta Chesapeake Bay Monday that matches her description."

"She still have her hands?"

"Yeah, but not her head. That was downstream. And you remember that Chief Inspector Brown?"

"Also dead?"

"Naw. He phoned half past. Seems he hadn't called 'cause he's been busy, jamming on 'nother case, gut job, some poor slob name of Henry Sykes."

"Glad to hear there's somebody still breathing."

"Ain't it nice. Bye, Charley."

"Bye."

Charley hung up, looked down at his feet; the rug was down to a nub. He wandered into the lavender bathroom and stared at his reflection in the mirror on the wall. His face was somebody else's, a stranger's. Turning his head to one side, then the other, with his hand, he examined his mustache. No matter how grim his efforts with scissors and razor, it would never be even. It bothered him in the same way the cup on the runway had, and with one ear cocked for the phone, he applied soap and lather. Using a fresh blade, he shaved with care, scraping the right side of his upper lip clean. Before he could turn his attention to the left, the phone rang again. With the moist lather tickling his nostril, he hurried to snatch up the receiver, certain it was Lisa.

"Hello?"

"Mr. Tone?" Intuition wasn't always Charley's strong point; the voice was male and familiar. It was also more agitated than Charley had heard it before.

"Señor Suarez?"

"Yes. I'll get right to the point. I just had a call from Paul Renaud."

Suarez hesitated, seemed to expect shock or astonishment, but didn't he know?—nothing surprised Charley anymore. Charley listened intently, trying to catch the color of a lie in Suarez's voice.

"The call, as you might imagine, came as a real shock. So I did what he told me."

"Which was?"

"That he had been instructed by the American lawyer, the one I mentioned—"

"His name is Dake. Lawrence Dake." Charley saw Suarez's face changing, the way it had when he'd confronted him about the oxford shoes and saffron socks with stirrups embroidered on the sides.

"Dake?" Suarez said. It was as bright as the oxfords.

"He taught last year in Caracas, guest lecturer at Universidad Central. You met him there. You got him together with Cedillo."

The silence got up and walked. Charley waited it out. After a while, Suarez came back, heavy with resignation. "How did you know?"

"I didn't, but it's the only thing that makes any sense, the only thing that adds up. You met Dake there and—?"

"And he was searching for something in his life. Like me, he needed something more, an edge, some excitement, a bit of melodrama."

"Don't we all. So you introduced him to Victor, who was exciting and melodramatic, liked John Wayne."

"Yes. I introduced them. Victor told him about his problem and its possible solution, a profitable new start in a profitable new land. Dake felt he could help him with his plans, felt they could help each other."

"Why'd you lie before about knowing Dake?"

"For the same reason I didn't want to admit knowing Victor. I didn't want to seem too involved. I didn't want your people coming around."

"But you told me about Cedillo. Why not Dake?"

Charley had to wait again. He could hear Suarez's labored breathing. When he spoke, his voice was strained and frightened.

"Because," he explained, "I didn't know what would get back. If something had somehow gotten back to Victor, well, he has sentimental loyalties, I might manage to stay alive. But Dake is different. There's no emotion to the man. I knew I could count on nothing except dying if he found out I had given you his name. And I was right, which is what I called about before we went off in another direction—Paul Renaud phoned tonight and told me that he had been instructed six months ago, by Dake, to kill me. I wondered out loud why he hadn't. Because of sentimental reasons, he replied. Because of better times when we were both close to Victor and the world seemed to make sense. He said he had told

Dake that he had followed his instructions. I don't think he particularly cared if Dake found out otherwise."

"Did he tell you why Dake wanted you dead in the first place?"

"No. He asked me, very politely, just to listen. With Renaud, following his requests seems to be the best policy."

"You believed him, about the sentimental reasons?"

"Yes, I think that might have been true, I can understand that, but I can't understand the rest of what he told me."

"Which was?"

"Why he had really called, and I can't understand it at all. He wanted me to pass some information on to the FBI, very pertinent information. Do you have paper and pencil?" Charley told him yes.

"He gave me directions. A hundred miles from Washington, D.C., there's a house just off a lake in southern Pennsylvania, up in the Tuscarora Mountains. The lake's in such remote country that it doesn't have a name, but you can reach it by taking 270 to Frederick, then 70 to Hagerstown, where you pick up 81 through Greencastle to Highway 16, then Route 30 to the first house past Summit Ridge—he told me that was where Victor could be found."

Charley stopped writing; he could still be surprised. "What?" he said softly.

"You see, you don't understand it any better than I do. Do you see what I mean? It doesn't make any sense. If there was anything in this dismal, devious world I was certain of, it was Renaud's loyalty to Victor. Why would he betray him? Can you tell me that?"

Charley couldn't, it was all yardbird chess, pick a move. He felt the blood jet to his head, but he tried to keep his excitement manageable as he asked Suarez what he'd asked K.C.

"Why tell me?"

"It should be obvious. Another favor to encourage you to keep Mr. Jones and his colleagues from untimely visits to my humble home. And perhaps others—somehow I don't feel as safe as I once did."

Charley had seen the movies, he knew the next question. "How do I know this isn't some sort of setup?"

"What could I or they possibly gain by letting you know where

Victor is? Do you think they have the Red army waiting out there to annihilate your friends?"

"I don't know what I think and you're right, I don't understand it."

"No matter. I did what Renaud asked of me. That's all I can do."

"How do I know I can believe you this time?"

For a moment, the irony crept back into Suarez's voice, took the shape of what they'd done to his wrists. "Trust me," he said, then the line went dead in Charley's ear.

Charley calmly replaced the receiver. The restlessness, the feeling of being in limbo, had left him. He knew precisely what he was going to do, he had all the moves.

First, he made a copy of Suarez's directions and put it where even a Valley cop could find it. Next, he phoned Hanlon's home and left a message on the machine, letting him know where he was going. Then he phoned the front desk and told the clerk what to do if an Indian wearing a toothpick showed up. Then he finished shaving; wiping his face, the skin looked pale but clean where the mustache had been.

Slipping into his coat, he straightened his flat, rumpled cap over his forehead, opened the dresser drawer, removed K.C.'s .38 and matched its six chambers with six shells; it was all ritual, like crossing yourself, like spitting up blood—had to be done right.

As he rode down in the creaking elevator, he considered bringing in the law but junked the idea; explanations could take too long and besides ritual was trial, or was it TV? He hoped he'd be around tomorrow to figure it out. He wondered what happened to Marlowe in the book, regretted not reading the end.

Outside, Charley saw the stone loony in the Ben Hogan cap talking to the fake blind lady and her dog. Hunching his neck and shoulders deeper into his coat, Charley hurried past them to his car, afraid that if he so much as broke stride, the man would tell him that Marlowe was dead and the sky was about to come tumbling down.

34

Tracking Charley

Staring out the window, Lisa watched Washington National draw near as the LC-10 descended with the evening darkness. Her reflection in the glass seemed distant, obscure, that of a casual acquaintance or a ghost.

The tarmac below took shape, leveled off. Fastening her seatbelt, she shifted her shoulders, loosening the tension. Sighing, she switched off the reading light and waited to tolerate disembarkment; airports were the loneliest of places, a futility of programmed activity and delayed goodbyes. With the sweep of engines in her ears, she glanced at her watch. 5:32. She set it ahead three hours, adding to her sense of dislocation, and she sighed once more as wheels met ground, shivered, and held.

By 8:47, she was through the terminal and braving the gauntlet of porters and taxis and cold, clutching her camel-hair coat to her neck and her overnight bag to her shoulder. A door swung open and a hack with halitosis appraised her legs as she climbed in back. He leered at her in the rearview mirror when she told him the Three Seasons.

By 9:06, they were at the hotel. She hesitated before getting out, something fluttery insinuating its way through her chest, cat paws upon the nerves. She wondered how she looked, decided it didn't matter. Tipping the driver a dollar, she hurried through twin doors, brushing past a blind woman and her dog and something in golfing cap and tatters that looked like it wanted to talk.

Finding the front desk, which wasn't easy, she told the clerk she was looking for Charley Tone. He informed her, no attempt to be civil, that the gentleman was out, left twenty minutes ago, no idea where, and by the way, you wouldn't happen to be Indian, would you? She let him know she was the gentleman's wife and no, she wasn't Indian, unless someone a few epochs back had jumped the fence, which was pretty damned hard to do in yarmulke, gown, and four-foot beard.

While he was scraping his eyes off the wall, she asked if she could go up to her husband's room to wait. He studied her skeptically, adjusted his hairpiece, shrugged, and replied it was nothing to him and don't disturb the neighbors. A kid in molting green livery and squeaky sneakers took her up to 409 and let her in, switching on the overhead light before leaving with the remaining single in her purse.

Alone, she felt suddenly fatigued, senses spread out and lost. Putting her bag down in the room's only chair, she slumped stiffly on the bed, her back arched. She sat there, blinking back collapse, then, just before her left foot fell asleep or off, she got up, went to the dresser and opened the top drawer, searching for assurances that Charley had really been here. She sifted through folded underwear and balled socks, smiled at *Farewell, My Lovely* tucked under a shirt, then the smile faded into something sick as she gazed down at the empty ammo box, where one overlooked copper shell lingered. She felt her heartbeat quicken again, deepening its rhythms, and she lit a cigarette with the shakiness of a gathering despair. Then, turning, she saw the note, taped to the bedside shade.

She waited until the turmoil in her chest subsided, even checked her pulse with a thumb to her wrist, before she read the scribbled directions, the smoke from her cigarette blearing the page. When she was finished, she folded the note and stored it in her purse. Walking to the bathroom, she considered throwing up under the girl in bloomers and Coke, settled instead for flushing her More Red down the toilet in a frenzy of basin water and ash. Love is a burnt match skating in a urinal, someone had once written; she didn't know why she remembered it at that moment. She stood there, fingertips braced lightly on the sink, staring at herself in the mirror. She wondered how she looked. Somehow it mattered.

She was steadier now. Turning from her reflection, she went to the phone, dialed the front desk and asked, in a voice far calmer than she felt, where she could rent a car. By 9:20, she was out the entrance, past the lady and her shepherd and the certifiable loony who asked Lisa if she knew the color of rain. No, she told him, but she figured she was about to find out.

As she hurried toward a waiting cab, she felt the night clench about her and she shivered involuntarily; tension was riding the air, deepening the darkness, shifting north toward unseen, distant lights.

35

Nightsongs

Charley glanced out the wing window at the uniform ground; patches of black on deeper black, with only an occasional orchard of hooded leaves to vary the mood.

The narrow macadam road dipped sinuously and angled to the left. He switched on his high beams, dimming them almost instantly as a diesel roared by from the opposite direction, leaving behind a vacuum of sound.

There was a town up ahead, a Christmas-chain sparkle of lights a mile beyond in the clean, cold night. He looked at the illumination of the car clock. 10:23. The Buick's windshield was starting to sweat, ice working its way up from the bottom, and he turned on the defroster. Squinting over the wheel, he tried to make out a sign . . . SLOW TO 40 . . . Dropping his speed, he checked the odometer—he'd gone eighty miles—70 to Hagerstown, 81 through Greencastle, on Highway 16 now, and the towns—names like Upton, Mercerberg, Cove Gap—kept getting smaller, the space between them greater. He glimpsed a second sign . . . LIN . . . something. POPULATION 143. He wondered if he was in Maryland or Pennsylvania. He supposed it didn't matter.

He was entering the town now, driving past a one-pump station with a blacked-out sign, past houses with dirt driveways and shingle roofs dwarfed by TV antennas, past a skeleton of a one-armed man sketched in a circle of porchlight, past a graveyard of junked metal dying of rust, past a Foursquare Church where there were people, actually people, the first he'd seen since a quarter to ten, bearded men and women in Puritan dresses in six-poster buggies, faces set hard under round brim hats and black bonnets. He wondered if they were happy.

He dropped his speed to 20 as he entered the main drag; images of the Old West, slatted wood walkways fronting depression-styled stores. He could hear a song coming from somewhere, bar to the left, the only one in sight, a neon flashing HANK'S, rebel music and redneck whoops from within.

A jalopy crammed with teenagers snaked by—wild white arms waving beers and grinning country faces yelling Happy New Year!—Then he was clear of the town as quickly as he'd entered it, a town like a blink with nothing but loneliness ahead . . . something complete there, something of life and death, in the black-hooded men and women, in the shit-kickers and the kids and the skeleton on the porch, with nothing but darkness beyond, and it reminded Charley of where he was going, his headlights sculpting out a path, and he turned on the heater for warmth and the radio for company and he kept on going.

Up ahead, Route 30 and the Tuscarora Mountains loomed as if slumbering, ready to wake to life.

The mountains were so distant, much too far . . . Although I know the way, I'll never reach them, she thought.

Lisa started slightly as the static overwhelmed the newscaster's voice. She adjusted the dial. The crackle remained but diminished. She could just make out words . . . snow expected . . . Route 30 . . . She couldn't catch if 30 was open or closed.

She tried another station, picked up nervous chords. She shifted from the acne rock to a cracker voice booming death and damnation. It was New Year's Eve and the world was going to end at the crack of midnight, the sky, intractable and black overhead, would splinter in a flood of hallowed flame, Hallelujah, brother . . .

Twenty-nine degrees and falling . . . Hallelujah . . . She recalled a movie she'd seen with Charley, a born-again epic awash in bathos. Throughout the packaged glory, a token black, hair conked and eyes sodden with plantation misery, kept repeating the hopeful refrain: All God's chillun got wings. All God's chillun got wings; Lisa mouthed the words inaudibly.

Twenty-five degrees . . . Snow heavy in . . .

A rabbit shot out of the void to her right, a blur of brown-white fur under her lights, then vanished like memory.

All God's chillun got . . .

Snow, the static said.

Hallelujah.

It had started to snow, a pattern of gossamer flakes falling around him. Inclement weather . . . snow through 30 . . . chains required, the weak voice on the radio said. Yeah. Sure, Charley replied.

The snow flecked his windshield. He switched on the wipers. The blades grudgingly scraped the slush aside with a sound as abrasive as the grinding of glass. He was babying the Buick up a hill, nothing but inclines, dips, curves, and open country for the last half hour, a roller-coaster ride, easy one though, kindergarten variety. He glanced at the speedometer; ninety-three miles out of D.C. Should be getting close, if there was actually anything to get close to. The whole thing could be a joke—Suarez had that kind of humor.

The road led him to the left. A brute of a snowplow, big enough to worry mountains, crawled around the bend. Lost in flannel and wool, the driver pointed to Charley's tires and mouthed, "Chains." Charley shrugged and kept on going.

Angling around rock, the road straightened. Charley was still climbing. He felt his ears pop, the sensation not entirely unpleasant. He was entering woods now, a few pines greeting him like scouts, flanking him. The voice on the radio was fading, deserting him. He felt like he was entering another world. Snow was everywhere, filling space and time. The road was icing over, polishing the asphalt to a diamond glitter. Lacking chains, he slowed to 15, felt the tires beneath him probing for traction on the slick surface. He gazed at the landscape, at the trees, the sloping terrain, the banked shoulders gritty with dirt, all giving way to whiteness, to the beauty of geometric precision. It should be Christmas, he thought. I should be sixteen, drinking Primo from the can . . . should be . . .

And then suddenly he reached the crest of the hill and he saw it, no more than a shout below. He saw it and his heart started, stopped, started again as he braked too hard, and the tires lost what little grip they had on the road. He let the wheel turn with the skid, had no choice, and the Buick bucked and veered in a slow, dreamy slide. He stayed with the wheel, held it tight to no purpose at arm's length, felt the car shrug and start to go over on two wheels like the diesel in the park. It seemed to slide forever, locked in a lazy euphoria. Then it thudded into something hard and unyielding, quivered, and came to rest, upright, steam from its hood obscuring the snow.

The radio continued to drone. Hands still tight to the wheel, Charley remained motionless with his head down, then he looked up through the whiteness and the steam and the glide of the wipers, staring down the hill at what waited below.

36

The Knight of Swords

It was less than a mile away—just past the entrenched sign reading Summit Ridge—off to the right of the road and at the bottom of a steep slope. Visible only in patches through the trees, the lake seemed small, with limits. Not yet frozen, the perfect mirror of water had the dark luster of shaded moonlight, and closer light that fell from the windows of the house at the water's edge.

The Buick had come to rest against a snowbank. From its awkward angle, Charley stared down the hill; then, cutting the engine, he got out of the car, took a moment to reconnoiter. Good word, reconnoiter. A driveway of rapidly vanishing cinder curved down to the house, which was surrounded by a clearing—no trees for a good fifty yards, no other houses for as far as the eye could see. Charley let his gaze stray to the left. There were only a few infant pines and scrub bushes on the upper half of the slope; the closer to the lake, the more plentiful the woods.

Charley started down in the direction he was looking, away from the driveway and toward the cover of pines. He stayed low, hunched down. It was cold, incredibly cold, nothing in Washington to match it. His heavy coat kept neck, torso, and upper legs relatively warm, but the rest of him—face, feet, hands—was dully aching and numb. He watched his breath taper off and freeze in the air, shreds of vapor staying with him like a shadow as he walked, sneakers pushing carefully through the hardening mush. He watched the house with every step; no sign of life, only the lights touching the lake.

The slope leveled off near the bottom. When he was almost there he slipped, breaking his fall with both hands; then he was among an abundance of pines, bunched just a few feet apart, the rich tang of their needles overriding the chill. The trees sheltered him, made him feel secure. They came in all shapes and sizes—trees as bountiful as armies, trees as impoverished as skeletons, branches like leprous bear claws, like weaver's patterns or the magic of spun gold, branches straight and firm, others snow-heavy and drooping; near Charley's elbow, one quivered and released its burden with a crack as sharp as a gunshot.

He had moved to within three hundred yards of the house, which, despite the woods, was becoming defined: two stories of natural pine, shake roof pitched steep to discard the snow, closed garage to the rear. He crouched down, studying the windows, but could still see no one. His hands were stiffening, seemed as rigid as wood, and he flexed his fingers for circulation. He realized music was coming faintly from somewhere up ahead

Clap hands Charley

something Latino and sentimental, a caress of violins and guitars and a woman's fine, smooth voice. He moved closer to the song, tried to make out the words but couldn't. Off to his left, a bird screeched and wheeled across the water, its single sustained note harsh over the harmony up ahead. Charley was aware of life stirring around him—quail lifting into the air in a flurry of wide wings, a white-tailed deer climbing on delicate hoofs toward an unseen sanctuary, something diminutive and camouflaged scurrying away to the right—a sensation of flight on all sides of him, with only the snow and Charley settling in to stay.

Two hundred yards now . . . He could make out more detail from the house: three windows, all on the first floor facing him, light falling from only one. Smoke was drifting from a chimney.

The setting was pastoral, remote, a lazy, postcard beauty to it all—the lake, fifty feet away, a clear stillness through the trees, snow falling silently like motes of dust to its surface of dancing light. Pastoral, he thought, watching the thin smoke rise. Oh yeah. Pastoral.

A hundred yards . . . He still couldn't catch the lyrics of the song. A man's silhouette appeared in the lighted window, paused in muscular profile before shifting from sight.

Charley kept moving forward. He was approaching the clearing, almost to it, when he heard a door open from the front of the house, releasing the song. The woman had a good voice, husky with a thread of sadness. "Lo quería más que a mi vida," she was singing. She sang it twice over the violins and guitars; then suddenly, without warning, a dog bounded out from where the music was, an Irish setter, young with a glossy coat. Tail sweeping the ground, it sniffed at the snow, then raced up the slope toward the road, leaping high once at an imaginary prey or with the joy of unexpected freedom. Smiling, it rolled on its back, a red rag on an endless white cloth. It got up and shook itself. If it had caught Charley's scent, it didn't seem to care. "Una mañana de frio en invierno," the woman was singing.

A man's whistle, piercing, came from the front porch and the dog charged down the slope and back into the house. After he heard the door close, taking most of the music with it, Charley took a deep breath and quickly crossed the clearing—fifty yards of staying low and he was at the house. He touched the frame with one hand, as if amazed he'd gotten there. He remained motionless by the side, afraid that someone could hear his watch or his heart. Light reached from a nearby window—turning the snow a fading gold—and from the porch twenty feet around the corner, but where he was, it was dark. The snow continued to fall, fragile, remote. Brushing it from his face, Charley edged to the window with steps as small as an insecure child's. He paused, his back to the wall, away from the light, but before he could peer inside, the front door opened and closed, bringing the music outside again—a different song, uptempo, syncopated. Bracing, he heard footsteps over the mariachis and castanets and the woman's vibrant timbre. Unbuttoning the top of his coat, Charley touched the gun but left it where it was; no good using it if he didn't have to.

His broad back to Charley, the man strolled out alone into the snow. Portable radio to his ear, he gazed up at the road. Charley could see part of his face; he remembered the rest in grainy black and white, one of half a dozen coming down cool marble steps with Cedillo, only now the suit and tie had been replaced by parka, Levis, lumberjack boots, and a white cotton scarf.

Bending down, the man scooped up a handful of snow and pressed it gently to his face, his cheek, something soft and inexplicable in the gesture. He held the snow close before shaking it from his hand. There was an unfinished smile on his face, wistful and a little lonely. New Year's Eve for him too, Charley thought, and he pressed back against the wall, wondering what to do, as the man started back to the front door. Only he never got there. He stopped in midstride, then suddenly he was coming around the corner, maybe remembering something he'd forgotten to do, ambling toward the garage, head down, ear pinned to the radio

Ai yi yi yi . . . cante conmigo con gusto . . .

and he was within a handshake of Charley before he looked up and saw him. He had an unwashed, animal musk odor that filled Charley's nostrils, and his dark, muddied eyes opened only slightly, his surprise so complete that he stared at Charley not with amazement, but merely curiosity and a mild disbelief, and in that moment Charley leaned forward—did no more than that—and hit him on the side of the jaw, the punch traveling less than six inches but with all of his shoulder behind it, and the man dropped leadenly forward the way Peterson had, without drama or flair.

Charley looked down; the bodyguard was lying on his face, the blood from his swollen lower lip congealing in the cold. The radio was by his open hand

Ai yi

and crouching down, Charley bound the man's hands behind his back with his belt, his feet with Charley's own. His eyes were shut as if in sleep and his breathing was coming thick with almost a snore, but Charley gagged him just to be sure, using the scarf. After tightening the cloth partway into his mouth and knotting it behind his neck, Charley took off his pea coat and covered the man, so he wouldn't freeze to death, did it because of the way he'd touched the snow to his face. When that was done, he left the sleeping figure and the music behind. Taking out K.C.'s .38, he walked around the corner to the porch, not even glancing in the window, staying close to the house with the gun barrel up and tight to his shoulder.

Reaching the door, Charley paused and looked up at the moon. The man imprisoned there was grinning, singing for his supper above the snow. Charley gazed at the sad-happy face; then, drawing a deep breath, he delicately opened the door and slipped inside, going in quick and clean with the same puncher's chance he'd had against Turner in the tenth round so many years ago.

37

The Wheel of Fortune

There was no one. Not even the dog.

Charley stood there, gun held high. The sudden heat from the interior warmed his hands, removing the numbness as deftly as the drawing off of gloves. From where he was, braced against a wall and shadow, he could see the living room. The space opening out beyond him seemed immense yet somehow cloistered. The room was dark, except for the glow spreading from the fireplace set in the far wall;

the fire burned silently, flames as even as the snow falling outside. He could make out furniture in the center of the room, sofas and chairs and a coffee table as long as a short alley. The paintings on the walls showed cost. So did the Persian rugs, their gin-maze patterns taking up most of the floor. Up above, a chandelier shed tears.

He was perspiring even more now from the heat. Wiping his brow, he inched forward to the end of the foyer, the scritch of his sneakers muted by carpet. The living room stretched out to a kitchen, light falling from it—inside, a patch of spotless sink and gleaming white dishes stacked in a tray. Although the sounds must have been there before, Charley noticed noises for the first time; a slavering from the kitchen, a soft lift of music and voices from the second floor. Focusing on the kitchen, he saw the setter eating from a bowl, scarlet tail, flank and bent head.

Charley looked toward the second floor, past the darkness congregating like snakes in a stairwell, up a flight of banistered stairs curving away to the rear of the house, and a carpeted aisle fronting three doors. The first two were closed and dark, the third ajar the width of a large man's hand; the music and voices and a curtain of blue-white light fell from its unseen room, the drone dispersed in television bass rumbles and treble squalls.

Another sound now . . .

It was coming from another direction, off to Charley's right, past the stairwell and down a dark lean hallway leading to a lighted room without a door. It was a funny noise, a pocking—three, four, five times—then the pocking would stop only to start again, like the ticking of a reluctant clock.

Charley glanced at his watch. 11:42. He hesitated, once more not sure where to go, then he went on a whisper of soles toward the stairs. A door closed briskly. Charley heard spiked heels sharp above him; he melted into the stairwell, listening to the steps coming down other steps.

New sound now—sounds were snakes under his feet—from the room down the hallway, tough guy laughter and voices joking in Spanish. Charley felt penned in, squeezed between the flanking noises. He expected them to somehow converge, suffocating him;

then the high heels were moving away, toward the kitchen. Hidden in the darkness, he watched as a tiny white ball skittered across the room's parquet floor and feathered off the back wall, watched as a man crossed through the light from the doorway, smiling as he stooped, ping-pong paddle in hand, to pick up the ball, saying "Chinga!" as it eluded him; there was something comic in the obscenity—he was as jolly as the other was sad. Had a bodybuilder's physique, all flex and pecs under tight tan T-shirt and slacks, healthy tan face familiar from the documentary, grinning as he turned to the hallway and called "Carlos," calling for his friend lying bound and gagged outside as Charley edged deeper into shadow; Charley could sense the shrug in his laughter when he got no response. The pock-pock-pock started again, too delicate a sound for the man making it.

Charley twisted his head—the high heels were returning, something else, a padding, soft as a moth strutting across your nerves, coming with them. The high heels were starting up the stairs, going away, but the padding grew louder, became more insistent, was suddenly with Charley, beside him in the darkness. He felt the damp muzzle of the dog nuzzling him. He cupped the animal's jaw, felt the tongue wet and active against his hand

options, Charley

and then the lady said "Jason," calling the setter with a voice as brittle as cracked china. Charley tried to steer the dog in her direction but it stayed beside him, happy as a kid with another's toy. The woman was coming back down the steps. He could sense her on the other side of the stairwell, sense her body tensing, wary and alert. Pock the ball went and

options . . .

a switch clicked on. Light filled the hallway, reaching into his sanctuary; then the woman was there, facing him. She was pale and plain, young but with her hair tied back tight under a nurse's cap, body loose under a nurse's gown. She was holding a steel tray with a glass of milk, a toasted muffin on a plate, a goblet of pink champagne, and a thermometer off to the side, it was all sweet mercy and a Swedish movie, holding the tray away from her body as though she might drop it, only she didn't—she stared at Charley with watery eyes, like someone who'd been out in the sun too long, at Charley and the gun down at his side; then she looked away, up at the ceiling, Charley couldn't imagine why. Following her gaze, he saw the security camera tracking in slow circles like a predatory bird craning from its perch, didn't even have time to wave hi before its eye found him and moved on. He looked at the camera, looked at the dog—the son of a bitch was still happy, showing a gap-toothed grin—and Charley tried it on the nurse, the polite smile he kept in his pocket, but she was staring past him, never saw it, and the tray fell from her hands, and before it hit the floor, Charley was wheeling about to the jolly bodyguard in the doorway, only he wasn't smiling this time, and the paddle in his fist had given way to a gun, bigger than a revolver and joined to his hip.

For an instant, Charley thought of Peterson lazily lifting the satin barrel of the silencer toward him, a hint of irises behind the ski mask, and the image nearly held him too long—he flung himself away from the memory just as the woman screamed and the Uzi blossomed into yellow-dark flame, the convulsion of sound and fireworks filling the hallway, eclipsing the overhead light. Dropping down into shadow, Charley felt heat and brightness race by, searing his skin even as he fired toward the flame. Through the smoke and cordite he saw the thick tan chest open like a flower, a single petal of red appearing as the man staggered back, stutter-stepping, as if resisting the pressure of an invisible hand tugging on him from behind. His finger was still locked on the trigger, blunt silver barrel whipsawing from side to side as he went down.

Charley stayed crouched beneath the stairway, not moving until the drumming in his ears died. He waited until he could hear only the TV up above, its drone constant, as if nothing at all had happened, as though nothing ever would.

Shifting his weight from heel to toe, he leaned forward and peered down the hallway, past the dog on its side, to the room. He could see the bodyguard sitting against the wall. The gun was cradled in his lap, but his head was bent to his chest where his blood, rich and flowing, emptied from his shattered heart.

Turning, Charley looked for the nurse. She was lying dead-weight on a rug of infinite patterns, near a sofa of none, facing away from Charley, one pale arm tucked beneath her stomach, the other broken-doll twisted at her side, palm cupped; her white bonnet favored one side and her starched white uniform was stitched through the back with her blood. The tray and all its sweet mercy were spread out beside her hand, spilled champagne mingling with the milk and the blood pooling around her. Something of life and death, Charley absently thought, something of . . .

The dog whimpered. Charley turned to it. The setter was still on its side, a hind leg mangled, close to off, but it had raised its head, was looking at Charley, betrayed eyes pleading. Charley wanted to help but there was nothing he could do; he knew there was someone else in the room at the end of the hallway, not making a sound but waiting, ready to dance.

He gazed at the gun, warm in his hand; then, getting to his feet, he switched off the hallway light, returning the corridor to darkness. He guessed the corridor was a throw to first base. He started down its ninety feet, trying not to look at the dog, who continued to whimper, a high-pitched, keening moan, as Charley went by. He stayed closed to the wall, gun poised, his back against bullet-scarred wood, an image of dirty firing squad cement returning to him. His mind roaming, he thought of other walls he'd clung to: Janice Vaitonis's, those during the madcap spree through Washington, all of it too far to fathom now.

He was at the doorway. The lighting in the room was the kind that goes with hard questions under a bare bulb, the glare accentuating the features of the man slumped dead against the wall; the bleeding had almost stopped and he looked peaceful, eyes closed under lashes as long as a girl's. Charley wondered what the lighting had been like during Eddie's interrogation, wondered what to do next. He had no idea if the guy deep in the room carried heat—sweet Jesus, but there were so many kinds—but he could sense his presence as easily as he had the nurse's, could almost hear him holding back his breath. A voice, his own, was telling him, keep it clean, a game of chess, but something else was stirring within him, urging him to

clap hands

go through the door, and then he saw the shadow looming against the wall, arms raised, stretched out of all proportion. "Por favor, no me mates, yo me rendo," a voice, not his own, was saying; it was a song, comic opera—it was going to be easy, the man was surrendering—and Charley went down two short steps and inside the room saw green plywood and net and the barbells beyond, saw too late one high hand yank the overhanging chain; plunging the hot, close space into darkness.

Charley fired once wildly, glimpsed the bodyguard, bigger even than the others, in the flaring of light before he was upon him. The darkness wasn't complete—moonlight was struggling through a window—and Charley saw something iron and brutal swing down and the gun was no longer there, only pain more numbing than the cold outside. Charley clutched his arm where the weight had dug in, saw the man eager to strike again, and Charley shifted slightly, the way he would to avoid a punch—the bar hissed down snake-fast, missing his head but not his shoulder, driving in more hurt, and Charley used the man's momentum against him, grabbed his wrist with both his hands, the pain shooting through the right, twisting the Venezuelan's arm down hard against Charley's bent knee.

The man grunted and released the bar, which thudded to the floor, but he knew more than one waltz; his arms enveloped Charley, hugging him back against the wall. Charley struggled to decline, would just as soon have sat it out, tried to keep his balance, knowing it was his only chance. He felt the dead man's thighs rubbery against his ankles and feet, felt python arms tightening around him and firm legs flexed with a wrestler's hard grace. His breath close against Charley's cheek, the man was squeezing the life from him, inhaling deeply with the effort. Charley could feel his own breath leaving his body, could feel his spirit being sucked away, chest expanding and throbbing in waves, felt that he was breaking apart like a ship against sea-lashed rocks. Desperate, he brought one foot down savagely on an instep. The man grunted again, but no more than that as he locked in his grip. Charley felt his eyes clouding over, shifting toward something like sleep, which except for the constriction around his chest was not at all unpleasant—something dreamy and drifting, coming toward him; then he saw what it was, saw sunbeam shafts and black angels dancing through the sockets of a skeleton with a graveyard leer, and a voice was rising, something fierce and angry and thrashing within him, and he drove his foot down harder than before, once, twice, no more strength left than that, and he felt the coiled pressure around his ribs slacken as, ankle giving way, the big man reached out to the wall to keep from falling, and in that second, before the arms embraced him once more, the air rocketed back into Charley's lungs and he lashed out with his left, felt it smash into bone. The shape before him staggered back then came forward again, swinging a fist as huge as death into Charley's face. Charley felt his knees buckle, tasted the blood warm in his mouth. The man was closing on him. The man was much bigger than Charley, stronger than Charley—Charley thought he could see the grin on his face—only the man couldn't accept the pain, the agony Charley had learned to live with in a thousand rounds, and Charley threw the left, heard him cry out, and he doubled off the hook, left to the belly then up to the head, the punches whistling home with the precision of instinct, and he would have punched once more, but the big body was sliding away from his reach, slipping in loose rhythms to the floor.

Elbows tight to her sides, Lisa stared over the steering—past the Buick broken against the snowbank—to the second car parked just ahead.

The Datsun had passed her thirty miles back, when she stopped at a station to have chains put on. Driving through the snow, she'd been riding his taillights ever since, never much distance between them. When she'd slowed after cresting the hill, so had he, stopping beside the disappearing driveway. He had sat there behind the wheel, staring hard at her in the rearview mirror, small warm weather hat straddling his head, smaller blue eyes worried and perplexed.

When she parked as well, he had opened the driver's door, leaned out, and tried to wave her back; then they both heard the shot from the house, faint but hanging in the bell-clear air, and she knew somehow that Charley was inside and she drove the pedal almost through the floor, the man still trying to wave her back—hands thrusting in unison, as if pushing someone aside—as she sped down the driveway as far as the snow would allow. Then she was free of her car, running toward the house and the perfect lake below, with the worried man's footsteps crunching rapidly and resolutely behind her.

38

The Man in the Lake

When the shooting had started, first a fusillade then later a single shot, he had shifted each time toward the dissonance, but the expression on his face had hardly altered, merely creasing slightly into greater confusion. The sounds meant nothing to him, no more than the spectral illusions drifting before him on the screen, and he had turned from their mystery even before they had stopped.

Statue-still, he sat gazzing out the frosted window at the lake below. Troubling his sight, the snow, a soft, patterned inevitability, fell like gentle rain, became rain, was always rain, locked within his head, change without memory, memory without change, images repeating, turning back upon themselves . . . He saw once more the plane's wide wing, through the window, shudder and dip, felt his stomach climbing as the aircraft fell, drawing down terror and a futility of arms and eyes reaching for God knows what . . . He looked to his right and he looked to his left and there was nothing there . . . He heard the church bells pealing even as the steeple gave way, even as the great steel-gray bird plummeted, captive to a final irony, drawn down to the circle of water as black and dead as a shark's eye below, all of it happening in a wink of God's eye, no time for prayer or remembrance of power, litany of sound and a flash of light upon the lake, all of it turning, turning back upon itself, turning back, turning . . .

39

Skeletons

Charley's one good hand found the overhead chain. He yanked it down, pulling harder than he intended. He squinted under the abrupt glare from the bulb, its cord dancing above him. He was queasy, not for the first time. He felt like he'd left his head in another room, maybe another state. His ribs throbbed and the muscles in his chest were tied into wet rawhide knots. His right arm and shoulder were vacationing in Des Moines.

He sat for a moment on the ping-pong table, feet touching the floor, until the worst of it had passed. Turning, he looked at the biggest of the bodyguards; the man was out cold, face down near the splayed legs of his friend. Charley didn't try to make him comfortable.

He gathered up the guns instead. There seemed to be only two, his own and the dead Venezuelan's Uzi. He tucked the .38 in the side of his pants, where his belt had been.

Holding the submachine gun—so small that it looked like a toy—barrel down in his left hand, he went out into the corridor. The setter twisted its head to him. The light from the rec room just reached the dog. Its fur was matted and damp, the blood around it a deeper red. Charley bent down beside it. He still had to go up the stairs to where the off-light and the sound rose and fell, but he didn't want the dog to die. Tearing a strip from his shirt—it wasn't easy, for the cotton was thick with sweat and his right hand was of little help—he wrapped the fabric around the animal's nearly severed leg. The setter, its breathing labored, nuzzled his hand, its snout warm and dry, then, with dimming eyes, watched him twist and tie the cloth into something that might stop the bleeding. When Charley had finished, some of the fear left the dog's eyes and it lowered its head to the floor with a very human sigh. Charley patted him once, then, collecting his strength, he left the corridor to find the man in the lake.

His stride quickened as he went up the stairs, the Uzi held tight to his side; then he was going down the carpeted aisle, the blue-white light drawing closer, the artificial drone gathering around him; then he was at the door. He paused to put the Uzi down, left it lying on the carpet like a cairn. Taking the .38 from his jeans, he turned the knob and pushed the door, not hard, just enough to swing it open.

He watched the illumination from inside grow brighter as the room took shape, reflecting images of illness: catheter, IVs, and John Wayne blustering on a VCR screen. Charley felt his heartbeat double as the frail stick figure in the robe and the pj's and the wheelchair turned slow as a dream toward him. The front of the man was blotched where he'd soiled himself. His jaw was slack, his face as uncomprehending as an infant's. Charley imagined that was how he must have looked at the instant when all the bright, fervent candles in his head went out, never to be lit again.

Charley stood briefly in the doorway, gazing at Victor Cedillo, then he left, closing the door softly behind him. He got halfway to the stairs before he stopped as if he'd walked into a wall.

The bodyguard with the grip of a nightmare was below by the fire. He was standing groggy and head down, braced at arm's length by the sofa near the nurse's body, shadow within shadow, under the light filling one wall. Charley noticed he had a mustache, full and drooping like Zapata's, resembled him in fact. He also had a revolver, shiny as Aztec gold, dangling from one heavy, veined hand. Should have made sure of him, should have searched for other guns, should have done a lot of things, Charley thought.

He tried the weight of his own weapon in his left hand, maybe he could fire it, but at that moment Lisa

Flesh of my flesh

came through the front door, rapidly and without thought, was there before he knew it was her, before she saw the bodyguard turning amazed as Charley toward her, and Charley shouted her name, his heart reaching his throat, and Emiliano looked from her to him, a sly, blood-flecked smile forming on his face, as he realized that the woman meant something to the man who had killed his friend, and done a job on him. Still smiling at Charley, almost as if he might say something polite, he lifted the gun toward Lisa, and then the door she had rushed so heedlessly through was pushed open again. Backdropped by the moon, a silhouette yelled "No!", the voice pitched to an ultimate desperation—it was all prime time.

Zapata swung his revolver toward the plea and fired, two shots too close together to count, the other's gun returning the compliment just once, and both men dropped heavily to the floor, the silhouette, suddenly familiar, falling toward the light.

40

A Month of Headlines

K.C. turned from the lights of the house and adjusted the dial, clearing away static. He had the radio on low, coaxing Guy Lombardo waltzes.

He was parked in his '75 Dodge, body like a Buffalo nickel, sort of out of sight under a res of elms. There were mountains way off, proud as flexed muscles, and Dake's house a lot closer, give or take a hundred yards, and what a pretty picture it was, nothing but la-di-da lawns and cars, not a Datsun for fifty miles. K.C. wished he knew where Pat was, wished he knew what the hell had happened with Dake. Most of all he wished, hey yah, for a toothpick, but he was all out. He had been hunkered down for two hours, ever since tailing Byrne and his better half to the shyster's. He didn't think they'd seen him, though it was hard to tell; Byrne and his old lady drove in a real funny way, like they didn't have nothing to say to one another. Maybe, he guessed, that was gospel.

Arms restless over the ratty seat—thirty thou a year and abuse, ain't that the truth—K.C. yawned and looked around. It was a kinda lonely place, maybe not so pretty a picture after all. There was no fuckin' wind. You couldn't trust a neighborhood with no fuckin' wind, it wasn't natural. Besides, there were too many goddamned statues taking up space, some of them pretty cute nudes; a guy could get hurt if he happened to be stewed and horny.

Taking the neighborhood in from Dake's, there was a house with no lights a good ways down the road to the left, and a house a good ways down the road to the right. They were having a party at the second joint, lots of fancy cars and hot music and folks laughing from around a pool no way he could see. Across the street from Dake's, there was a two-story white dream, the kind dames with diamonds down to their toes sashayed through on TV. Nothing to worry about there; windows were lousy with boards, fat cats probably away starkers on a frog beach.

Lombardo was playing "September Song." K.C. remembered his watch. 11:24. Jesus, but he should've been holding a sweet, loving gal, dancing away all the dreary hours, and here he was, waiting on some guys in penguin suits to make a move might never come, story of his life, Sitting Bull would show a few tears. Switching off the radio, he turned on his CB to listen in on the police reports—maybe they'd have something interesting, a poodle on a tear or a four-wheel drive spreading some grief.

K.C. straightened up behind the hub as Dake's front door swung open and the porch light went on. The four of them, Dake, Byrne, and the wives, came outside looking snazzy, tuxes and sequins and hours under the hair gun. They were going out, someplace you'd need a second mortgage to pay the bill. He'd have to tag along. Maybe he'd get a New Year's kiss. Maybe he'd get a fuckin' pie in the face, if he was lucky.

They were strolling toward their cars, which were parked in a driveway shaped like a bow.

The CB had something to say. "Code 911 from McConnellsburg County, Route 30," the dispatcher said far away. "First house north of Summit Ridge Crest. All units in area . . . code 911. Request urgent. Respond to call from associate director of FBI . . ."

No, they were all going to Dake's chocolate Mercedes, car like a fuckin' candy bar, the mouthpiece leading.

"Code 911 . . ." "Wha . . . ?" K.C. said, blinking. "Associate director of the FBI . . ." "Wha . . . ?!"

Dake was opening the door for his wife. Byrne and his old lady were just behind.

". . . all units . . ." K.C. jerked his head around half expecting Pat to be there to explain it all, but he saw only the boarded-up dream

and a glint of light

By the driver's door, Dake said something mild to Matt Byrne, who was on the other side of the car, opening the door for his wife. Both men almost smiled.

"Urgent," the dispatcher said without urgency.

glint of light from an upstairs window

Dake slipped behind the wheel, taking a gold cigarette case out of his coat. His wife sat Eastern-school straight beside him.

"All . . ."

glint

And then K.C. realized it. He spun toward the second-story window, saw the head and big shoulders dark behind two boards nailed like a drunk cross, moonlight glancing off the rifle's gleaming stock, and suddenly K.C. knew—didn't know why, understood none of it, but he knew who was going to die and it was going to be big and bloody even from three hundred yards, and now, in a lost lonely place, understanding only enough, he dreamt himself into the real world, and he was out of the car, reaching inside his coat for a gun he'd never used as he sprinted toward the house.

From the upstairs window, Paul Renaud glanced at the hard-driving figure running toward him, then he looked away; it didn't matter.

He gazed at the rifle in his hands. The weapon was a bolt-action Ruger 77, pistol grip, tapered forearm, walnut stock, twenty-two-inch blued barrel, accurate up to twelve hundred yards. Resting the rifle against the wall, he pushed the window up, letting in the music and laughter from down the road. He had hoped for a sympathetic breeze, atmosphere, mood, but there was none. Sighing regretfully, he picked up the gun, poked the barrel through the boards, leaned forward and rested his elbows on the ledge. Staring through the cool, clean sight, he tracked the foursome across the street. They seemed vulnerable, close enough to touch. Dake was behind the wheel, lighting a cigarette. His window was down, to let out the smoke. His wife was leaning forward, checking her makeup in the rearview mirror. Byrne's wife was seated directly behind her, searching for something in her purse. Matthew Byrne was coming around the trunk to the near side of the shiny brown car.

Renaud turned as he heard a side door crash open from the first floor—unnecessarily, since he himself had already broken the lock. He heard footsteps pounding toward the stairs he had taken.

Ignoring their urgency, he adjusted the crosshairs and sighted on the director of the FBI; a rigid, slight man, no great loss. Renaud held the gun steady on him, then he delicately swung the barrel to another target.

Dake glanced up at the window across the street, saw the glint of the rifle, felt his heartbeat quicken. Behind him, Byrne was opening the passenger door to get in, unaware that what was left of his life could be counted in seconds. Dake felt the irony—Byrne was going to die because, in his bloodless way, he was perfect for his job, even too passionless for corruption. Dake felt a pang of regret for his friend, for what was about to happen. It was short-lived. Byrne would understand. It wasn't personal. After all, neither was Matthew.

Placing his cigarette in an ashtray, Dake reached for a button to close the window at his side.

Renaud hesitated before he fired. In that moment, disparate, faraway memories crowded his mind's eye—his parents, Enklaar, Victor—the faces, including his own, passing before him like melding portraits on a single canvas. He thought of where they were or where they were going. For an instant, he saw his parents again, his father bloodied, raising a hand from the floor imploringly before Paul separated head from body, his mother screaming to a pitch that stretched across time. He thought of them and then he thought of Dake. He hesitated for a fraction of a second more

God was time . . .

then he squeezed the trigger.

With the car window closing, the bullet took the back of Dake's head off with the taste of the cigarette still fresh in his mouth.

K.C. was halfway up the stairs when he heard the shot. His nose was bleeding, the same unprovoked response he used to get in the ring. The blood was streaming down his mouth and chin, but he kept on running, up the remaining steps. He could hear a woman screaming from somewhere over the good-time music. He wasn't built for distance and his breath was coming as fast as the seconds, but he kept charging, down a short corridor, gun where it was supposed to be, going like hell and six Sioux to that ridge, hey yah, to a closed door and he kicked it in nearly without breaking stride, the wood going three ways under his size fourteens, two left feet he always had, and he was through the door, sluing off balance into the room, eyes primed for a target and the target was there—he saw the business end of the rifle yearning for his drumming heart, turning it to stone.

K.C. froze, expecting a bullet from the man with Burt Lancaster's face. The face was smiling at him through the cordite and fading smoke, grinning real nice, lips parted slightly over too many teeth, then the barrel swung up away from K.C. and Renaud squeezed the trigger a second time, still smiling, as though the bullet were a gift; then the shock of the shell shattered his brain, ending all thought, flinging the strong body against the wall, the light gone forever from his dark, gently mocking eyes.

K.C. stood in the doorway shaking, the touch of death upon him, then he crossed to the blood-painted window. He stared at the body beneath it, down there with the broken glass scattered like leaves, then he stared across the street. The music and laughter had stopped. Dake's wife was screaming, couldn't stop. She was sitting in the car, body straitjacketed, staring at her white upheld arms dark with her husband's blood. Lawrence Dake was slumped lifeless against her shoulder, perfect blond hair in place, except for the part of his head that was missing. Byrne's wife was leaning over the front seat, supporting what remained, looking to help. Matthew Byrne stayed by the rear passenger door, slender body side-angled, his face turned back amazed toward the window where K.C. stood, wondering where Custer had gone.

41

The Informer

Charley remained locked in time as the two men dropped, then he went down the stairs two steps a stride to where Lisa met him at the bottom. He held her close and the pressure of her body against his aching ribs and chest felt fine. She was trembling, a flutter of soft, intimate flesh, and her eyes kept wandering to the bodies on the floor—Zapata's, the nurse's, the setter's, and the man who had so resolutely chased her.

Cupping her face between his hands, Charley found a smile in his pocket and shook his head, too amazed to even wonder why she was here, only glad they were both alive. She looked up at him, her eyes asking for answers he would have given her, except that Pat Hanlon was lying in his own blood, just barely in the light. Her face in his hands, Charley gently told her, "Call the police. Find a phone and call the police." She lingered for a moment, eyes still asking; then she went to do just that.

Charley checked Zapata first, made sure he was dead, before he went to Hanlon. The big Irishman was conscious. His service revolver was on the carpet behind him, his comic small hat flat beneath an arm. His face chalk white and slack, he watched with curiosity as Charley approached.

Crouching down beside him, Charley eased Hanlon's bulk back against the wall. Hanlon was bleeding through his coat where Zapata had shot him. The lines across his brow tightened as Charley moved him, but the glow from the fireplace softened his anguish and his blue eyes managed a twinkle as he looked up at Charley and said, his voice working against the pain, "Pittsburgh and it's raining."

"Yeah," Charley said. Yeah. He opened Hanlon's coat and shirt. The bullet had caught him high on the left shoulder. There was a fair amount of blood, but it looked like he'd live if Charley could stop the flow. Bunching Hanlon's handkerchief up in his hand, he pressed his palm to the ridiculously small ragged hole near Hanlon's bull neck. The redness seeped through the cloth, staining the edges of Charley's spread fingers.

"Just take it easy," he told Hanlon as he pressed down. "We're getting help."

He could hear Lisa's footsteps coming up fast behind him. She was suddenly by his side, eyes still asking but willing to wait. She didn't speak, simply nodded to let Charley know that help really was on the way.

Hanlon didn't seem to notice that she was there. "Let me tell you a story, Charley . . ."

"Shh . . ." Charley said, keeping the cloth clamped to the skin, but Charley couldn't stop him, not unless he doubled off the left. Hanlon continued to talk, the kind of jag shellshocked soldiers sometimes go on. His gaze had traveled to some distant place and the words came quick, gathering their own momentum between his short, sharp breaths.

"A story, Charley. It's about good guys and bad guys and maybe something in between . . . starts almost a year back with Peterson, here in D.C. I hadn't been out of Heavy Traffic that long and he used to come around to rap, and one day I mention something I'd picked up on the grapevine, about muscle coming in from down South, nothing to it I figure, only Peterson gets evasive, mostly in the eyes, and I knew then that he was on the take . . . There'd been rumors and besides I'd seen the look before, and I knew it was something big, could see it there in his eyes, and I needed something big, Charley. Ann was dead a month and I needed something righteous to make the nights a little better. So I let him know I knew, only I let him think it was okay, that I wanted in, that I was getting old and tired and needed something more than a gold pen and a handshake at the end . . . I was going to nail them, Charley, I was going to nail them all . . . So I let him know I wanted in, only he didn't trust me at first, damn fool if he had. He denied it, denied it all, said, 'You don't actually think I'm taking it under the table, I mean I went to *Princeton* for Chrissake!' Yeah, ivy coated he was . . . but I kept on, kept on working on him, and he must've gotten the word from Dake letting him know how much it was worth to bring me in, because one day he said, 'What if . . . ?' and that was it, that was all I needed, what if, and I took it one step at a time, sent Peterson to L.A., before the rumors caught up, showed them I was on their side, then one day I get this call saying someone wants to meet me in this lousy tenement at midnight, and I go out there and it's Dake with his robot's voice, selling this scheme about how we'd all be rich, with Byrne dead and me as the director of the FBI, nothing to arranging it, all for a little protection from my side, and all along I'm thinking what a righteous bust it was going to be, went home thinking how I was going to work it, and then it all started to get mixed up, all started drifting . . . I thought of Ann and how without her it just didn't matter anymore, and I thought of Matthew and how I was a better man than him, and yeah, I thought of the money, yeah,

Charley, I thought of that, and I just let it slide . . . The guilt was eating at me, but I let it keep on going because I just didn't care, even after people started dying. Perfect scheme, Dake kept saying that night, only I knew better, knew there was no such thing, and the bodies kept piling up and the guilt kept growing, big as monsters it was, something raw and tearing, something of the soul—you'd know about that, Charley—only I didn't stop it, even before I knew about Eddie's tape I didn't stop it, not even the last, the bullet for Matt Byrne, because it just didn't seem to matter, not even the people on the plane, didn't know them, but I knew you Charley, and that mattered."

Hanlon inhaled, then released his breath, a weariness coming with the exhalation. Lisa wiped the perspiration from his brow. They could hear the TV, growing large then small, could hear that and nothing else, and hand pressed tight to Hanlon's shoulder, Charley stared down at him, trying to weigh his words against what he knew of the man

and the man in the moon sings for his supper . . .

and finally after seconds that seemed longer, Charley said softly, keeping the thread of it going, "They were going to kill Matthew Byrne . . ."

"Tonight, already dead by now."

"And Dake would take over for Cedillo . . ."

"Who was as good as dead."

"And Dake would keep working through his name, which inspired confidence and loyalty . . ."

"Which Dake never had."

"Use his name as long as he could, and use his own influence . . ."

"Not much needed."

". . . to see you were appointed head of the FBI, to keep their operation . . ."

"To keep us all . . ."

". . . safe from interference."

"Plan worth its weight in gold, three genies and God on a

string and the pigeons left out in the cold. Gave it all to you before, Charley, only one name was wrong."

"And you stayed with it . . ."

"Hating myself, taking chances, playing games, hoping more than a little to get caught."

"Yet you stayed with it, until tonight."

"Until I got your message on the machine." Hanlon nodded, his voice winding down. "Should've called the police then, but it was still all mixed up, so I drove out here, just hoping to make sure you came out all right." He turned his head to Lisa. "And she was with me all the while."

"My wife," Charley said.

"Yeah," Hanlon said, as though her presence needed no explanation. "And we heard the shot and I called them then and came in fast, did what I could."

"I know."

Sirens were closing in from somewhere, too soon for Lisa's call. Hanlon let their loneliness settle over him, then a smile as wise as centuries came over his face.

"It's a sad old story, Charley," he said, "one that's been told before, will be again . . . something of money and power, worth a month of headlines, or maybe a week, the way the world is now . . ."

He drew in his breath once more, his features creasing into an expression of pain as subtle as grace. Suddenly, he got very pale and still. He reached for his left side with a slow hand and said, "Christ, but it hurts," said it almost apologetically, and then the hand fell to the floor; drawing back his coat, Charley saw where the other bullet had entered, finding a lung, passing through clean, not leaving much blood.

"Should've been my heart." Hanlon smiled faintly, then he said no more. He stared at Charley, who held his hand as tenderly as he would a woman's, held his hand while his breathing slowed until it became something like sleep.

42

The Color of Rain

Charley and Lisa stayed by Hanlon's side after the sirens stopped, stayed while the attendants in immaculate white jolted his chest with the brutal heels of their hands and tried to give him the kiss of life. Soon the house was crowded with state troopers in gray and black, filling rooms and corridors and waiting for the M.E. to define the shape of death with his chalk. The troopers were big men, probably good men. Some were beginning to understand that important people had died here. They would take this night home the way the black boy had, turning it into a different kind of legend, no more like the reality of what had actually occurred, and no less, than any other legend. But for the moment, they simply moved quietly about, talking in hushed voices and executing the small formalities of procedure, and Charley and Lisa stayed through it all, through the questions and the troopers carrying Victor Cedillo down the stairs like a child, and the dog, still alive, in another's arms; stayed until the sheet was drawn irrevocably over Pat Hanlon's face, and then an attendant looked at Charley and said, "You're hurt," and Charley just nodded, his expression as fixed as a mask.

They took him out then, Lisa on one side, the paramedic on the other. It had stopped snowing. A mist was in the air, drifting up the hill, and they took him to the top, to where the ambulances and K.C. waited.

K.C. turned from the mist to Charley and told him Dake and Renaud were dead. Charley said so's Pat, and K.C. bit his lower lip and said Jesus, his voice breaking. Charley asked without interest about Byrne. K.C. told him he was okay, would have told him more, only he saw that Charley was hurt, knew they both were in ways that couldn't be measured, so he just told him how it all could wait, they'd talk when there was time, then hands were helping Charley into the back of an ambulance, with Lisa climbing in behind. Somewhere a car radio was playing "Auld Lang Syne."

"Happy New Year, Charley," K.C. said, his voice low and drawn and breaking again over the sweet sad joy of the drifting music.

Charley looked at him for a long moment, wished he could have found something strong and fine to say, but "Yeah," was all he could manage, his voice filled with irony and rue and something resembling affection; then the doors closed and the ambulance pulled away. Through a halo of ice, he could see K.C. standing motionless, big hands buried in his coat pockets, watching the ambulance, growing smaller until Charley could see nothing but the road and whiteness.

As the distance rolled out before him, Charley thought of all that had happened. He thought of the living and the dead, and the prayers he'd be saying. He thought of how some people he'd liked had died and some he didn't hadn't, and he wondered if what he'd done had really mattered, knowing only that the faces would stay with him always, like strays in the rain.

And then, as one year passed into another, he thought some more, about what Pat Hanlon had said about abuse of power, and the damage that could have been done with God on a string. He thought of how Cedillo was a mystery, Dake a machine, and Hanlon a tragedy, for he was a decent man gone bad; yet in a sense they were all the same, for they had all become corrupt, and corruption was a turn, clap hands, twisting spirit and soul and lives, one's own, the lives of others. And because of that, and because perfect schemes never were, Charley thought of the others who would have died at some unforeseen time, if he hadn't been what he was and kept on going, and it mattered, mattered that they would continue to see the sun and the rain and the shifting of seasons in this gift we call life, and turning to Lisa, he smiled, the one he kept deeper than his pocket. She was at his side, always would be if he was lucky. He kissed her softly then. She rested her head against his shoulder and he held her hand and they rode in silence, like two kids new to love, hoping to catch the brass ring.

Not so very far above them, the moon glistened in the bright darkness of early morning, and began its slow, immutable descent toward dawn.

Riffs, the face in the moon said. Riffs.